.. ⊔1 ꓘ

Kit Fisher

Wayward Books

WAYWARD BOOKS

ISBN 1-903531-01-2

Published by Wayward Books

This book is set in Times 11pt
Printed and bound in Britain by Biddles Ltd of Guildford
Cover design by Orchard Print Services Ltd of Daventry

This book is lovingly dedicated to everyone
from the Weekends by the Lake

1

London 1981

The evening was close, almost unbearably hot; the weather unseasonable for early autumn in London. Byrne, barefoot and sweating even though he'd not long showered, padded to his front door and smiled as he pulled it open.

"Hello, Peter."

"Byrne." A nod.

Byrne stood aside as the young man brushed past him, then closed the door, setting the locks before turning to his visitor. "The money's on the bookcase."

Payment in advance, sandwiched between the latest Len Deighton and an unused Rubik's cube. Byrne watched as, without comment, the roll of fivers disappeared into a tight pocket. Then he noticed the bulge swelling next to it and had to smile: there really was something gratifying about a whore being so eager.

"It's nice to see you too! Go on, you know where the bedroom is."

Without a word the young man went; all easy, carefully enticing walk. Byrne followed, pulling off his shirt as he went, jeans unfastened as he walked, stripped off as he pushed the bedroom door closed behind him. The window was open, letting in whatever breeze was there, along with the sound of a car radio playing Blondie's latest hit at full blast.

The sound of an engine revving, then with a squeal of tyres the car was gone, leaving blissful silence.

The young man had paused by the bed. As Byrne moved he turned, eyes carefully wary.

Naked, Byrne stalked him, smiling. In the faint amber glow from the bedside light he savoured anticipation, his cock hard, pushing up as he walked forward until it brushed against soft cotton jeans.

Byrne stopped, grinned. "Glad you could make it."

The wide mouth twitched, amused. Sharp features, pale skin, supple body, eyes that were all invitation to iniquity. Perfection. Byrne reached up and tugged gently at a lock of long dark auburn hair. "Good week?"

"Yeah." A shrug.

"Mine's been bloody awful."

"Oh."

"I really want to fuck you tonight."

A nod, and a slight shiver in answer.

"Right now." Byrne reached out and ran his finger down a flat belly, finger snagging under the tight waistband. "You can take these off."

A moment of almost hesitation, then long, strong fingers were working at buttons and the trousers were pushed off, shoes and underwear kicked away at the same time.

"And this."

The dark green shirt was fingered. And removed.

"Better."

Byrne took a further step and cupped the back of the man's head, fingers tight against the shape of his skull. "I'm warning you, it really has been a bad week."

A flicker of amusement. "Better do something about you then, hadn't we."

"I was hoping you might."

"How do you want me?"

"Screaming."

A smile. "I expect I can manage that too." There was a catch of anticipation in the husky voice.

A couple of months of sex and they were still strangers. Intimate strangers, bound by need and commerce. Yet there was more ease between them, more acceptance, than Byrne had ever found.

Byrne shifted slightly and their cocks rubbed together, pushing eagerly one against the other. He was fiercely aroused and the touch made him groan softly.

Two paces to the bed. Byrne guided the man back, then gently pushed until he was spread across the mattress, long limbs pale on dark blue cotton. Following, turning him away, belly down, Byrne was over him, mouth around one shoulder, biting deep enough to make the hard body arch back, fingers clawing at the sheets. He bit again, finding muscle, feeling the whore writhe under him, the curve of his bottom tight against Byrne's groin.

Byrne licked at the reddened shoulder, tasting salt. Holding wide shoulders, knees easing thighs apart, he pushed the young man flat, sliding his fingers between their bodies, pushing into the soft cleft, finding tight flesh already slick and ready. He gave an appreciative growl, and took hold of himself, finding the right angle, cock there, just waiting, paused, loving this moment when everything was in perfect balance, when it was all to come. Then with a twist of his hips he pushed home, gasping out loud as the tight muscle gave and in one long, forceful stroke he was inside.

One hand was still wound in auburn hair. He tugged the softness gently and then untangled his fingers. Very slowly he pulled back, cock almost sliding free, but stopping just where the flaring head kept him deliciously trapped. Shifting gently, rocking, just in, just out, waiting as the body he fucked gave, opened; as the tight muscles in the long, strong back eased. Then, at that moment, as sweat dripped from his face, he drove in again, hard and fast, with a brutality that made them both moan.

Eyes closed, he leant forward, weight supported on his arms and began to fuck in slow strokes that darkened his vision and shuddered through bone and muscle and nerve, that took away thought, and volition; everything but animal need.

He was cursing softly under his breath, the words without sense, his voice raw and uneven, the sound woven through the slap of skin against sweat-slick skin. He was close. Very close.

Through sweat-blurred eyes he watched the whore. And then he moved, hands sliding under the taut body, pulling it back, making it kneel. He felt the man shudder as his weight settled back, Byrne's cock spearing him so deep he was sobbing at each stroke, sobbing as Byrne's fingers found his nipples and pinched. Harder. Again, until he came, crying out, wrapped in Byrne's arms as Byrne watched him: watched him, and came too in a blinding rush; orgasm destroying everything but the feel of the body in his arms.

He stilled, into a silence broken only by the rough sound of their breathing. Groaning, arms still holding tight, he let himself fall to the bed, the whore crying out softly, shuddering as Byrne's cock ripped from his body.

Blinking away sweat, breath still uneven, Byrne touched his hand to one bruised shoulder. If it was an apology, it wasn't needed. But Byrne was smiling as he slipped into sleep.

And slowly woke as an observer. In the spill of street-light through the curtains he could see his body, could see the light where it touched the long fingers that were cleaning his cock: long flesh-spare fingers that really should have belonged to the hands of a priest.

The thought made him smile sleepily, lazily stretching. The warm cloth was delicious against his skin, and every now and then he felt the teasing touch of flesh against flesh. Eyes half-closed, curiously distanced, he watched as his cock thickened, curling away from its dark nest of hair, lifting, swelling. It was a nice cock. A lovely cock, really. Uncut, thick, long enough; longer than most. He'd never lost any locker-room battles, that was certain.

The cloth was tossed onto the floor as long fingers gently skinned him back. Byrne gave a soft sound of encouragement, letting himself slide away under the ministering hands, letting himself float easily into arousal, into the delicious greed of being ministered to, and of not even pretending an interest in the other man's arousal.

Selfishness: it was what he paid for.

With one sure hand ringing his shaft, the other cupping his balls, massaging gently, Byrne opened his arms, spreading himself on the bed. Closing his eyes he concentrated on the minutiae of pleasure, wanting to feel everything as the neat tongue teased its way around his glans, licked inside the slit, flicking like a snake until, breathless, he arched with need, oxygen suddenly absent. Only then did the wide mouth swallow him deep. He cried out, feeling the strong throat hold him tight, slide free, then push deep again, lips around the base of his cock, then teeth were skimming skin, moving back, and the mouth was sucking, tongue twisting around and around until he thought he would die of bliss. And then, only then, did the throat slide back, a tight glove of flesh. And didn't let go, strong muscles merely swallowing around him as the hand around his balls squeezed tighter and tighter and shuddering, he came, the pleasure dislocating time for a fraction of infinity.

In the moment before he slept he murmured, "Jesus, that was good." The words were slurring. "Worth every penny." A yawn, a pat on a nicely rounded buttock and Andrew Byrne curled onto his side.

Within moments he was breathing deeply, fast asleep.

When Byrne awoke it was morning and the alarm was screeching next to his ear.

Cursing, Byrne batted it into silence and lay still for five heartbeats. The flat was very quiet, just the faint murmur of Radio One from downstairs, and kids laughing in the street.

Without looking he knew that he was alone. Ever since the first time when the rules had been laid out, Peter always left sometime in the night. Byrne couldn't help the fact that he liked being alone in the mornings. Always had and always would. Though part of him did wonder what it would be like to wake with someone else. Well, this someone else in particular. It might not have worked before, but maybe with Peter Duncan …

The thought caught him by surprise, and for a moment he toyed with it. Then laughed it off as ridiculous; the product of too little sleep and too good a session of sex. Muttering to himself, he pushed back the covers, climbing out of bed to stretch and yawn. The room reeked of sex. He stripped the bed of sheets, pillow slips and cover from the duvet, leaving them piled together on the floor. The woman he paid to clean would get the hint.

Whistling the song he could just about hear on the radio, something catchy, sung he was pretty certain by overly pretty men dressed as, of all things, pirates, he headed for the shower, stepped into the stall and thanked the heavens for hot water.

It had been a good night. No need to be anything other than himself. No need to wine or dine or even care if the other person got off, not that Peter left that in any doubt. He tipped his face into the spray, content. The chance meeting with the hustler had proved the perfect solution to a too busy life and too strong a libido. All it took was a phone call and he could have what he wanted; rough, uncomplicated sex. With a man.

A goose walked over his grave as he wondered what his boss would think, then he shrugged the niggle away. He'd never find out. Why should he? Besides, it wasn't a sacking offence. Not really.

Well, it didn't matter. The illicit quality to what he was doing only added a certain edge. As if it needed one. Peter was actually worth every penny he got paid, and that was a first for Byrne; the sex he'd paid for in the past had always lacked something, leaving him faintly unsatisfied.

Whatever the difference was, he'd got it right with Peter. Very right, and he wasn't in a hurry to call a halt.

Picking up the soap he slowly rubbed it over his skin, allowing himself the luxury of slow sensuality. Satiated, his cock did no more than pulse half-heartedly, even when it was lovingly cleaned.

It really had been a good night.

Perhaps he'd give Peter a call, set up something for the weekend. After all, everyone needed something to look forward to.

A month of routine at work made the weeks pass slowly. Then out of the blue a juicy case came up, one he wanted so badly he could taste the success of it. Except it was given to someone else.

Against his own judgement, Byrne tried remonstrating with his boss. "But, sir ..."

"No. I know that you think yourself above the normal procedures of this department, but you are not. I'm understaffed and you are available." Cadell was tapping unconsciously at the buff folder on his desk, his eyes fixed on the rain streaming outside the window. "So no more complaints about what I do assign you or I'll put you in Records for a month." He looked across sharply. "And I mean it, so help me."

"Yes, sir."

"Oh, 'yes sir'. For once try and mean it as well as say it."

"I always do, sir."

Cadell sighed, and relented slightly. "You chose to work solo, Byrne. The Ascot/Weston case needed a team, it was as simple as that. This business with soon-to-be ex-Superintendent Paget may seem to you like a waste of time, but trust me, it isn't."

"It's just police corruption."

"Just?" Graham Cadell shook his head. "You know better than that. Don't you?"

"Yes, sir."

"Good. You might not make the front page of the *Evening Standard* tomorrow, but be patient, make friends, lead him on about your corruptibility and hopefully we can persuade the cautious bastard to give away enough so we can hang him up high and dry." Cadell took off his glasses, and held them lightly, carefully tapping them against his fingers. "I know that this type of slow operation doesn't come easily to you, you've made that plain enough in the last year, but we can't have running gun-battles in the London streets every day of the week."

With a glare he put his glasses back on, his mind clearly already concerned with other problems. "Now get out of here, and in future you obey orders without question. Coming in here and demanding explanations! And, what's more, me giving them ... Go on, Byrne, off with you, before I forget that I'm in a good mood."

Curiously enough, Andrew Byrne went.

Hands in pockets, he wandered disconsolately through the Whitehall offices. It wasn't as if he wanted a shoot-out every day. Or even every month. Hell, there'd only been one in the three years he'd been working for Cadell. But he did want something to do that involved more than just waiting for information, more than just asking questions. Of anyone. Except maybe Peter the whore. That would be an interesting game. He could imagine that lithe body tied to his bed, tied down and fucked. Maybe a little candle wax for added interest.

He caught himself there, already half-hard. This really wasn't the place. The Commander really wouldn't approve. He grinned at the mere thought and wandered on, more cheerful than before.

Four weeks later Byrne was still being a good boy, and he'd impressed himself if not his boss. He'd spent hours drinking with Derek Paget, and had finally become interested in the whole case and actually fascinated by the bent copper's thought processes. Part of him had even gone so far as to like the tall Londoner. Part of him. The rest despised the bastard for the immoral, shameless crook he was. But great on a pub-crawl, that was certain, he'd had the hangovers to prove it.

Paget was big, blond, and almost as tough as he thought he was. Byrne had known men like him before, undoubtedly would again. Men who never quite saw reality as anything other than on their own terms. In the end it usually made them easier to bring down. Usually.

And Paget was finally trusting his new associate enough to show his true self. It had been an amazing moment when Byrne had realised there was more to his quarry than the bigotry and ignorance that comprised the surface man, and more and more he was getting tantalising glimpses of the ingenious mind beneath the coarse facade.

Paget was definitely interested in the easy corruptibility he saw in Byrne, but so far he'd given nothing away about why. He might pretend to be as thick as shit, but the policeman knew what he was doing. And nabbing him wasn't going to be that easy.

Their friendship had progressed to the 'all lads together' stage, the imaginary character Byrne had invented for himself being as hard drinking and immoral as Derek Paget could possibly want. He was also slowly letting the copper know that he was as unscrupulous as was necessary for his own gain. Even Paget could trust money as a motive.

Playing the villain had been the saving grace of a case he had thought pointless. Paget wasn't exactly going to destroy the nation and besides, corruption in the police was hardly earth-shattering news. Byrne mentally shrugged his shoulders, resigned to fishing for minnows while the sharks smiled as they swam past.

The pub in Lisle Street had finally got too crowded, and as they stepped out into the street Byrne immediately regretted the amount of Scotch he'd knocked back on an empty stomach, though the effect was nowhere near as bad as he let Paget think. He swayed slightly, eyes a fraction out of focus.

"Great evenin', Derek, shame you've got to go on that bloody course! We could've had a night on the town." Byrne enjoyed the petulant tone in his own voice.

Artistically he reached to grab the support of a railing and missed, falling against it instead. "Reckon I've had a couple too many ... You shouldn't let me drink so much."

"I'd like to see anyone try and stop you. Come on, here's a taxi." The blond man flagged it down, grabbed Byrne by the jacket sleeve and shepherded him towards it. "Go and sleep it off. You'll be okay?"

"Yeah. Thanks for the cab. I'm going home to bed, all this bloody paperwork's getting me down."

"Serves you right for being a naughty boy. Besides, there must be something interesting in all that crap they've got you sorting through?"

Byrne leant on the side of the cab, biting his lower lip. "Interesting ..." Letting bitterness tinge his voice, he turned and opened the cab door. "Not what I'd call it." He shrugged. "I'd better be off ..."

"How about dinner on Wednesday? Might cheer you up a bit."

"Thanks, Derek, you're a mate." He yawned hugely. "I'll be dreaming of bloody paperwork tonight."

"Yeah, see you."

"Night." Byrne closed the door of the taxi, just catching the interest and anticipation that flickered across Paget's face.

It had been a good evening's work. In the darkness as they drove up Charing Cross Road, he was smiling at the simplicity of it all: put out the bait, wait for the bite, reel in the catch. Easy. And he got to get absolutely drunk on Government money.

There had to be worse jobs.

He watched London sliding past him, all the laughter, the fun. On one corner a couple were kissing, bodies close, his hand curved around the slight swell of her breast. On another a hooker was bargaining softly with an older man dressed for the City.

The night was young, for some.

In the time it took to reach home, he had almost sobered. Paying the driver he waited until the taxi had driven off, just standing on the curb, breathing in the night air. He wasn't sleepy. At all.

Peter.

The thought made his cock swell expectantly.

In the last two months he'd been too busy, too controlled by work and the need to remain in his undercover persona to see anyone socially. Peter had been around a few times, no more, and not at all in the past three weeks. Byrne was beyond the point of being eager. In fact, it was hardly a decision. Turning on his heel he reached for his keys, fumbling them into the door, inside, up the stairs, flat door unlocked, slammed behind him and fingers dialling. After three rings it was answered.

"Hello ..."

"Peter. It's Byrne." He was slightly breathless.

"Oh, hi."

"Yeah. I wondered if you were free tonight?"

Pause. "What are you talking, an hour or longer?"

"Longer."

There was a moment's silence, almost as if 'no' was going to be the answer. Then a sound that might have been a sigh. "All right. I'll be over in about an hour."

"Great. Bring some wine with you, I'll pay for it when you get here."

"Sure." The phone clicked on an empty line.

Byrne was smiling as he put the phone down, giving it a little thankful pat.

Showering quickly, he slipped into a soft towelling robe, scorning even the pretence that re-dressing would have offered. Anticipation made him edgy, and he prowled around the flat touching objects; leafing through books; watching the clock, his blood beating loudly in his ears, every sense heightened.

By the time the doorbell rang he was already half-erect, and he cupped his own flesh reassuringly before walking to answer its summons. The voice over the intercom was tinny and remote. Pressing the door release he waited.

After a minute the lift doors opened and Peter stepped gracefully out, walking slowly towards where Byrne stood in the doorway.

With his eyes Byrne paid lustful tribute to the whore's slender-bodied attraction, the silent approval the most he'd let the other man see of his fascination. Dressed in dark, slightly flared velvet trousers that shimmered from black to green as he moved, and a tight silk shirt under a suede jacket, the supple form looked edible. Not that Byrne was going to be doing any eating.

He swallowed sharply, a frisson of simple lust catching his breath. Stepping to one side he let the other man in, closing his eyes as peppery scent brushed past him. It was as much as he could do not to throw him on the floor and fuck him here; the possibility searingly tempting.

Christ, close to three weeks of abstinence and he was almost rabid.

Then Peter turned, holding out a plastic carrier. "Blue Nun, two bottles, right?"

"Great." Handing over a roll of cash, Byrne took the bag and pulled out a brown glass bottle. It was cold to the touch.

"The receipt's in the bag." Peter tucked the notes in a pocket. He didn't count them.

"Great." Byrne sounded distracted; he was watching the way the soft velvet contoured long muscles and sweet curves.

"No problem."

Intent on other things, Byrne missed the wry edge that roughened the words.

He jumped slightly when Peter came to stand quite close, one hand lightly curved around the strong column of Byrne's neck. He smiled.

"What?" Byrne frowned slightly. "What's so funny?"

"You're eager tonight."

"That a problem?"

"No." Duncan shrugged, letting his fingers trail down towelling until they just brushed against the bobbing shaft that parted Byrne's robe. "Want it now?"

Byrne licked his lips.

"Here on the carpet?" Duncan slowly grew closer, his breath warm, scented delicately of mint. "What do you fancy tonight?" His husky voice imbued the simple words with centuries of carnal knowledge and he tilted his face. "Fuck me? Once, twice? Or do you want my mouth …"

Byrne did. He looked at the teasing curve and was lost. He kissed, and the world was consumed by the intense response that sparked flame out of nowhere. Bottles thudding unnoticed to the floor he took the slim body in both hands, groaning as the action was mirrored, fingers clutching, digging into flesh to draw it closer, each of them seeming to try and claw inside the other while their mouths met and their tongues tangled wildly.

Had they even kissed before? Byrne wasn't sure: didn't know, didn't care. He sucked at Duncan's full lower lip, biting it, almost coming as Duncan shuddered against him, pushing him up against the door, thigh pushed hard between Byrne's as he took control of the kiss, driving it deeper, taking possession until Byrne was light-headed, his hands tight around velvet, pulling Duncan close, grinding sex against sex, urgent, until Duncan stilled, mouth releasing, hands suddenly pressing him hard to the white wood door.

"Eager doesn't seem to describe it." His mouth was swollen, wet. "What do you want?"

Byrne hissed and bucked his hips.

Peter was smiling wickedly. Weight canted forwards, hips still pressing Byrne to the door, he leaned back and pushed the towelling robe off the broad chest. Slowly, with delicate sensuality he licked his forefingers and then pinched the hard nubs of Byrne's nipples until Byrne swore softly and groaned. "Now tell me what you want."

What did he want? Byrne swallowed, and spoke the first thing that came into his head. "Suck me." The words were spoken on a strangled breath; Byrne sweating, eyes closing as Duncan massaged his flesh with strong fingers.

"Right here?"

"Yes."

He bent, long wavy hair falling over his face, mouth hidden as he took first one nipple into his mouth then moved to the other, his hair soft against Byrne's chest, his mouth hot and hard.

Groaning, Byrne held on to the door-frame, bracing himself, watching every movement as the tie belt at his waist was loosened and his body exposed, Duncan kneeling gracefully as his body was bared. Dark-eyed, the whore ran his tongue up the soft skin of Byrne's inner thigh.

"No ... no." Assessing eyes flickered up. Byrne begged, "Please."

"Trust me."

"I do!"

"Then shut up."

Byrne nodded, and shivered as a wide, wicked tongue licked him from root to tip.

Sighing, Byrne let himself relax as sensation flooded him. The talent was almost inhuman. No one, man nor woman, had ever made it like this. From his cock the pleasure reached through his body, every nerve alight with desire. It was so good, at this moment better even than fucking. He let go of the door frame and wove his fingers into thick russet hair, imposing a slightly different rhythm, pushing deep and groaning out loud as his cock slid deep and, taken by surprise, Duncan almost gagged.

"Yes ... Jesus!" He thrust again, harder into tight, wet sweetness, felt the throat open to him, take him whole, give everything as the kneeling man sensed the nearness, the need. Blanking out for a second Byrne came, a pulsing stream of semen emptying him, convulsing through him with deep satisfaction.

Slowly relaxing his grip, Byrne let the other man pull back, conscious that his face was wet, dark patches staining the pale silk shirt. Byrne smiled, blinking as reality restored itself. Peter was still on his knees, chest heaving as he controlled his breath, his face tilted up. If he was expecting anything, he was wrong.

Byrne leant against the door, pulled his robe closed and sighed happily. "Great! Time to open one of those bottles I think." Offering a hand he tugged the other man to his feet, though Duncan pulled away immediately, making Byrne raise an eyebrow in enquiry.

"Give me a minute." Peter hesitated, then shook his head, moving away toward the bathroom. Walking though to the kitchen Byrne heard water running. He gave a mental shrug and reached for the corkscrew.

When Duncan walked in to join him, the skin of his face was rosy from being briskly towelled dry, and the ends of his hair lay damply against his cheeks. He took the offered glass and downed it almost in one.

"Good job you got two bottles." Byrne watched the expressive face flush. "It's okay, I was teasing. Besides, you deserve it."

"Thanks." The voice was dry, almost but not quite amused, and Byrne wondered how he survived in his trade with such a spiky attitude.

"Come on, let's sit down." He didn't wait for an answer, just led the way into the living room, switching on the tape-deck as he passed by, Genesis softly filling the room as he put the wine down on the low glass table. "Come on, Peter, make yourself comfy." Duncan nodded, and carefully folded himself into the sofa's farthest corner.

Caveat emptor. Byrne smiled at the thought.

Hazel eyes slid across and an eyebrow lifted in interrogation. "What's so funny?"

"Nothing. I was just thinking that you can't be everybody's cup of tea."

Peter Duncan almost smiled, his mouth twitching, then he turned away. "Oh, I get by."

They sat on the sofa, Byrne wrapped snugly back in his robe, watching Duncan's long fingers play with the wineglass. It was a reminiscent gesture. And yes, he probably had a stream of clients queuing for his services. Frowning, it took Byrne a moment to place the strange emotion the thought provoked as anger. Something like jealousy, perhaps.

Uneasy with the thought, he was deliberately coarse. "You give great head, must be all that practice."

Duncan was clearly startled, he turned back, his eyes meeting Byrne's, a curious expression on his face. After a long pause he simply leant his head back against the cushions and shrugged casually. "Yeah, and natural talent."

"You've got enough of that."

"Thanks."

Irony? Maybe. Byrne frowned, looking at his companion. At some point Duncan had shed his jacket. His shirt and trousers were tight over long, finely-muscled limbs, flat belly, wide shoulders. He was dressed as an invitation; one impossible to resist.

Byrne took a long drink of wine. "Still, unless we're actually fucking, you don't come on like a hustler. Not that I've know many. Doesn't your attitude lose you customers? Or don't you have any regular clients?"

"Apart from you?"

Byrne blinked, then nodded.

"No. And I didn't think you were the type for plastic hearts and paper flowers."

Byrne was beginning to doubt what sort he was. Slowly, he shook his head. "No. Suppose not. Wouldn't you get more money if you were more, well, amenable?"

15

"Money isn't everything." He laughed hollowly as he said the words.

"No?"

"No."

Byrne watched and wondered, the conversation only deepening his interest in the enigma who sat so uneasily on his sofa.

"Could've fooled me." The contradictions surrounding Duncan were fascinating. He owned no car, never took taxis and if his telephone number was to be believed, lived in one of the less prepossessing areas of North West London. Yet he wore an expensive, if limited, selection of clothes, his nails were manicured and he was always deliciously clean. He had long hair, though that was more likely fashion rather than necessity. Byrne himself still went to the barber he'd first visited when he left school, and still had the same short haircut. He liked Duncan's hair. Liked touching it.

He took a short breath. "Not exactly chatty tonight, are you?" If Duncan ever was. Byrne remembered the vicious exchange of insults that he'd overheard the first time they'd met. "Though I know you've got a tongue like a razor, when you want."

Peter's eyes cast down, seemingly intent on where his fingers rubbed patterns into soft velvet. He gave a slight shrug. "It's usually described in rather different terms." As he spoke, he looked up, a wicked glance through lowered lashes.

"Oh, there's no complaints here." Shifting, Byrne stilled the moving hand by reaching across to touch it lightly with his forefinger, wanting more, but somehow unable to admit it even to himself. "But I am curious, you're not like any other pro I've ever met."

For a moment Byrne thought he saw a flash of something like recognition in Duncan's face, then it was gone, his eyes averted.

"Don't."

"Don't what?"

"Don't disappear. Sometimes you're like the bloody Cheshire Cat. I'm sorry. I won't pry if you don't want me to." Byrne hid his curiosity about the man's present, turning instead to his past,

16

reaching out and stroking his cheekbone, just where a small scar curved away from his eye. "What happened here, your mouth get you into trouble?" All his concentration was focused, and with surprise he realised his own deep fascination for all things concerning Duncan: and that the fascination was, if anything, getting stronger the longer they were involved.

Duncan shook his head slightly. "It was nothing, an accident. Look, Byrne, can't we talk about something else? How about something to eat? I'm starving."

Byrne gave up on everything but the now. He put his glass down and shifted across the sofa, pulling the slighter body towards him, fingers busy undoing the shirt's pearl buttons. "There's cheese, bread and pickles." His thumb swept abrasively over one of the small nipples, making it peak. "Soup." Another brush of flesh over flesh. "Whatever you can find in the kitchen, but get undressed first. Go on. I like to see you naked; you've got a beautiful body."

The body in his arms held quite still, then shivered slightly as if suddenly defenceless.

"Okay." Duncan nodded and slipped away from Byrne's grasp.

Byrne watched as slowly the shirt was shrugged away, loving the play of muscle under warm, pale skin.

"I don't do this for everyone, you know."

Byrne was glad. He sat forward as the coffee table was pushed away and Peter was there, just in front of him, fingers skimming the line of his waist, lingeringly, and the stud was released, the zip slowly lowered, the sound of metal rasping softly on metal loud, extraordinarily erotic.

Fly open, belly bare, a faint curling of hair just visible above where his cock pushed against velvet, weight balanced on one leg, hands on hips, Duncan was the archetypal hustler. "I wouldn't like you to think I was easy."

Byrne heard him laugh, the sound deep and so utterly arousing. "I never thought that!" he said.

"Good." Peter turned, arse just at the level of Byrne's face. "As I'm only easy for you, sweetheart."

"I bet you tell that to all your punters." Byrne laughed, but he couldn't hide his flaring response. Eyes bright, face slightly flushed, he leant forward and pushed Peter's hands aside, sliding his own under the warm velvet, letting the weight of his hands push the tight fabric down.

As arses went, it was just about perfect. Byrne cupped the curves with his hands, thumbs stroking skin so smooth he wanted to bite it.

It was his. All this perfection was his. Tonight. And that knowledge was utterly arousing. Byrne growled, tried to pull Duncan back, but he was eluded as Duncan stepped out of his trousers and was suddenly back, pushing Byrne by the shoulders and straddling his lap.

He was grinning. "So you like a little strip-tease, do you?"

Byrne cleared his throat. "Apparently so."

"Well - I expect we can do something about this." He reached down, and squeezed. Byrne moaned. "But I'm having that sandwich first."

"What!"

"You'll cope."

Byrne wasn't sure. Especially when he found himself kissed, long and deep. But then he heard a gurgle. Duncan laughed ruefully. "Sorry, truth is I'm bloody starving."

Byrne nodded. "Go on. A little abstinence will do me good." He licked at dry lips as Peter climbed off him, all lithe, unselfconscious nakedness.

"Sure?"

"Yes." He took a steadying breath. "Don't be too long ..."

Peter grinned and went.

Abstinence, that must be it. These days he was too busy to go through the long process of enticing some bird into bed, and when he did get any free time it was always Peter who was easiest to call.

Yeah, that explained it: his libido saw an available body and ran riot. That was the explanation. Simple. Byrne nodded to himself and, easing himself upright, went to steal half a sandwich.

The second orgasm was always the best.

The first was like a taster, whetting his appetite but not really satisfying. The third could often leave him exhausted. But the second! By far the most intense, it seemed almost to have colour and texture, as if every sense fed on the sensations that radiated from his cock. Sexual nirvana, he courted it, played with it and tried to make it last as long as humanly possible, savouring every nuance of expectation and need.

Braced on stiff arms, his cock buried deep in the responsive body curled beneath him, he rested, fighting against the desperation that pushed him towards the edge, moving slowly, rocking back and forth in small movements; deep, deeper, deep, deeper, sliding back so slowly until just the head of his shaft was held tight, then deep again and the slow rocking.

Peter arched slowly, his legs around Byrne's shoulders, his body doubled on itself. A shift of muscles and he gasped aloud. Byrne pushed in deep, angling high, aiming up to Peter's heart, his throat, as if wanting to make him taste it in his mouth, to pierce right through his body, claiming it all.

A wicked twist of his hips, then Byrne was back to toying again, drawing a soft complaint, then a string of curses as Peter tried to pull him back. The curses changed to pleas as he was ignored. As Byrne arched away, almost pulling free, Peter clutched at him, fingers clumsy as they tried to bring him back. Holding tight to control, Byrne just held quite still, then brought up a hand to touch a small, brown nipple, to squeeze hard until the slim body was writhing, clenching with need around his cock.

It was almost too much, and Byrne groaned aloud. Control slipping, sweat dripping from his spiked hair onto the twisting body, he just managed to hold back, his breath fast and erratic. They were both so close, the whore as exposed as he had ever been, filled and fucked, thighs splayed, body opened. Palming his hand down the honey-skinned belly, Byrne felt muscles ripple against his touch as the man fought his battle with need. He was perfect, beautiful, sexy as hell, his long slim cock dripping pearls of precum onto his belly, his balls so tight, pushed hard against the base of his cock.

Byrne shifted very slightly from side to side. The sight of his cock stretching and filling so perfectly the ring of flesh was sublimely erotic. Perfect, he thought through the haze of need, and once again pushed in deep, watching as his slick cock slid smoothly in until his balls slapped against warm skin. Mesmerised, he pulled out again, watching the whore's body seeming to turn inside out around his shaft, hearing the catch in the man's quick breath, head pounding against the bed as he whimpered.

Byrne had drawn this fuck out to its extremity, no longer really aware of time, focused entirely on the tightness holding him, on denying the need that weighted his balls. Peter moved again and moaned softly, one word, "Please ..."

It made Byrne smile. Duncan hadn't come yet. He was shuddering, his hair dark with sweat, out of his mind with need. Just as Byrne wanted him.

Lifting one hand off the bed, shifting his balance, he touched the heat of the weeping cock, cupping it, loving its feel in his hand, his own body shivering in response as Peter groaned. With a quick, ungentle squeeze that made the other man's body buck beneath him he let go, dipped his fingers in the pool of sweat and seed that glistened on his skin, and slowly trailed his fingers down to touch the dilated ring of muscle. He circled his own flesh with the whore's, making them both gasp as he pushed the tip of one finger inside, then another. Lush, it was all so lush …

A push and his cock was in deep again, fingers too, sliding home until there was no air between them, just skin against skin, heat, free fingers pressed tight to the swell of his balls.

Through almost blind eyes he saw Duncan reach for his own cock. "No! Don't."

"Jesus, Byrne, please."

His voice was ragged, its harsh sound a goad. Byrne bucked with his hips, making the body under him shudder, arms spread wide on the bed, hands clutching at the sheets. "Say that again."

"Please."

Again. Deeper, more strength behind the angle. "Ask me."

"Fucking, bastard. Please!"

Stillness.

A sob, and Duncan was twisting on the bed, wild-eyed. "Please, please! "

Slowly, fingers pulled free, then took hold of Duncan's cock, squeezing. A slow rhythm.

"I'll - Please." A whisper this time.

"All right." And Byrne gave up on control, fucking hard and deep until almost screaming the whore came, his fierce spasms triggering Byrne into release, losing him, obliterating him as he came again and again, his mind splintered by desire.

Gasping and trembling he slumped over.

After a while, he felt Peter move cautiously beneath him. "Sorry." His voice was slurred. Carefully he lifted himself, unsticking their bodies, pulling free with a twist that made them both gasp.

"Nah, 's all right." Duncan explained no further. Byrne had rolled off to one side and was snoring gently, instantly asleep.

2

Careful not to wake him, Duncan propped his head on one bent arm and watched the sleeping man.

Byrne, without tension, without the control he wore like a mask, was young, not much older than himself, late twenties, maybe. Dark hair, almost black, and silky dark lashes curving against pale skin. He needed to shave, the stubble a light shadowing on his skin. The sheets were still pushed away, despite the chill of late September whistling against the windows, inside the room was warm enough to be naked in comfort.

It was a strong body. Wide-shouldered, deep-chested, muscles close to the skin. Very little body-hair, a nice bum, even nicer cock. All pretty perfect, really, as if dial-a-fantasy had got it right.

Not that there was any point getting ideas. None at all.

Duncan was quite aware of that.

He was paid for one thing, well, several actually, and all rather pleasant. But he wasn't paid to be interested, wasn't paid to be affectionate.

Or to be in love.

Which he wasn't.

At all.

And he might not be paid for affection, but there was something that kept Byrne coming back. Something more than the skills he paid for, surely?

Or maybe not. Stupidity surely could only go so far.

Very carefully, Duncan straightened. He eased his abused body flat, turning gently on his side, wincing as his back reminded him what tomorrow would feel like. Reaching down he pulled the covers over them both, careless of the sweat that chilled the sheets, just needing to be still, to be here. Slowly, his breathing returned to normal.

Almost peaceful, he rested his head on his arm to wonder at his own infatuation; curious that the other man's pleasure could be as exciting as his own. Aches and bruises? Well, maybe he was more masochist than he'd ever thought. Besides, Byrne ended up with his share as well.

Ridiculous, though, to build any hopes around what was basically a good fuck. Byrne would wet himself laughing if it turned out that his own personal whore had been stupid enough to fall in love.

Plastic hearts and paper flowers, eh? Must be better at lying than he thought. Counterfeit coin presented as truth. Very gently, he leant across and planted a soft kiss on a rounded shoulder, then lay back. His legs felt like melting wax, and his back was protesting violently. But it had been worth it.

It had been quite an evening: 'please' and 'sorry'. Miracles would never cease. A lot had certainly changed since their first meeting. Still, even after that less than delightful encounter he'd come back, the dark-haired man more than just his image of physical perfection; the difference between them fascinating in a way that neither familiarity nor contempt could ever be. He buried the wish that he could have met Byrne under different circumstances. Byrne would have undoubtedly despised him.

Careful of every muscle he possessed, he weakly made his way to the shower. Shrouded in steam, standing isolated under the running water, he remembered the women who had dominated his childhood talking late into the night when business was slow. The bitter advice had been absorbed by his young mind, never to be forgotten: never believe what they tell you, punters always lie; always tell them they were the best; your body is all you've got, look after it. Even strange arcane details, like how to put a rubber on a man without him knowing; how to give good head. Tricks and techniques all absorbed by a small boy they thought was asleep. He wondered what they would think of the use he had put their advice to. Sound advice as well, most of it, the older girls letting the new ones in on the secrets of the game: how not to get hurt, and, most important of all, how not to mind when you did.

He remembered their voices rather than their faces, lilting Irish and Northern rhythms weaving around his childhood dreams. And his mother. He'd loved her so much, seemingly as beautiful and mysterious as the night itself, with a deep, beautiful voice that could sing like an angel and tell stories he never wanted to end. He'd idolised her, and when she died he'd gone crazy, wanting to destroy the world that had taken her away.

Six months in care had made him wise, older by far than his years, and he'd learnt to turn all the violence inwards, letting himself appear withdrawn and introverted, until he ran for the last time, taking his wildness with him, hiding it on the hard Manchester streets.

At sixteen he was a convinced loner, seeing himself as street-sharp and dangerous, up for anything, fit and hard. A few months later he was drowning in a sea of drugs, money and sex. Sex with women, sex with men - though he made more money out of them than the women. Just pretty enough to be interesting, just hard enough to be more than a pretty boy, he'd had his pick, learning as he went along until he could project innocent vulnerability or brazen sexuality at will, pandering skilfully to every fantasy.

The money he spent on drugs and the feeling of control, of power, that the drugs gave him. Well on the way to being burnt out by the time he was seventeen, it had only been a month in hospital that had slowed him down and made him realise that he actually wanted to see the grand old age of twenty. And he was lucky, going straight had been easy, the past sloughing off like a dead skin.

Somehow, in a warped way that made him laugh bitterly at

himself, the police had seemed to be the ideal solution. He'd hit London where, reverting to the name on his birth certificate, for years he'd been the model citizen. He had joined the police; trying to be one of the lads, playing darts and drinking beer, carefully ignoring any advances from other men, trying to burn out his sexuality with an endless series of women. For years he'd existed, trying to forget that the world had ever held other excitements, and it really hadn't been that bad. Until the day it dawned on him that the police were as crooked as the criminals. And he'd come across the means to prove it.

Looking back, he wondered now why he hadn't left then; why he'd tried to make an issue of it, do the right thing, make his dead mother proud. Fucking waste of time. He should have known better.

Instead of being the end of the nightmare, seeing four of them put behind bars had proved the beginning. So much for the scales of justice. Though a whispering voice told him what he knew too well: that the pain was only what he deserved. After all, Blind Justice carries a sword in her other hand.

His past unearthed, rumours about his present running rife, he'd finally lost his temper, leaving the police under a cloud so large that it was impossible to get a decent job. Okay, so he'd taken four of the bastards with him, but they were only the tip of an iceberg. The book he was writing would finish that, though. If he could ever get enough money together to keep the informers happy, and get the bloody thing published.

So many ifs and buts, they spun around his brain in a whirling morass of frustration.

Away from the Met he'd changed his name and gone back to living on his wits, carefully avoiding the easy options. Living in a squalid Willesden flat that was borrowed from a friend, with only a portable typewriter and his notebooks for company, he sometimes wondered if he were going mad. He survived the isolation only by anticipating the bastards' reactions when they got sent down for a long, long stretch inside.

The water was running cold and he turned it off. Meeting Byrne that night had been a godsend. A hundred pounds.

Riches.

Trouble was, he'd found - and he had tried - that he couldn't do it with anyone else. Must be love.

Or insanity.

A week later he had tried it again, letting himself be picked up, exchanging the use of his body for cash up-front. But he'd hated it. Despised and loathed himself. Quite mad. He hadn't planned what happened with Byrne at all and it was as if, by his mind's own convoluted reasoning, that made it all right.

Christ, it was more than that. In moments of despair he wondered if it were becoming too much, the sweet need that flowed through him at the memory of Byrne's capable hands and body.

He laughed softly and wondered what Byrne would think if he knew, how he would react to finding out, that his whore sometimes sat by the phone begging it to ring, desperate for him to call.

Mind you, at other times he decided equally clearly that he never wanted to see the man again.

Bloody stupid.

Byrne and purity. Now that was a laughable comparison. Yet to Duncan their times together held a certain ... innocence was too strong a word, but something like it, so that even when the hours they spent in each other's company were concerned only with undiluted sex, he found himself returning afterwards to the underworld of thieves and informers calmer, somehow cleansed. Bless me, Father, for I have sinned. Sex as a confessional. He paid a silent, mocking compliment to the priests who had had the education of him as a child.

Towelling himself dry, a twist of his lips ridiculing himself along with the rest of the world, he pushed it all away. Then, quietly, he dressed in the half-light, going to stand silhouetted in the doorway as he bade a silent goodbye. Though he would come back.

As long as Byrne continued to asked him.

Another sigh, and he turned away, letting himself out, pulling the door firmly shut behind him. Light-footed he ran down the block's main stairs and through the double-doors into the chilly night. For a moment he stood still, then, huddled into his jacket he began to walk towards the Edgware Road. There'd be a night bus if he was lucky.

"Byrne, what d'you fancy in the 3.10?"

"Fancy! You must be joking. Load of broken-down nags if you ask me." Byrne paused. "Except for Tiddly Pom, of course. Just look at her history: won last two out of four times out, not carrying any extra weight and Hughes is on board. What more could you ask for?"

"I take it you mean all that as a tip?"

"Yeah."

"Thank Christ for that, I thought you were just giving us a lecture."

"Fuck off, Walsh, you've got a nerve."

"Now, now, boys, no fighting." Byrne turned to see Paget smile, his moustache bristling at the good-humoured argument.

"Well, I don't see who'd arrest us as drunk and disorderly, do you?"

They all laughed, five policemen and Byrne, sitting in a first-class compartment on the race train, most of them hunched over the racing pages. It was the first time that Byrne had been included by Paget in any of the group socialising, and it was the first concrete proof that he was going to be accepted by them as one of their own. Though the odds were heavily against anything being said today; the mood of the group was certainly not serious. They hadn't even got to the racecourse yet and they were all already half-cut from the effects of a slap-up meal washed down with endless liquid refreshments.

Byrne watched them all with well-concealed satisfaction: Derek Paget, as far as they knew, the leader; Danny Walsh, Adrian Lurie, Bill Cohen and Chris Kerrigan. A nice little group that would light up Cadell's eyes when he was told. Not one of them lower than a Detective Inspector. In fact the only one of that lowly rank was Lurie and he seemed to be out to impress the others as much as Byrne was. Two new boys being given a taste of how good life on Paget's side could be, both eager to please.

Through the smoke-filled compartment Byrne observed them, seeking for some common denominator other than greed and power. There was nothing. So much for the experts who believed that you could read character from faces: Kerrigan looked as if he should be a history professor, and even Cadell would have bought a used car from the open-faced Cohen.

They had been topping up the alcohol levels with regular trips to the bar, and the small compartment was littered with empty cans and discarded paper cups. Byrne thanked the misspent youth which had given him a hard head.

Kerrigan was getting restless. "Hey. Dan the man, close the curtains, will you." He nodded to the grey hessian. "Time for a little pick-me-up!" Kerrigan sniffed loudly and smiled, and Byrne changed his mind about him looking like an academic, unless they were giving courses in corruption.

Walsh did as he was bid and closed the curtains, he also jammed the door shut with his foot. All the men had focused their attention on Kerrigan, and Paget spoke: "Off you go then, try and make it equal shares for everyone this time." The three old hands laughed, it was obviously an old joke, one that Kerrigan didn't look as if he shared.

"Fuck off, Paget. You try cutting this stuff when you're high as a kite. I couldn't even see straight, let alone cut powder into fifths."

They laughed him down, good-humouredly teasing.

Reaching into the inner pocket of his anorak, Kerrigan brought out a clear plastic bag of white powder.

Damn, thought Byrne, the things you do for Queen and country.

Kerrigan's eyes were bright with anticipation. "Great stuff this, only came in last week. You were right, Derek, it's uncut and clean as a whistle." As he spoke his fingers were busy, preparing the coke. "Who wants the first line? Derek?"

"No, Kerry, let Byrne."

What did they see this as, an initiation test? A treat? Whatever, Byrne took the offered card and, using a rolled tenner, snorted half a line into each nostril. The rush was instantaneous, the cocaine as pure and clean as Kerrigan had promised.

"Wow." Byrne swallowed on the metallic taste that filled his mouth, and with a sniff passed the doings to Paget.

"Told you it was good stuff," Kerrigan said.

Sitting back, head numb, heart suddenly racing, he felt the rush of counterfeit power and energy. He sniffed again, and grinned across at Paget, who was wiping his nose. "Very nice!"

"We look after our own. Don't we, Kerry?"

Kerrigan nodded, but his eyes were watching the powder. He was next in line. "Of course, and there's plenty enough for all."

Cohen grinned. "Just being careful."

Byrne watched them all take their turn, took his own again when it was time. The bag was only put away just before the train arrived at the racecourse stop.

"All ashore who're goin' ashore."

"Ah shuddup, Danny. Just because you once spent a week on the Woolwich ferry." Kerrigan was pulling the sliding door open, the train slowing.

"Yeah, and he was seasick the entire time. God, that operation was a waste of time. Back and forth, back and forth. Don't know what we were up to, even now."

Paget answered Cohen. "You don't have to, Bill. Just be happy that it went well and we all ended up better off because of it." A sharp look with the mild words, no dissent allowed in the ranks.

"Sorry."

Paget slung an arm around the wilting Cohen and smiled at him. "It's all right, mate. Just remember, there's a point to everything." A gentle shove and they were out in the packed corridor, then down onto the platform.

A seething mass of people was making its way past a harassed ticket collector. Pushing past them, Paget and his men waved warrant cards and were through, laughing, walking across the windswept car park towards the course entrance.

Programmes bought, they made their way to the private box that had been lent to Paget for the day, all of them heading unerringly for the drinks table.

Beer in hand, Byrne wandered over to the huge plate glass windows that overlooked the course, and stared down at the crowd, at the bookies and the tick-tack men. As he watched, the first race was announced, runners and riders already making their way down to the start. The crisp, late September day was quite perfect for racing.

Kerrigan came to stand next to him. "Lovely!"

"Nothing like it." Byrne agreed.

"Fancy a wander?"

"Sure."

Kerrigan turned back into the room. "Anyone want us to put a bet on?"

There was an immediate clamour and Kerrigan and Byrne ended up going to the tote with bets for them all. Mission accomplished, they wandered through Tattersall's to the track side listening to the tannoy commentary as the race started.

"This must be nearly the last of the flat races. Prefer watching when it's over the sticks myself." Kerrigan took a sip from a hip-flask, passed it over to Byrne.

"Yeah. Still, this is good enough."

"Mmm. Look, they're off."

They watched in silence as the pack of horses came up the straight and thundered past in a blur of sweating muscle and bright silk. Byrne grinned. "Looks like you're onto a winner!"

"It's not over yet, wait and see." The horses disappeared from their view and they sipped from the flask again, watching the crowd.

"Kerrigan - " But Byrne was interrupted, "Call me Kerry, everyone else does."

"Cheers, Kerry!"

"What about you, is it Andrew, Andy?"

"Just Byrne, usually." He shrugged. "I was in the army for a while and got used to it."

Kerrigan nodded. "Here they come again."

31

"And yours in still in front, you lucky bastard!"

They cheered, roaring with the rest of the crowd as Archduke cantered home. Byrne clapped Kerrigan on the back. "What are you in for?"

Kerrigan did a brief calculation. "Fifty quid, not bad for the first race." He grinned.

Byrne tore up his own useless ticket, letting the pieces scatter to the ground. "So much for that. I never have any luck here anyway." He shrugged as they pushed past the crowd of punters trying to get to the tote.

"Still, you know what they say about unlucky at gambling." Kerrigan winked. "So who's your lucky lady? A long leggy blonde, I'll bet."

"No, a redhead."

"Natural?"

"Of course."

"Right goer, then. Knew a redhead once myself, bloody near wore me out she did. Fucking nympho if you ask me." He smiled lecherously, denying his aggrieved words. "So what's yours like, eager?"

"Begs for it half the time."

"Lucky bugger."

"Yeah, I am."

If Kerrigan thought Byrne's laughter excessive, he hardly showed it.

Byrne nudged Kerrigan's arm. "Hey, how about a quick trip to the Gents."

He wiggled his eyebrows expressively at Kerrigan's pocket, winning a sly smile in return.

"And by the time we're done the queue here will have gone down a bit. You always get such good ideas?"

"All the time, mate, all the time."

The toilets were just around from the tote. They took it in turns to step inside and lock the cubicle door, Kerrigan taking a huge hit, Byrne a small one but managing to place a pinch in a bag in his wallet. It was a long shot, but with any luck Cadell would be able to get the actual consignment identified, which would be another nail in Paget's coffin.

Buzzing with goodwill they picked up the winnings, placed more bets then clattered their way back up the metal stairs to Paget's box. The men had made inroads into the whisky and the beer and all clamoured for the packet that Kerrigan had so inconsiderately taken away.

Jesus, thought Byrne, much more of this and I really won't be able to see straight. Though apart from general rowdiness there was little change in the group, all of them hardened drinkers. And drug users. Resigned, Byrne laughed at Cohen's crude jokes, drank with Paget and snorted coke with all of them. The afternoon passed.

And later, most of them dozed through the train journey home.

Decanted at Waterloo, they stood together chatting before the group slowly dispersed. Paget was talking to Walsh, and Byrne was trying to listen in when Kerrigan came over to him.

"You seeing her tonight then, Byrne?" Byrne looked mystified "Your bit of crumpet! She must be all right, I can never find a bird who'll put up with the hours." He was well on the way to being maudlin.

"I know. But this one's nicely amenable. Always ready to come round when I call her up. You need to train them right, Kerry, let them know who's boss. Eh, Paget, isn't that right?"

Paget waved Walsh goodnight and strolled across to join them. "What's that?"

"Women. Kerry was saying he has trouble finding one who'll put up with the hours."

"Ah! Poor bastard - "

"He just needs to get the training right." Byrne grinned. "Hard and fair, just like dogs."

"Absolutely, my son, the little bitches don't understand anything else."

They all laughed in gentlemanly accord.

Paget turned before he left. "We're all going to the Coach and

Horses on Monday, come along if you want to. They've got a stripper on, she's really - " He gestured expressively.

"That good, eh?"

"Better!"

"He had a fling with her a while back, didn't you, Paget."

"Had? No had about it, Kerry my son. She'll see me all right, anytime I fancy it. Good night."

"'night." And Byrne left them, heading for Victoria Street to flag down a taxi.

What a day. It had been years since he'd indulged in quite so many drugs. Sniffling noisily, he wondered if he could claim off Cadell for the wreckage of his sinuses. He smiled to himself at the thought, there would be no sympathy there. Cadell expected you to do what was necessary and shrug off any consequences.

Settling into the back seat he patted his wallet; the day hadn't been a complete waste of time, what with the drugs sample and a large wedge of winnings stashed next to his heart. Tiddly Pom, stupid name for a horse, but Hughes had brought her home and even at short odds Byrne had made a neat killing. The day had been in all worthwhile, especially as he'd learnt about Paget's little group, and picked up on a few of their foibles, especially Kerrigan's.

Watching the shimmering lights flicker past the window, he admitted the truth in the lie that he'd told Kerrigan. Peter Duncan was his. Gender was immaterial, as was the little matter of payment. Peter was his, beyond any argument. Still cushioned by drugs from the reality of his thoughts, he smiled, his features imbued with such sexual awareness that he startled the cab driver, making him anxious to get rid of the fare before the dark man voiced the proposition so obviously on his mind.

Impervious, Byrne waited to reach a telephone. Peter would be free. He had to be. Jesus, Byrne thought, he'd probably cry if he wasn't. He felt the wad of money that he'd won; there'd be no problems about cash tonight. Laughing out loud at his thoughts, Byrne paid off the cabby, not even noticing that the man was in gear and foot off the clutch before the door was properly closed.

Yeah, Peter would be in, always was when he was needed. The sweet ache in his balls firing his quest he ran up the steps three at a time, not even taking off his jacket before his finger was dialling the well-remembered number.

They were kissing as soon as the door closed, walking blind through the hallway, making it into the living room before clothing became too much and Byrne was tearing at Duncan, baring skin with a sort of desperation. Jacket and shirt were tossed onto the floor, belt undone, buttons ...

"Jesus, I hate button-flies."

"They're meant to make the wait more interesting."

"Sod that!"

Finally, Byrne ripped them open and taking a deep breath he stood back, watching. Duncan caught a glimpse of himself in a mirror; naked to the waist, trousers half open and pushed back from his hips, his sex bare, dark red hair curling around the base of his erection, he blinked, seeing himself as wanton, as desirable.

A pause and he dragged his gaze away, meeting Byrne's eyes. There was a wicked smile on the handsome face, and Duncan realised that somehow Byrne was already naked. He blinked, licked his lips.

Byrne stood very close; all heat and skin. He took a deep breath. "I think you should know, I've had more coke today than's decent."

Duncan nodded slowly, reaching out and lightly rubbing one nipple with his fingertips. "Mmm. And?"

"I want ... "

"What?"

"Everything!"

Peter laughed softly. "And, of everything the world has to offer, what would you like first?"

"You."

"Which part of me?"

That smile again. Then Byrne took Peter's fingers, pulling them from where they brushed against his nipple and pushing them down,

35

holding them roughly against the heat and solidity of his arousal. "Kiss me again."

Obedient, Duncan closed the short distance between them, his mouth slightly open, eyes heavy. The kiss was delicate, delicious, he drew their cocks together and squeezed, his other hand skimming flesh, travelling around to cup the muscular swell of Byrne's arse, pulling him close.

His mouth slipped away from the kiss, nipped down the length of strong neck, found the spot just under an ear and licked, making Byrne groan and his shaft pulse against Duncan's own. He smiled, and slowly lowered himself to the floor, mouth tasting all the way down to the saltiness that dripped from the tip of Byrne's cock.

He sucked for a little while, just at the tip, then licked down the thick, corded vein to the heavy sac, opening wide and taking one ball into his mouth, rolling it across his tongue, pressing up, rasping his tongue across the shiny, hairy skin, feeling it tighten. With both hands he stroked thighs, calves, arse, curling around to smooth the flat, hard belly, dipping into the shallow navel, before lifting them up and, finding the hard nipples, teasing them just as he sucked all of Byrne's sac into his mouth.

Both men groaned. Peter could only hold them there for a moment, then he slid them free and, greedy, needing, he took Byrne's cock and swallowed it deep, moaning softly as it filled his throat, fucking himself on its length, fingers biting hard into resilient skin as Byrne shuddered and came, flooding his throat until seed spilled from his mouth, trailing down his chest and belly, pooling in the dark red of his pubic hair and the faded blue of his jeans.

Breathless, he was pulled upright, and saw himself again in the mirror, captured for a moment, half-naked, mouth glistening, wanton indeed. He met Byrne's eyes and shivered.

"Turn around."

"What?"

"You heard."

He had. Slowly, Peter obeyed, pressing his back to Byrne's chest and belly, letting warm arms curl around him as Byrne held him close. Faint stubble rasped against his shoulder and he shivered again, just as Byrne's large hand took hold of his shaft and began to pump. He moaned, head falling back onto a solid shoulder, tilting, twisting to meet dark blue eyes and another kiss. It was enough, too much and gasping into Byrne's mouth he came, spilling into Byrne's hand, held up by his arms.

It took a moment for him to able to stand. Then he smiled in hesitant apology. "Sorry, I was quick off the mark ..."

"Don't apologise. That was a compliment."

And it had been; he hadn't come that fast in years.

"Be okay if I have a shower?"

"Course." Byrne turned and walked away, arrogant even down to his walk. He picked up his shirt, wiped his hands, tossed it to Peter. "Want a drink?"

"Yeah, great."

"I've some wine open ..."

"Fine." Duncan slowly wiped his hands, his face. The shirt smelled of Byrne, utterly delicious, arousing enough to make him shiver. Glancing up he watched Byrne, still naked, in the kitchen. He was whistling tunelessly. Peter had to smile, and picking up all his scattered clothes he wandered into the bedroom, dropped them onto the floor and headed for the shower.

Much later, they lay side by side, touching at arm and thigh, the slick wetness of their skin a reminder of hard-fought passion. Hard-fought and utterly involving: the sexual act as interpreter. Telling of things neither could admit in the cold light of reality.

It had all changed so fast. From months of impersonal sex to something else. Something he wasn't sure he wanted.

He wondered if Byrne felt it too, the change from strangers to - to what? Certainly not lovers. Not really, not as the romantics meant the word. Then what?

Byrne was asleep, and in the half-light Duncan's eyes followed the tracking patterns of cracks in the ceiling, knowing that he should get up, his own personal witching hour nearly at hand.

Wryly, he smiled at the white plaster. Crazy. Just crazy, to find someone special, to want to give them something, and find that the only thing they want from you is not to see your ugly mug after a night of fucking your arse off.

There were distinct disadvantages to being a whore that had never occurred to him before.

Crazy. He turned onto his side, heavy-lidded eyes transferring their attention to the blind sprawl next to him.

Byrne was sublimely unaware that his whore was anything but a whore, and it was going to remain that way. Exerting strong will-power Duncan restrained himself from touching the quirky arch of dark eyebrow, knowing that he should be out of the bed and dressed already, not hanging on till the last minute. He knew that he shouldn't give in to this irrational need to try and take strange comfort by staying. But he did. Had needed this for a while, this hour that was his alone when, weighed by a sweet melancholy, he let himself dream.

Bloody stupid, but what the hell.

The room was in twilight, the only illumination the filtered glow from the street lights. He raised his hand and shadowed it across Byrne's chest and arms, across neck, eyes and nose, the features relaxed, beyond stress and strain, and wished a silent benediction on the sleeper.

Duncan was certain that Superintendent Paget would trace him soon. He also knew that his chances of surviving the experience were remote. Paget forgave nothing. Ever. And he must know that ex-D.I Peter Duncan had enough information to take him down. Or almost enough.

And Duncan didn't want to draw Byrne into the mess. Paget had a nasty habit of throwing his nets very wide indeed. Yet despite himself Duncan kept returning to Byrne's bed; he just wasn't strong enough to stay away.

He sighed gently. What had started in anger and disgust at the corruption in the Met had become a race for information. Paget searching for Duncan, and Duncan searching for evidence that would irrevocably convict Paget and his fellow bastards. Four in prison already, but how many more still in the Met? It had been easier from inside the force. Much easier. But he hadn't know about Paget then, had only caught some minnows and unwittingly left the shark.

He had found out the truth though, after being thoroughly smeared by a campaign of gossip, lies and truth bent irrevocably out of shape. Well, he was going to even the score. Hopefully before Paget tidied away the nasty little inconvenience that Duncan had become.

It was, however, going to be a close-run thing.

In a moment of loneliness, he wondered what Byrne would do if he knew, how he would react. The temptation to talk to someone was so strong, but the likelihood of Byrne believing his story was remote.

He lowered his hand, resting it feather-light on the deep chest. Byrne had no idea, just as he had no real idea what Byrne did, though it was probably something illegal. There weren't many professions where you carried a gun, and though Byrne had never been obvious about it, Duncan recognised the smell of both cordite and gun-oil. Just how far over the line he was Duncan didn't know and, as he was never going to ask, was unlikely ever to find out

Anyway, he didn't really want to know, because if Byrne was ... what? What would make him beyond Duncan's personal pale? He searched for crimes he considered Byrne capable of. Too many. But none of them irrevocably awful. He'd never be a rapist, or a killer, at least not in cold blood.

He blinked, stopped his thoughts up short. Byrne might eat babies for breakfast for all he knew. Oh, and the moon was made of cream cheese. He twisted his lips into a half smile. Bloody enigma. Bastard enjoyed it too, very calm and collected on the outside, until you got him in bed; soon sloughed off, that did. Just as well, it wasn't the done thing to be rabid with lust while your partner lay there like an ice-maiden.

He glanced at the digital clock: 4 a.m. Time to be going. He never let himself sleep here, not even dozing, too afraid that he'd break the one promise Byrne had asked of him. Sighing silently he shifted, readying himself to be going. Very gently he lifted his hand, but firm fingers caught hold of his wrist.

"Don't." The voice was buttery with sleep.

"It's nearly time ..."

"I don't care, stay."

"But ..."

"Shuddup." His wrist was tugged hard, and Peter ended up lying close to a snuffling Byrne. "Go back to sleep ..."

"You don't want - "

"Yes, I do. Sleep."

And fitting himself into the nooks and crannies of solid warmth, Peter Duncan obliged.

The alarm went off at seven, and they woke together for the first time.

"Morning." Byrne was disgustingly alive.

"Garumph." A warm hand insinuated itself between Duncan's thighs, tickling at his balls. Immediately his cock swelled from morning interest to full erection. "Byrne ..." His voice was caught between irritation and arousal.

"That's me. God, you smell good, don't know how I ever let you get out of bed."

"You're usually asleep." Peter's voice was dry.

"Knew there had to be a reason, I'd never be that mad awake."

Duncan turned, causing a few seconds tangling as Byrne's trapped hand got in the way. The flesh he sought was hot and gently seeping moisture from its tip. "Wow. And good morning to you."

Pulled close until they lay nose to nose, their cocks rubbing together, crushed into their bellies, Peter offered a kiss. It was very gentle, barely more than a meeting of open lips, dry softness and wet, an exchange of breath; the arousal as serene as a summer's sea. Stiffening, Peter cried out first. Head thrown back he moaned as Byrne's teeth sank into the strong column of his neck, the pleasure-pain intensifying the orgasm, as Byrne was there too, his hot face buried in tangled hair.

They waited until their breathing quietened, then slowly disentangled themselves, skin peeling away from skin. Byrne, seemingly quite happy, kissed the tip of Peter's nose. "Now I know why I didn't want you to stay." Peter just caught the devilment glinting in Byrne's eyes. "I hate mornings, and now I'll have to set the alarm an hour early every time!"

He just reached the safety of the bathroom before a pillow thudded against the closing door. It pushed open. "Hey, you going to be there all day or go and cook breakfast?"

Climbing out of bed, Peter surprised even himself by wanting to do just that. He pulled on his clothes, quite content with the world.

In the kitchen he cooked absent-mindedly, rummaging in the cupboards to find everything he needed. After about ten minutes, the smell of frying bacon had to have drifted though the flat, for Byrne, dressed in his robe, padded into the kitchen and rested his chin on Duncan's shoulder, peering at the frying pan.

"Go and have a shower ... I'll finish this lot off."

Duncan turned an omniscient eye on him. "Yeah, finish the cooking then eat all the results."

Byrne gasped as if wounded. "How could you say such a thing? Just because I ate the last pancake roll last night."

"That was my pancake roll and you knew it. So behave." Peter leant back, and felt Byrne's arms curl around him.

"I always behave, hadn't you noticed?"

Byrne's breath was warm and sweet, raising the small hairs on Peter's neck, making him shiver. "Jesus, Byrne, you'll never get to work." His breathing was unaccountably ragged.

"Damn, I know." He groaned but backed away.

Released, Peter took a deep breath. "Go and sit down. Two eggs?"

"Please."

They sat quite companionably, eating in silence. There was no need to talk. Each of them was completely aware of the other, of every glance, every casual, accidental touch. A perfect circuit, they fed on each other; the levels of awareness and enticement a deep, intense delight.

Hardly the behaviour of a whore with his client. The thought was in Peter's head as suddenly Byrne pushed aside the remains of breakfast, knife and fork dropping with a clatter to his plate.

Two minds with but a single thought.

Except Peter knew that Byrne was less happy with the result.

Across the table Byrne was frowning, anger darkening his face. Abruptly, he scraped his chair back and stood up. Peter looked at him uncertainly, watching as the anger turned into something like rage.

"You finished?"

Duncan's plate was half-full and his knife and fork were still poised in mid-air. He swallowed his mouthful and neatly abandoned his knife and fork.

"Looks like I have." He glanced obliquely at Byrne and knew miserably that the interlude was over.

Already distancing himself he stood up, meaning to leave but hesitating. He didn't want to go, not like this. He glanced at Byrne's averted face, and against his own better judgement gave a slight shrug. "I'll wash up."

"Fine."

Piling plates Duncan crossed to the sink, scraping leftovers into the bin, filling the blue plastic bowl with water, adding a squirt of Fairy Liquid, ignoring Byrne's glowering presence. He found a washing-up brush and started on the plates, and all the while a voice was shouting at him inside his head, calling him a fool, telling him to go before even the mildest of his illusions was shattered.

But he couldn't. Instead he washed his way through the dirty dishes and cutlery.

Waiting it out.

Until, against reason, it worked.

Peter would have paid money to know exactly what Byrne was thinking, to know what had gone wrong, what thoughts were behind that beautiful, quite impenetrable facade.

Though really there was little doubt.

It would just have been nice to be certain, but a whore at the breakfast table? It was enough to make any man upset.

Shaking his head slightly, Peter poured away the dirty water, looked for a tea-towel. He was so lost in his gloom that he was startled when Byrne spoke.

"I invited you." Byrne appeared to be talking to himself.

Duncan sighed softly. It was true, he had been invited.

Byrne was leaning on the kitchen table, eyeing Duncan's back, avoiding his eyes. Seemingly almost against his will he pushed upright, then shrugged apologetically. "Look, I'm sorry."

"What for, unless it's for wasting half my breakfast? There can't be anything else for you to be sorry about." Duncan tried to turn back to the sink, but Byrne was there, hand gripping his chin. "Hey!"

"Peter, I'm trying to get you to understand."

"What?" He forced the hand away, holding on tight to the sudden bitterness that soured his mind. "That having a whore to breakfast wasn't such a good idea after all?"

"No!" Byrne blinked, then nodded. "Well, maybe."

"Suddenly ashamed of me?"

"Don't be stupid."

"Oh, stupid is it?" He turned. "Jesus, I wonder about myself sometimes." He was looking for the towel when Byrne's arms went around him. He stiffened, unyielding in the enforced embrace, deliberately coarse. "Watch it, darling, or we'll be into overtime."

Peter felt the tension that suddenly tightened Byrne's muscles. Well, that was that. He'd stepped over the line. Still, it was probably for the best. He stared bleakly ahead, waiting for Byrne to release him. But instead the arms curled tighter and an earthy chuckle stirred the fine hairs at his neck. "What's so funny?"

"Shut up for one moment, will you." Byrne manhandled the resisting body around. "And listen. I didn't mean it, and if you want I'll cook you some more bacon to prove it. It's my fault, I'm not used to having anyone here in the mornings, and I'm not renowned for being sane before 11 a.m."

"Bastard." Duncan tried for aloof dignity but, at the spark of

43

humour in Byrne's dark blue eyes, was lost before he even realised that he was at sea. All the anger had melted from Byrne, as if it had never been there. And Byrne smiling at him was too much, too irresistible. Peter smiled back, laughing softly, until the sound was taken into Byrne as they kissed with little passion, but warmth and affection instead.

"Forgiven?"

Peter nodded, feeling almost light-headed with relief. "Forgiven. But give me warning next time, okay?"

"Right. No unflagged fits of unreasonable temper."

"Only unreasonable?"

"Of course!"

They kissed again, and parted slowly.

"Peter, I've got to go to work, I'm late already." Byrne sighed. "Come on, I'll drop you off if you're going anywhere near town."

"Thanks, but I'm heading in the opposite direction so I'll get the bus."

"Sure?"

"Yeah."

In five minutes they were ready, and were almost at the door when Byrne cursed. "Damn, I nearly forgot, sorry." He rummaged in his pocket and came out with his wallet, handing over five notes. "There you go."

Duncan hesitated, then reached out, his fingers brushing against Byrne's warmth as he took the cash. He didn't want the money. Didn't want the lies that went with it. But there was too much he couldn't explain, too much he didn't really understand. Sighing softly he shoved the money into a pocket. "Thanks."

"You all right?"

Duncan shook himself and made himself smile brightly. "Course!" He watched obliquely as Byrne frowned, unsure. Duncan deliberately looked at his watch. "Come on - you'll be late."

Byrne cursed. "Yeah."

And the moment passed

3

The logical part of Byrne's brain acknowledged that he had to put in a certain amount of time, for appearances sake at least, in Records and Personnel, the rest of him refused to admit anything of the kind. He hated the work, and made no bones about it.

Bent coppers. As far as he was concerned you found four and missed ten. The whole system stank, the rusting wheels of law enforcement too archaic to deserve anything but being thrown on the scrap heap.

Sitting in front of a blank computer screen, he wondered exactly what Paget would try and get out of him. Cadell probably knew, but that was a lot of use, as it was doubtful if he was even telling himself.

Leaning back he tilted the office chair and plonked his feet on the desk, crossing his arms, yawning at the walls of grey files.

Perhaps he would call Peter. Last night, despite this morning's little upset, had been amazing. Satiated as his body was, he shivered at the thought of seeing him again. These days, he seemed to want little else other than to see Duncan as often as possible. True, their encounters had got a little out of hand since that first time.

It had been a filthy pub, tucked somewhere shitty at the back of the Old Kent Road. Duty done he had headed for a pint and a pastie, and was quietly getting it down when, out of idle curiosity, he'd started listening to an argument at the bar. There, facing up to one of the bouncers had been a young man, seemingly all fine bones, hair and fury, he had looked ridiculous; a David trying to pick a fist fight with Goliath. Byrne had been amused, and almost in awe of the slim man's command of the coarser uses of invective.

Then the bouncer had made a comment about hustlers. Well, the huge guy hadn't even seen the right cross that knocked him over. And that would have been that, except that the bouncer's friend had turned up and two against one wasn't fair. Byrne had thoroughly enjoyed himself; though he never did get to finish his pint.

He'd left when the barman pulled out a sawn-off. Well, it had seemed sensible. He'd dragged the still furious spitfire with him, taking him home to bandage a badly cut hand. And ended up propositioning him.

Quite what it had been that drew Byrne the instant they touched, he didn't know. After all, the man had hardly thrown himself into Byrne's arms.

"How much do you charge then?" Bandaging the nasty slash, Byrne was answered by a frigid stare that dropped the temperature by at least ten degrees. "It's all right, I'm not the Old Bill trying to set you up. I heard what the muscle-bound monolith was saying. Come on, how much?"

Nostrils flared and an arrogant profile was presented for his delectation. "A hundred pounds."

"You used to Arab princes or something?"

Obliquely, the man was staring at Byrne, almost daring him agree to the outrageous amount. Byrne remained silent until the lithe body moved away, preparing to leave; the sinuous curves were enough to tempt Saint Jerome away from the wilderness.

"Okay."

"What?"

"Come on then, I want my money's worth." Getting up off the kitchen chair he walked into the bedroom.

"Oy, no funny business, nothing kinky! Just you and me. And all night."

"As long as you're gone before I wake up in the morning." He narrowed his eyes, catching a slim hand as it rubbed obviously tender ribs. "And presuming you're up to it, of course."

The tousled head came up, challenge issuing from icy hazel eyes. "Oh, I'll manage. You'll get a good return for your investment."

Byrne changed the subject as he started to undress. "I'm sure. What made you pick a fight with someone that size anyway?"

"Miscalculation." The over-careful enunciation warned him off.

"Hope I get more than just a blow-job for the money."

This time it was fire. "I told you ..."

"Yeah, I know, value for money."

And it was.

He remembered it with postcard clarity, the whole evening: his own total abandon, letting go for the first time in years and fucking the braced body hard and fast, scarcely giving the poor sod time to breathe. He'd made up for it later, drawing a crystalline response that left them both gasping, adrift on a tide of passion.

After four months he was just as intrigued, just as aroused. And he still paid for the privilege.

Every time, like this morning -

Alone in the office, Byrne sat up, leaning on the desk, and remembered the look and almost imperceptible sigh that Duncan had given when he was paid. Strange, very strange, almost as if he was going to refuse the offered payment. Not that Byrne would have let him; it made life so much simpler that whores were for sale. You could say goodbye whenever you wanted to.

Goodbye.

His mind froze on the thought. Who did he think he was kidding?

The moment of revelation was shocking, and he wondered how he had ever deluded himself into thinking that what he wanted from Peter Duncan was a simple issue and could be resolved by a fuck or two or even twenty. Cold with self-knowledge he gripped the table with bone-white hands and then jumped when the door slammed open.

"Byrne?"

"Here, sir."

47

"My office. Now." And Cadell was gone.

Yes, sir. No, sir. Three bags full, sir. He muttered under his breath, but he obeyed, burying his own confusion under years of discipline, straightening his jacket as he went.

"Are you sure this is the man?"

"I am not in the habit of inventing things. Of course it's him." Cadell was the soul of impatience.

He swallowed and tried out a sentence in his head: Well, Mr Cadell, sir, it's like this, I've been paying to screw him for months, and now, I think, I ... He didn't have time to complete the thought.

"Well, spit it out, man, do you know him or what?"

Byrne nearly laughed, it was definitely more 'or what'. "I see him occasionally."

"Do you now." Cadell removed his glasses and waited.

"In fact," Byrne took a deep, calming breath and tried not to squirm under Cadell's icy scrutiny. "I see him. I employ him quite often. He's a prostitute."

"Aye, at least he was."

Byrne looked up, his face paling. "You don't mean ..."

"What? Oh, no, no, he used to be a prostitute, he's not dead." Cadell frowned at what he undoubtedly saw as excessive emotion. Then he just frowned. "So you see him in his professional capacity. Indeed, and how long has this been going on?"

"About four months."

"Has he said anything to you about the police?"

"No, he doesn't even know what I do." Byrne realised what his intuition had been trying to tell him, what he should have seen. So much for being a detective. "But I should have guessed that he wasn't what he seemed."

Byrne knew he should have paid more attention to the details, seen beyond the attraction he felt. How had he ever thought Duncan was a pro? He had too tight an arse for one thing; which was another carefully observed insight that he didn't repeat to Cadell.

"He's undoubtedly got enough experience to get by." Cadell

consulted the grey folder on his desk. "He spent at least a year on the streets up in Manchester when he was in his teens, made an impressive amount of money which he spent on supporting his drugs habit. He was lucky though, he lived through a vicious beating and he survived addiction to heroin. The combined experience was enough to make him clean up his life and after a couple of years he came south, changed his name back to what he was born with and joined the Met, quite a considerable achievement for someone with his past. He even did the marksmanship course, turned out to be a crack shot."

He scanned further, nodding with something like approval. "And we've been looking for him."

Byrne's mind was almost blanking out. This was all Peter Duncan? His own Peter Duncan? Cadell was looking at him though and he fought for some sort of clarity. He cleared his throat. "I didn't know we were looking for him."

"I should hope not, or you would have, I'm sure, informed me. He wasn't top priority until we realised quite how keen Paget has been to find him." Cadell stood and walked around the desk. "He's quite an interesting chap, your Mr Duncan. An honest policeman, a seeming rarity these days. No wonder they used such force to get him out."

"What happened?"

"He grassed on some bent members of his own squad. Testified in court too. Either he didn't know about Paget, or didn't have enough evidence right then to go after him too, which was a shame. Paget saw to it that he was disgraced and thrown out."

"And since then?"

"We think Duncan's been going from bad to worse. Paget hounded him for a while, made sure he didn't keep any of the jobs he found, then lost him. It was only because he was looking for him so hard and so obviously that we found out about it at all."

"And he's been seeing me."

Perched on the edge of the desk Cadell's gaze was uncomfortably intent.

"And I want you to continue seeing him."

"Why?"

"So we can use him to trap Paget."

"What!"

"Whatever information Duncan has, Paget seems prepared to move heaven and earth to cover it up. We can use that, use that Paget wants him silenced. With any luck, with Duncan as bait, we can actually get this wrapped up."

Smarting at the implied criticism, floundering on the idea that Duncan was to be used as any sort of bait, Byrne straightened. "I have been trying, sir, but he's a cautious bastard. I'm sure I only need a bit more time, there's no need ..."

Cadell interrupted. "Time is a luxury! I want this cleared up and Peter Duncan should do the trick nicely. Talk to Paget, drop Duncan's name into the conversation, let him know that you see him, tell him you employ Duncan as a prostitute, that should stir things up. Do what you do best, provoke him into some rash move."

And get Peter killed? Byrne swallowed the thought and tried to come up with an alternative suggestion. "I'm sure, given the right misinformation, Paget would try to blackmail me. Wouldn't that be better than risking Duncan, after all we could use his information as much as Paget."

"If he'll tell us." Cadell nodded. "Do what you think, you're the one on the inside, I'm not fussy, Byrne, as long as Paget goes away. That man is dangerous and we need him and his lot before they rot the police force from the inside."

Andrew Byrne swallowed. There had to be a way to protect Duncan, and still get Paget. He stood up, uncharacteristically uncertain. "Sir, Paget could, if he takes the threat seriously, just shut Duncan up permanently. It could be nasty. Paget's not the type to slap Duncan on the wrist and tell him nicely not to say anything." He faltered under a searching pale gaze.

After a long silence, Cadell asked, "Tell me, what's Duncan like?"

Byrne tried to find the words, but he wasn't really sure exactly what Duncan was like. Apart from someone he suddenly found he didn't want to lose. "Difficult, wary, bright. I - I like him." Byrne looked Cadell in the eye. "And I won't throw him to the wolves."

"Even if you have to?"

"There has to be another way. If I get Paget after me, then that should do the trick. He already thinks I'm crooked, maybe he just needs more of the same."

"Maybe." Cadell looked thoughtful, and Byrne was uncomfortably aware that his superior was seeing far more than Byrne really wanted. "Well, as you appear to be championing him, you will have to look out for him, I don't have the resources. Besides, I doubt if he'll want any sort of police protection."

"After what he's been through? I wouldn't either."

"Maybe not. Byrne, believe me when I say Paget is more important than Duncan. We need him. Duncan is only important for whatever it is he knows, and I doubt if we can persuade him to trust us enough to tell us outright what that is."

"I could try."

After a moment, Cadell shook his head. "No. I can't risk it, we can't be certain that Duncan's information will be enough. Paget first, everything else after."

"I'll get the word out about my hobby. Paget will love it."

"Good. If it doesn't work in a week, I'll use Duncan."

Byrne nodded, then stood up. "I'd better get on."

"Yes."

He turned, made it to the door where a sharp voice stopped him. "And Byrne, we'll discuss your liaison with a male prostitute at a later date."

"Yes, sir." Byrne left, closing the door and, in a moment of cowardice, wished he was never coming back.

"How's the Met faring this week, more exciting than my lot I hope?" Byrne asked.

"We like to keep the criminals on their toes."

Byrne put down the two pints he'd just carried from the bar. "I'm sure, I'm sure, just don't know how you put up with all those fresh-faced babies just up from Hendon with their, 'Oh! It's not Johnny's fault, his dad smacks him and now he just can't help beating up old ladies'. The police in this country are bloody morons." He shook his head. "I don't know why you didn't join my mob. When you're not being tied to Records, like me at the moment, you at least get some fun."

"Yeah, I envy you, carrying a gun, no questions asked. Bloody lucky. And you're right, the do-gooders get right up my nose."

"Who's the worst you've ever met, and what did you do to him?" Byrne let his face smile with feral interest. He knew he shouldn't be probing, but it was impossible not to, he needed to know what Paget had planned.

"Christ. There's too many bleeding hearts around for my liking. Mind you," Paget's eyes focused on the middle distance. "There was one slimy bastard worse than the rest. Got four of my division put inside. He's a fucking shirt-lifter as well." He twisted his lips, almost smiling. "We soon did a little number on him, though. Last I heard he was out on his ear."

"I should hope so! Maybe he should have been a social worker rather than a copper."

"Yeah, they're all bloody poofters. Though come to think of it, a session with a real man would've worked wonders - a nice dose of aversion therapy. Me, I'm keener on bodies shaped like that." He gestured to the barmaid and her overflowing charms. Both men stared in a moment of silent appreciation.

Byrne sipped his beer and tried not to feel ill. He risked another question. "How come he got away with shopping his mates?"

"Little toad went to a different division to report it, it was all over before we could do anything. He didn't last long afterwards, though." His smile was wholly malicious. "The chief doesn't like bum-boys on the squad. Heffernan up in Manchester did a bit of asking around for us. That fixed him quick enough. We couldn't have a past like that polluting the Queen's upholders of the law, now could we? We kept tabs on him for a while afterwards, made sure he had trouble getting jobs, that sort of thing. Had quite a bit of fun until he disappeared." His face darkened. "Mind you, we should have fixed the sod permanently, seems he's been around asking awkward questions; looks like he might be writing a little work of fiction."

"Naughty." Byrne spoke whilst bitterly thinking to himself: *You stupid bastard, Peter, how could you be so careless?*

"Yeah. And he'd better keep his head down, or we'll blow it off."

Oh, fuck! Appalled by the unadulterated hatred in Paget's voice, Byrne lifted his glass, at once toasting the proposition and hiding any shock that might have found its way to his face.

"Anyway," Paget looked over the rim of his glass, "we've been doing a bit of asking around. You've quite a chequered past, know you're sympathetic to us, in fact we've got a proposition to put to you. We need a contact just where they've got you beavering away. We need to know a few things see, and your department will know exactly what's going on."

"Only my boss knows that, come on!" Byrne protested.

"Yes, we know, but he must put some things down on the computer."

"I suppose I could get something." He tried to sound doubtful yet faintly hopeful at the same time. "For the right remuneration."

Paget grinned. "I thought so. And I expect we can come to a mutually agreeable arrangement."

"I like the sound of that."

"Good. We're efficient, Byrne. I like to know what's happening, what's what. Take you. Does Cadell know about the piece of arse you see every week or so? Oh, don't look like that, we did a bit of research, tapped your phone, needed to know a bit more about you, that's all."

"No, he doesn't know."

"Calm down! I'm not threatening you; just letting you know we do a thorough job."

Sweet Jesus they already knew!

Byrne was sure that he'd gone white as a sheet, though in the pub's dim lighting Paget didn't seem to notice anything untoward.

He managed to keep his voice normal, slightly outraged rather than completely dumbfounded.

"You certainly do that." Byrne took a swig of his drink, putting the glass down with exaggerated care. "I thought you didn't like queers?"

"I don't." Paget looked surprised. "But you see women as well, we know that, and we all need to let off steam from time to time. Nothing better for that than a pro who can take it and not scream the house down." He grinned knowingly. "Bet you had a high old time out in Africa, lucky bastard. What does your little fairy think of some of the habits you brought home?" He leered over the rim of his pint.

"Not a lot." Byrne tried to play along, though even for Cadell it wasn't easy. "But I pay him enough to keep him sweet, so why should I worry."

They both laughed, though Byrne had to drink to hide the hollowness of his amusement.

"Yeah, money and sex and power, the only things worth having. So will you still do it?" Abruptly he was serious, fixing Byrne with his intense eyes.

Byrne stared back. "Money?"

"Of course!"

"Let me know what you want."

"I will. It won't be for a few weeks. Rest easy till then, okay?"

"And look forward to the sex and power?"

"Looks to me as if you've got the sex bit sorted, mate! I might have to ask for his phone number!"

And though he knew Paget was joking, Byrne still had to fight the urge to tell him to fuck off, to keep away. For one thing was certain, if Paget ever found out the identity of Byrne's anonymous whore he'd want a lot more than just his phone number.

They chatted for a while longer, finally going their own ways at closing time, Paget to his intrigues and Byrne to a sleepless night.

By the time morning arrived he was pissed off and furious with himself. A lifetime of careful non-involvement and now this. Bloody stupid. Yet however he berated himself, there was no getting around his need for Duncan. Physically, certainly. He tried not to think that it could be anything other than that; that and the need to protect Duncan from a man he wouldn't have let loose on a dog.

Peter Duncan, caped bloody crusader. No, that was unfair. Byrne wondered what he would have done in similar circumstances. Been honest as Duncan had been, or just ignored it all as none of his own business. There was little doubt. Byrne didn't see himself as any sort of moral hero.

And Duncan did? After all that time on the streets when he was a kid as well. Poor bastard. Though at least it explained why he was so good at giving head. Probably could give lessons. Maybe had.

And what else was there, what other secrets were in that file that Cadell was keeping so close?

For the first time Byrne looked forward to his stint in Records. Showered, shaved and dressed with unaccustomed speed, he headed for work, on time for the first time in weeks. Whistling, he ran up HQ steps heading for Records. A voice stopped him half-way down a corridor.

"Byrne, wait up!"

"Hello, Aidan. How's things?"

"Don't ask, I'm fine. But you're wanted by the old man. And I think he wanted you an hour ago."

"I'm here early as it is!"

Murphy grinned and looked at his watch. "Mmm, by three whole minutes."

"Better than late!" Byrne was faintly aggrieved that his accidental efforts at punctuality were so scorned.

"You'd better get on with it."

"Bugger."

"You on for lunch?" Murphy was backing away.

"Sure."

"It's your turn to pay."

"It can't be!"

"'fraid so!" And, grinning, Murphy was gone.

Walking up to the next floor, Byrne knocked on the outer door of Cadell's office suite and peered around it. Alice, tall, blond and belonging only to their boss, was as cool as ever. Seemingly fixed at her desk she surveyed him perfunctorily, as if he were a small boy with mud on his knees.

"Morning, darling." He pushed into the room, grinning with evil delight as she winced. "He in?"

"Yes, he's waiting for you."

"What does he expect, a dawn chorus? It's only 8.30 now!"

She frowned at him. "Most of us start at eight and he's been here since seven so don't sound so hard done by." She relaxed her severe pose. "Go on, I'll bring some tea in a moment."

He winked at her, and knocked briefly on Cadell's door before walking in.

"Morning, sir. Lovely morning."

"Hurumph." Cadell, deeply engrossed in a document, only gestured for his officer to sit down. After a while, Byrne's fidgeting upsetting even his steely concentration, Cadell put the folder down and looked up as if noticing Byrne for the first time.

"Ah, Byrne, good morning." He pressed a button on the desk console. "Alice, bring in some tea, please." He leant back, tapping his finger against a stack of papers on his desk. "You'll be pleased to know that the lab reports on that cocaine sample have come in. Apparently it was part of a batch seized at Dover three weeks ago. The initial intelligence led the drugs squad to believe there should be over twenty kilos, in fact they found only sixteen. It was a joint operation with the police, your Mr Paget was in charge of the London end."

"Yeah, with contacts all down the line, I'll bet."

"You wouldn't get any odds. So we have the first piece of hard evidence. He was there, he stole a few kilos and we can actually pin that on him. But it is not enough."

He broke off while Alice arrived with a tea tray. "Thank you." She smiled neutrally, poured two cups, handed them out and then simply left. Cadell watched her, then turned back to Byrne. "There's another consignment coming in very soon. This time it will be heroin and I don't want it getting out onto the streets. Especially I don't want it put there by the police themselves. If Paget follows the pattern from last time, he'll want this for himself, except this time we get to catch him and as many of his cronies as possible."

Finally there was a way to catch Paget that didn't involve Peter Duncan: Byrne could have hugged his boss, though he didn't. "Perfect, surely?"

"Maybe, but I'm not prepared to let other options drop."

Suddenly he leaned forward, hands flat on the desk. "I hate this case, the corruption sickens me, that man using his position to feather his own nest at the expense of innocent lives. Bloody Hell! How do the police vet their intake, with a tape to measure their height?" Shaking his head, Cadell picked up his cup, sipping the fragrant, steaming liquid as the flash of temper passed. "Now, tell me how last night went."

"He's taken the bait."

Cadell looked up. "That's more like it! What did he say?"

"He asked if you knew about me seeing a male prostitute. He has no idea who it is, thank God. He also knows that I spent time in Africa, and had the front to insinuate that we're alike." Byrne's lip curled in distaste. "He's got my phone tapped as well."

"Aye, we know - happened a few days ago. Chap fitted it to the outside junction box. Neat job according to Masters. We've left it in place."

"You could have warned me! Jesus, sir, I should have known: I could have given who knows what away!"

"You might have, and it was an oversight that you weren't told, one I'm investigating. Luckily, as it is we got exactly what we want. Well done." Cadell was close to smiling. "Between the drugs operation and this we've got him cold. Good. Now tell me, exactly what does he want you to do?"

"No idea. He couched a threat as proof of their thoroughness and told me I'd know more soon. That was it. Jesus! I could have told him Peter's name and that would have really screwed things up!"

"It's not usual to call someone by their full name on the phone. Though we were lucky."

"Too right!"

Cadell sighed. "Now drink your tea and stop sulking."

"Yes, sir." Sarcasm dripped from the words but he drank up nevertheless.

"Have you spoken of any of this to Duncan?"

"No."

"Good." Cadell pushed himself away from the desk and stood up. "And you're sure he doesn't suspect that you know who he is?"

"Absolutely. I really don't think he'd be seeing me if he knew that." Byrne almost blanched at the thought. Time for explanations later when this was all over, and he could explain everything without need for concealment.

"True." Cadell was at the window, staring out into the cold day. "You know, I look out here and see all these lives, and know that so many would be ruined, are being ruined, by selfish bastards like Paget. And you know what I hate the most? That a policeman can behave in such a way. We need to stop him, Byrne."

"I know."

"You changed your mind then?"

"I catch up eventually."

"I knew you would." Cadell nodded, and almost smiled. Then he was all business. "I'll get Murphy and his team working a parallel operation to the one Paget is heading. That way, hopefully, we can catch him and as many of his lot as possible red-handed." He turned back into the spartan room. "If it comes down to it though, we need Paget most. He's the lynch-pin. If we get him the rest will fall apart anyway. You'll be on the inside so make sure you go along."

"He'll only spook if I push too much. He might be an ignorant bastard but he's not stupid."

"I know, but I'm sure you'll think of something."

"Thank you, sir." For nothing. "What about Duncan, can I tell him what's going on?"

58

"No. He doesn't need to know." Cadell glared. "You can tell him afterwards."

"Thank you, I was going to."

"Indeed."

They stared at each other, then Cadell nodded. "Be careful, Byrne."

Startled, Byrne nodded. "Yes, sir." Though he wasn't entirely certain what his boss was telling him to be careful about.

"I'm fuckin' bored."

"You in Records still?"

Back with Paget, on the town, drunk, Byrne was close to enjoying himself. "Yeah, reckon I'm getting corns on my arse. Fuckin' Cadell, he really hates my guts. Just can't cope with an honest opinion, the sanctimonious old bastard."

"You shouldn't give him so much lip, should you."

"Deserves it. Treats me like I'm a leper half the time, only fit to go out and shoot people when he needs his dirty jobs done."

"Sounds like you're more upset that you haven't been allowed out to play with that toy you carry under your arm than anything else."

"Maybe."

Byrne swigged at his whisky. They were this time in a private club, though the atmosphere was no different from the succession of pubs he usually met Paget in. The man certainly liked a seedy ambience for his drinking. Byrne frowned into his empty glass then put it down on the table.

Paget lowered his voice. "Byrne, what're you up to next weekend?"

"Nothing, mate, why?" At last.

Byrne looked up innocently.

"We're planning a little day trip to Dover. You won't get a chance to use your gun, but it should prove an interesting and nicely profitable day out."

Byrne allowed himself to twig. "I see, extra-curricular police activity, eh?"

"Got it in one. Interested?"

"Is the Pope a Catholic?"

"Good." Paget grinned. "There's a batch of heroin coming in, almost pharmaceutical grade, and ours for the taking. I'll cut you in on the profits in exchange for information." Byrne raised an eyebrow. "Your computers link with all the security services, including Customs, yes?" Byrne nodded. "Well, just find out where the units are going to be stationed on Sunday, so we can work around them, and I'll run a slice of the profits over to you."

Byrne didn't even pretend disinterest. "You're on. I thought there was some sort of big operation going down, the computers have been going like crazy. When do you want to know by?"

"As soon as possible, of course." Paget smiled at him. "And in as much detail as you can get. Two of us are in the drugs squad so that's no problem. It's Customs we need most details on. We go in, get the goods, put ours aside and off we go. Leaving everyone happy. The police and Customs have a nice meaty haul of drugs and we have some tasty stuff to sell."

"You're a genius, anyone ever tell you that?"

"Only me mum. Come on, drink up, it's your round."

"Well done, Byrne. With any luck it should all go like clockwork." Cadell was positively enthusiastic in his praise.

He watched as the man retreated from his office and sat back, his stern face betraying a rare moment of satisfaction. The information that Byrne would feed to Paget should hook him nicely. It would be a satisfying moment when Paget went down. Byrne had done well. He was good man, one who had earned his trust, despite his often irritating habit of believing he knew better than his boss.

In fact the slight unpredictability that had dogged his career had calmed at roughly the same time that Peter Duncan had appeared in his life.

Anchors can appear in many strange forms.

Cadell mused to himself about the character of that other young man. If things had been different, well ... Turning his mind back with a wrench to the business at hand Cadell tutted at his drift into the land of ifs and maybes. He'd be consulting fortune tellers next. Setting back to work, he began to go through the plans for Sunday. Yes, he thought, it should all go like clockwork.

The phone hadn't rung. Well, what do you expect, nitwit? Love notes? Serenades? Fuck him.

It had only been a few days, but Peter Duncan was already past the point of rationalisation.

Giving up, there being no sound reason to sit pining by the telephone, he hit the rounds of his contacts with a vengeance, wandering in and out of pubs, clubs and pool halls. A ghost at the wake, all he seemed to do was wait for one of his informers to repay the large amounts of money he handed out by coming up with the goods.

Too tense to eat anything apart from the occasional sandwich that only seemed to lie heavily in his stomach, he slept uneasily, spending hours every night poring over his notebooks, sure that something was there that he was missing but unable to get a clear enough picture to see what it was. The itch nagged at him, the instincts he'd always relied on shrieking loudly that something was wrong, and it was this certainty that something was brewing that had him out on the streets whenever he could afford it.

On the Friday night he finally got lucky.

The pub was one of the seediest in Kilburn; sawdust was strewn on the floor, more to mop up the inevitable blood than the ever-present beer slops.

Duncan had been visiting the place for years: first as a copper, then as part of his never-ending search for information. The pub's regulars, mainly Irish, all had long stories to tell about the indignities thrown at them by the police. Even discounting nine-tenths of the yarns spun to him it all still amounted to a damning indictment of London's finest. Homes raided, people harassed, strip searches, beatings, all because the victims had the misfortune to have Irish accents. In other parts of London the intonations were more exotic but the results were exactly the same.

Duncan had no sympathy with the IRA but he was aware of the other side of the coin: that not all the Irish were terrorists. The pub and its mix of ageing Irishmen who still clung to the accents of their childhood, even after forty years on English soil, and the young people of both sexes who mixed their Irish lilts with North London cockney, accepted him. It may not have exactly welcomed him with open arms, for he had been a policeman after all, but his dismissal from the force had earned him a sort of inverse respectability. The landlord had even been known to pour the odd free pint when it was obvious that he was skint.

Always nodding neutral greetings to the regulars, even taking the same corner table whenever it was free, he was left alone but never made to feel like an interloper. It was a long time since the word had got around, and all he had to do was sit silent over a pint for the seat next to him to be filled. Sometimes they came to exchange words of greeting, occasionally with stray bits of information about all sorts of things that they thought might interest him.

Rosie O'Neill was the archetypal tart with a heart overflowing with love looking for a deserving home. She had looked at Duncan and seen a skinny boy who desperately needed mothering. Sure he was not in the least in need of maternal care, Duncan been very wary. But she was so kind, and he felt so sorry for her, that he couldn't quite bring himself to the cruelty needed to dislodge her attentions. Except for that once when she'd bought him a bag full of groceries, and found her rose-tinted view of him discoloured by his response. Since then she had always smiled shyly at him, waiting for an answering softening of his face before moving to sit at his side.

Her resemblance to so many of the women from his childhood was so strong that he felt it like a hand squeezing his heart; lost innocence, lost youth, desperate need buried beneath the easy support of drugs.

His treatment of her was erratic at the best of times, malicious at worst. But as she seemed to remember only the good days, even Duncan had finally realised that she must genuinely like him.

It was a strange enough phenomenon for him to have been utterly surprised.

Tonight she was sitting at the bar, fiddling uneasily with the strap of her voluminous white bag. When he looked up, she smiled.

Without asking she bought a Snowball for herself and a pint for him, taking them over to his table. She pushed the pint towards him. "Hello."

"Cheers, Rosie."

She sat carefully, easing her short skirt down to an almost respectable length and genteelly keeping her knees together. "You look a bit down, love."

"I'm okay, Rosie. What you up to these days? Don't know about me, but you're looking in the pink." He picked up his glass and toasted her. "And I'm flush today, so I'll get the next lot in."

"Good for you!" She sounded genuinely happy for him. "But I'll have to be off after this one; got to get me quota in, you know what it's like - a working girl's life and all that." She twiddled with the ends of her teased and bleached hair. She had once confided that she aimed to look like the blond one from Abba, but he hadn't ever had the heart to say quite how far off she was.

"Yeah, woman's work is never done."

"Not when you've got a pimp, that's for certain."

"He treating you okay? Just let me know if he isn't and I'll sort him out for you."

"I know you would, love, but 'e's all right, better than most." She wouldn't have told him if her man beat her black and blue every night, Peter's slender build convincing her that he'd be pulverised in seconds by her six-foot-two man.

She drank daintily, pink tongue coming out to lick froth from her lip between sips. "What 'ave you been up to? 'aven't seen you for a while."

"Bit of this, bit of that. Still hunting up evidence, some things never change." He shrugged.

"You should give that up as a bad job." The stress lines that webbed across his temples told their own story.

His face tightened. "Never. They'll pay eventually."

"Was being chucked out of the police that hard?"

How to explain that it had been home? Along with more disillusionment and pain and more misery than he had ever wanted. Even more than he'd got from his real home.

"Sorry." As if unsure, Rosie spoke very softly. At least he didn't snap at her.

"No, it's not you, Rosie, just me. All I seem to do is run around in circles." Depression pulled at him, and he fought it, smiling tiredly at her exquisitely over-painted face.

"Yeah, life can get you down."

"Too right."

Swallowing down the last of her drink she took a look at her watch. "Oh, shit, look at the time, I'd really better be off." She leant over and planted a brief, chaste kiss on his cheek. "Be good, Peter, an' if you can't be good ..."

"I know, be careful." He almost laughed at the cliché, wondering exactly how he could apply it in his life. But she wouldn't understand. "I am, Rosie, always am."

Picking up her bag she hurried out, sailing a smile back at him just before disappearing out of the swing doors.

After a while he ambled over to the bar and bought himself another pint, chatting in a desultory way with the landlord before returning to settle down at his table.

By ten-thirty the pub was packed. Duncan had spoken to two old blokes lonely for company, and bought them both drinks; they'd been good enough to him in the past, and he enjoyed this opportunity to reciprocate. Neither one of them had any useful information for him. There was nothing buzzing about on the streets that was even hopeful.

Finally convinced that his instincts were lying to him, he was on the verge of getting up to go when a teased blonde head appeared at shoulder level through the crowd.

Rosie was breathless. "Peter! I can't stop but thought you'd like this. Bloke said it involved Paget. I've written down what he said.

Don't let on where you got it, please," and she was gone, burrowing through the crowd, leaving him speechless, holding a scrap of torn paper.

Reading it, he understood how Moses must have felt on being given two lumps of stone.

The words on the paper were ill-spelled and the hand as unformed as a child's, but to him it was the Ten Commandments and the Holy Grail rolled into one: a place, a time, a date and a simple sentence that spelled out Paget's downfall.

Suppressing a powerful need to shout out loud he left the pub, stepping out onto the filthy Kilburn street, smiling blindingly at the night. Finally.

Proof!

This would really fuck the bastard.

Almost light-headed, he wandered down the rubbish-strewn street, kicking empty cans as if they were cup-winning goals.

It was Friday night, thirty hours to wait.

He walked home through the deserted back-streets, taking short cuts through wind-blown alleyways, smiling inanely. A thread of what he finally recognised as happiness sang through his blood.

Paget.

Yes!

Letting himself into the room that he couldn't quite bring himself to call home and setting the kettle on the gas, he leant on the fridge while waiting for it to boil. Taking the slip of paper from his pocket he read it again, trying to persuade his disbelieving brain it wasn't imagination. Yeah, there it was, written in slightly smudged biro.

Whistling interrupted his reverie and he stopped gloating over Paget's imminent downfall long enough to make a cup of instant black coffee. Happiness, it was such a strange sensation. And life would be perfect - if only Byrne would ring.

That the only friend he had was someone who fucked him as a pastime was like ice-water poured on his thoughts. Especially as that someone seemed to have forgotten him. The bubble of elation burst far too quickly, and he was left feeling morose. Holding the mug he sat himself down on the sofa bed, and firmly told himself that he wasn't really waiting for the phone to ring.

He wasn't.

Finally, by two in the morning he admitted defeat. Not bothering to open the sofa into a bed, he curled up on it as it was, tucking himself under the blankets, quite still, eyes closed. Only to remain resolutely awake, his mind whirling with thoughts. At some point close to morning he drifted off, but his sleep was restless, torn apart by strange dreams that verged on nightmares he couldn't remember when he awoke sweating to a cold dawn.

The room was grey and unwelcoming. He stayed under the covers and consoled himself with fantasies about Paget's arrest. It was hard to believe that there had been a time when he had idolised Paget. But he had. Especially through the whole corruption trial, when Paget had been an outraged supporter of Duncan's case. It was only when it had all turned sour and he'd found himself about to be thrown out of the force that all the pieces had clicked into place and Duncan had seen exactly who was the real villain.

By then it was too late, and it was all to do again, for no one was going to believe anything he said without hard evidence to back him up. Paget had been very thorough.

For a long time all he had wanted was to bring the bastard down, the need so strong that he could taste it, bitter in his mouth, through every hour of every day of hating the way Paget used his power and authority to further his own ends. His single-mindedness had left room for little else. Until Byrne had turned up, and casually changed the way he thought about so many things. Now he wanted it all to be over and done, for he had finally remembered he had a life. He still wanted Paget inside, but finally he could imagine a time after that, a time when he would be free.

As gifts went, it was pretty amazing.

Sometime around mid-morning, Duncan climbed out of bed. Dressing in jeans and an old sweater, he wandered into the kitchen to make himself a coffee, taking it back to the sofa, sitting in silence, watching the walls.

A couple of hours later, aimless, restless, he locked up and ended up walking over to Camden, losing himself in the crowds, casually admiring the stalls piled high with junk. Crossing the canal he wandered down the tow-path to sit for a long while at the lock, watching houseboats negotiate the gates. But after a time he grew too chilly and walked on, hands deep in his jacket pockets, the wind tangling his hair, his mind carefully in neutral.

Avoiding the patrolling pairs of police with the skill of long practice, Duncan walked past the tube station and up Parkway. Stopping to buy himself a lasagne in an Italian café he ate four mouthfuls, leaving the rest, his restless stomach complaining at the sudden influx of food. The waitress, offended at his lack of appreciation, demanded to know what was wrong. He smiled at her: the food was great, but he just didn't feel well. It wasn't far from the truth.

Staring out at the street, watching the world, he nursed a single cup of tea and considered tomorrow. The way to deal with it was to go down to Dover and take photographs of Paget and company caught in the act of stealing the heroin. That should do it.

There was no point just ringing the police and telling them what was going to happen, they wouldn't believe him, not for one moment. One of ours, stealing drugs? Doesn't happen, sonny.

Briefly he considered the Police Complaints Bureau but discounted them, unsure how far his own Paget-enhanced reputation had spread. For all anyone knew, Peter Duncan was a worthless little shit who had grassed up some colleagues in an effort to take the heat off himself, and whose past was dirtier than the Thames.

So, he would go alone: it wouldn't be for the first time.

Putting the money down for the meal, he left, faintly cursing the darkening sky that promised rain. He needed it to be fine. For tomorrow to be fine. Photographs could be ruined by bad light.

He walked back up towards Chalk Farm, idling through the crowd, the dull ache in the pit of his stomach a physical expression of tension. He thought about Byrne, and regretted not having taken the other man into his confidence. But it was too late, far too late.

Besides, he briskly told himself, it'll all work out fine and you can tell Byrne your life history next time you see him.

Hopping on a 31 bus he gave up on Camden, getting off at Kilburn to walk the rest of the way back home. The rain came when there was still a mile to go but he ignored the trickles of water that ran down his face and dripped from his sodden hair, plastering it to his face and neck, almost making him wish it was short and neat like Byrne's. Though Byrne did seem to like it the way it was. Had liked it, anyway. He sighed, breath warm on his rain-chilled lips, and knew himself for a fool.

He turned into his road with a quickening of pace, waved through the window at the owner of the downstairs Chinese Restaurant, and let himself in, running up the stairs. Back in his rooms he stripped off his sodden clothes and quickly towelled dry before changing into the first clean and dry clothes that came to hand, all the while considering.

The urge to be doing was very strong, and part of him really wanted to get the Dover train that night. But that would have meant staying at an hotel. And besides, a day return on the train was cheaper and he needed every penny in his possession for purchasing rolls of film.

Be sensible, he told himself. Sensible.

He convinced himself and, finally resigned to another night of waiting, he slumped down onto the sofa to watch TV, though nothing really registered. By ten o'clock he was tucked up, trying vainly to sleep, mildly regretting that he'd always turned down Rosie's offers of various different uppers, downers and a few things in between.

Rosie. He'd have to get her something to say thank you. Guilt for all the times he'd snubbed her enforced the thought. Who'd have believed that of all the contacts he'd made she'd be the one who would come up with the goods? He considered the things that she'd like best. Cash wouldn't be any good: her man would have that off her before she'd gone twenty paces down the road. A bottle of perfume. Something sweet, heady, and with a name she could impress the other girls with. Yeah, something exotic, bestowing a temporary glamour.

His mother had, on the rare occasions when she'd had some spare cash, always treated herself to a bottle of Chanel No.5, using it with abandon, its promise of dreams come true pervading her life until it ran out and she went back to Boots' cheapest. Sometimes she would wait a year before she could buy another bottle, the rash expense too much for her income to bear. Duncan remembered with clarity the bright glow that would light her face when, teetering back from the shops on impossibly high stilettos, she unwrapped her purchase, the first spray of scent an almost religious experience.

Wonder if Rosie would get the same sort of pleasure? Not that she ever seemed as sad as his mother. Perhaps she was more suited to the whore's life. More likely she just hid it better. Still, perfume would do nicely. When he could afford it.

Every thought circled back to Byrne. Damn.

Lying alone in the neon-shadowed darkness, listening to the wet sounds of cars driving by on the street, Duncan conjured Byrne's presence. The touch of sweet-smelling skin, soft-downed glide of flesh against flesh, smooth, textured like warm silk. He wanted to be wrapped in it; held tight by strength and muscle. Taken. Loved.

Even the idea was comforting.

See you next week, Byrne, tell you everything then. Shocked by the thought, dark superstition whispered in his mind, and reaching an arm out of the covers, he touched wood. Just in case. Half-laughing, half-reassured, he pulled his chilled arm back into the warmth, and told himself: it's only a reflex action, like going in to light a candle whenever you pass a church. It means nothing. A placebo for the soul.

Wide-eyed, sleep as far away as the moon, he stared blindly at the cracked ceiling, trying to persuade himself that the itch at the back of his neck wasn't presentiment. After all, what was there that could go wrong?

4

The Ford Granada began to descend the long road into Dover at 2.30 in the afternoon exactly. The closer they got to the docks, the more the adrenaline and excitement stirred amongst the car's occupants.

Driving with his usual expertise, but none of his usual concentration, Byrne chatted sporadically to Kerrigan, whilst his mind circled on the events that were already under way at the docks. For all that Cadell had planned the operation with his usual meticulous attention to detail, there were still far too many loopholes.

The operation was set to run parallel to, but unknown by, the police, though the Dover Harbour Board were aware of what was going on, there having been no way that Cadell could set up an operation so big without their knowledge. Yet Byrne fretted, for even in that he could see problems. The only good thing was that the Harbour Board was innocent of any complicity in Paget's schemes.

Glancing into his rear-view mirror Byrne checked that the Rover with Paget and the other two coppers inside was still on their tail. He smiled viciously to himself; for all his guile, Paget was still making the basic mistake of over-confidence. What a show-off, bringing five men on a job that only needed two. Still, it was all the better. Catching as many as possible red-handed: just what was needed in court.

Paget's plan was very simple: he would monitor the drugs bust by radio, then swan into its aftermath and disappear a few kilos into his own car. Simple. And easy as long as you had half the on-duty policemen in your pocket.

"Nervous?" Kerrigan inquired. He'd spent a large part of the journey telling Byrne how he was going to spend the money. He was hyped-up from expectation and wanted Byrne to be the same.

"Why? Not going to be any trouble is there?"

"With Paget in charge? You must be joking. He's got it all sewn up nice and tight."

Complacent bastard, thought Byrne. Just you wait and see.

As they pulled into the dock area, Kerrigan glanced at the dashboard clock. "2.37, right on time. Byrne, it'll all be sitting there waiting for us." He rubbed his hands together gleefully, and looked over with curiosity. "What are you going to do with your share?"

"Christ knows, money runs through my fingers like water."

"Yeah, I know exactly what you mean."

Byrne ignored Murphy who was standing in as a petrol pump attendant across the road, and slowed down to let Paget overtake.

"How often has Paget done this? He seems to have it all off pat." To Byrne the admiration in his voice was sickening, but Kerrigan seemed to concur wholeheartedly.

"Two or three times. All you need is friends in the right place and it's like taking candy from a baby." Kerrigan grinned and Byrne could only agree.

"Yeah." Byrne ceased listening as up ahead the other car had stopped. He pulled into the side and turned the engine off. "A nice afternoon's work, if you can get it."

"Better than most, my son, better than most."

They got out of the car and strolled over to where Paget was standing talking to the officer in nominal charge of the operation, right by a heaped pile of packs of confiscated drugs. Paget's Rover, its boot open, was conveniently close. It was all very neat. The theft was effected in full view, the very ease with which it was done giving no rise to suspicion amongst the few officers not involved in the deal.

Beaming all over his face, Paget turned to Byrne, and put a jubilant arm over his shoulders. "Told you, easy as pie." He gave Byrne's shoulders a shake. "I am a very happy man."

Kerrigan was casually lifting packs into the boot.

Byrne smiled widely in return, staring into his eyes, savouring the moment of Paget's imminent downfall. Walking together, they looked uncommonly like soul mates.

Kerrigan banged the boot lid shut on their contraband and Byrne thought, now, Cadell, come on. The urgency for movement swarmed in him, and it was only because he was waiting for Murphy and the others to move that he even saw the figure who was suddenly running towards him.

Byrne cursed softly. Peter? Here? Thinking to block Paget's view, Byrne moved to shield him, and only belatedly realised that Duncan wasn't heading for Paget at all, but for himself.

What …

Caught in a moment of surprise, he turned just as a lightning-hard fist knocked him flying and the impact of his skull with the stone curb took all conscious thought away.

In the silence of the operations room Cadell cursed; of all the stupid, idiotic, mad-cap ... Impotent, he could only watch as Paget casually walked up to where Duncan stood glaring wildly at Byrne's still body, and without pause hit him hard across the back of his head with his gun.

Cadell winced as Duncan collapsed, though almost before he hit the ground Paget had hold of him, and was bundling him into the back of the Rover before simply getting behind the wheel, waiting two seconds for Kerrigan, and then just driving off.

As the Rover sped away in a cloud of burning rubber, Cadell was issuing orders for roadblocks and interception. But they had all been geared up for a stakeout and a drugs bust, and Paget was through the barriers and lost in the backstreets before they could even set up pursuit.

It was a neat trick, vanishing into thin air. One that Cadell refused to admire. He cursed vainly at everything: from the inefficiency of his men, to the winding streets that had hidden their quarry so effectively, for even though an APB was put out immediately, no trace was found, the car disappearing completely into one of the most densely policed areas of the country.

By the time Cadell reached the scene of the fiasco what was left was under control. Two of Paget's men were in custody, and they had some of the heroin, but not the rest which had been taken by Paget.

Footsteps hard on the concrete, Cadell found Byrne leaning heavily against his car, tenderly nursing a head that was obviously bleeding, having just regained his senses. If that's what you'd call it. Cadell wasn't sure, convinced as he was that Byrne must have told Peter Duncan about the set-up.

"Fuck it, sir, there must be some trace of them. That bastard's got Duncan, he'll kill him. He'll think I was with that lot too. Bastard. Paget will kill him! He's got him - "

"Yes, yes, I noticed. But what was he doing here anyway?"

"Don't look at me like that, I didn't tell him anything. I've been so busy with Paget that I haven't even seen Duncan recently. Jesus, I don't know what the stupid idiot was doing here ..." He broke off as Hoskyns loped up carrying a camera.

"I found this next to the van, sir."

Cadell took it. "I think this explains Duncan's presence." He looked up. "He was after his own proof." Cadell nodded to himself. "Hoskyns, get the film processed as soon as possible." He dismissed the agent and turned to his most pressing problem. "What did he say to you? I could only see it, damn it all. I couldn't hear anything."

White-faced, Byrne closed his eyes. "Nothing. He just hit me. Looks like it wasn't just Paget I managed to fool." Frowning, pain lining his face, he asked, "What happened then?"

"He was looking down at you when they got to him. Paget knocked him out; Duncan was probably only half-conscious when they pushed him into the Rover and drove off."

"And we let them." He closed his eyes.

"Yes, it's a complete fiasco."

They stood in silence for a moment.

"He'll kill him. I don't think I've ever seen such hatred directed at one person. Even when we were talking in the pub he was unbalanced when it came to Duncan. After this, with all restraints taken away, God knows what he'll do."

Cadell sighed. "I know. But in this case Paget should be thankful. It was only Duncan's appearance taking us by surprise that let him get away."

"I shouldn't think he'll see it like that."

"No." Cadell inspected his agent. "Get yourself to hospital, you look as if you've got a spot of concussion."

"I'm all right, sir, it was only a knock."

"Hospital. Murphy can take you."

"Yes, sir."

"I'll keep you informed." Cadell's voice was surprisingly gentle and, startled, Byrne looked up. Cadell continued, "I hope we find them. Mr Duncan deserves better than this."

Silenced, Byrne nodded.

"Catching flies, Andrew?"

"No." Byrne shook his head to clear it, regretting the movement instantaneously.

"Come on, mate, off we go to hospital." Murphy guided the clumsy figure into the car's passenger seat. "There's one on the way back to town."

"Thanks, though I really don't - "

"Now, now, you heard the man. Just sit there and Auntie Aidan will make sure you're fine."

Byrne gave a small snort of amusement. "All right." He clicked the seat-belt shut with a sigh.

They drove in silence, and were halfway up the A2 before Byrne muttered, almost but not quite to himself, "He won't believe it. He can't."

Murphy gave a baffled shrug. "Who and what?"

"Duncan. Believe what he saw. That I'm as crooked as they are."

"Well, that's a tough one. I suppose that depends on what he thinks you do for a living."

"He doesn't know anything. I always got the impression that he thought I was some sort of villain. I never told him what I do, it never seemed necessary."

"In case it scared him off." It was a statement.

"Yeah, that too." Byrne shifted in his seat, and stared morosely at the landscape as it speeded by. "I didn't tell him anything."

"It's one of the things you get paid for. You did the right thing."

"For Cadell, yes." But for Duncan? Not at all.

Hands sure on the wheel, Murphy glanced at his passenger. If he was curious about Duncan's place in Byrne's life he hid it well, and simply drove.

Beside him Byrne relapsed into silence, keeping the darkness of his thoughts to himself. After all, it wouldn't matter what Duncan believed of him. You couldn't hate someone when you were dead.

Though dazed and nauseous, Duncan managed to retain enough awareness to know that they hadn't travelled very far before the car turned off the road and started to bump slowly over uneven ground.

He'd spent the journey pushed half on the floor, head down, Paget's gun ground hard into the back of his neck. Sweat dripped into his eyes, and he knew quite well that his life hung from a very fine thread.

As the engine clicked off he finally felt the tension ease between his two captors.

"Jesus." Kerrigan sounded limp with relief. "That was close."

"Too right." Paget was out and on his feet. "Come on, close the garage doors and let's get inside."

Kerrigan opened his door, and Duncan blinked as the interior light came on.

"What about him?"

"I've got plans for him." Duncan twisted as Paget reached into the back and casually hit him across the shoulders. "Come on, get out."

Awkward and cramped, Duncan carefully uncurled himself,

listening as the garage doors slid shut. For a moment there was darkness then a light was switched on. As he stepped away from the car Paget was there, his hands hard, shoving him into the breeze-block wall. Duncan blinked, seeing a double garage, empty except for the Rover and a heap of old crates on the far wall. Apart from the metal shutters that Kerrigan was noisily closing, the only exit was a single door that must lead into the house. He shifted, and a gun was suddenly nestled viciously against his neck.

"There's no point trying anything. Understand?"

Duncan nodded slightly in response. "Yeah, I heard you, I'm not deaf."

"Kerrigan, get your cuffs."

The tall man came up behind them and roughly clamped Duncan's hands behind his back, the snick of metal on metal frighteningly final. Pushed into the wall, crowded by the two men, Duncan straightened his back, hiding every glimmer of fear.

"So what happened?"

"This little fucker is what happened." Fury darkening his face, Paget whipped his hand, gun and all, hard across the side of Duncan's head, stepping back as his prisoner slumped to the floor.

Duncan knew he was moaning, the pain in his head so sharp he wondered if he was going to be sick.

"Bastard!" Dazed, Duncan looked up in time to see Paget's foot move. The kick caught him in the ribs, and he gasped.

"Feel better now?" Kerrigan was talking to Paget. Duncan shuddered and looked up, seeing the amused, somehow academic, face relax.

"Yeah."

"It wasn't him, you know, they were on to something anyway. This maniac ruined their plans as well as ours."

"I'll thank him properly later." Paget kicked out again. "Never thought the day would come when I'd be grateful to the cunt. What a fucking mess!"

"Remember, he got us away. And he's still our insurance."

"Yeah, a ready-made hostage."

"Let's hope we don't need one, I want to be out of this nice and easy."

They exchanged a look. And curled on the floor, Duncan wondered if there was any hope at all.

"Come on, let's get inside. All we can do is wait."

Paget was walking away.

"What about him?"

"Bring him along. I'll find somewhere to lock him up."

Only half-conscious, Duncan gritted his teeth, biting down the moan of pain as he was dragged inside and dumped in a hallway. Utterly despairing he opened his eyes, seeing peeling paint on old walls, bare floor-boards, little else.

"There's a downstairs bathroom, we'll keep him there." Paget came back, slipping his gun back into its holster. He peered down, and smiled. "Still awake? Little bastard - "

A slap almost took the last of reality away. Duncan felt them pick him up, heard them talking as they dragged him along.

"Jesus, you wouldn't think he could weigh this much."

"Skinny little shit. At least between us we won't have any trouble with him."

Pulled through a doorway and dumped without care onto the floor, Duncan held still for a moment, then eased onto his side, blinking his eyes open.

It was a big, old bathroom, maybe a room that had been converted when plumbing was invented. It was cold and Kerrigan was rubbing his arms as he checked the security. Duncan did too: one window, barred, and one door into the rest of the house. Duncan could have wept.

"Not exactly home from home, is it?" Kerrigan kicked at the wall.

"He doesn't deserve any better."

"Too right."

"The rest of the house isn't up to much, but it's better than the cell we might have ended up in. And at least we won't freeze to death, Gerry left a Calor gas heater in the living room."

"Bloody cold in here though."

78

"Yeah. Oh dear, never mind!" Duncan watched them smile. Watched Paget watching him in return.

"Don't worry." Paget came to stand over him. "The minute we get the all clear, we're off to sunny Spain."

"You bastards."

"Hear that, Kerry? He can still talk!" Paget crouched down. "But it won't be for long."

A slap rocked Duncan's head. Another. Then, his hand tight around Duncan's jaw, Paget deliberately punched him in the belly. The third blow brought no reaction at all. And Paget smiled.

Duncan awoke slowly, reality wavering until he finally knew he was lying with his face pressed to cold lino. Dark blue lino, with what appeared to be slightly surreal fish swimming across it. Curious, sure he was imagining things, he tried to touch one, but the attempt at movement only sparked aching discomfort that at least served to clear his mind. And made him remember he was cuffed, tightly from the numbness in his arms.

Duncan cursed himself. He'd been an idiot. Again.

He shivered suddenly, discomfort acute as he lay twisted on the floor. He was cold, his head hurt and he was absolutely certain that things were only going to get worse.

With an effort he pushed his body upright; sitting marginally better than lying. Peering around, squinting past the headache that pounded at him, he almost laughed. Trapped in a bathroom. Well, at least he wouldn't die of thirst.

Bath, toilet, sink and the stink of old piss for company. Lovely. It was also bloody cold, and the fish-print of the lino made him feel slightly unwell. Or maybe that was the knocks on the head.

The room was big, high-ceilinged, all the fixtures old. A window, dark with ivy, let in a trickle of faded daylight. Vaguely he wondered if it was still the same afternoon or early the next morning. Probably the same day. Maybe. Was he stiff enough to have been here that long?

Legs curled under him, he pushed upright, using the wall as

support. After a moment he steadied and with a few steps made it to the door.

Locked, of course. But he'd had to try.

Upright, the room looked smaller, but just as uninviting. The walls were green with mould, running with damp. The enamel of the bath was cracked and brown, years of lime-scale crusting around the taps, a few small black insects clustered around the overflow. The toilet bowl was unspeakable, stinking and cracked, seatless.

Still, if the worst came to the worst he could always hang himself on the pull-chain. If it wasn't too rusty.

Faintly amused at the darkness of the thought, he slowly paced around, stopping by the sink. How cruel was Paget? Would he have left him in a bathroom with the water turned off? Duncan twisted around, got his hands around one of the taps, and winning a battle between its stiffness and the numbness of his fingers, managed to turn it on. The water was ice cold, clean. So, not that cruel then.

Leaning over the sink, lips angled under the pouring water he swilled out his mouth, spitting blood, watching it swirl away. Then he drank, the water so cold it made his teeth ache. He found he was very thirsty.

It took a while for him to realise that he wasn't gagged.

Straightening, he held still. Considering. After a moment he just relaxed, wiping his mouth awkwardly on his shoulder. There was no point shouting for help. Paget wouldn't have let a detail like that escape him; they were probably in the middle of nowhere. Even listening hard he could hear nothing but the odd bird chirruping away in the distance. No traffic noise, nothing. No rescue on hand.

It didn't seem as if he would be walking out of here soon. If at all.

Turning the tap off he went back to where he'd sat before, and slowly eased down to the lino, sitting back with a sigh, shoulder to the wall, cautiously resting his head on damp plaster.

He felt nothing. Discomfort, yes, but no emotion. The most he felt was desolation.

Byrne and Paget.

Paget and Byrne.

The names turned in the aching void of his mind, leaving room for nothing except keening loss. His face was damply cold and he hurriedly wiped the treacherous salt away on his shoulder.

Damn you to hell, Andrew Byrne, he thought. And sniffed loudly.

Staring sightless into the shadows, he knew himself for a fool, and burned the misery away in flames of self-hatred. Fancy being stupid enough to trust so blindly! He'd had that lesson beaten into him years ago: don't trust. It doesn't pay.

But what had made him forget something so painfully learned? Something quite new, for he hadn't trusted, exactly. He'd loved. And that truth he avoided, stepped around, ignored, unsure if there would be any surviving of the answer.

Jesus, Byrne probably knew all about him and had laughed up his sleeve every time they'd met; the spice of fucking an ex-cop just what the bastard needed to get off. Humiliation burning into the back of his eyes, he curled against the wall, the sharp pain in his head at least serving to distract his thoughts.

As long as he carefully thought of nothing it would be all right. Nothing. He could do it. Quite still in the near-dark, growing colder, he grimly counted off seconds. It was as good a way as any of passing the time.

At some point he must have drifted off into a state that was part sleep, part oblivion for when the high overhead light clicked on he awoke with a start, scrunching his eyes against the blinding brightness. Ridiculously, both Paget and Kerrigan were laughing. Duncan hadn't heard the joke, though he was quite sure he was the punch-line.

"Wakey, wakey. Come on, Duncan, we want to have a little chat. Oh, you are awake."

"Quick as ever, Paget." He grunted as a kick caught him sharply on the thigh as he scrambled to his feet. "And eloquent as always."

Duncan leant back against the wall, watching, wary as hell. Both men were flushed, at least partially drunk if not worse.

Paget took two steps forward and pushed himself close, curling his fingers around Duncan's neck, breathing whisky fumes into his prisoner's face. "I'd be very careful if I was you. Don't push your luck with that mouth of yours. We might be here for a while and I don't give a damn one way or another what happens to you. So, you can make all this easy, or hard; it won't make any difference to me."

Personally Duncan couldn't have given a damn either, convinced that the only way that Paget would leave him would be with a bullet as a keepsake. He coughed painfully as the fingers gave a squeeze then let him go. He stared up as the big man straightened, his flat, emotionless defiance speaking louder than words.

"Jesus, you haven't changed a bit, have you. Well I've got news for you, mate, after a couple of days you'll be begging to talk to me."

"I doubt - " Duncan's words were lost as Paget backhanded him.

"No mouth! I told you." Another slap, rocking Duncan's head hard into the wall.

Blood was dripping from his lip. Duncan licked it away. He didn't say anything.

"That's better, you're learning!" And he hit him again anyway, a low punch that left Duncan retching and on his knees.

"Kerry, look at this! I think we've got him tamed."

Kerrigan, cigarette in his mouth, came close and looked down at where Duncan was doubled over, fighting for breath. "Maybe. But we both know what'll really do the trick - " He reached up and, after a long drag, took the cigarette from his mouth and casually stubbed it out on the back of Duncan's neck. Stepping back he was laughing out loud as the kneeling man cried out in shock and pain and was suddenly pressed back against the wall, eyes fixed on the blackened stub in Kerrigan's hand.

"Look, it's all gone!" Kerrigan twisted his fingers, letting tobacco and shredded paper fall onto the floor. And then casually pulled a still wrapped packet of John Players out of his pocket. "But I've got plenty more."

"You're bloody sick!"

"And you're scum who deserves anything it gets!" Kerrigan was suddenly angry, the veins in his forehead pulsing. "I'll do what I want and enjoy every bloody minute."

Paget was next to him. "Come on, Kerry, show Mr I'm-So-Righteous our real surprise."

"Yeah." Kerrigan relaxed, and tucking the Players away pulled a case out of another pocket. Slowly he opened it. He was smiling, knowing that Duncan's eyes were following his every move, enjoying his power, the helplessness of their captive. He clicked the case shut and lifted what it had contained into the light, so that the spike of metal and glass flared into incandescence.

"No." Duncan was shaking his head, staring at the brown liquid that filled the syringe.

"No? And after I went to all the trouble to prepare it. How ungrateful - "

Pushing back, trying to disappear into the wall, Duncan could hardly speak he was trying so hard not to beg. "No!"

"Oh, don't be a spoilsport, Peter, it won't hurt a bit!" Kerrigan held the syringe up, tapped the glass and expelled a little liquid through the needle. "All ready. Roll your sleeve back."

"Not fucking likely!" Duncan shuddered at the thought and without warning kicked out, slamming his feet against Paget's legs. But he was too slow, Paget danced away from the glancing blow and was back, all his weight behind a punch that knocked the prisoner away from the wall's slight protection. A knee across his neck and the cuffs were unlocked, flopping his body open. Paget moved, trapping one of Duncan's arms, pushing the wrist high into bony shoulder-blades, twisting the other out straight, laying it on the floor, holding it tight, his knee in the small of Duncan's back, his weight close to breaking Duncan's spine.

Finally, held absolutely still, the prisoner gave in, whimpering as Paget ground his wrist higher.

"Want me to dislocate your shoulder? Then move, all right?" A slight nod in reply. "There, get his sleeve up."

Kerrigan obeyed, pulling back soft green cotton to expose an arm corded into anatomical detail by panic and despair.

"I bet you remember what this feels like: they say junkies never forget." Kerrigan's voice was utterly normal "Still have dreams about it, do you?" With Duncan's arm twisted so unnaturally, the blue veins stood out starkly in the soft flesh inside his elbow. Kerrigan's fingers brushed against skin, tracing a meandering line with something close to a caress. "No tracks. What did you do, shoot up between your toes to keep your body clean? Well, we're not going to worry about anything like that."

The needle hovered over his arm and, staring into Kerrigan's intent face, Duncan realised with shock that the man was enjoying himself; he was aroused, turned on, loving every nuance of pain. As Duncan watched, Kerrigan licked his lips and trailed the sharp point down pliant skin, drawing a thin line of darkly beading blood before suddenly jabbing the needle expertly into a vein.

The needle was a discomfort, then the cloudy liquid slowly slid home. Duncan shuddered convulsively.

"There you go." Kerrigan was all fake geniality, an uncle at a child's party. "I made sure it's nice and strong, mixed in a little something to make it interesting. It won't kill you, don't worry about that." He laughed, sending clouds of whisky-breath over Duncan's face. "We don't want you to be bored, do we?"

They both stood back, and brokenly Duncan eased himself onto his side. Paget was leaning on the wall, hands in his pockets. Kerrigan was standing in the doorway, smiling. They were waiting, anticipating, both of them clearly eager. In the cold, shabby bathroom Duncan understood what lab rats must feel while the scientists watched. Softly, he cursed them both as bastards, then closed his eyes as all they did was laugh.

The room was beginning to spin, and the beat of his heart was growing louder, pounding its pulse into his brain. Sweat dripped from his face, chilled his body, and as the rush hit he convulsed, vomiting dryly, quite suddenly unable to understand thought any more.

Later, inverted, gutted, reassembled by the drug, Duncan lay quite still in the silence. They had cuffed him again and gone, locking the door behind them. The light they had left on. Enfolded by harsh brilliance, truly alone, his mind delineating despair with steel-edged clarity, Duncan shuddered, and understood finally that there was no hope at all.

5

A week after the abortive operation, Cadell called all his men in for yet another briefing. He opened it bitterly. "This operation has been a fiasco from start to finish." Wisely, there was only silence in reply to such an accurate summation. "A dozen highly trained men and they slip right through your fingers! Now they seem to have disappeared into thin air." Cadell slapped the papers he was holding down onto the table.

It hadn't been an easy few days. Cadell and his team had travelled back to London, leaving the local police to deal temporarily with the continued search. As Cadell trusted none of the police on principle, he was as irritable as hell about the entire operation.

He glared at the averted faces in front of him. "It is ridiculous. *We* are ridiculous!" In the face of such derision, all the men in the room wished themselves comprehensively elsewhere.

"We can assume that they haven't managed to leave the country, we at least managed to seal off all the ports and airports immediately. They could of course have had a fast boat waiting somewhere, but I'm hoping that wasn't the case, there was certainly nothing in what was told to Byrne to make us suspect that. The main roads were closed within ten minutes; though Kent is a maze of lanes. They're holed up somewhere down there, either close to Dover or Folkestone at a guess." He turned to one side. "Murphy, have you had any luck with the two of Paget's team we did manage to catch?"

"No, sir. Both Lurie and Cohen claim categorically to know nothing. Of the two, Lurie seems the likeliest to crack. But, according to Byrne's information he was reasonably new to the group so whatever information he has," Murphy shrugged, "who knows if it'll be any use. Anyway, we're working hardest on him, but it's all going to take time, they both seem more afraid of Paget than us."

Cadell nodded. "And where's Byrne?"

"He had his last check at the hospital this morning. I think he's down in Records, seeing if he can come up with anything from Paget's past."

"Well, he should be here for - " The door opened, and a close-faced Byrne walked in. "Glad you could join us, Byrne." The sarcasm managed to be quite gentle. "Have you found anything?"

"Not yet." The flat voice discouraged comment.

Cadell closed the meeting. "You all know what's to be done. We'll leave the ground search to the police, though they report to me. There must be enough of them who are honest to make it work. Murphy, use as many men as you need for round the clock interrogations. The rest of you: there must be a clue about their whereabouts somewhere in Paget's past, find it. Byrne, my office in five minutes."

Waiting a moment, Cadell watched Byrne standing alone, isolated in the sea of milling agents, being very carefully ignored. Then with a sigh he gathered his papers and left, heading for his office.

Byrne was hard on his heels.

Three hours later Cadell had gone over every scrap of information Byrne had ever known about Paget. Unfortunately none of it seemed to have any relevance.

Byrne was wound tight with frustration, even when he sat still, a finger was tapping incessantly against the arm of his chair. "They obviously had a bolt-hole ready. Jesus, a door-to-door search is going to take for ever. If it can be done at all out in the middle of bloody nowhere."

"Aye, but unless we come up with something from either of those two men, it's our only option." Cadell tiredly rubbed at his eyes, then looked at Byrne, speaking softly, urgently. "Come on, let's go through it all again, there must have been something we're missing, some hint, some clue - "

"Look, sir, you know everything I do. There's nothing else." His eyes were bleak, dark-ringed; clearly being patient in the face of helplessness was not one of Byrne's virtues.

Cadell straightened his spine. He was tired, and inspecting Byrne closely he realised that the agent was exhausted.

"Go home, Byrne. Get a good night's sleep. You'll be no use to anyone if you don't get some rest. The hospital did give you the all-clear about that bang on the head?" Cadell was suspicious, even though Murphy had checked with the hospital.

"Mild concussion, I'm fine, sir." But he remained seated, the effort involved in going home temporarily beyond him. He started when Cadell spoke.

"How tough is this Peter Duncan of yours?"

Of mine ... Yes, he'd made that pretty clear, even to himself.

"I don't know. Tough enough I hope. Considering his past, certainly more than he looks." Byrne gave a noncommittal shrug. "But I don't think anyone can face down a bullet."

"He won't be dead yet, not as long as they need him as a hostage."

"I know." Byrne's answer was a whisper, as if even to hope such a thing was tempting fate. "But what else are they doing to him?"

"You can't think of that."

"I can't stop. You know, don't you? About what I feel for him?"

Cadell looked into Byrne's eyes and nodded. "You're quite easy to read, when you understand the signs."

"Unlike you. I never have guessed you'd be so calm about it."

"I'm far from calm! I'm angry about what happened, and also angry that you didn't see fit to tell me you were involved with someone, anyone. And it wouldn't have mattered if it was a man or a woman, the department still needed to know." He sighed, rubbing his eyes. "But emotion won't catch these men, and I very badly want them caught."

"I'm sorry." Byrne gestured emptily. "I didn't mean for any of this to happen."

"The operation going wrong, or what happened between you and Peter Duncan?"

A shake of his head. "Both, either."

"Work to get your friend free, then go from there." Cadell sat back with a creak of leather. "Try thinking of one thing at a time. It can help."

"Like finding out where he is. You're right." He stood up. "I'll see what I can do."

"Good. Get some sleep first, you won't do anyone any good falling over."

Byrne paused at the door. "Thanks."

"Get off with you, I'm busy. You can send Alice in, though."

Dismissed, Byrne went.

"Not so pretty now, is he?" The voice was far away, out on the edge of Duncan's perception.

"Pretty? Always thought he was an ugly bastard myself."

Through a rush of ecstatic pain and deepest nausea Duncan felt himself being turned over. He heard a harsh groan and belatedly recognised it as his own.

"The stupid fucker still hasn't told us anything."

Had they asked him questions? At this moment it was beyond his ability to remember. He listened instead.

"He looks pretty rough, are you sure whatever you're mixing up isn't too much?"

"He's okay, I told you. It's dodgy with heroin; but too little and he'd only be enjoying himself, too much and you won't ever be asking him anything. Besides, what d'you expect him to look like after all this time?"

Paget seemed to consider, then he nodded. "You're right. Besides, who cares if he talks or not, half the fun's asking the questions. So you just watch your hand when you measure that stuff."

"Don't worry, I'll be careful. Christ knows, having him to torment at least makes it less boring being stuck here." He stood up. "Come on, let's get a drink. Gerry should be here soon and we can find out what's going on. The plane has got to be ready!"

"I'm fast losing patience with Gerry. But you're right, a large drink will go down very nicely. I'll pour, you get him tied up again." Paget picked up the syringe and turning around, left, whistling softly.

Alone, Kerrigan waited until the sound faded, then knelt to refasten Duncan's wrists, his hands taking far too long, fingers touching far too intimately.

Softly, he spoke to his victim. "You need a bath, know that? I might give you one too, see what you look like naked. You'd like that." He clicked the cuffs shut and turned the dead-weight onto its side. "I know you would, little whore, begging for it like the cunt you are." His hand reached under Duncan's shirt, pulled it up, baring his chest. The nipples were dark, small. He squeezed each in turn, then dug his nails in, enough to make the still body twitch under his hands. "Yeah, knew you were hot for it. Could tell ..." His hands went lower and he gripped hard, bruising.

Not that it mattered. Duncan was where he really couldn't feel any pain. Distantly he tried to resist the touch on his body, but the nerves that sent messages to his muscles weren't working, and all that came out was a slight moan.

From another place he cursed and fought and ran to freedom. But here, in the cold, there was only this nightmare and, lost to everything he gave in, closing his eyes against the light, blissfully unable to feel anything at all.

His own bed was so wide and so empty that Byrne felt lost in it. Lying slap in the middle, trying to deny the expanse with the sprawl of his limbs, it still wasn't enough. Not when there should have been another body, a hard, companionable body lying next to him. Which he knew was stupid, as Peter had only stayed over that one time.

Now, though he tried his damnedest to obey Cadell's orders, sleep eluded him, the bed itself seeming to mock his plans. In the end, after an hour of lying staring into space, he got up and made a mug of whisky-laden tea.

Sipping the hot liquid he went to stand against the window, looking out from the high vantage point over the shadowed square of moonlit gardens. The thought of what they could be doing to Duncan was a horror that prickled under his skin.

He could imagine such appalling things that he almost surprised himself. In some of them, he came close to believing that Duncan would be better off dead than maimed, or insane. Maybe.

But the true horror was that of Duncan already dead.

God, it was crazy, he was crazy to be so wound up by something over which he had no control.

Though that was the trouble. He'd had the control but hadn't used it.

He realised now, with clear hindsight, that what he should have done was to tell Duncan everything and tell Cadell to get stuffed. Once he knew who Peter Duncan really was he should have searched him out and not only told him the truth, but demanded the truth in return.

He gripped the mug hard and pressed his burning face to the cold glass, close to desperation.

You fuck him, grow closer to him than you've let yourself get to anyone for years, but talk to him? A simple thing like that? Oh, no, that's beyond you!

He tore at himself with recriminations, ripping at his self-esteem with guilt-barbed talons until he turned and hurled the mug against the far wall.

For a moment he stood, staring wide-eyed at the dark mess of liquid and broken china. Then the absurdity of it caught him and he laughed. Leaning back against the glass, arms wrapped around himself, he laughed out loud, the sound perilously close to hysteria.

Finally he stood still, his expression closed. There was nothing of humour left.

Moving to the dining table, he sat and, resting his arms on the surface, stared at his hands. Clean, square, capable, somehow they looked most at home when wrapped around a gun. Yet they'd held Peter Duncan as if created solely for that purpose.

And been good at it. As good as they were with any weapon, that was true, surely? Peter had always responded so beautifully, just remembering made him ache with bitter happiness, with need.

This wouldn't be the end to it all. It couldn't.

Peter Duncan deserved more. Would have it, too. One day.

Byrne glared at his clenched hands and gravely considered his friend, his lover. Duncan was a strange man, not unsurprisingly all things considered. Passionate, remote, vicious, tender, such a multitude of complexities in a single person.

Eyes blank, he stared into nowhere and thought back over the months he'd been seeing Duncan and, for the first time, saw everything clearly. What had started with a transaction, the exchange of sex for money, had changed so gradually he wasn't sure if either of them had been aware of it. Curiosity, desire, affection, ease, were all equal attractions. That they had all blended neatly into what had to be love was very strange.

Yet love it was. And, despite wariness, dismay and downright disgust at his own fallibility, Byrne knew that it wasn't going to go away.

In his own way Byrne could be just as stubborn and pig-headed as Duncan. He rarely committed, rarely gave himself to anything or anybody, but once he did so then that was that. And he was pretty certain that Duncan was the same. That he felt the same. He had to.

Besides, why else would Duncan have thrown away his chance of getting Paget? What else would have induced such a surge of temper that all his careful planning counted for nothing?

What a strange way to find out you loved someone. Byrne laughed at himself softly, pain like a knife cutting high under his ribs.

Well, Duncan just had to be alive. Paget would need a hostage. Cadell had said so. And Cadell was always right.

But what if this was the exception that proved the rule?

Or if their escape route was efficiently planned and they were already abroad? If that was so then he might as well go and order the wreath of lilies tomorrow. He clenched his fists. They still had to be in Kent. They had to be.

The key had to be somewhere in Paget's past, maybe with someone he knew as far back as his time at Hendon, or school even. Byrne knew that he would find the answer; he was prepared to comb through every week of the man's life and interview anyone he'd ever met if need be.

As long as it didn't take too much time.

If it did, or he failed, then he wasn't sure if he would be able to live with himself.

He shook his head, wondering how he had ever become so dependent on the welfare of another being. When exactly had it happened? Why? The sex had been great, but somehow he'd taken that for granted, neatly pigeon-holing Duncan in a box marked 'whore'. Yet no other paid fuck had come even close to giving such pleasure. And then he had stayed the night, and everything had changed.

It was something he could get used to, was going to get used to: waking up with Peter Duncan. He refused to believe the future could unfold in any other way.

He felt too much guilt as it was.

Getting soft in his old age, that's what he was doing. When had he ever felt guilty before? The answer was never. But now ... Christ, you never had an equal relationship even in bed, and if he gets out of all this alive, and sane, you expect him to forgive and forget everything?

Yes.

He did.

He had to.

He rubbed at the bruise on his jaw, the pain dull enough, the memory far too sharp. He could see Duncan's eyes as he hit out. Remembered the defeat in them, and also the hate.

If love wasn't enough to keep him alive through whatever was happening, then maybe that hate would be. There was some hope in that.

A small hope indeed. But it was all he had.

The darkness was a movie theatre playing a strip of celluloid that looped again and again, stuck forever in the grip of an insane projectionist.

It had been countless hours since they had last visited him. The only way he knew that it was hours was because the last bout of sickness had tailed off, leaving him almost clear headed, for usually the drug left him with no grasp of time at all. Duncan wondered if the smack they were using was cut with some hallucinatory crap, or just bathroom cleaner. Kerrigan would enjoy that.

Weakly, he eased himself upright and sat back against the bath. For the first time in what seemed like days he registered that he was cold. Cold to the bone, aching with it. And unbearably thirsty.

Carefully, thankful they had started cuffing his hands in front of his body, he made it to his feet and across to the sink.

Awkward, with numb fingers, he managed to turn on first one tap then the other. Only one worked, spilling a rush of clear water into the basin. Bending painfully, he put his sore lips to the running water. It was cold, but that was fine. Rinsing his mouth out, he spat again and again before taking a long, much needed drink. Feeling the cold liquid trickle down into his empty belly, he waited, then drank again. Tap carefully turned off he went back to his usual patch of wall and gratefully eased himself back to the floor.

Worn out, he rested his head against the wall and felt unwell. He wasn't hungry. There was a plate of cold tinned potatoes by the door. Yesterday had been corned beef, before that - he frowned, but couldn't remember. He'd eaten some, thrown up more. Water was what he craved, and that it was available was a never ceasing source of relief.

He hoped, quite hard, that they didn't realise how much it meant. There was no doubt at all that they'd move him. To somewhere dry.

Mind-games, games of any kind. Paget and Kerrigan would have made ideal Inquisitors.

Silence crawled by.

Thinking didn't help, when all he could think about was Byrne. Byrne as he wanted him to be, Byrne as he was. Had the bastard ever seen Duncan as anything other than a casual fuck?

Self-delusion, an art form he'd managed to live most of his twenty-eight years without, really had made its mark with a vengeance. He'd had such ideas, such dreams. Pathetic.

Byrne, with Paget's arm around his shoulders.

Bosom buddies.

Bitter disillusion rose to mix with the bile in his throat and he was nearly sick again.

Black despair, a figure with pale sardonic features and hot blue eyes, haunted him, and ice-cold to the depths of his being he waited in the silence for the door to open, already wanting the drug, needing the oblivion it promised, even with the pain that it brought.

Come and finish it, Paget. He shivered and knew that his body was protesting the absence of the drug. Come and get it over with. Hollow-eyed, he waited, recognising that he didn't care what they did, as long as they did it quickly.

The tensile thread of anticipation was as bad as their presence.

They loved hurting him so much. He ached everywhere, the small burns inflicted by Kerrigan each a pit of burning light in his skin. At least they no longer bound his wrists behind his back, or cranked the metal cuffs too tight. His shoulders and wrists still protested violently, especially when he moved. But the drug would sort all that out anyway.

Oh, the drug.

He'd first sniffed heroin when he was twelve. Mainlined when he was fourteen. Come off being hooked when he was seventeen and never looked back.

Until this nightmare.

How had they known? He'd covered his tracks so carefully: but clearly not carefully enough.

And Kerrigan was so bloody skilled. Duncan shifted uneasily against the wall, his skin itching with sudden ferocity.

They'd be here soon.

He peered though the ivy-tangled window, and nodded. It was evening. They always came in the evenings.

He stared at the ruin of his wrists and wondered at the depth of his need. They'd got him this needy so fast. Or was it once an addict always an addict?

He didn't care. Not now. Maybe one day. Now all he wanted was the sweetness of absolute oblivion, and it would be here soon.

It would.

But it was a whole day before they returned.

In the long, terrified hours of the night and through the next day, Duncan called out, shouted, kicked at the walls and the door and paced in a sweat of panic, convinced they'd left and that he was alone in the house. That he would die there.

Hours into the day, he kicked too hard on the door, and finally a voice shouted at him. He stood back, so relieved that he hadn't been abandoned that it was an hour before he remembered to need the drug.

He did need it. And wanted it too.

Misery churning his gut, he curled up on the floor and tried to be sane. It wasn't easy.

He watched the light fade, watched the shadows gathering in the corners of the room. Exhausted, at some point he fell asleep. And it seemed only a few minutes before the rattle of key in lock woke him.

Gathering what was left of his wits, Duncan watched them, blinking in the bright light as they pushed into the room. He swallowed, heart plummeting; they were both roaring drunk. The cold lethargy was cleared from his brain by a sharp frisson of fear: numb indifference could only go so far.

"Did you miss us?" Paget kicked him almost playfully until he lay panting against the wall. Sitting themselves on the side of the bath, they watched him sweat.

Kerrigan reached into a pocket and pulled out a bag of white powder and grinned at Paget. "Want some?"

"Of course!"

Duncan eyed them warily as in turn they snorted coke, spooning it up their noses straight from a plastic bag.

Kerrigan looked at Paget. "Why don't you give him some?"

"What, waste it!"

Crouching at Duncan's side, Kerrigan examined him. "Listening, are you? Do you want some, or would you rather have some smack." He traced his finger over Duncan's sweat and blood-stained shirt, the gesture coldly sensual. "How long 'as it been?"

Duncan didn't answer, just swallowed the saliva that filled his mouth, knowing better than to spit in Kerrigan's face. He'd done that once and learnt his lesson. He shivered. Jesus, Mary and Joseph, prayers from his childhood clear in his head. He tried not to believe that any of it was happening. It didn't work. The shivers just got worse.

Kerrigan was so happy. "Our drug fiend seems to be getting a little restless. How long's it been, Paget?"

"Two days." Paget leaned towards Duncan and wrinkled his nose in distaste. "Bloody hell! He stinks! Doesn't he believe in washing?"

"Can't do. A duchess would feel at home in here, it's bloody palatial enough."

"Maybe he's just wilful."

"Nah, just couldn't be bothered, could you, Pete? Addicts are all the same."

"I'm not."

The two men stilled. "Did you hear someone speak?"

"Don't think so."

"I'm not a drug addict."

"Little bastard thinks he can have a conversation with us now."

Kerrigan went to the prisoner, gripping Duncan's beard-stubbled chin and heaving him up until he sat against the wall. "Such a little bastard, aren't you. And I've news for you, you're hooked, well and truly fucked, matey." He turned his face to Paget. "Derek, how about running a bath?"

"What a good idea." Sniffing, Paget was standing up, pushing up his shirtsleeves. "Can't have filth like that lying around, can we?"

"It'd be unhygienic ..."

"Yeah." He leaned over the bath and pushed the plug home, twisting the taps until the rushing sound of water filled the room. "Oh dear. And there's no hot water, what a pity."

Kerrigan was upright again, slightly unsteadily. "With his clothes off, I think."

They took Duncan between them, keeping him trapped as they ripped off his shirt, buttons bouncing onto the lino. Twisted around his body it snagged on the handcuffs. Paget tutted. "Can't have that, can't keep your shirt on in the bath!" He produced a pocket-knife and clicked it open. "Yeah, that's kept you quiet!"

The knife was sharp enough, though it was still an effort to cut through the fabric. Finally the ruins of the shirt fell to the floor.

"There." He patted Duncan's cheek. Kerrigan was supporting Duncan's body, arm around his chest. Over a bare shoulder he watched as Paget unfastened Duncan's trousers and pulled them down, underpants and all. "Step out of them."

Duncan did nothing.

The knife was suddenly sharp against his neck.

"Go on, tempt me."

Duncan swallowed dryly, and obeyed.

"That's better." Paget kicked the clothing away and stepped back to examine the bruised length of Duncan's body. He smiled, and walked over to the filling bath, turning off the taps and dipping his hand in the water.

"How is it?" Kerrigan asked.

"Freezing."

"Very nice. Time for a swim ..."

Paget lunged for him just as Duncan tried to kick out, and between them they lifted his twisting body into the air and, heaving, dropped him into the bath.

Breath taken by the icy cold, Duncan shuddered, crying out loud as he slipped under the water, choking instantly, drowning in panic until he fought his way up, finding purchase with feet and elbows and bound hands and finally finding the blessedness of air.

Breath whooping into his lungs he coughed, blinking water away, desperate to see, to know what they were doing. Both of them were laughing, but at least they were drenched as well. It was almost enough to make him smile. Almost. Then Kerrigan put a hand on his head and pushed. This time at least he took in air rather than water. And held it until the world turned to crimson behind his closed eyes.

He came to, retching violently, his body voiding water. Dazed, he knew himself still alive, the pain in his chest too sharp for anything else. Leaning against the side, the bath's enamel almost warm against his cheek, he knew they were only playing with him.

And wished he were dead.

"Again?" Paget's voice.

And before he could even think of reacting he was under again, a roaring in his ears. He held his breath, could do it, it was better than the horrible sensation of drowning. Until someone punched him hard in the belly, driving what little air he had up, pushing it out of his lungs, opening his mouth, and letting the cold water rush in, filling him with pain and darkness and leeching everything from him, everything.

Scarcely conscious, he felt himself pulled from the bath, dropped hard onto the floor. He knew he was shuddering, cold deep in his body. But that was all.

A hand slapped him, and it was an irritation. Harder, and he finally opened his eyes. Paget. Byrne's bastard. Holding a syringe.

"Here you are, Peter, all your troubles taken care of. Ask nicely."

From somewhere he remembered how to speak, found the muscles that controlled his jaw. "Fuck off ..." It was a whisper, but he meant it so much.

Paget was tutting. "Just ask, beg if you'd rather ..."

Words, dragged from pain. "Go fuck yourself."

"Whatever you say." And he was laughing. Walking away.

The door slammed close. Duncan shivered, pressing his body to the lino for warmth. He wasn't weeping. Couldn't be. It was just water, seeping from his body.

He did hate though. And it was almost as warming as fire.

At some point they did come back.

"Ready to beg?" The light clicked on, unbearably bright. "Ready for another shot?" Kerrigan's voice was darkest temptation.

"No." Duncan forced himself to speak, though he was shivering so hard it nearly made him bite off his tongue. He watched the two men warily, hating them, hating the way he tried to move away from them but was completely unable to stop himself.

"Are you sure?" Kerrigan was coaxing, though Duncan could hear the mocking laughter in his voice.

"Yes." He came up against the wall.

"That's not the way to get what you want."

"You're miserable bastards ..." The words were whispered, but enough for Kerrigan. The blow was vicious, cracking Duncan's head against the wall.

Tasting fresh blood, licking it from his dry lips, Duncan kept silent, though the sound of his harsh breathing blended with their laughter.

"God, this is getting boring." Kerrigan punched the defenceless body again and stood up to watch Duncan try and curl onto the pain. "Pass me the stuff."

The body at his feet froze into stillness and Kerrigan smiled into the suddenly wide, staring eyes. He took the prepared syringe from Paget's hand, crouching, tracing the bruises that trailed down one icy arm. He smiled, rubbing his hand over Duncan's chest and belly, fondling skin with hands so warm they felt like brands.

Duncan looked away, only to find Paget's eyes. In their pale depths he saw arousal, and a dark, animal hunger. He shivered and suddenly fought. Weak-limbed and despising himself, he twisted away from Kerrigan's hands, cursing out loud as Paget held him too, their hands brutal.

Crushed under their weight, he knew the deepest of despair. Watching the syringe when it was held in front of his face, seeing the tiny push that made sure there were no air bubbles to end this too completely, he was shaking his head, sobbing, denying his need but wanting, just wanting so much.

Kerrigan hissed in his ear. "Too proud to beg? Just wait till next time."

There was little doubt. For like balm, the drug slid into Duncan's veins, like fire into ice. Moaning aloud he gave in, welcoming the rush of oblivion with open arms, lost to everything and no longer willing to care.

Releasing him, Paget and Kerrigan watched as the drug took control, and all the tension, all the fight, just faded away. Relaxed, eyes darkly dilated, their hostage lay quite still, utterly soft. Willing. Inviting.

And they were ready to be invited.

Paget looked at Kerrigan and saw arousal to mirror his own.

An arse was an arse.

And it would serve him right.

And Byrne too.

"Let's get him into the warm."

"And play?"

"Yeah."

Paget touched cold skin, curled his hand around Duncan's neck and tilted the bent head to look straight at him.

"Paget. I remember you - "

"Good. In a bit you'll remember me even better." He squeezed gently. "When I've fucked you." Paget was smiling. He bent his mouth to one shoulder, teeth biting, and leapt back when the body in his arms convulsed violently, again and again, every muscle clenched in violent spasms as it arched painfully high, bare feet slapping hard against the floor.

"Jesus!" Paget scrambled away and was on his feet in alarm. "What's happening?"

Kerrigan was at the door, hand over his mouth. "He's having a fit."

"For fuck's sake, what did you give him?"

"The usual!"

"It can't have been."

"Maybe he's had too much - " Kerrigan shrugged.

"Well, do something, we might still need him."

Completely at a loss, Kerrigan knelt and rummaged on the floor, finding Duncan's own belt, cursing as he tried to force it between the teeth of the convulsing man. Paget bent, holding Duncan's head as it slammed into the floor. Between them they forced the leather home.

Standing back, breathing hard, unsure, they watched, as the wild shudders eased and slowly stopped, turning to stillness broken by sporadic shivers that ran the length of Duncan's entire body.

"Get a blanket."

Paget crouched down, eased the belt from between bloody lips, then felt for a pulse.

"He's alive."

"Good." Kerrigan tossed a couple of blankets over the unconscious man. He stood by, uncertain. "What do we do? He needs a hospital."

"Well, he'll have to do without."

"But - "

"Shut up! He'll live or he'll bloody die here. What a fucking mess." Paget stood up, pulling his fingers through his hair. "The sooner we get away the better."

"Tomorrow, yes?"

"Yes."

Stone cold sober, as far from arousal as it was possible to be, Paget walked away, waiting for Kerrigan to follow him out of the small room. He closed the door, not looking once at the figure huddled against the wall.

6

Bright as he was, Adrian Lurie only slowly realised that being one of Paget's select band had disadvantages. Ones he had never really considered.

Like prison.

Cadell watched him from the moment he was brought into the vast basement complex under Whitehall, using a hidden camera to spy as he was left alone in a huge, echoing room that was about as hospitable as a cell.

Because it was a cell.

The pale green paint-work and miles of exposed piping were a neat foreshadowing of where he would end up. Cohen was in another room. Neither man was allowed to speak to the other.

Not being entirely stupid, Lurie clearly realised soon after Cadell started the first interview that they knew enough to destroy him, and that the only way out would be to co-operate in full.

He was also wily enough to know that the more time he wasted the better. Cadell sighed as he watched, knowing exactly why Lurie behaved as he did. Paget exerted a strong influence, even from a distance.

Fear was all that held Lurie's mouth closed. Fear that only lost its hold with time. In the end it was eight days after being taken that he finally began to answer when they talked to him. In his eyes he'd proved his loyalty, now he was trying to secure some leniency.

Cadell could almost admire him.

For the next eighteen hours Lurie had answered every question that they'd asked him, and even some they hadn't thought of, all in an effort to appease the coldly cynical interrogators. Unfortunately, what they really wanted to know he couldn't tell them.

And Cohen wouldn't.

Sitting in a smoky, cramped room watching a screen that was far too small, Cadell cursed softly. They knew Cohen had the information, Lurie had said so. But would the bastard talk? As far as he was concerned the whole establishment could fuck itself.

He wasn't saying anything.

Ever.

Cadell's gaze slid across to Byrne.

Dressed in black from head to toe, the pale cream leather of his shoulder holster stark against the breadth of his shoulders, it was not only his body that looked menacing. White-faced and hollow-eyed, bones carved from stone, his violence was barely leashed. Cadell hesitated, wondering about the wisdom of letting Byrne loose on either of the two men.

Byrne never coped well with having his toys taken away. If that was what Duncan was, Cadell thought. But he had to be, he was simply a toy another boy had stolen, instantly giving that one plaything more desirability than anything else in the toy cupboard.

Well, it was a possibility; one that would be very easy to believe. But staring at Byrne's haunted face, Cadell slowly admitted to himself that it was not at all likely.

Cadell knew as much of Duncan's background as was on record and believed that he could read between the lines to guess a lot more. He was a singularly unlucky young man. Except that he had found Byrne.

Byrne, who looked at this moment as if he would tear down whole buildings with his hands just to find Duncan alive.

Cadell knew he had hesitated too long. The decision had to be made. He sighed, and turned to the other men in the room. "Murphy, get Cohen into an interrogation room."

Murphy nodded and went, taking Hoskyns with him. Knowing what was to happen, Cadell could almost felt sorry for the prisoner. Almost, but not quite.

"Byrne." He watched as ice-cold eyes turned to acknowledge him. "You can have Cohen."

Byrne was on his feet, his smile holding not a single iota of humour.

"But remember, I need him alive."

"He can't tell us anything if he's dead, sir, can he?"

Logic. Cadell nodded. "And sane."

"If he's that now."

"He is. Just leave something we can put on trial, okay?"

Byrne didn't bother to reply, just left the room.

It was one of the most unpleasant interrogations Cadell had ever overseen. Twice he was on the verge of sending Murphy in to pull Byrne off. But he didn't, and after an hour the information they needed was in their hands. And there was not a single mark on Cohen's skin.

"Fucking police, should have known Paget would have been holed-up with his own kind."

Cadell just nodded while concentrating on the M20 traffic. Byrne had been saying much the same thing since they left London.

"The bastard, he - "

Cadell ignored him, his mind thinking ahead. He'd sent a team in front of them, keeping Byrne with him in London until the last moment, somehow feeling that things were only in control as long as Byrne was in his sight and tightly leashed.

He didn't want Paget dead.

They were heading for a farmhouse about five miles from the old Lympne Airport. Paget was apparently waiting for a short-hop flight to France from where he planned to go on to Spain, but the contact he needed had proved slow in finding a pilot who would take them with no questions asked.

Cadell knew that, at every stage, the success of the operation had depended on luck. But he wasn't ashamed to make the most of it. It had been a tough case, and they had needed every piece of help they could get to crack it open. And it wasn't over yet.

Murphy and his team would be there already; five of them to take two. It should be enough. Would be enough.

By the time they reached Sellindge, Byrne was quiet, intense: his presence in the car almost overwhelming. Cadell turned down a lane, passing some of the team waiting in an armoured personnel van, nodding in acknowledgement before driving slowly up the narrowly twisting road.

"I want him alive."

Byrne grunted in acknowledgement.

"Alive, okay?"

"Yes, sir. And I want Duncan alive."

Cadell nodded. That was something no one had any control over. Except the men in that house.

The RT crackled and he picked it up. "Yes."

"We're in place, sir." Murphy's voice, breaking up with static.

"Five minutes. If you look towards the main road you should see the Rover approaching. Oh, and the police are on their way."

"I've got you. We'll wait."

Cadell clicked the radio to off. He drove on for another half mile, then pulled over, silencing the engine. He climbed out of the car, Byrne already outside, the brisk wind ruffling his short hair. He waited, though.

Murphy stepped out, gun in hand. "The house is around the next bend. They don't know we're here."

"Good."

"Do we wait for the police?"

"No." Cadell looked at them both. "Good luck."

Almost in unison his men nodded and together disappeared silently into the undergrowth.

Leaning against his car, Cadell waited. After a few minutes the radio crackled. "Yes."

"We're in, no casualties, sir."

"Good." Cadell let out a breath. "And Duncan?"

"We're looking."

"I'm coming in."

Tossing the radio onto the driver's seat, Cadell walked along the road, then turned onto the track which led to the old farm-house. Distanced, he looked up, seeing the Kent sky very pale, the trees, russet or bare, moving in the wind, the ground thick with leaves. His feet crunched as he walked. As he approached the house Murphy was there, "Sir," leading him inside.

In the living room, furniture pushed aside, Byrne was fastening metal cuffs around Paget's wrists. Paget was smiling into his eyes, mocking him.

"Where's Duncan?"

"Missing your pretty boy, are you? Must be difficult getting to sleep without his sweet little arse to keep you warm." Paget's lips were curled with scorn. "You're nothing but a bloody queer. Well, let me tell you, we fixed your piece of meat well and truly. With any luck he might even be dead."

He was silenced by Byrne's fist smashing his mouth into blood.

"Whatever you've done, you'd better pray he's still alive or I'll come after you, wherever they put you. And don't you think that being inside will make any fucking difference at all."

Breathing hard he turned away as Murphy came into the room.

Byrne hesitated at what he saw in his friend's face. "Where is he?"

"Second door on the left. I've called for an ambulance."

Byrne was running. The door was old, paint peeling in strips away from the wood. He pushed it open. Anderson was kneeling on the floor, swearing under his breath.

Transfixed for a moment in the doorway Byrne hesitated then, stumbling, he too was on his knees, desperate hands feeling for life.

"Peter!"

Duncan was curled on his side, hands behind his back. Byrne, his hand unsteady, felt for a pulse at Duncan's neck, fingering ice-cold skin until it was there, fluttering weakly under his finger-tips.

Alive.

It was almost too much. Byrne took a long shuddering breath and steadied himself. Reaching around the bound body, hunting for the rope, he found instead the bite of metal binding bloodied wrists. "Jesus!"

"Here." Murphy was there, key in one hand, blankets in the other. Byrne held Duncan's body while the cuffs were peeled away, then very carefully turned him over, easing him flat as the blankets were wrapped around him, handling him with great care, avoiding seeing the worst of the marks that covered the thin body. Duncan had been beaten, more than once.

Beaten and more.

Pulling the blankets around him, Byrne checked his eyes, finding dilated pupils. He fought down panic. He'd seen men battered to death, knew that the body in his arms was barely alive.

"Peter ..." Duncan was cold, starkly pale around the bruises, eyes sunk deep into his skull. He held still, close to shock. A hand touched his arm and he looked up.

"Hello, sir."

"Byrne."

"He's alive."

"Good."

Startling them both, Murphy reappeared in the doorway. "It's going to take too long for an ambulance to get here, there's been a fire in Canterbury, everything's tied up there." He took a step into the bathroom, looking around, his face tight with tension. "We'd better get him there in the car. There's a hospital in Ashford."

Byrne shifted, lifting Duncan even as Murphy spoke. As he began to hoist the dead-weight up, one of Duncan's arms slipped free of the blanket. All three of them stared at the filthy, naked limb, at the livid path of injection marks that traced the veins close to the skin.

"The bastards!"

Murphy was gone again, Cadell close on his heels.

In silence Byrne traced his finger along the path of the bruises. And hated Paget more than he had ever hated anyone. Lowering Duncan carefully to the floor, tucking the blankets around him, he nodded to Anderson, and walked back to the room where Paget was being held.

Cadell was shouting, demanding, and Paget was smiling again. Byrne just stood in front of him, waiting.

"So you liked your little present."

Byrne shuddered. "What was it? What did you give him?"

"Smack, speed, a little acid."

"Why?"

"We were bored." Paget shrugged.

"Did you give him anything else?"

"Who fucking cares!"

Byrne took hold of Paget, one hand around his thick neck the other around his balls. "I do. Tell me."

"Fuck you!"

"Tell me!" Byrne was squeezing.

Paget squealed out loud. "All right!"

Byrne eased up when Paget gasped out, "Nothing."

"Sure?"

A nod.

Byrne backed away. "You'd better hope he lives." And he was gone, calling Murphy after him.

He was walking down the hall, Duncan cradled in his arms, when Cadell caught up with them. "Take my car."

"Thank you."

"Murphy, you drive, I'm coming too. Anderson's going to liaise with the police and get Paget and Kerrigan back to HQ. And Byrne, the police have offered a fast escort to the hospital." He tossed his keys to Murphy, following his men out of the house, across the garden and out into the road.

Byrne walked quickly, his feet quiet on the tarmac. He held Duncan's body, feeling its seemingly slight weight, its absolute chill. There was no room in his mind for anything, not thought, or anger, or bitterness. He was too busy willing Duncan to live.

At the car he let Murphy take the still body, sliding into the back seat, the two of them easing Duncan in after him. Byrne settled him, and realised the cold body was shaking, subtle tremors running faintly through his muscles.

"Jesus - "

Cadell turned from where he sat in the passenger seat. "What?"

"He's shivering."

None of them knew if it was good or bad, but Murphy had the Rover in gear and was turning, rubber burning on the road as he floored the accelerator. Cadell was radioing ahead, his voice soft and urgent.

They picked up the police escort as they pulled onto the main road and, sirens blaring, the three cars speeded off.

Byrne eased himself back against the door, trying to cradle Duncan's body with his own warmth.

He was shaking. He was alive.

But heroin!

He'd kill Paget. Rip him limb from limb. Later.

"Byrne."

The word was a faint murmur, hardly more than a breath, but it made Byrne's heart leap.

"Peter?"

"I thought I was dreaming - "

"No. I'm here."

"Wonderful." Duncan frowned. He tried to shift a little, then groaned softly. "Sweet Jesus, I feel awful."

"I know. I'm sorry."

"Not your fault, is it?"

"I don't know - "

"I'm sure it isn't." He shivered hard. Turning to curl tight on himself. "Byrne. Hold me."

"I am, sweetheart, I am."

"I can't feel you properly, ache too much."

Byrne gently eased Duncan higher so that they were wrapped together. "Better?" He stroked lank hair away from Duncan's bruised face.

"I love you. Bet you didn't know that." The words were soft, slurred, but the drug in Duncan's veins spoke the truth for him, declaring it without sentiment or disguise.

"I did." Byrne could hardly speak the words, his tongue swollen, his eyes burning with tears. "And I guess I love you, too."

Duncan's head was nodding and then he was gone again, scaring Byrne even though his fingers were welded to Duncan's wrist.

"Fuck it, Murphy, can't you drive any faster than an old woman?"

"Nearly there, Byrne."

Cadell was on the RT alerting the hospital of their imminent arrival.

"Hold on, Peter, it'll be all right. I promise."

Awareness came slowly. The third time he opened his eyes he actually knew who he was, and was so pleased to remember something that he fell straight back into darkness.

The fourth time, it was all for real.

He tried to speak, but there was something down his throat, and in panic he clutched at it until a voice was there, soothing, and hands were touching him, bringing more pain, but taking the vile thing away so he could breathe alone. Someone was talking, but it was a very long way away. He was so very tired and, turning onto his side, he slept.

And wasn't sure he wanted to wake up. For when he did all the memory was there, and along with memory came pain.

It was an uncomfortable conviction, knowing sin had to be paid for. Somewhere in Duncan's feckless upbringing that philosophy had been so firmly instilled and so carefully observed to be true, that nothing had ever changed it.

He knew that he had sinned, at least in the eyes of God. Even occasionally in his own. But it seemed difficult to believe that he hadn't already wiped his slate clean and that this was just fate's maliciousness.

Heroin.

Mother of God, Sacred Heart of Jesus, not again! Why did the

113

past have such a nasty habit of catching up?

Flexing his hand, he felt the strangeness of being alive. Through barely open eyes he looked at his arm, seeing the tubing laced into his veins, seeing the dark tracks that wove unsteadily up to disappear under what had to be a hospital gown. He shivered, feeling other chemicals buffering him from the truth, cocooning his nerve endings.

Smack.

Gathering his strength he lifted his hand and placed it over his eyes. Alive after all. Jesus.

With dream-like disassociation he wondered what had happened; the last thing he could remember was Paget's face. Hardly a comfort. But, unless hell was a very strange place indeed, something had gone wrong with their plans.

By the feel of it there was more plastic hooked up to his body, liquid in, liquid out. Something attached to his chest. Monitors? Alive, maybe, but he felt like death warmed up with extreme inefficiency. Drifting off, faint tremors running along his muscles, it was a while before he thought anything much.

He slept and woke hazily, knowing he was still heavily sedated. Doctors and nurses came and fussed. They smiled emptily, asked if he was all right, and at least removed the worst of the tubing from his body. He drifted again. Happy to feel nothing. And slept.

Waking to desperate thirst. Tongue running slowly over dry lips, he wanted liquid, but the effort needed to sit up and reach the glass that sat by his bed was almost too much. He stared at it, tantalised.

And out of nowhere, remembered.

Byrne.

The name brought a flood of memory and he squeezed his eyes closed and fought with his thoughts. Stop it! Byrne's a double-dealing bastard. He never promised you anything, get it straight! You were the one who made a plaster saint out of him - and you should know better.

The pain lay in the space separating how it had been from how he'd wanted it to be. He stared wide-eyed at nothing and tried to accept the logic, but his heart screamed back: You loved him!

He was shivering again, nausea catching at the back of his throat. Christ, he had troubles enough without crying over what Byrne might or might not be.

Well, he wasn't going to throw up in bed. But trying to move he found himself shaking with weakness, and simply pushing himself up in the bed left him panting for breath, close to exhaustion.

Cursing, he knew it was too late, was loathing himself, when strong hands came around him, steadying, gentling, holding a bowl while he tried ineffectually to be sick.

Gasping for breath, white and sweating, he lay back with eyes closed.

Byrne looked at him and could have wept. Around the bruises Duncan's skin was translucently pale, temple and eyelid traced with blue veins, hair damply matted against the pillow. Two days in a coma had worn him to a thread, the deep hollows in his face making the scarred cheek painfully obvious. The sheet had slipped down and with warm hands Byrne tucked it carefully back.

He was exhausted himself.

Cadell had called in from time to time after Duncan had been transferred to the London hospital, but Byrne had stayed through it all: the transfer, the tests, the hours of despair. Now, hopefully properly this time, Duncan was awake. Byrne, unnoticed, planted a swift kiss on Duncan's head and slipped out to find someone to tell.

"He's come round again."

"Good." A doctor followed Byrne into the private room. Duncan was scarcely awake, sweating freely, shivering.

"He was trying to throw up."

The doctor examined the monitors that flanked the bedside, then went to the notes hooked on the end of the bed. "How long has he been an addict?"

"He isn't."

The doctor raised a disbelieving eyebrow.

"Look, don't you people talk to each other?" Byrne sighed, turning away to hide his anger. "Read the notes. He's been forcibly given high doses of heroin. Apart from that, as far as I know he doesn't even smoke dope." He pressed on a far more important matter. "All that matters is that he will be all right. He will, won't he?"

"In time, yes." The doctor cleared his throat and continued reading. He looked up after a moment, and shifted defensively under Byrne's intent stare. "I do need to know if he has a history of drug use. Have you any idea where he might come from, where we could find his medical records?"

"No." Byrne shook his head. "All I've seen is his police service record and there's nothing in that about drugs."

Though Cadell had mentioned something. Byrne tried to remember what exactly had been said all those weeks ago. Cadell had spoken to a different doctor; if only the medical profession talked to each other. "He's clean."

"No."

The voice was faint, roughened, but clearly Duncan's. Byrne said quietly, "Hello."

Duncan ignored him. "I was a user. Years and years ago." Duncan closed his eyes to hide the hopelessness.

"Why can't we find your medical records?"

Duncan's mouth twitched into something that was almost a smile. "Listen, I've had three different names and I've hardly ever seen a real doctor. I'm surprised that you have anything about me at all. I expect that his lot know it all; they seem to know everything else." He broke off with a shiver.

Byrne went to stand by the bed. He took a deep breath, but didn't touch, just stared. "It'll be all right."

"Fuck off, Byrne. Why are you here anyway?"

The doctor was standing close by, oblivious to the tension between the two other men. "There'll be some symptoms as the drug gradually leaves your body."

"Thank you, doctor. Fancy that." Duncan turned his face away.

"They're little worse than gastric flu." The doctor flushed as two sets of eyes glared at him.

"Really? If you think it's easy you should try it." Duncan looked feverish. He was sweating, his eyes still dilated, slightly dazed. Byrne frowned and wondered if he should just leave now, let the poor bastard be ill in peace.

The doctor went to the door. "I'll get your treatment sorted out. I won't be long."

"Don't trouble yourself too much."

Unsure what to answer, the doctor just left.

Alone, the two men were silent. Then Byrne took a pace forward and hesitantly touched cold fingers. "Look, I can help."

"No, you bloody can't." The fingers were snatched away, tucked under the sheet.

"Why not?" Byrne was shocked by the bitterness in Duncan's voice.

"Get out. I don't know what you told them in order to be here but you won't con me again. Get out of here." His voice was quiet, intense. "Just get out of here. Find somebody else to fuck, I'm finished with it."

"Peter, you don't understand. Paget and me, it was ..."

"Byrne, fuck off!"

Backing off in the face of an ill and shaking Duncan glaring at him, Byrne went to the door. "Okay."

"Don't come back, Byrne, just leave me alone."

"We do need to talk. I'll come back later, when you feel better."

"When I feel better? Really rich that is, when your friend did this to me."

"He's not - " Byrne stopped and made a lunge forward as Duncan, all rage, was free of the sheets and reaching for his neck. He fell before Byrne made it, weakness and drugs taking his strength, leaving him collapsed, on his knees. Byrne crouched next to him, utterly unsure of what to do, watching the blood drip down Duncan's arm where he had wrenched the IV tubing away.

"Peter!" Byrne reached forward.

"Don't ... touch ... me." There was exhaustion and anger yet even so, even stricken and shaking, Duncan's voice brooked no opposition. "Just go away."

117

"I'll go and get the doctor."

"Yeah, you do that. Don't bother to come back."

"I can't. I need to see you, to explain!"

"Don't."

Byrne slowly stood up. He took a deep breath and walked away, pulling the door shut behind him. He stood still for a moment, taking one last look through the glass panel at where Duncan sat so forlornly. He didn't doubt his own ability to make Duncan see sense eventually. After all, what else would he be telling but the truth.

Knowing that Duncan was out of danger and in competent hands, Byrne gave in to his own exhaustion and went home to sleep for twelve hours straight.

Showered and, for the first time in three days, dressed in clean clothes, he returned to the hospital to be greeted at the main door by Cadell.

"Morning, sir, doing your bit for the sick as well?"

"No, Byrne, I'm here because Duncan has walked out."

"What?"

"He stole some clothes and walked out in the middle of the night."

"Who was guarding him?"

"Patterson."

"And why did he let Duncan leave?"

"I don't believe he actually asked."

"Jesus, he's too ill to be wandering about."

"I know. And I should have guessed he'd make a run for it, put more than one man to look after him." Cadell sighed. "Anyway, do you have any idea where we might find him?"

"Maybe. I think I know the area his flat's in."

"What are you waiting for? We need him as a witness."

"Sir."

"And Byrne …"

"Yes?"

"I spoke to the doctor. Duncan will be unwell for a few days, but he won't die of the withdrawal from the drugs."

"What about the rest of the stuff they did to him? Did you see him, did you know they bloody well tortured him?" Byrne's voice was far too loud. He took a deep breath. "Sorry. I know you've seen the report."

"But not the reality. It makes a difference, I know."

Looking up, Byrne nodded. "One day I will kill Paget." Then he shrugged, almost apologetically. "After I've stubbed out a few lighted cigarettes on his skin, see what he thinks of it."

"He's not worth it, let the courts deal with him. But your friend is. So go on, go and find him."

"Yes, sir. And thank you."

"What for?" And Cadell smiled, for he was speaking to thin air.

7

Getting out of his room had been easy. Duncan waited until his guard went to the bathroom then just walked away. Penniless and dressed in a hospital gown, he found an empty staff room and stifled his scruples. There was a row of lockers, all locked. A quick search had turned up a screwdriver and in minutes three were jimmied open and he was dressed in jeans, sweat-shirt and slightly-too-tight Clarke's lace-ups. There was also a wallet, with a sheaf of notes in it. Leaving the bulk of the cash, he'd taken one twenty, needing it to get away.

Disorientated, he found himself standing on Westminster Bridge in the middle of the night. A cab was there, orange light a beacon, and he flagged it down. Ignoring the strange looks he got from the driver he asked to be taken to Willesden, even agreeing to pay up front, and was on his way. He sat back in the wide seat, resting his head. And had to be woken when they arrived.

Shivering, he rescued the spare key from under a brick and let himself in, closing the door behind him with utter relief.

The flat was sanctuary.

Without bothering with lights he went straight to the sofa, crawled under the blankets, just about finding the energy to kick the vile shoes onto the floor as he curled up.

In body and spirit, he ached so much. For everything. For the fact that he still lived. For Byrne. For himself.

He stared into the darkness, nose and fingers and toes like ice.

What a mess.

He sniffed, and firmly closed his eyes. Despite everything, it was a long time before he slept, and then it was only fitfully. It wasn't until dawn that he really found some rest, and then he slept like the dead; unmoving and quite without dreams.

When he woke it was day, and bright daylight was spilling through the net curtains. Eyes gummy with sleep, Duncan moved cautiously, easing his body until he was sitting. He was still cold, and his body simply ached with need.

Pushing out of the blankets he stood up, and caught sight of himself in a mirror. Peering into the glass he realised why the cabbie had been so reluctant to take him as a fare. Gently, he touched a finger to mottled red and blue patches of bruising, and sighed into his own drawn face.

At least he looked as bad as he felt. That was a curious reassurance.

Remembering he was cold he finished his journey to the living room, crouching down to light the ancient gas fire. Then he remembered, before he'd left for Dover the gas had run out. Standing, rummaging through the pockets of his borrowed jeans, he came up with only notes.

Change, that's what he needed. And maybe something to eat. His stomach lurched at the mere thought and he gave up on that idea.

Change anyway, he needed warmth.

The brash freshness of the late morning air revived him and he walked down to the local shops. The pub on the corner had just opened and he decided to quench his thirst with a pint.

Barely awake, he sat over it, watching the working men come in for their two hour lunch breaks. Normality. How did some people end up so bloody normal? Shaking his head he sipped at the warm liquid and jumped when his name was spoken, spilling some of his beer.

"Peter!" A girl's voice, sounding shocked.

He looked up and smiled. "Rosie! Look what you made me do."

He mopped ineffectually at his purloined jeans.

She sat next to him, her hand on his arm. "Peter! Are you all right? Look at you!" She hesitated, unsure. He was sweating, yet his skin was cold. "Who beat you up?"

"Nobody." He shrugged.

Of course. The answer they all gave. She sat closer, still holding his arm, feeling the tremors that ran in shivers through his body. "Can I help, Peter?"

"I'm okay."

She stared into his eyes, and with a slight gasp saw the truth. Rubbing his arm she almost casually pushed his sleeve up, and caught her breath at the extent of the fresh tracks. "How long since you had a fix?"

He shrugged, wiping sweat from his face with the back of one sleeve. "Don't know. I was in hospital." He frowned. "They gave me something. I think - "

"It would only have been rubbish." She bit her lip. "But I can help you out. If you want?"

Yes, he wanted. "Are you sure?"

"Yes, I've spare enough for you." She smiled, happy. "We can shoot up together, cosy."

Cosy. Oh, yes, just like it had been with Paget. Duncan shivered hard.

"You still staying close by?"

"Yeah."

"Come on, then."

She dragged him out onto the street, holding his arm, chattering about nothing until they'd walked the five minutes back to his flat.

"Jesus, Peter, it's so cold in here."

"I know. I went out to get coins for the meter."

"Feed it then, silly! I'll get everything started."

He went into the hall and carefully inserted ten pences into the meter, clicking each one home, not thinking at all. He stood for a moment, then went back, standing in the doorway, watching as she carefully lifted everything she would need from her bag: spoon, matches, lemon, foil, syringe, and lastly a small bag of the precious drug.

It was more complicated than a ritual to raise the devil.

Arms wrapped around his body, Duncan watched with deadened eyes, curiously distanced from the small part of him that told him he was a fool.

"Come on, Peter, it's good stuff." She took his hesitation as caution. "My bloke got it for me, he wouldn't give me crap."

Without realising it, he was suddenly sitting at her side, and holding out his arm to let her tie a cord around it. Avid, his eyes followed every move as the liquid filled the syringe and she made it all ready.

"Okay?"

He nodded. There was a vein, pushed high by the tourniquet and the needle tip slid sharply home. He licked his lips, and sighed as the drug slowly eased into his blood.

Peace. Joy. A rush of pleasure and the promise of absolute oblivion. His spine arched as pain faded. This was so different from the times with Paget. He was in control of this, wanted this. Nothing else mattered.

"There." Rosie slid the needle free and began to ready her own fix.

For Duncan she might as well no longer have been there. Slumped back into the sofa he was dumb and blind, lost to a thousand broken dreams.

Yet afterwards, when the evening was making the room dark, lit only by the glow from the fire, Duncan came to a strange realisation. He could kick heroin easily enough; what the doctor had said was pretty much true, if slightly optimistic. It would be uncomfortable, but possible. He could get clean, cure his body of the longing for the drug. Easy.

But he also came to understand something else: that the worst of his addiction wasn't to heroin at all, but to one Andrew Byrne. His body might protest the absence of the drug but it was nothing to the pain and the desolation he felt from that bastard's treachery.

But he couldn't waste away like a girl in a romance. However much the thought appealed.

He would mend. In every way.

So, that decided, he would get on with his life.

He knew it wouldn't be quite as easy as that. Physically he was weak, still badly battered, and prone to irrational bouts of emotion - and there was the nausea that his treatment in Kent seemed to have left as a legacy. All of it was a nuisance. But he could cope. Would cope.

Irrationally he blamed the telephone, its bright red plastic having only ever rung when Byrne wanted him. In a moment of pique he came close to throwing it out of the window, then nearly jumped out of his skin when it rang.

If it was Byrne then his eardrums would never be the same again.

He snatched up the handset and snapped: "What?"

"Hello, Peter darling, friendly as ever I see. Look, I'm in a bit of a hurry, but I'm back in town and well, I'll need my flat back rather quickly. Sorry, but you know how it is. In this business, no engagement lasts as long as you think."

"Sure." Duncan tried to arrange his thoughts into some semblance of rationality.

"Sorry, darling. Will you be okay?"

"Er, yes. Where are you now?"

"At a dreadful greasy-spoon on the way back from lovely Portsmouth, and let me tell you I am never going back. It's been awful, sorry and all that, but I just need to be home. I tried ringing before, but you haven't been there."

Duncan swallowed, and voiced the thought that was swamping every other: "Where shall I go?" Immediately he wished the pathetic words back.

"I've thought of that, sweetheart," Stevie said. "I've got this run-down old boat moored down on the south coast, you can have that until next summer if you want."

"Yes, of course, I'd love it!"

"I'll be home in an hour to give you the keys. She won't be sailing anywhere but you're welcome."

"Thanks."

"Don't mention it. You've helped me out often enough, sweetheart."

"Really, thanks."

"Silly boy!" And he was gone.

Replacing the receiver Duncan looked blankly around the room that had been home for too long, though to look around no one would ever know. Giving himself a mental shake he stood and carefully began to round up what things he did possess, ready to be off as soon as Stevie appeared.

Anyway, it would be ideal getting out of London. No Byrne. No temptation.

Slightly cheered by the thought, he packed his things into two canvas holdalls, one of which was nearly filled by notebooks alone. It had been so long since he'd bought any new clothes that his wardrobe was dwindling, and what he had looked old and tatty. Even the few good silk shirts were getting a bit threadbare, and if they got any worse he'd have to cut the collars off.

Folding faded jeans and his one last decent pair of trousers he smoothed the deep soft fabric. They were the ones he'd worn for Byrne.

Oh, damn it all!

There were so many easy ways to be miserable.

Well, at least he'd always looked good when they met. It was ridiculously easy to look expensively dressed if you made the effort to get to Portobello early on a Friday.

He'd learnt the technique of market stall shopping from the girls when he was still about twelve, part of his education being to learn that outward appearance meant more than almost anything if you wanted to make money as a hustler. They'd loved having a pretty child to play with, laughing as they taught him how to manicure his nails, cut his own hair and how to pick a silk designer shirt out of a pile of thirty cotton ones.

If Byrne had realised that the silk and velvet outfits that he had

126

admired so much had cost Duncan about a pound he'd probably have demanded his money back, claiming under false pretences.

That first time - bloody hell! One hundred pounds. With enough bartering he'd have done it for ten.

Still, that was his secret and one Byrne was never likely to know. Never.

The thought made him unaccountably depressed. Which made him angry. Which came close to making him laugh.

Leaving his bags by the door he had a hurried tidy round, gave the flat one last look. It had been a very strange few months. Ones at least he would never forget.

The doorbell made him start.

"Stevie."

"Good lord! Were you run over by a bus?"

Duncan had to smile. "No."

"Walked into a door I assume?"

"Something like that." He shrugged, and pointed to his bags. "I'm ready."

"I knew I could rely on you. But are you sure you're well enough to go? I could try and make other arrangements."

"No, I'll be fine. Where is this boat anyway?"

"Newhaven. Here's the keys, instructions about everything and a little bit of cash. I thought you might need it, don't know why."

"You're an angel." Duncan took the envelope, then opened his arms and gave his friend a quick hug. "I don't know what I'd do without you."

"You'd manage." Stevie sighed. "But a lift to Victoria Station would help?"

"Well, yes."

"The car's outside, off we go." He picked up Peter's bags and just walked back out of the flat. "Come on, you know I can't take no for an answer!"

So, bemused, Duncan followed.

Tracing Duncan's flat had been easy. Well, comparatively so, once he'd persuaded the harridan at the telephone exchange that he was genuinely from the police. He'd almost had to swear on the Official Secrets Act, but in the end he was sure it was charm that had won the day.

So far so good. Then Cadell had needed him urgently, his inside knowledge wanted for part of Paget's interrogation. Only an hour the boss had said - and to his frustration it was now nearly a whole day since Peter Duncan had disappeared from the hospital.

A-Z map in one hand, he found the right road and the right building. Parking, he sat and watched. Even in the streetlight, he could see the 1930's block was falling apart at the seams. He took a deep breath, and, locking up the car, went across the road. There was no front door and the lift looked like it was permanently out of action, yet the tenants seemed to keep the place reasonably clean and, for what Byrne suspected was really a slum, stench free.

He walked up the stairs with none of his usual vigour, taking them one at a time, dispassionately seeing in himself physical symptoms that he hadn't felt for ten years: dry mouth, sweating palms. The truth was so simple, yet he was suddenly certain that Duncan wouldn't be easy to convince.

On the second floor he found the right door number and knocked politely. Then again. After the third attempt he gave up and casually kicked it through.

The one-bedroom flat was clearly lived in. Furnished in a style he could only think of as shabby, it was sparse but comfortable, but absolutely empty of anything he recognised as Peter's.

There was always the possibility this was the wrong address. Byrne chewed a callus on his hand and fretted. Unlikely though, they usually got it right. He went back to the bedroom and started to search again.

Then, in the wardrobe, he found a silk shirt that he remembered Peter wearing. He fingered the cool, supple fabric, seeing it as it had moulded elegant muscle, parted to reveal sun-warmed skin. He crushed the silk in his hands, holding it tight as if he could squeeze some essence of his lover from the cold fibres, putting it to his face and breathing in, wanting to smell, to remember, to be reassured. But it was clean: essence of washing powder.

He tossed it aside and went on looking, but there was nothing in the flat that gave any clue to where Duncan had gone, even though with disbelief he went through it twice more. The need to find the man was close to pain, he would have done or paid anything for Duncan to have answered the door when he knocked.

Anything but let Paget off the hook.

But he should have been here earlier. So much could be happening, damn it! He wanted to find Duncan, take him home, and make him stay there until he was better. If Duncan wouldn't come willingly, then he would be persuaded. He needed -

Byrne was so engrossed in his thoughts that the sudden loud creak of floorboards had him flat on his stomach, gun out, before he could blink.

"My, now that's what I call a welcome." The figure in the doorway was completely unfazed.

Byrne stared up in embarrassment and got quickly to his feet, though the hot eyes behind pink-tinted glasses devoured him as much when he was upright as when he had been prone.

"I don't suppose by any chance you were looking for me? My luck couldn't have changed that much, I suppose."

Byrne was utterly silenced. The voice, the small, balding vision in skin-tight denim, the make-up –

Every interrogation skill he had ever learnt skittering out of reach, Byrne stood slack-jawed.

"Look, sweetie, put your nice gun away, close your mouth and tell me all about it."

The apparition managed to sound remarkably like a queer agony aunt.

Clearing his throat, Byrne belatedly holstered the .38 and straightened his jacket. The other man's gaze seemed fixed at crotch level and it took all Byrne's self-control not to cross his hands in front of himself. He coughed. "Who are you and what are you doing here?"

"You're asking me? Well, this is my flat and that was my door you, I presume, demolished. Try again, shall we, and introduce ourselves like real ladies." The apparition minced forward, hand extended limply. "My name's Steven Dyes, but you can call me Stevie."

Hand propelled by unseen forces, Byrne dazedly shook the other man's hand. "Er, I'm Byrne, sorry about the door, I thought somebody might be in trouble."

"I could only wish." Pink-shielded eyes fled heavenwards as Stevie sighed. Then he frowned. "If you really thought somebody was in trouble you must have been looking for Peter, and from what he said I don't think he wants to see you."

"You've seen him, how is he, where is he?"

"Hold your handbag! One thing at a time, mate."

The camp mannerisms were on hold as Dyes turned suddenly wary. "Yes I've seen him, and I haven't seen him look as ill in over ten years. He mentioned you to me, talked quite a bit before I dropped him off at Victoria. I hope you feel pleased with yourself destroying a defenceless soul like that."

Open-mouthed, Byrne gathered himself. Ill Duncan might be, but: "Defenceless?"

"Be quiet. You, you traitor, I can read between the lines of what happened and I can see when a boy's been jilted."

"He hasn't."

"Maybe not for another man, sweetie, though I think that's part of what Peter believes. You certainly did something to hurt him badly." Steven crossed his arms and managed to look indignantly down a very short, snub nose.

"You're a good friend of his?"

"How can you ask!"

Byrne sighed, and gave in. "Yes, I did hurt him, but it was an accident. He thinks something is true, but it isn't. Please tell me where he is. I only want to talk to him."

"Talk with those big fists maybe. Someone's given him a pasting, was it you, loverboy?" Steven's words dripped with sarcasm.

"No!" That was one thing Byrne could defend himself about with alacrity. "I've never laid a finger on him."

"Umm, laid him though, haven't you. You are the man he's crying over, aren't you? His lover?"

Crying, Peter?

"I was, am. Yes."

"Well, then. You've got a lot to answer for."

"I know. I made a mess of things with him, but now I need to sort it out. In person, if possible."

"I'll let him know you were here, and that you want to see him." Steven turned away, conversation ended.

"Look, you thick-skulled ..."

"Do you always think you can get through people with bluster? It might work with the others, sweetie, but not with me. I've been harried by tougher girls than you." His nostrils flared magnificently. "Go on, you can leave now. I need to settle in, get my frocks unpacked before they die in those horrid cases. Off you go."

Ignoring this enigmatic comment as being beyond him, defeated, Byrne turned to leave, then paused. "Why was Peter living here?"

"I was away and I wouldn't see anyone out on the streets. Those bastard pigs who lost him every job he tried for also managed to get him chucked out of his flat. Community policing with a vengeance."

His voice softened. "We go back a long way, Peter and I. I would have helped a dog who'd been kicked as often as he has, let alone a friend."

Byrne nodded. "Are you sure you won't tell me?" He knew he could try and force this strange man into telling, take him down to HQ if need be, but something told him that he'd keep to his word.

"Absolutely, darling. But if you give me your number, I'll ring you on Monday."

"You won't forget?" Byrne rummaged in his wallet for a card with his personal number on it, then handed it over.

"How could I?" Stevie's eyes glanced downwards. "Wave your gun at a girl like me and I'll remember you for ever." He laughed at Byrne's reaction. "Don't worry, Peter's about the only person in the world whose territory I don't poach on." He waved his fingers in farewell. "Off you go ..."

"Yeah. Bye."

Byrne departed feeling - edgy, disconcerted by Dyes' blatant exhibition of sexual preference. There was no doubt he was gay. Queer. A shirt-lifter.

And so what was Byrne? Never having gone quite as far as queer-bashing, he'd still, over the years, dished out his own share of verbal abuse. None of which he was proud of, but it was the truth.

Which raised a problem. What if he did get Peter Duncan to live with him, what then? He unlocked his car and slid behind the wheel, slamming the door closed. Was that really what he wanted? He frowned, considering that possibility; Duncan, living with him. As a lover. Even if it meant being labelled a faggot?

Being a faggot.

No excuses. No women. Just one man.

He shivered, and hated the cowardice that made him want to run.

But Duncan was the opposite of camp. So what was the problem, love, sex or holding hands in public? Sex was fine, very nice in fact, thank you very much. Love, well, he was finding out about that. The last? Well, maybe Duncan wouldn't want to.

But what if he did?

Muttering under his breath Byrne put the car into gear and drove off. Before anything else he had to persuade Duncan that he wasn't an unmitigated bastard. Then maybe there would be some hope. Holding hands? A cinch. In comparison.

Three days. Which felt like three months.

Even though Byrne was kept busy interrogating the police who had been implicated in the drugs swap, the thought of Duncan rarely left his mind. Images haunted him: Duncan ill, Duncan hating him, Duncan lying mindless in ecstasy beneath him.

He was not at his most efficient.

And time crawled.

Cadell kept Paget to himself, wanting the trickiest of all the policemen to be his own. Paget, even now that the game was truly up and he was caught fast, still made his interrogator fight for any scrap of information.

It was late on the Sunday night and Byrne, bleary-eyed with tiredness, yet with his brain spinning madly, was sitting in the rest room trying hard to gather up the enthusiasm to go home when the door banged shut and he looked up, surprised to see Cadell walking towards him.

"Evening, sir."

"Byrne." Cadell nodded and sat down to stare in silence at his folded hands. For the first time in their association Byrne understood that the commander was not a young man; he looked wearied by his years, as if a lifetime of experiences had suddenly become too heavy a burden to carry.

"Sir, would you like some tea?"

Cadell almost smiled. "Aye, I think I would."

Standing, Byrne filled the kettle and switched it on. He hovered awkwardly over teapot and mugs while it boiled and wondered what had brought Cadell to this outpost of non-civilisation, the slightly seedy room furnished with junk shop furniture not Byrne's idea of an ideal place to choose to relax. Pursing his lips, he admitted that Cadell needed to grab any chance of relaxation he could get.

The kettle boiled and, a mug of tea in each hand, Byrne sat at the table. "Sorry, but there's no cups." The chipped, thick china sat strangely in the liver-spotted hand.

"I've drunk out of worse than this." Cadell sipped at the hot tea. "And I've tasted worse tea. Cheers." He raised the mug in salute. They sat in silence for a while. There was no clue for Byrne what Cadell wanted. If, indeed, he wanted anything. Though the idea of Cadell amiably, inconsequentially socialising was not easy to take. Byrne remained quiet, too tired to initiate whatever Cadell wanted. Finally, after several minutes, Cadell placed his empty mug down on the table and looked at Byrne.

"Have you heard anything from Mr Dyes?"

"No, he said it would be by Monday evening. I didn't think it would help to pester him." Byrne cleared his throat. "He seemed the type who'd deliberately jump in the opposite direction of where he was pushed."

"What will you say to Duncan when you speak to him?"

Hey, guess what? I love you, come back and live with me, everything will be all right. Maybe that would work. But then again -

"Umm, that we need his information and his testimony. I think we'll have trouble getting him to prosecute Paget for the physical damage he inflicted, though the bastard deserves to be."

Byrne felt a rush of rage as he remembered the state of Duncan's body, and wondered what civilising influence had stopped him from breaking Paget into little bits. Releasing his stranglehold on the mug, he wiped damp palms on his cords, willing the fury away; there were far more efficient ways of destroying Paget than physical ones.

"You know Peter Duncan better than anybody." Byrne looked startled at the remark. "He hasn't many friends. This Steven person is about the nearest he's got, apart from you, and as far as we can make out, they only meet very occasionally." Cadell leant back in his chair, looking doubtful. "So, how do you think he will cope with what's happened to him?"

Nonplussed, this was about the last topic he'd expected Cadell to broach, Byrne shrugged. He'd managed to think no further than the immediacy of emotion; rationalisation beyond him, but he tried. "Well, he's certainly tough and resilient. Once he's physically over the battering they gave him I think he'll be fine. He isn't an addict as such, I know that."

"I hope so." Cadell stared at his hands where they rested on the table. "You know that despite everything they did to him he didn't tell them anything - a point Paget seems really very aggrieved about."

Cadell shifted, the hard chair creaking, and he watched the muscles bunching in Byrne's jaw. "He's an interesting man."

"Paget?"

"Don't be obtuse, you know I mean Duncan. I wouldn't like to

134

think of him being irreparably damaged by this experience."

"He's a survivor."

"Very true."

Byrne looked at his watch and glumly counted the hours until Monday night. "I'll know more tomorrow. Steven Dyes did say that he'd make sure Peter was okay."

Cadell nodded and stood up. "Get some rest, Byrne, and keep me in touch with what's happening. Good night." He patted Byrne's shoulder as he walked to the door, not looking back as he left.

Alone in the empty room Byrne turned over in his mind the things Cadell had said and asked, yet could find no rhyme or reason behind them. Unless ... But no, Cadell might ask but Duncan would spit in his face. After Paget it was doubtful if Duncan would even want to look at another policeman, let alone return to being one.

Byrne picked up his jacket and shrugged into it. There were so many 'ifs': if Duncan was okay, if Dyes rang back ... Byrne cursed at the unwelcome thought. If Dyes didn't ring back he'd skin him alive.

Still, patience was a virtue.

He was talking to himself as he made his way down the stairs to the car park, muttering under his breath. Eighteen hours. If he slept for eight that would only leave ten, then with working all day, it wouldn't be long. Not really.

Unconvinced, he went home and curling around the pillow that Duncan had slept on, finally managed to sleep at least four of the promised hours.

At 6.08 on Monday night, Byrne was at home and waiting. By 9.00 he'd eaten four doorstep sandwiches, a chocolate log and downed a bottle of wine. The only reason he hadn't turned to the whisky was in case he needed to drive anywhere. If Duncan needed him. Switching to coffee he sat in the silent flat and felt a subtle cloud of depression settle around him. He tried hard not to think, but the voice that spoke to him was very insistent.

Convinced of the unlikelihood of persuading Duncan that anything

135

he said was genuine, Byrne nearly panicked when at 11.36 the strident tones of the telephone brought him back to reality. Clutching at it, he didn't give the caller a chance to speak.

"Steven, did you see him, how is he?"

"It's not Steven."

"Peter!" Byrne felt his heart and stomach change positions.

"Stevie persuaded me I ought to call." Duncan's voice was arctic. "Stupid sod thought you were upset."

"Jesus. Upset doesn't begin to describe it. I've been frantic." He swallowed, trying to keep the urgency from his voice. Peter didn't sound as if he'd appreciate promises of undying love. He tried again. "Are you all right?"

"Yeah." Byrne could almost hear the shrug that accompanied the terse word.

"I mean, are you ...?"

"I'm clean, Byrne. Yeah, it was no big deal."

Byrne ached at the casual dismissal of what he couldn't conceive as being anything but cruel. "I'm glad you're okay."

The disembodied voice thawed a fraction. "Yeah, well, thanks."

"What about the bruises?"

"Technicolor, but doing what bruises do, going away in their own sweet time."

"Great." Byrne reached for words. "And you, how are you?"

"Byrne, I'm fine. Get on with it, what do you want that's so urgent?"

"To talk to you, to explain. It wasn't what you think, you know." He could hear the tension in his voice and wondered what Duncan would make of it.

"Course not, silly me to believe what I saw."

"Believe me, I was working undercover, it was a set-up. I hate Paget and his kind as much as you do."

"That much, eh?" Dry, ironic, Duncan sounded less than amused.

"Please, I've got to come and see you. Show you proof."

"It'll make a change from etchings."

"It will be the truth."

136

There was silence between them, then they both spoke at once.

"Byrne."

"Peter."

There was a moment of uneasy silence.

"Please, I only want to talk." Byrne could feel the other man's resolve waver. "Do you need anything?"

"No." Instant mistrust.

"Look, I've got a day off tomorrow. Wherever you are, I could come and meet you. We could meet somewhere neutral." He paused, dry-mouthed. "Please."

"Why, want a quick fuck, do you?"

"Jesus, no! I want ..."

"A long fuck, a blow-job, a quick rimming to - "

"Stop it! It isn't like that any more."

"Oh, decided to go back to your girlfriends, have you? Well I'll be damned and there I was ringing up to arrange some business." Duncan's voice was pure sarcasm, refined and undiluted. "I forgot for a moment that you only fuck me under orders."

Byrne's indrawn breath was clearly audible. "That's not what I meant. Look, this is ridiculous. I need to see you, talk to you in person."

"No." The word sounded so defeated that it made Byrne wince.

"Please."

"No."

"But, Peter ..."

"I rang tonight, Byrne, wanting to hear the truth however unpalatable it might be. Whatever you are, I'd persuaded myself that it didn't matter as long as you were honest with me. God, it makes me laugh. You wouldn't recognise honesty if it was strangling you. Undercover? So you're telling me that you're a copper?"

"Yes."

"Oh, highly likely. In case it escaped your notice, you've been seeing a prostitute, fucking a male whore, for months ... Unless they don't know?"

"They know."

"Poor you." Duncan laughed, the sound soft and bitter. "I bet that was a fun meeting with the boss."

"He understood."

"What! It doesn't happen, Byrne. You'll be telling me next that you took my fee out of expenses."

"It's the truth." The word was losing its meaning. "Not the expenses, but everything else."

"Bye bye, Byrne. If I ever find myself in town I might call, give you a freebie for old time's sake."

"Peter!" Byrne's despairing voice was answered by the purr of a disconnected line. Slowly lowering his hand Byrne carefully replaced the receiver.

So that was that.

At sea in the darkness Byrne cursed his own stupidity. He should have played it differently, said different things, been less clumsy, more persuasive. There should have been a way to be convincing. But, playing back their conversation in his head, he found no hint that Duncan wanted to believe him. In fact it seemed amazing that he'd rung at all.

But he had called. Byrne repeated it again to himself. He had called.

Which meant? Maybe more than Duncan knew. And maybe there was a small pinch of hope.

Standing on shaky legs he went to get a drink. Whisky was there, and he poured a large measure, drinking it down in one. The spirit burnt all the way down into his gut, where it settled into ice. He shivered, cold to the bone.

Hope. Was he a fool to still need it? Or was he a worse fool for not having done something already, found Duncan, made him listen, made him understand. Misery, utterly bleak misery made him stare hollow-eyed at the bottle. He picked it up and took it to bed.

Two hours later it was empty: and not even then was he granted the grace of sleep.

Wan-faced and feeling ill he entered HQ the next day to find that

138

Cadell wanted to speak to him. On a list of priorities, seeing Cadell would have fallen off the bottom.

From behind her desk Alice watched him, mildly interested in how subdued he was. The steady stream of pseudo-witticisms and flirtation that he usually showered on her were an irritation, but they were Byrne. This man was - different. She was still watching as he went into their boss's office.

"Morning, sir."

Gimlet eyes surveyed him and passed on without comment. "Byrne." Cadell nodded to the chair and Byrne sat down. "Last night, seeing that you had neglected such basic procedure, I had your call from Duncan monitored and traced."

"You what?" Byrne was on his feet, dismay and anger moving him before he thought.

"Sit down." Cadell had perfected the art of soft-voiced command, and obediently Byrne sat. "Now then, less over-reaction, please. I took the precaution for various reasons, not least because Peter Duncan is a witness for the Crown and we can't have him wandering the country at will. He undoubtedly has a vast store of information that we need. Do you really think I would just ignore him? Your conversation was taped for these reasons only, not to find out any secrets about your private life." Cadell sighed as Byrne subsided into the chair. "Why are you making such a complete mull of all this?"

Byrne opened his mouth to answer, then thought better of it. He shrugged instead.

"Very eloquent. Why didn't you think to trace the call?" It wasn't really a question. "Look, Andrew, I may have a certain, distaste shall we say, for your private life, but it is just that. I'm not judging you. All that concerns me is that through you and this relationship we actually have a chance at Paget. We need Duncan, and we need to know where he is and hopefully do a complete de-briefing as soon as possible. The wire-tap was a basic precaution."

"I have a right to know when I'm being investigated."

"Good grief! Is that what you think? Don't be so stupid. I just want Duncan, whether he wants to be found or not."

"Perhaps that's why I didn't arrange to have the call traced."

Cadell doubted it; such altruism was beyond his experience of Byrne. Unless Byrne was changing. "Anyway, this is all beside the point. At least we now know where he is."

"Where?" Just don't let it be the Outer Hebrides! Mentally, Byrne crossed his fingers.

"Newhaven in East Sussex."

Byrne searched in his mind and finally came up with a town on the coast. Newhaven, the ferry sailed to Dieppe from there, he'd been once as a boy.

"Aye, that friend of his whom you met the other day, he owns a run-down old boat that's moored there. He lets it out in the summer to holidaymakers. Duncan has use of it for the winter."

He could be there in two hours. Byrne's thoughts were intent, though he was aware of Cadell's words.

"I'll go now, sir." Two hours. He was on his feet and at the door.

Cadell's voice reached him before he opened it, though his boss spoke almost hesitantly. "Byrne. No interrogation tactics. Try listening to him as well as yourself - we need him on our side." Byrne stared at him and Cadell gave in. "Oh for goodness' sake, be off with you. I don't know why I bother."

Byrne smiled, boyish pleasure lighting his face and smoothing it of tension. "Can't think either, sir."

8

The small town of Newhaven was set around a long estuary, and most of its livelihood seemed to come from the ferry terminal. What livelihood there was. Byrne drove around winding, steep streets and saw endless empty shops, a lot of pubs, dreary women and very little sign of prosperity. It might have been better in summer of course. At least it wouldn't have been so drab.

Not really concentrating, he managed to get stuck in the one-way system and fifteen minutes later was still cursing. He'd driven over the bridge spanning the estuary three times, once ended up in a supermarket car park, once in a dead end and once done a U-turn on the main road right in front of a Mazda driven by a little old lady with a really remarkable command of invective.

It had almost been enough to cheer him up.

The mess that 60's developers had made of what must have been a quaint old Sussex port was amazing. In fact, the only good thing about it was that it sat within easy driving distance of London.

Oh, and that Peter Duncan was there.

He knew Duncan was living on a boat, and there was only one place for a boat to be, and that was on the water. There was an awful lot of the stuff, but discounting the working fishing boats, the ferries, the tugs and the weekend sailors' pride and joys, there was only one boat that was at all likely. A victory lap later and he pulled into a side street.

Parking, Byrne got out and stretched his legs. Car locked, he went to the end of the street and walked down some steps to the main road. It was a clear day, the air clean enough, scented of the sea. There were hills in the distance, fields, the water still and dark by his side as he went down the hill, the pavement sandwiched between the road and the low-lying estuary. White metal railings acted as a barrier, and he followed them along for about fifty feet. There the fence opened, giving access to a small, slatted wood jetty that led to a disreputably battered old boat.

If Steven Dyes ever managed to con people into paying good money to stay there either he was a more gifted salesman than the devil, or Newhaven had delights that Byrne hadn't noticed.

Broken down, with peeling paint and a hotchpotch of rusting metal adornments, it was a ramshackle affair. Byrne felt distinctly disinclined to set foot aboard: apart from being convinced that his weight would be the last straw for her aged timbers, it just looked so damned dirty.

He was faintly shocked. Peter Duncan was one of the most fastidious people Byrne had ever met, one who, even broke and living in what Byrne could only describe as a flea-pit, had always been sleek, his personal appearance exquisite. That he should be reduced to living here, on this old hulk was outrageous.

Standing on the edge of the pavement, just where the walkway began, gulls squawking above his head, Byrne realised, maybe for the first time, that Duncan was utterly serious about what he was doing. That his life had actually been torn apart. That he had come close to being destroyed.

Apart from when Duncan had been held by Paget, which had all too obviously been rough, Byrne hadn't really considered what his life had been like.

Suddenly he saw what it must have taken to deal with no job, no money, no security and with only a distant friendship to keep a roof over your head. He frowned, shouldering deeper into his sheepskin, the cold grey winter day finally penetrating his absorption.

Duncan's life had been upended. But there was no need to live like this. Surely he'd only need to be shown the sense in coming back to London, coming back to Byrne. No more living on freezing boats; bloody stupid anyway. Gentle persuasion was all that was needed. Byrne knew he could do it, he could charm the birds from the trees on a good day. Knew he could. Charming a vulnerable man back to town and into his flat couldn't be that hard, could it?

Course not.

Heartened, he set one foot firmly on the unsafe-looking slats, tested them, then walked gingerly over to the boat. The old thing was a reasonable size and had probably been some sort of trawler. The ship's wheel was still in place, though it clearly hadn't been used in years; maybe about the last time the boat had been seaworthy, which, in Byrne's estimation was about 1910.

Fat-bellied, propped permanently aground, wetted only by the estuary's tidal flow, the boat for all her forlorn aspect did have a certain appeal. An appeal Duncan might relish.

Doubt slowing his feet he looked at the boat again and wondered if, despite the dirt and dinginess, it might be somewhere Duncan would be content. After all, he wouldn't need shag-pile carpets and three-piece suites to make his life complete. For all his love of fine things Duncan had a sense of balance that came unequivocally from within. There was no way he would have survived otherwise. Unlike the boat, Duncan didn't depend on props for support.

Cautiously Byrne continued on his way, eyeing the smelly, silted estuary bed with disfavour as he stepped over the side and onto the deck. Standing still he waited for a second to see if his arrival stirred anyone, the sound of his footsteps having been noisy enough to alert Peter of approaching company.

Nothing.

The doorway to what had to be the living quarters was at the raised stern and carefully arranging his face into a neutral mask, he went and knocked.

Still nothing.

Bloody typical, Duncan was out. Though surely after three days Duncan would have used up Newhaven's dubious delights. Unless he really hated the boat, in which case maybe he was spending as much time as he could in the town. Byrne frowned, wishing he could guess how Duncan was feeling about the boat.

About everything.

Wrapping his jacket more closely around his body, Byrne parked himself in a sheltered spot; sitting on sun-warmed planking and resigning himself to wait. He'd give it an hour. If Peter was longer than that he'd go to the pub and warm up. An hour. It wasn't long to wait, really.

Considering the fact that the main road ran along the waterside, the boat was amazingly peaceful, the cawing of seagulls seeming to add to the quiet rather than detract from it. He watched the beached fishing boats with idle interest, his eyes travelling from them to scan the pedestrians walking by. Even from a distance he knew he would recognise Duncan's straight-backed, easy walk, and eagerly anticipated it.

After a while, Byrne became aware that the tide was rising, the gently lapping sounds of water against the boat's hull suddenly separate from the general background hum. The hour was up but, surprisingly content, he decided to give Peter a bit longer.

Byrne had always hated sea journeys, finding the old adage that it wasn't the destination but the journey that counted, a load of bollocks. If he wanted to be somewhere, then he wanted to be there, not caught somewhere in-between. In fact, he'd rather be there yesterday.

Any romance the sea might ever have had for his juvenile brain had been thoroughly washed away by six months on a cargo ship. He shuddered delicately as the memories came back and search though he might, he couldn't find a single good one.

Mind you, at least this boat was firmly attached to dry land. No seasickness, thank heaven for small mercies. Boats were fine to look at, but for comfort, nothing beat a nice big jet. Followed by a five-star hotel somewhere hot. With Peter Duncan as a companion.

The thought made him smile.

The faint winter sun broke through the clouds and warmed him where he sat. Very pleasant. His eyelids slowly closed, weighted by inertia. Forty winks, he promised himself.

Well, maybe fifty ...

And was suddenly startled awake.

"Byrne! Okay, how the bloody hell did you find me?"

Byrne, caught off-balance by the depth of sleep that he'd been in and the shock of Duncan's appearance, could only look. And want. Though after a minute he found the muscular control to speak.

"Hello, Peter."

"Yeah, save the reunion for another time. Get the fuck off my boat."

He looked ill.

Byrne blinked up, seeing a thin body in faded jeans and baggy jumper. The swelling on Duncan's face had subsided but the bruises had emerged as a spectacular swathe down the left side of his face. Byrne knew the feel of that skin beneath his fingers, knew it as well as his own and he wanted to touch now. Comfort it. If it had been possible he would have taken the pain into himself, somehow made everything right.

He pushed up off the deck, standing slowly, almost reaching out, not quite. "Peter, I came to explain."

Duncan seemed to hesitate, then his face hardened. "I told you last time. I don't want to talk to you and I don't want to see you. Go away." He turned to unlock the door, dismissing Byrne with a casual twist of his shoulder.

"Cadell sent me. He's the one who found you."

The name seemed to work. "Graham Cadell?"

"Yes."

Duncan stilled, his head slightly down, face hidden by his wind-blown hair. Byrne held his breath.

"Okay. You've got ten minutes. Come downstairs."

Byrne could have grinned. Instead he took a sharp breath and found refuge in humour. "Don't you mean below deck, or something?" He brushed dust off the seat of his trousers, carefully avoiding staring too hard at the bruises patterning what was visible of Duncan's pale skin. He looked gaunt, sick. But not in the least bit in need of sympathy.

Side-tracked, Byrne only noticed that the door was opening as a waft of damp sea smells hit him and he wrinkled his nose in distaste.

"You won't be here long enough for the stink to worry you, come on." Duncan disappeared into the stairwell, leaving Byrne to catch the swinging door before it slammed shut.

As he followed down the stairs, Byrne managed to be amused at himself and his 'come and let me take you away from all this' plans. Duncan was hardly fainting into his arms. Even if he looked frail enough to be fainting all over the place.

Though preferably not on the carpet.

Byrne eyed the living quarters and reconsidered what Duncan might need in the way of interior design in order to be happy. His own flat suddenly seeming palatial. Here everything was old, broken, damp and downright cramped. The sole sign of Duncan's occupancy was a typewriter set up on a spindly table that was flanked by piles of notebooks in varying stages of scruffiness, a used mug and a pile of blankets heaped on an old sofa.

Tongue-tied, charm utterly deserting him, Byrne looked around and fought for something to say. "So Paget told the truth about that." He nodded to the table. "You're thinking of writing a book."

Duncan glared at him. "Yeah, though I'm doing a bit more than thinking. I have to if I'm going to fuck Paget with it. And you can stop looking like that; I've been in worse places than this. Besides, who invited you?"

"Sorry." Byrne had the grace to be slightly shamefaced. "I wouldn't recommend some of the places I've had to live in either."

Truce. Though neither of them sat down, just stood and stared at each other.

"How did Cadell find me?" Duncan spoke quietly.

"Divination, for all I know." He stopped at the look on Duncan's face. "No, he tapped my phone and traced your call. It's easy when you know how."

"I wondered if you would."

"I didn't think. Cadell, well, he thinks of everything. How he found out about this boat, though, from you ringing from a call-box, I don't know."

"He could have talked to Steven."

"Could have done, though I didn't get much out of him."

Duncan almost smiled, and obviously thought better of it. "Oh, I wouldn't say that. I think you got quite a bit of admiration out of him. He was very complimentary about this butch queen who held him up at gunpoint. Did you have to bring one of his favourite fantasies to life?"

"Ah, yes - "

"When he told me about it, I could have laughed; to make his day complete all you'd have to have done was search him. Wish I'd been a fly on the wall."

Lips tightly compressed, Byrne willed himself not to make a rash comment. At this moment Duncan didn't look as if he'd ever laughed at anything in his life, the well-remembered face planed into austerity.

He shrugged. "Made a right idiot of myself. It was one of those things."

"Stevie likes you, God knows why ..."

Wearily Duncan sat down on a long, cushioned locker and rubbed his hand over his face as if brushing cobwebs away. For a prolonged moment he sat still, eyes fixed on the floor, then he nodded, as if an internal argument had been resolved. "Okay, Byrne, tell me the story. How come you know Cadell?"

Byrne dug into a pocket and found his ID. He proffered it to Duncan.

A nerve was pulsing by Duncan's eye. "It looks genuine."

"It is."

"I suppose I can't argue with that."

"I've worked for him for a couple of years. We were after Paget, and it all sort of came together with you. I wasn't one of Paget's lot, it just looked that way."

"I see."

147

Did he? Byrne wondered what was going on inside Duncan's head, searched for the right things to say. He didn't understand why Duncan suddenly looked utterly defeated.

As if deathly tired, Duncan slumped back against a cupboard.

"Are you okay?"

Duncan stirred himself slightly and looked up. "Yeah. I must have overdone the walk this morning. I wondered if three miles was too much."

"Are you well enough - "

"Yes." Though he shivered slightly as he said it.

"Do you want some tea?"

Byrne, tea-maker extraordinary. Well, if Cadell liked it ... He caught Duncan's slight nod and went to find the galley. All brisk efficiency in the tiny kitchen, he filled the kettle, lit the Calor-gas stove, rummaged around to find where Duncan kept his food. Then he realised: the tea, the milk and an ancient bag of rice were probably all there was.

Leaning against the sink Byrne fretted, knowing Duncan would be too proud to take any money. So, what to do? A food parcel? Byrne could see that being consigned to the fishes. Out to dinner? Better. Maybe, if there was anywhere in this pox-hole of a town that served food worth eating. He watched the kettle as it started to heat and frowned.

It would be a good way to get Duncan to talk more. In a getting-blood-from-a-stone sort of way.

If he would come back to London ... That seemed an unlikely option. Byrne sighed, and chewed his lip.

The water took ages to boil on the ancient stove and it was nearly ten minutes later when Byrne stepped back into the main cabin holding two chipped mugs in one hand, and an ancient half-packet of biscuits in the other. Perseverance in all things was Byrne's motto and he'd found them in the top of one of the cupboards, after an exhaustive search that would have made Sergeant Dixon proud. They weren't much, but anything would do to fend off starvation at least for a while.

On the verge of opening his mouth to joke about it, Byrne stopped. Duncan was asleep. Sitting upright, back resting against a cupboard, head tilted, lips slightly parted. Fast asleep. Byrne's gut clenched. A pulse was visible at Duncan's bare neck, the fast beat disturbing the skin, emphasising the frailty that seemed to have come from out of nowhere.

No, not from nowhere. From Paget.

Byrne stood still, watching. He couldn't help but compare this tired, bruised man with how he had been, all vibrancy and ease. He hated this remote vulnerability that was so new and so unwanted. Even asleep the gaunt face couldn't escape the lines of stress and pain. The pale features were bruised, though none of the fading marks were as bad as the black smudges that lay under the fan of dark lashes. Long ragged locks, matted by the sea wind, twisted in dull disarray framing a face as dissolute and damaged as Adam's on the wrong side of Eden's firmly locked gates. He was beautiful, and Byrne had to swallow hard to move the stone that had lodged in his throat.

Careful not to make any noise, he put the mugs and biscuits down and sat opposite the sleeper. He was in no hurry and there was great pleasure in just watching, just simply absorbing the other man's presence. That he was here, alive, close enough to touch. Byrne was sure that he wouldn't be allowed to even look, let alone stare, once Duncan was awake.

In a silence that was lined by the faint purr of the fire and the seagulls' distant cries, Byrne sipped his tea. He didn't even open the biscuits in case the rustling was too loud and Duncan woke up.

Limply sprawled, dressed in jeans and jumper so disreputable that Byrne had trouble believing that anyone would wear such garments by choice, Duncan looked as ragged as his clothes. Through contentedly drowsy eyes Byrne watched, and was warmed by Peter's silent company, the worry finally dissipating now that he could see for himself that despite it all, Duncan was safe.

His eyelids drifting shut, Byrne tried to fathom the complex pattern of thought that motivated the other man. There seemed to be little doubt that Duncan believed him, that he accepted Paget as their common enemy. But instead of the expected relief, Peter seemed even more remote and distanced from Byrne than ever. If they had spoken different tongues there would have been more likelihood of communication.

Maybe it was because Cadell's group was affiliated to the police. But Duncan had to know that they were as much against police corruption as he was. Besides, Cadell's name had gone down well with Duncan. At the very least it had got him invited in.

Not even able to put a name to the feeling, Byrne knew he wanted Duncan to believe him, to trust him again. He wanted things to be as they were.

He wanted his friend.

Lover.

As if they had ever been either. But they could be. There was hope for both. There had to be.

In his sleep Duncan made a low sound of distress and, instantly alert, Byrne sat forward. He put his mug down and clasped his hands together, not knowing what to do. In the space of a few heart-beats, Duncan's sleep had gone from rest to nightmare, the muscles of his face drawn tight into a frown. A soft whimper made Byrne flinch.

Should he wake Duncan up, or let him ride it out? He hesitated. Though surely any sleep was better than none. Even this. If every attempt at sleep ended up in nightmare, no wonder he looked run into the ground.

Another whimper.

Knotted with uncertainty, Byrne watched the sleeper's face, hating not knowing what to do.

He took a deep breath and made a decision. He'd wait. If the dreams turned into a screaming nightmare then, well, then Peter would wake anyway. He sat back, still tense. Wary. Ready in case the sleeper needed him.

Any excuse. He needed to give comfort as much as he was certain Duncan needed to receive it.

Considering how long they had known each other, and how intimate they had been, it was ridiculous that there was no normal structure to their relationship; nothing to fall back on except sex. Which was very nice, and not something he had ever before even mildly regretted, but here and now - He sighed deeply. And wished that at least once they had met as friends, true friends, before all this had happened.

He should have admitted the truth long ago. Or at least come close to seeing it. Maybe that morning when he'd woken with Duncan wrapped so perfectly around him, and he had known contentment as well as desire. Had their futures been linked from then? Or from earlier, from that first meeting. Looking back it was easy to see there had been more than simple attraction even then. Certainly more than commercial transaction.

Truth? Peter Duncan was the only person who had ever come into his life and really meant something. There, that was the truth; one he had known but just never admitted. Until it was rather too late

Now it was all to build from scratch. Which was possible. Of course it was.

He frowned, thinking hard; something he wasn't usually pressed to do. But there was nothing like wanting something he couldn't have to make a man introspective. The thought made him smile very briefly. Then he was utterly sober. He wanted Duncan, body and soul; even to the hidden recesses of self that he shared with no one.

Everything.

Byrne knew he had changed, that Duncan had changed him, and that everything with Paget had made him see reality for what it was. Made him admit what he wanted. Which, for maybe the first time ever, was whatever was best for someone else.

Dry-mouthed Byrne looked back at his life and knew there was not one previous lover who would recognise Byrne as he was with Duncan, even in their client/whore months, as the man they had known. Now he would be a stranger to them all.

Utterly unnerved, Byrne sat very still. In the silence he admitted the real truth, that what he wanted more than anything was to experience waking with Duncan forever. If that was possible. If Duncan wanted it. If ...

Damn, it was all so bloody unlikely.

He sat lost in thought while his tea cooled and then went cold. He only came back when Duncan finally stirred and, achingly slowly, sat up.

He peered around, spotted Byrne. "Still here?"

Byrne shrugged. "Didn't seem polite just to leave." It hadn't occurred to him to try, but he didn't explain that to Duncan. "Anyway, I didn't want to wake you, you looked like you could do with the sleep."

"Yeah." With thin fingers Duncan rubbed at his reddened eyes.

"You sleep that well all the time?" Byrne enquired cautiously, slipping the words out as if asking the time of day.

"Worse, usually." It was as if the admission was out before Duncan's tired mind caught up with his mouth. Dropping his hands he glared at Byrne's innocent face. "Not that it's any concern of yours."

Byrne ignored the jibing comment, and changed the subject. "I'm here for Cadell, too. He would like to talk to you."

"Why?"

"He wants Paget put away, he knows you can help do that. He wants to know more about when you were in the force, and after. He knows you've information Paget wanted destroyed, and I guess he's hoping you'll share."

"Hoping? More likely assuming." Duncan shrugged slightly. "All right, though I expect it'll be more like an interrogation."

"No, it won't."

It certainly wouldn't be if Byrne had anything to do with it; he hid a flush of protectiveness by reaching for the biscuits, side-tracking Duncan who, though he hadn't looked very hard, was certain that Stevie had left the boat devoid of food. "Where on earth did you find them?"

"In the galley, want one?"

"Good grief, no; they've probably got more weevils than the boat."

"More protein," answered Byrne obscurely. "I'd been eyeing up the woodwork till I found these." And you. He tried to control the aching hunger that he felt, dragging his eyes away from the unconsciously sensual body. He coughed. "Want to go out and grab a bite to eat? There must be somewhere decent near here."

"No." Duncan shook his head.

"I'll pay if that's what's worrying you." Ruefully Byrne remembered that Duncan was undoubtedly broke. "It's on expenses."

Duncan gave a snort that could have been laughter. "Oh joy, what an offer, but all the same I'll pass this time."

"Well then, come back to London with me. Please?"

Narrowed eyes assessed him coldly. "Are you asking for yourself or for Cadell?"

Fascinated by the dark pupils that seemed to pierce right through him, Byrne answered with the truth that he thought Duncan wanted to hear. "Cadell."

Feathering lashes hid the reaction, but the reply was succinct. "No."

"Look, Peter ..."

"Peter, Peter, yes, it is my name."

"Is it?"

"Yes."

Byrne nodded. "Cadell said you'd used more than one, and I wondered."

"How long have you known that?"

Byrne heard the tension in Duncan's voice, but could only answer the truth, as he had no idea exactly what was upsetting the other man. "Since before the Paget op."

Very pale, very quiet, Duncan nodded. He took a long breath then looked up, though he didn't look at Byrne. His voice was pitched low as he asked, "What do you really want, Byrne?"

"You. You can't hide out here for ever."

"I don't suppose Cadell would let me."

"No."

Duncan smiled. "Just watch me." He turned away, and continued in a completely different tone of voice, "Thank you for calling, but don't call again." Suddenly he was on his feet and marching up the stairs. "I'll just escort you off the premises in case you get lost."

After a second, Byrne followed, walking up the stairs, past where Duncan held the door open with a hand that held the wood so tight its skin was bone-white. Stepping past he blinked in the daylight and turned back, standing so close to Duncan that they almost touched.

"I would never have thought you a coward, Peter. But burying yourself out here comes pretty close. You can't hide for ever."

"I'm not hiding, I'm getting on with my life, thank you very much."

"But - "

"What? Oh, I see, this is about you. Well, Byrne, tell me this. If you knew about me, and about what Paget wanted, what stopped you mentioning it? Or perhaps even letting me know who you were, or that you knew who I really was? What about that? It couldn't possibly have been cowardice, could it?"

Byrne shrugged. "It was orders."

"Great excuse!"

"Look, come back to London. You'll be better off with me."

"Better off?" Duncan was incredulous. "Why? In what way? Because you'll be able to fuck me twice nightly? Oh, great, thanks for the thought, I really appreciate it."

"That's not what I meant." Byrne only just managed to stop himself from taking hold of Duncan and shaking sense into him. He spoke, keeping his voice low and reasonable. "I want to take care of you."

"Take care ..." The white line around Duncan's lips deepened. "Get off this boat, now. Before I throw you off!"

Despite himself, Byrne couldn't hide the condescending glimmer of disbelief and, from the corner of his eye, he just caught the fury that narrowed Duncan's eyes. He moved fast, just saving himself a broken nose, but still ending up unbalanced and sprawled on the deck. After a moment he dabbed at his mouth with careful fingers.

"Fuck off, Byrne. Just leave me alone." He didn't look angry any more, just tired. "Go back to London. I'm fine."

"I only - "

"Don't!" Duncan closed his eyes briefly, then punched the door, the noise setting a group of seagulls flapping into the air. "I don't want any pity. I don't want any help. I am quite all right, thank you." He breathed in deeply and shrugged.

"Duncan ..."

"Sweet heaven! Byrne, get over it!" And with a shiver of some emotion, Duncan stepped back inside and slammed the door home.

Finally getting his feet underneath him, Byrne stood, and leaned back against the door. He glared at the distant hills and wondered if there was any way he could have made a more thorough hash of the entire meeting.

After a moment's consideration, he decided not.

Though Duncan's unreasonableness didn't help. Grumbling under his breath at himself, he wiped his face clean of blood and, braving the walkway, walked back along the pavement to his car.

Turning on the ignition, revving the engine in an effort to encourage the heating, he peered at his face in the rear-view mirror. Despite it feeling four times its normal size, his lip was only slightly swollen; in a day or two it wouldn't even be noticeable. Though it was a good job he'd been moving back at the time.

Peter had been so angry. Perhaps it hadn't been the best idea in the world, calling him a coward, and it wasn't even as if he'd meant it. Byrne sighed, winced, and wryly admitted that it was his own fault. Reaching up he realigned the driver's mirror and sat back, trying to make sense of it all.

Duncan clearly thought that he had been used by Byrne. Understandable as long as he believed that Byrne was still cast as a villain. Yet he'd accepted he wasn't. And there had been no doubt in his face when he looked at the ID card, only resignation. So why?

Putting the car into gear, he headed back to London, the problem diverting his mind sufficiently for him to be blithely unaware of two sets of road-works and a Porsche that cut him up ten miles out of Tunbridge Wells.

What did Duncan believe that could have made him so angry?

Close to the motorway the answer came to him in a light brighter than nuclear fission. How could he have been so blind? So stupid. He berated himself and thumped the steering wheel so hard that it made his hand ache. Calling himself forty kinds of fool, he did an illegal U-turn and headed back, reaching his destination just before dusk.

Breath tight with uncertainty, Byrne walked back across to the scrap-heap of a boat and, without knocking, tried the door; it opened at his touch. Counting under his breath to ten, he stepped inside and, in the shadows, went down the stairs.

Duncan had been asleep. As Byrne reached the bottom of the stairs a light clicked on and, pushing back his bed-covers, Duncan sat up.

"What?"

"Don't say anything, please. I just needed to tell you something."

Stopping where he was, Byrne let the other man get his feet on the floor. He was still fully dressed and Byrne wasn't surprised as the cabin was icy. Captured by a compassion he still never expected to feel, Byrne smiled.

"Well?"

Well, indeed. Disconcerted by Duncan's direct gaze, Byrne straightened his shoulders. And gave his speech. "I don't think we were on the same wave-length earlier. Or I'm just crap at explaining things."

He took a deep breath and, emotion raw in his eyes, gave a small shrug. "I'm an idiot, too. I should have explained more clearly. You see I gave you the wrong idea. When I said I'd known about you since the beginning of the operation, I should have been clear that I meant the drugs bust at the docks, not the beginning of the whole thing." Byrne gestured with his hand, stilling any reply. "From the day that I met you until a few days before that day in Dover, I believed you to be who and what you said you were. The Peter

Duncan I knew was absolutely real to me. So real that I ..." He hesitated, berating his own cowardice. Then with a shrug he gave in, letting the truth spill free. "That I fell in love with you."

Still sitting half-wrapped in the blanket, Duncan didn't seem unduly moved. "Nice of you to let me know."

"I had to tell you. And I didn't want you to think I'd just been using you."

"No?"

"No. I'm not trying to hurt you: not any more than I already have."

Duncan lowered his head, staring at his fingers where they picked at the rough-edged blanket. "Thank you."

Sarcasm? Byrne ignored it, whatever it was. "Think about it, please. I had to come back."

Glancing up, Duncan somehow flinched. He spoke quietly, his voice roughened. "Thank you. Really."

No sarcasm. Nothing much of anything really.

"It's the truth, you can ask Cadell if you want." Byrne had a foot on the stairs. "I'll be back the day after tomorrow. If you want, you can come with me then. I won't try and force you; as if I could."

"I'll think about it."

"About everything?" Byrne gave an empty gesture with his hands, and turned back. "I meant what I said. I love you."

Before he could regret the impulse he was crouched at Duncan's feet. He took a thin hand in his own and turning it over, kissed its palm. Awkward, he swallowed and spoke to the floor. "Believe me. And please don't disappear again." With a squeeze, he released the unresisting fingers, and stood up. "I don't honestly know if I could cope." A half-smile and he turned to leave.

Halfway up the stairs he paused, peering under the lintel to where Duncan sat in bemused silence. "By the way, there's something for you up on the deck. Don't throw it overboard; the fish won't appreciate it."

A slightly manic grin and he was gone, the thud of the closing door quite final.

9

Duncan blinked and stood up, quite beyond coherent thought. Flinching at the betraying surge of hope that swamped him, he slowly made his way up the stairs and opened the door. It was dark, the boat lit by street-lights. At the right of the door stood a large box with 'P. Duncan' written in marker pen across the top. Wary but curious, he hefted the package down the stairs.

He clicked an overhead light on and, putting the box on a table, ripped off about ten yards of packing tape, opening the flaps with a fair amount of caution.

And blinked hard. The box contained tins of soup, bread, cheese, cereal, milk, and two four-packs of beer. At the bottom was an envelope. In brisk, clear handwriting was a short letter curled around a twenty pound note. The message read:

> *Peter,*
> *Pay me back when you can. I hope the food is OK,*
> *I didn't get anything too fancy, just in case. Take*
> *up eating again, it's a hobby to be proud of. The pale*
> *and interesting look can only be taken so far.*
> *See you on Thursday.*
> > *And I do love you.*
> > *Remember that.*
> > > *Byrne.*

It was signed with a flourish.

In spite of himself Duncan folded the paper and tucked it safely into one of his notebooks. The cash he held between the finger and thumb of both hands, glowering at the Queen's placid face.

Byrne was such a prick.

He wanted to rant and rave and hold his disbelief like a shield but there was such abject honesty in Byrne's words that Duncan knew that this was indeed the truth. Even if it was the truth on Byrne's terms.

Tucking the cash into his jeans, he crawled back under the blanket. At least with the money he'd be able to buy another gas cylinder and stop freezing to death. For a second he contemplated the food, but his stomach lurched and that was that. Scrambling clumsily as far as the kitchen, he made it to the sink in time to retch, though having put nothing in his stomach except for water, nothing but water returned.

Weary, cold, and faintly shivering he leant his forehead against the cupboard above the sink and despised his body's weakness. He was going to have to get over this soon. Eating was an essential, after all. Byrne always thought he was right, shame that on this occasion he actually was.

Byrne.

The name flickered in his mind. Irritation and caution warred with hope. How could the prat think he had some right to control Duncan's life? Because he didn't. But it did show he cared. Didn't it?

Yet, if he cared, really cared and not just because Duncan was useful for his work and maybe getting up another notch of the career ladder, how long would it be for? Was Byrne the type to remain interested in anyone for very long? Not a woman and certainly not a man.

It wasn't as if he was really gay.

Was he?

Duncan rubbed at his cheek and wondered. Just because Byrne enjoyed sex with another man, was that enough to make him queer, or did he just bow both ways as the fancy took him? There was little doubt that Byrne saw himself as straight - well he certainly wasn't out there campaigning for Gay Rights. In fact he probably wanted kids, a mortgage and a semi in Barnes.

Though what Byrne thought, what he wanted, all of it was a mystery. If only they had ever done anything other than have sex. Like talk.

But the answers might have been the wrong ones, and Duncan was suddenly sure he preferred the hope he had now to the certainty of Byrne's answers. Love? Never heard of the word, guv. Despite what he said.

Rubbing at his aching belly and wondering why being sick should give you a sore throat, he went back to the cramped living area, turned the light out and, lying down, tried to mummify himself against the cold.

Sleep was a singularly depressing prospect and instead, tucking his nose under the itchy wool, he lay quite still, watching the shadows made by passing car head-lights and tried to make sense of it all.

God, to try and make sense of Byrne, what a prospect! Though he had to admit Byrne's good intentions, Duncan couldn't evade the nasty thought that whispered about ulterior motives. Byrne had countered every charge that Duncan had laid at his door; he wasn't a crook, and he hadn't known about Duncan's connection with Paget. All that was gilt-edged, but what about Byrne himself?

With him, was it possible to be certain of anything at all?

If only love hadn't come into it. If only he hadn't been so stupid. The fantasies he had woven as his own version of the future had been of equality, of sharing. Byrne didn't seem to want to share anything but Duncan's bed. If that was love, well ... Duncan ground his teeth in aggravation. As far as he was concerned, Byrne wouldn't recognise the emotion if he tripped over it. Oh, he could say the words, but anything else?

Give us a break.

He was probably so used to telling girls he loved them that it was a habit. Even if it had all felt so wonderfully real.

Then the bleak thought hit him: what if that was Byrne's version of love, and self-obsession all he was capable of? Turning toward the wall Duncan tried to dismiss the thought, to keep the anger he felt from being smothered by self-pity. Damn it all.

Sleep? It lived a million miles away on a far off planet. Maybe one that he and Byrne lived on together as Mr and Mr Happy-Ever-After.

That thought at least made him smile. Uncurling, he stood up and wandered into the kitchen, running water into a glass and drinking thirstily. With deliberate concentration he wiped his mouth dry using the tips of his fingers and refused to let his mind pivot on the thought of Thursday.

For all that, he would go back to London. What Paget had done, or more accurately what he and Kerrigan had done, was the icing on a cake of corruption. Duncan was certain he would happily have cheered as Paget was hung, drawn and quartered. Though settling for seeing him and Kerrigan in prison for the rest of their naturals would probably have to be enough. It would happen too, the information he had gathered along with everything else would see to that. As long as the legal system had any justice left.

Unsure how much Cadell had found out, Duncan knew that he would have to go and present his own evidence. It was needed. Though the idea of getting up in court and telling what they had done to him -

Maybe he could keep it impersonal. Just tell the parts that didn't involve himself. Maybe. Though if that meant the bastards got off more lightly than they should have, how would he live with himself then?

Paget and a suspended sentence. He shivered; hard enough to make all his bruises ache. Well, there was no way he was going to let that happen. He'd testify in court about everything. However miserable the thought made him; the reality couldn't be that bad. Humiliating maybe, but for Christ's sake, he'd been humiliated before and survived.

He'd survived Kent.

The thought made him smile, his teeth a glint of white in the shadows.

His brain numb, exhaustion making him dizzy, he wrapped himself back into the nest of blankets and tried to hold his spinning thoughts together. Though spin how they would, Byrne was always at the centre.

When the bastard came back, he was going to be torn apart. Peter grinned suddenly into the darkness. Yeah, ripped apart and then eaten up.

Not quite arousing, it was a warming thought, and without him really being aware of it he was soothed, comforted. He sighed, closing his eyes. After a little while, he slept.

Returning from a five mile walk that left him with irritatingly shaky legs, Duncan scanned the roads as he went, not that he was really looking for Byrne's car of course; more checking, just in case.

Thursday. Even though it was only lunch-time, he felt that it was getting a bit late in the day for Byrne's promise to be true. After the easy rest of Tuesday night, Wednesday had produced nothing but a fierce insomnia broken by patches of sleep shredded by nightmare. All resolutions forgotten, he'd even abandoned his attempt at eating normally.

Walking wearily across his own private drawbridge, Duncan completely failed to notice the dark red Jaguar that was parked along the main road.

Settling down in front of the typewriter, Duncan looked at the pile of typescript, then at the other pile of notes and was lost for a point to begin. He sighed deeply, and rested his beard-shadowed chin on a propped hand, while his eyes stared into space.

His absence was so complete that it was five minutes before the banging noise coalesced in his brain into the reality of someone knocking on the door. Ruthlessly suppressing a wild surge of hope, he went to answer it.

Stomping up the stairs, convinced it was going to be Byrne, Duncan pulled the door open.

"Good morning, Mr Duncan. My name is Graham Cadell, may I come in?"

Duncan stared at him, then in silent acknowledgement held the door back.

"Thank you." Cadell nodded and slowly walked down the sharply inclined steps that led into the boat. In the middle of cramped living quarters he turned, waiting until Duncan joined him. "I - "

"I know who you are," Duncan interrupted. "And I think I know what you want. Though I thought you'd have sent your errand boy, rather than come yourself."

Cadell smiled. "Byrne doesn't usually see himself as anyone's errand boy. I assume you did mean Byrne?"

"As he's the only one of your mob I've actually met, yes."

"He was detained. And as I had to be out of London this morning anyway, well it wasn't much of a detour to come here myself."

"How was he detained?" Duncan ignored the rest of Cadell's sentence, concentrating on what he felt was the pertinent part. Then he realised that they were both standing. "Look, have a seat. I'll clear those papers."

He moved some stuff, and awkwardly gestured for the other man to sit. He sat opposite, dumping the sheaf of papers onto the floor by his feet and leaning back.

"I'm afraid that was my fault. He wasn't very happy about it, but it was fairly important." Cadell settled in the lumpy chair, looking around as if he were mentally cataloguing every feature of the old boat and its occupant.

Duncan shifted uneasily, suddenly aware that he was too thin, too ill, and remarkably uncomfortable with this man. He caught Cadell's eyes staring down, and following their line saw his cuffs had ridden up. Casually he pulled them back down, covering the red, raw marks that still circled his wrists.

Cadell leaned forward. "How are you?"

"Oh, just hunky-dory." Duncan crossed his arms. "Look, skip the small talk and get on with it. What exactly do you want?"

Cadell nodded as if in agreement. "You're very direct. Well, without preamble, I want what you know about Paget. Everything. Every last piece of information so we can put him in gaol for so long he'll never see the outside world again."

The sudden intensity in the older man's voice found an answering chord in Duncan. For the first time they looked each other in the eye, faded blue meeting wary hazel, assessing and somehow, after a moment, reassuring.

"I won't beat around the bush. We know a fair amount about Paget, but I think you know more." Cadell pointed to the heaped notebooks. "Is it all in there?"

"Some of it." Duncan grimaced and dragged his fingers through his hair. "There's more in my head." He sighed. "I'm working on getting it all on paper, everything from how they worked the more basic scams to who they beat up because they were the wrong colour or had the wrong accents. I've noted forced confessions, harassment, the protection they offered in exchange for money, blackmail, drugs, lies." Feeling the pressure of it all swamping him anew he tailed off, taking a shaky breath.

"Aye, all of that, and more. You personally have just cause to hate them."

"Yes." Duncan nodded, blinking slightly.

"If it hadn't been for what happened, you would have made a good policeman. You could still."

"Not in their force."

"No, in the police as it should be. Will be. Whatever you saw when you were in uniform, whatever they did to you afterwards, they'll pay. I promise. We're concentrating on Paget and Kerrigan first. Cleaning up the rest will take quite a while longer." His disgust was palpable. "Paget's fall, though, will be an object lesson for all the others. You could go back then."

"No."

"You sound very certain."

"I am."

"But you're willing to help anyway?"

"Of course. I've got stories about him that would make your hair curl. But I should warn you, you'll only get them corroborated if he's going away for ever. Paget's a vicious bastard and everyone knows it. No one's going to risk their families or themselves to get him a two-year suspended sentence."

"If that was all we could get I'd pull the trigger myself. I despise him and what his like have done!" He eased off. "I apologise. I'm up on one of my soapboxes."

Duncan smiled, genuinely appreciating Cadell's passion. "Rant away, I'm up there with you. Are you sure you're not a figment of my imagination?"

"I should hope not," Cadell laughed, "or you'll have a strange journey in my car."

He was suddenly quite serious. "I'm parked at the end of the road. Come back with me so that I can debrief you properly. Apart from anything else, we still only have Paget and Kerrigan's version of what happened in that house in Kent. A few days, then you can come back to your hideout."

Suddenly the boat was just that, somewhere to hide from the world and equally suddenly, Duncan hated it.

Yet, as always, there was the matter of money.

"We have a safe house ready, if you'd like it, unless you'd rather stay with Byrne?"

"Jesus, are you pimping for him too?"

Cadell was absolutely unmoved by the vehemence of Duncan's words. "I don't think Byrne needs me for that, do you?"

"No." Duncan took a breath then shrugged, almost apologetically.

"Well, would you like to stay with him?"

"Has he been asked if that's okay?"

"I doubt it."

"Perhaps it would have been polite."

Cadell smiled and admitted a truth. "Maybe I'm out of the habit of asking."

"Ah. Then don't bother."

Cadell nodded. "A safe house it is then. If you want, I can wait in the car for you?"

"Won't take five minutes, if it really is only for a few days?" His slight enquiry was greeted by an absent nod.

Packing took four minutes exactly. A soft nylon bag still containing clothes was emptied and refilled with notebooks, a spare pair of jeans, two T-shirts, underwear, spare jumper and a hastily filled wash-bag. Changing into his boots, Duncan was ready as he pushed his trainers into the bag and zipped it shut.

All done, he ushered Cadell off the boat, locked it up, tucking the keys into one of the pockets of his thin leather jacket.

Back across the walkway and onto the pavement, the noise of seagulls loud enough to rival the traffic, Cadell led off to the right, Duncan at his side. They walked up the hill, and found the Jaguar parked on double-yellow lines, a chauffeur patiently behind the wheel.

"Sir."

The figure got out as they approached. It was a woman, which Duncan found mildly surprising. Was it a sign of prejudice, or lack of it, that Cadell's driver was female? Did it matter, anyway? He nodded at her greeting, and opened the rear car door nearest to him as Cadell settled in the back behind the driver's seat.

"Any trouble, Anne?"

"No, sir. I've been reading." She waved the latest Dick Francis at him. "Didn't have to move once. Back to London then?"

"Yes."

Cadell settled himself, staring out of the window as they slid into the traffic. Duncan's attitude was interesting, there was a certain forced quality to him, as if he were uncertain, unsure, maybe acting the way he thought the world wanted him to act. Was that it? Cadell frowned, then tutted to himself. There were better uses of his time than out and out conjecture. He reached for his briefcase and pulled out a handful of reports.

The car was warm, quiet, and driven by a skilled person at the wheel. The two men sharing the back seat settled into a sort of silent companionship. Engrossed in his paperwork, Cadell was unaware at which point on their journey Duncan fell asleep. He was, however, completely enlightened when the dream began.

Cadell rarely shared a bed, or any other sleeping arrangements, with anyone. Of those he had had to share with, most had been restrained enough to keep their dreams to themselves.

Duncan had no such compunctions.

A flailing arm caught his papers and sent them scattering to the floor. It took a second for Cadell to realise what was happening, and that under his rapid breaths Duncan was talking in his sleep. Moving too, his body racked by shudders that ran from head to toe. Alarmed, Cadell turned, reaching out, frowning at such utter vulnerability. He touched a bony shoulder, his expression softening as he tried gently to wake the dreamer.

But somehow the touch must have translated itself into part of the nightmare. Grunting as a fist caught his arm Cadell was suddenly tangled in fighting limbs as Duncan, his hands on this occasion free, attacked.

"Wake up, Duncan, wake up!"

A life of issuing orders made the command imperative. He caught the flailing limbs and trapped them with little effort. "Anne, don't pull over, it'll be all right."

He caught her eyes through the mirror and she nodded, easing the car back into the fast lane. As far as she was concerned, if he wanted to drive along a public road snug in the embrace of a young man, that was entirely up to him. She did, however, keep her amusement carefully to herself.

Cadell spoke again. "Wake up." His voice was low and coaxing. "Duncan, come on, wake up."

Duncan was sweating, his face twisted into a mask of distress. But slowly, as if Cadell's voice permeated through the layers of dream and memory, he quieted, and his eyes flickered open to meet Cadell's assessing blue gaze

"Oh, God." Duncan flushed crimson and pulled back.

With absolute calm, Cadell disentangled himself and straightened his tie. Choosing to ignore the burning humiliation clear on

Duncan's face, he picked up his scattered papers, though he made no effort to read them, merely straightening them as he settled back into his own corner.

He spoke conversationally. "Do they happen often?"

"What?"

"The nightmares."

Duncan nodded, then switched his gaze so that he looked out at the blurring scenery. His whole body was tense with embarrassment, his fingers picking at the cotton of his jeans.

After a moment he cleared his throat. "Yeah, on and off for years. More since ... since what happened in Kent, I suppose."

"I believe that's to be expected. If you'd stayed in hospital they would have offered you help."

"Oh yeah, I'm sure. Look, I'm sorry." Duncan's colour was back to his normal pallor. "I didn't mean to crawl all over you, but there's no point telling me off as if I'm a child - or one of your bunch of merry men. I'm not. And as far as I see, hospitals know sod all."

"Why?"

"Because they wanted me to see a shrink. Bloody stupid idea. Oh, and they wanted me to take methadone to get me off the smack! No idea at all." He crossed his arms and glowered at the leather seat-back.

"They said it would take longer, but they also seemed to believe you would be less unwell." Cadell was genuinely curious. "And why no psychiatrist?"

"I wasn't raped." He glared sideways at Cadell, challenging him to argue with the bald statement.

"I know, but you were treated badly. Probably in more ways than the marks on your body could tell them. It can help to talk."

Duncan seemed to shrink back into the seat. "I know. But not to them."

"Then who?"

A series of stark emotions fleetingly touched Duncan's eyes. Then he sat quite still, looking utterly worn. "I don't know."

Cadell nodded, as if that were in itself an answer. "Tell me about the heroin anyway. Why didn't you need the hospital's treatment?"

Sighing, Duncan tried to explain. "Paget and Kerrigan had me for about ten days, yes?" Cadell nodded. "I thought so, but I wasn't sure; they kept me pretty much out of it." He shrugged. "You see, I didn't want it. Even when my body said 'yes', my mind was there screaming 'no'. At least, I hoped it was."

He closed his eyes, and Cadell wondered what memory precisely made him look so grim. "When I woke up in hospital, I knew where I was, in my body I mean. I'd been there before, years ago. That idiot of a doctor, he knew nothing at all, treating me like a fool."

"I'm sure he didn't intend to."

A sharp glance dismissed that idea. "No? Well, I told him that I knew what was happening and he still insisted on giving me a shot. God, talk about the rights of the individual." His fingers clutched at his upper arms, digging hard into the leather-covered flesh. "Anyway, that's why I walked out. If you ignore it and don't pander to it, coming off smack's horrible and uncomfortable and messy, but it doesn't kill you."

"I see." Cadell thought he did, though he still frowned slightly.

"Do you?" Duncan bit his lip, then asked, "Do you really?"

"You needed to be in control; you had been tortured."

Duncan made a revolted noise.

"That's what it was. Abused, if you prefer."

"No!"

"Well then. It isn't shameful, you didn't ask to be there."

"No." Duncan closed his eyes, then opened them, rubbing his hand over his face. "But I was stupid enough to get myself there. And nearly fuck up everything in the process."

"It worked out, in the end."

"Don't tell me you didn't curse me." He smiled suddenly. "I certainly cursed myself. After I'd done with Byrne, of course."

Cadell's mouth twitched upwards. "Maybe I had a few choice words for both of you."

"I bet."

"Tell me, do you think you're up to these debriefings?"

"Well, we'll soon know if I'm not, won't we." Duncan shrugged, apparently resigned.

"Just let me know if it's all going too fast."

"Sure."

In fragile silence they finished the journey to London, Cadell trying without success to complete his paperwork while Duncan considered the problem of Byrne; neither man benefited from either exercise.

Staring blank-eyed at the depressed and depressing vistas of south London as the car slowly navigated them, Duncan finally decided with calm resignation that he was being ridiculous. In fact, the mountain he was making out of this particular molehill could have rivalled Everest for altitude.

So Byrne might think himself in love. Fine.

When the idiot calmed down it would all be back to normal. It was sex and pity, nothing else. Duncan tutted softly, and knew he couldn't let himself clutch at straws. Whatever he might want. There was no excuse, and the reality of Byrne, at some point in the future, either throwing him out or inadvertently reaching for his wallet was too much.

Clients did not marry their whores.

They didn't even take them to live with them.

Especially when they were both men.

Duncan glowered blindly at the shoppers, then shook himself. It was all too stupid, and he was being a fool. It was quite clear there was no hope for the relationship. Guilt was the only emotion making Byrne do odd things. Not love.

Love was too improbable. Too breathtakingly impossible.

When the guilt and the pity faded he'd take a huge breath and thank the heavens he was still free. Duncan nodded to himself, and knew he was right.

Besides, whatever he felt for Byrne - and it might be love and fifty other needs combined - he'd survive.

Him and Gloria Gaynor.

He sighed softly, and wondered absently if Byrne could dance.

Without warning the Jaguar slowed and braked. Refocusing on the world Duncan realised that they were in a car park outside a huge red-bricked building.

"Our offices." Cadell spoke in explanation, already reaching for the door handle.

"Yeah."

It was where Byrne worked.

For God's sake!

Irritated beyond belief by the direction his mind had taken, Duncan stepped out of the car, slamming the door too hard, which elicited a tut from Cadell and a pointed comment about the precision of British craftsmanship.

They entered the barren corridors with Duncan dragging in Cadell's wake, absorbing the utilitarian bleakness of the building. Typical government interior: cream paint that was fading nicely to nicotine yellow, bare wood floors and not enough radiators. It reminded him of nearly every police station he'd ever been in. It was also bloody cold, though luckily Cadell had made sure that his own office was adequately heated.

"Please, sit down, Mr Duncan." Cadell gestured to a leather-padded chair. "I'll just get my secretary to rustle us up some tea, and then we'll get started." He reached to flick a switch on his desk panel, then hesitated. "Unless you'd like some lunch first?"

Politely, Duncan refrained from shuddering. "No, tea'll be fine."

The order given, Cadell sat back and over steepled fingers observed his guest. Unaware that they were doing anything more complicated than waiting for the tea, Duncan said nothing, making his own inspection of the utilitarian office.

After a while, Cadell nodded as if in answer to some unspoken question. Then, reaching into one of his desk drawers he placed two sets of keys on his blotter.

Duncan raised a brow in enquiry.

"I'm not sure how long this will all take, so for now this," he prodded the larger bunch, "is the set of keys to a flat in Chalcott Street and this," he indicated the single key, "is for a car. You'll need to be mobile, I can't rely on public transport to get you here efficiently."

Duncan stared at the keys. Then up at Cadell. He sat in silence for a long while, wondering about the man in front of him, and if he was a mind-reader. What to say? How to thank someone who waved a magic wand and made life as simple as it was likely to get?

In the end he settled for one quiet admission. "Thank you. It will make life much easier."

He would have asked. Would have had to. Being offered though, it made it all so much better. Duncan smiled, and met an answering amusement in Cadell.

Boundaries posted and seen to be observed, they settled down to four hours of taped interview. Rummaging in his bag Duncan occasionally consulted one of his notebooks, but most of the information was as accurately recorded in his head as on paper. There were also names, dates and a list of witnesses.

Cadell more or less just let Duncan talk, only guiding his revelations occasionally down particular avenues. Duncan tried for a straight accounting, wanting to be cool and unemotional. It seemed to work. Cadell nodded here and there, and occasionally commented. Everything seemed to be of use.

Towards the end of the session, despite being lubricated by water, having refused the whisky that sat so comfortably at Cadell's elbow, Duncan's voice was gravelly and the grasp he held on the room's horizontal axis was beginning to waver.

In the end, he just ground to a halt.

Cadell looked up, startled. "I'm sorry, Mr Duncan. You're tired. That's enough for one day, you should get some sleep." He switched off the recorder and sat back, satisfaction reflected on his lined face. "I'll take you down to the car pool."

They both stood up and, cursing the dizziness that dogged him, Duncan had to hold on to the wall for a moment. He took a deep breath, waiting for it to pass.

After a moment he straightened. Cadell was standing at his side, assessing but not over-reacting in any way. "Thank you."

"Indeed." Cadell granted Duncan the privacy of not pointing out the obvious and they went out into the corridor.

Forty-eight hours' sleep would just about be fine. Though Duncan wondered if even four was within his ability. Still, just telling someone else his story seemed to have lifted some of the weight off his mind, especially as it was all going to be put to good use. So much for expecting Cadell to pace the interviews though, the man was like a terrier. He glanced across and reconsidered; more like a piranha.

They rounded a corner and came slap up against another group.

And there, as if straight from one of his more lucid nightmares, was Paget. He was grinning.

"Hello! Well, if it isn't Peter Duncan. How's the smack habit, you cunt?"

The words were a goad. Possessed by fury, Duncan didn't think, he just lashed out, the sound of fist hitting flesh utterly satisfying.

Dimly aware of Cadell's voice shouting orders, Duncan wildly followed up the assault, stopping only when determined hands gripped him and pulled him off. Breathing hard he watched solemnly as Paget staggered, blood on his face dripping onto his shirt, upright only because he was handcuffed by both wrists to Cadell's men.

Breathing hard, the berserk fury passing as fast as it had come, Duncan took a deep breath. Carefully he relaxed, letting the men who held him know that it was okay and he wasn't going to kill anyone: whatever it might have looked like.

"I'm okay." He held a hand up, felt their hands release him.

"Bastard, I'll do you for assault!"

"Just try." Duncan was laughing, though there really wasn't anything funny. A hand touched his arm, and blinking, he looked around and saw Cadell. "You could have told me he was here."

Cadell nodded. "Get Paget out of here. He's had an accident it seems, get him cleaned up."

Finally released, Duncan watched as Paget was led away. He leant back against the wall, suddenly needing its impersonal support as he shakily wiped the sweat from his upper lip.

Frowning, he looked across and saw Cadell glare at him, knew he was saying something, but couldn't quite hear it. The world was rushing around him, and though he shrugged in rueful apology, he didn't mean it; the feeling of fist hitting flesh had been too good, like oil poured on an open wound.

Wiping his sleeve across his face Duncan tried hard to concentrate. From somewhere in the echoing corridor he could hear his name. But nothing made any sense, and never having fainted before he was totally confused as the world turned to flashing yellow and black, and he collapsed into an unconscious heap on the floor.

At the moment Duncan hit the floor, Byrne turned into the corridor.

The whole day had been a waste of time. Bloody Cadell. All he wanted was to be away and on the road to Newhaven. And as for the stupid piddling little job he'd been kept here to do -

He was grumbling to himself as he rounded a corner and ran into a crowd. He stopped, and watched as a slightly worse-for-wear Paget was escorted away by two of Cadell's men.

He swallowed the feeling of foreboding, and pushed through the group all standing looking down at ...

"Peter!"

Shouldering past people he didn't even know were there, blood draining from his face, Byrne knelt and touched the pulse point on Duncan's exposed neck. Reassured, he took a deep breath and looked up at Cadell for an explanation. "What happened?"

"Duncan attacked Paget."

"Good. Why is he unconscious?"

Cadell continued as if the interruption hadn't happened. "When he was pulled off he just collapsed."

"Peter." Byrne gently brushed the lank red hair from Duncan's eyes. Directing his glare at Cadell, he asked, "Where's Doctor Anderson?"

"On his way. Luckily he was in the building."

"And why is Duncan here at all? I thought I was going down to pick him up later."

"I went instead. Ah, Anderson." Cadell explained no further, as the medic arrived and brushed them all out of the way.

A quick check and the doctor nodded. "He's fine, but can we get him off the floor?"

"My office has a couch."

"Thank you, Graham. There's a stretcher on the way."

Byrne didn't wait, he simply crouched down and eased Duncan into his arms. Standing carefully he nodded at the doctor and walked towards Cadell's office. Alice was there, holding the door, fussing as he placed Duncan on the old leather sofa, though she was shooed away with the others.

The examination didn't take long and Byrne watched with ill-concealed worry as the doctor stood up. "He'll be fine. The closest diagnosis I can give you is that he's simply exhausted."

Two voices spoke in unison. "What?"

The doctor raised an eyebrow. "His system has just shut down. He's malnourished, exhausted and still suffering from the effects of extreme trauma." Snapping shut his bag, he frowned at Cadell. "I thought that you were going to bring him for a check-up before you started the debriefing."

Looking almost shamefaced, Cadell admitted, "You're right. I should have remembered."

"You mean you've been interrogating him?" Byrne glowered at Cadell and was about to unburden some of his anger when the doctor hurriedly continued.

"Still, there's no real harm done. A week in bed should set him back to normal. I should think that he'll be out for at least twelve hours, maybe longer." For some reason he spoke directly to Byrne. "When he wakes up make sure he has plenty to drink and actually eats something; there's no need to hospitalise him unless he deteriorates further."

"Are you sure?"

"Yes. Just keep an eye on him."

"But - "

"Byrne!"

"It's all right, Graham. Byrne, I have all his files, and I examined him the last time he was in hospital. The last thing he needs is more time in any sort of an institution." He smiled suddenly and patted Byrne on the arm. "Just look after him, he'll be fine. Well, if that's all the drama, I'm off. Graham, Byrne." He nodded at each of them, gathered his things and was gone.

Cadell glanced at the doctor's departing back and then turned to Byrne. "Take him to safe house four. The keys are in his pocket. Stay with him until he comes around." He paused. "Well, why are you looking so doubtful?"

"Unless you arranged otherwise, there won't be any heating on and there won't be any food apart from tinned stuff in the cupboards. I think he'd be better off at my place. And I'll be able to look after him."

The message in Byrne's eye challenged Cadell to try and deny him the right. Even under the pale, direct scrutiny he didn't back down.

Cadell hesitated. Then he nodded. "Very well." He walked around his desk and hit a switch on the intercom. "Alice, get Aidan Murphy in here, would you?"

"Sir."

Byrne was at Duncan's side, just looking, as if trying to absorb everything about the limp sprawl. He was quite oblivious to everything else, including Cadell's intense scrutiny.

A knock at the door startled them both.

"Sir, you wanted me?"

"Aidan. Help Byrne get Duncan home, would you? Byrne, you'd better take the rest of the day off."

"Of course." Curiosity glinting in his eyes, Murphy came into the room and went over to Byrne, touching him on the shoulder. "He okay?"

"Apparently he's just tired."

"Understatement, from the look of him."

"Mm."

"Well, when you're both ready."

"Sir." There was a slight echo as both men answered at once.

"Go on, I was wanted in a meeting ten minutes ago." And with that he was off, issuing orders to Alice as he went.

Byrne let out a long breath and stood up. "Right then."

Murphy was shaking his head in astonishment. "And how on earth did you manage that?" Cadell was hardly renowned for his philanthropic tendencies.

"Christ knows." He pantomimed wiping sweat from his brow. "But I'm not going to ask any questions. Come on." He bent down and with a little effort picked Duncan up again. "You can drive."

"Sure." Murphy held the door open. "Want a hand?"

"No."

They left the office, Byrne carrying his unusual burden. In the car park they settled Duncan into the back seat, his head on Byrne's lap. It was all uncomfortably reminiscent.

Leaning in from the side, Murphy looked ruefully at Byrne. "At least he looks better than the last time we did this."

"That's for certain." Byrne smiled suddenly. "Thanks, Aidan."

"Don't be an idiot." Murphy settled into the driver's seat. "Right, where to?"

"My flat."

There was only a breath of hesitation. "Sure."

Twenty minutes later they'd parked outside Byrne's block, extricated the still sleeping Duncan and got him up to Byrne's flat. Murphy watched as the limp body was laid carefully on the bed, meeting Byrne's eyes as he straightened. "Good job he's light."

A small smile. "Wait till he's started eating again."

"Home-made soup?"

"Sainsbury's best at the very least."

Murphy grinned. "Right, I'll leave the rest up to you. I'd better get back to Cadell before he starts yelling." He slapped Byrne on the shoulder. "Best of luck." And the next thing to be heard was the front door closing.

The room was remarkably silent. From where he stood Byrne looked down at where Duncan lay in a loose sprawl on the brocade cover.

The images that the sight conjured were all too pervasive and Byrne tried to shutter them away.

The man was ill. There was nothing erotic about insensibility.

Nothing.

But the memories were so strong, and the reality of having him back, alive, was so incredible.

Byrne shivered, and wondered if he was some sort of pervert. Yet for all his self-castigation, when it came to undressing the still body, when it came to touching … He flinched as a sweater-disentangled arm trailed across his groin and cursed softly, muttering under his breath, half-amused, half-frustrated. However, it all faded as he slowly stripped clothing away. Naked, there was nothing erotic about Duncan's body at all.

With his fingertips Byrne touched the sharp definition of a hip-bone, then ribs, skimming across skin that was deeply bruised, shoulders that were dotted with the dark scars of cigarette burns, wrists which were scarred from how tightly they had been bound. The bruises were a richly mottled expanse that stretched the length of the long, pale body, clustered at belly and thigh, along both sides. He had to have been kicked whilst he was on the floor. Over and over again.

Byrne swallowed faint nausea.

I'm sorry. He apologised mutely, unsure exactly what for but needing to say the words; if only to himself.

Shaken, Byrne stood up, and rummaging in the depths of a drawer found a couple of pairs of Christmas pyjamas, pulling out ones that were pale blue with white piping. He couldn't remember which aunt had thought they'd suit him, which aunt thought he was Christopher Robin. Well, they were perfect now. He went back to the bed and carefully eased them onto Duncan's laxly resistant body, dressing him with gentle, clumsy care.

The doctor had been right about one thing, Duncan was certainly out of it. He didn't stir at all, his face relaxed, breath even. Byrne tucked him under the covers and stood back, wiping sweat off his forehead.

There, done. He stood quite still, just looking, then turned away. There was so much to do. A check that the heating was on maximum and then, propping the door open with a book so that he'd hear if Duncan called out, he went to make an inventory of his store cupboards.

Five minutes later he realised that the sort of food that was perfect for eating in snatches between shifts was not really ideal for an invalid. Mentally weighing the chances of Duncan waking up in the next half an hour, Byrne went back to the bedroom. He touched a warm hand, brushing his fingers against it. Nothing. Was it worth the risk? He chewed his lip for a moment then decided it was.

Almost running to the corner shop and then back, Byrne returned armed with two bags containing everything he could think of that would tempt a fussy eater. And went straight back to the bedroom.

Duncan was still asleep, though he had turned slightly onto his side.

Letting out a breath he had forgotten he was holding, Byrne stripped off his jacket and went to unpack. Humming softly, he sorted bread, tinned soup, tinned meat. Fruit he put in a bowl, vegetables in the rack. Milk and butter, cheese and a pound of mince went into an almost empty fridge, packets of cereal he just left on the side. Enough food to feed an army.

Satisfied, he made himself a sandwich and settled down with a beer, all the while listening for any noise that would show the sleeper was awake.

He made himself eat slowly. Hardly daring to think, to plan. He had no idea what would happen when Duncan did wake up, but at least he was here. And hopefully would remain so.

For better, for worse, wasn't that the wording?

It would work. He would make it work.

Carefully shying away from picking at the future, he read the paper, filling in the crossword as he finished his beer. After a while he realised it was almost dark. Scraping his chair back he went to the door and switched on the light, blinking in the brightness.

Duncan was alive and asleep in bed. Delight shivered through him, and he was smiling as he washed up his dishes. Still happy when he checked on the sleeper.

That night he found something new about himself; he could be patient. For this, at least.

Settling in the living room, another beer in hand, he watched TV. *Minder,* the news, and a late movie which he could never later recall a single thing about.

At ten to eleven he switched off the box and, turning off the lights, went to sit by Duncan's bedside. Just for a moment. A few minutes here then he'd make up the spare bed. But comfort was very beguiling, and he stayed still, sprawled in the wide arm-chair, watching nothing, just being. It started to rain, drops spattering heavily against the window panes. And he was very warm. Drowsy. After a little while he simply fell asleep.

10

The feeling of well-being that permeated Duncan's awakening was marred only by definite hunger pangs; something so unusual he'd almost not known what the sensation was. Eyes closed, he luxuriated in the cocoon of warmth that surrounded him, in the feeling of relaxed well-being, happily amazed that his body was contemplating food all on its own.

Bread and soup. Yeah, that would do nicely. Maybe one of the tins that Byrne had left: celery, or farmhouse vegetable. His stomach gurgled in response. For a moment he just lay limply, content to anticipate the chilly moment of getting out from under the blanketing warmth.

The blanket was different; the cover was definitely not the scratchy wool that he had gone to sleep under. Puzzled, but not really worried, he opened his eyes and then sat bolt upright.

Remembering.

Some of it. Though none of the things he could recall explained why he was tucked neatly into Byrne's bed, dressed in what he assumed were Byrne's pyjamas, or why the supposed perpetrator of all this was fast asleep in a chair by his side.

Byrne's room.

He took a long steadying breath, letting it out slowly. God, everything was so familiar, the pale cream walls glowing in bright daylight, the dark carpet, fitted wardrobe with its long mirrored doors. A big room, simply decorated, carefully luxurious. Like the king-size bed, the abstract prints that hung on the walls.

He rubbed a hand over his face, feeling the beginnings of a beard. And he needed to use the loo.

Carefully climbing out of bed, he made a slow path to the bathroom, taking his time, washing his face afterwards, getting the gum of too much sleep from his eyes. He didn't shave, but he used Byrne's toothbrush.

The bed was a haven, and he fell back into it, sitting back against the headboard frowning, breathing unsteadily as the world righted itself. Someone had taken all his clothes off and dressed him in what looked like old men's pyjamas, which were about two sizes too big. Someone. As if there were any doubt.

He couldn't remember being asked.

Mild irritation being slowly superseded by slightly less mild vexation, Duncan frowned at the other man, and spoke his name softly. "Byrne."

Starting to uncurl slowly, Byrne was suddenly awake. "Peter!"

"Explain things, Byrne." Duncan couldn't help sounding indignant.

Byrne cleared his throat and rubbed his hands over his face, trying not to stare.

"Oh, good start, Byrne. But I'm not fluent in grunts." Impatience did little for Duncan's equilibrium.

"Sorry." Byrne sat forward, holding out a calming hand. "You're here because you needed somewhere to stay."

Duncan frowned, clearly trying to recall events. "I was with your boss." He paused, then paled further. "And Paget was there, in the corridor."

"You gave him a pasting then collapsed. The doctor gave you the once-over and, well, you just needed somewhere to rest. While you were out of it Murphy and I brought you here. You've been sleeping ever since."

"How long?"

Byrne looked at the clock. "Eighteen hours."

"Oh." Duncan looked unsure for a moment, then suspicious. "Why here, why not the flat Cadell gave me the keys to?"

"The heating was off at the safe house and the doctor said that you'd need warmth and food. I've got all that here. At the time it seemed the best thing to do." Byrne was clearly already doubting its wisdom. "I thought you might be better off here, that's all. I didn't think you'd want to be in hospital again. I thought it was sensible."

"Sensible." Duncan spat the word into sibilance. "And I suppose that Mr Cadell went along with this merry scheme? What is he, some sort of procurer for his staff?" Duncan swung the bedclothes back and in a flurry of swift movement went to stand.

Would have stood, but his body had other ideas. He was just about upright, then his knees gave way, and he would have fallen, except Byrne was there, holding him before he hit the floor, arms secure and tight. Warm.

"Peter!"

"I'm fine ..."

Duncan heard Byrne swallow any reply he might have been about to make. Felt the arms lift him back to the bed until he was sitting on its edge.

"Really, I'll be fine." The world was spinning slightly, but it was the truth. He was fine. Would be, anyway. "Thank you."

"Peter, for - "

"Don't. I won't fall to pieces!"

"You might."

And Duncan turned, met a starkly pained expression. He blinked, suddenly unsure. "Why did you bring me here?"

Byrne gave a soft, weary sound, and gave up on lies. "Because I couldn't bear to think of you anywhere else."

Duncan's face twisted, as if bereft. "I could hate you so much."

"I know. But I never lied to you. I promise."

Duncan laughed, the sound callously without humour, until a large hand cupped his face and stilled him, gentled him. Despite its instigator's best intentions, the touch was somewhat less than clinical, rocking them both with a shocking intensity of response.

Byrne tried to speak, choked, then tried again. "I'll get you something to eat."

"Fine." For Duncan food was there in sight in the shape of dilated blue eyes and perfect lips. He could feel himself being sucked towards the lodestone that was Byrne and although his mind screamed out that he was only being used, his body couldn't have given a damn.

"Oh, hell." The whispered word was taken from him as their mouths met and hunger was suddenly too mild a word for what he felt. Subsumed, obliterated, transformed, enlightened; the simple kiss stole each of their selves for the other and gave back more than either could believe.

After a moment, it was no longer clear who supported whom.

Drawing back, staring into hazel depths as if they threatened his sanity, Byrne recalled why Duncan was there.

"If ..." He cleared his throat. Holding the man in his arms carefully, shivering as Duncan's dishevelled head slowly came to rest on his shoulder. "If you aren't going to fall over again, you really ought to eat something."

"I know."

This was desire. Need. Duncan required nothing from Byrne but this moment, this now, this here, this strength that held him and took all the hurt away. So what if the promises were lies? It didn't matter, nothing mattered. Not when he wanted this beyond any sane method of reasoning, when all he felt was the need to be held, wanted, loved. What were truth and honesty compared to this? Nothing. Nothing at all.

He lifted his arms and held onto the solidity of Byrne.

A fool.

Certainly.

Maybe two of them. For he felt the response. Knew Byrne felt the same. Could hear the rush of heart-beat that echoed that of his own. It gave him some hope.

Whore. He laughed silently, remembering. Oh, it was so true. With this man.

"Food, Peter, remember?" Byrne tried coaxing, fighting past Peter's scent and touch for reason. Yet of its own accord his mouth fell towards its fate. At the last minute he jerked back. "No. No, we can't."

"Why?" Duncan murmured. "Byrne, please."

"Peter, you're not well enough!"

"No?"

"I can't - " Byrne's voice was uneven, yet somehow he drew strength from an untapped source. "No. Food first, and then ... then ..." He shivered as a hand brushed against his groin. "Oh, Christ." The word was a sigh that stirred the curling tendrils of auburn hair and dusted across a beard-shadowed cheek.

"Kiss me."

"It's not as if I don't want to ."

"Then do it."

Byrne did, moaning softly as if in pain as their mouths met.

If perfection could be two mouths meeting, this was it. More. Duncan reached for solidity and held on tight, holding warmth and need and joy.

With a sudden dip the world disappeared, and they were lying on the bed, wrapped tight together, limbs tangled close. Belly to belly, mouth to mouth, it took only a moment of touch, of nearness, of cloth-wrapped flesh burning against the same and they came, the moment as hasty, as sweet as either man had ever known.

Breathing hard, blinking sweat from his eyes, Duncan let Byrne's weight hold him down, surround him, and could have cried. There were suddenly no doubts. He would take what was offered, whatever that was, for as long as Byrne offered it. Pride? He had none. And couldn't have cared less. Not here, not at this moment, when all he felt was belonging, and the strangeness of it was almost beyond his ability to comprehend.

He would take this and damn all the consequences.

The decision made him weak, and he released his hold on Byrne's back, letting his arms fall to the bed. Love? That it didn't matter was the clearest thing in his life. Wrapped in the warmth whose absence had cost him so dearly he knew that this was the closest to happiness he was ever likely to get.

And his stomach rumbled.

"Peter!"

"Mmm?" Lost, wanting only more of the same, Duncan reached for disappearing warmth. But the hand that met his didn't react as he wanted, instead he was pulled up until he was sitting. Upright, blinking uncertainly, he sat and peered at Byrne. "What's the matter?"

"I'm sorry."

Sorry. Duncan tried hard to think what Byrne might be sorry about. And couldn't come up with anything. He sniffed. "For what, exactly?"

"This." A big hand gestured across the bed. "I, you're not well, it's … "

"Idiot." Duncan smiled, his tone really quite affectionate.

"I didn't want to make you, force - "

"Be quiet. I wanted it too. I wanted you very much; it wasn't rape, I promise you that." He blinked away the shadows.

"I could still have waited."

"I couldn't." He grinned suddenly as his stomach made a louder noise.

Byrne cupped Peter's face in his hands. "Hey, I think your stomach's trying to tell you something."

"Noisy bugger, isn't it?"

Pulled into an easy hug, Duncan knew Byrne was feeling his ribs. And probably planning a six course meal.

As if galvanised Byrne pulled away, resolutely ignoring the hands that tried to keep him still. "Come on."

His gaze fixed somewhere around Byrne's belly, a smile was spreading across Duncan's face.

Byrne shrugged, and looked down at the damp patch darkening his trousers. "Well, at least I won't have to wash the sheets."

"True."

"What about you?"

Duncan carefully stood up. He tested upright for a moment, looked pleased when he didn't fall over, then picked carefully at slightly sticky cotton that was plastered to his groin.

"I'll survive. Anyway, I don't usually wear anything in bed."

"I know." Byrne looked at him. "But I've another spare pair, so get 'em off."

"Why?"

"Because you are going back to bed and I like clean sheets."

"Oh."

Duncan took a breath, then sat back. Suddenly utterly exhausted, he curled into the bed and let himself be stripped, cleaned, redressed, tucked in.

With a smile that was without any shadow or complication, he settled down. "I never took you for a nursemaid."

"Nursemaid? Where you're concerned it feels more like a keeper."

Sharply reminded of his deficiencies, Duncan stilled. "Thanks."

"No problem."

"No." Duncan wished that were true. "What are you going to feed me then?"

Byrne hesitated, knowing there was something he was missing. "Anything you want."

"Anything?"

"Well, maybe not lobster, but I can have a good crack at most other things." He stretched easily, spine uncurling as he reached up then relaxed. "And I'm starving."

Rubbing his hands together he recited a menu that would have given Escoffier pause, and before he'd finished, Duncan was half-laughing in protest.

"And you'd better make the most of this; my normal culinary skills tend more towards something instant from Vesta, or going round the Chinese. But today, I'm cooking."

"I'm not sure if that's good or not." Peter shook his head, the faint shadows gone. "I don't mind, anything, but certainly not lobster. In fact nothing fancy, I don't want to throw it back up at you."

"Definitely not a good idea." Byrne almost hid his concern.

"Besides, your stomach wouldn't dare. Come on, make a decision."

Duncan rubbed a hand over his distinctly concave belly, pale blue cotton rucking up around his fingers. "Okay, bread and soup. It's what I was dreaming of when I woke up." The last words were smothered by a yawn.

"Bread and soup it is, then sleep. Do you want a shower first?"

Wearily conceding that for the moment he was happy as he was, Duncan just waved a hand.

"You can nap while I make it, but I'll wake you up to eat!"

"I consider myself duly warned." He yawned on the words, eyes closing.

Listening he heard Byrne leave the room and go to the kitchen. He was humming softly. Duncan sighed into the pillow and let himself hold the memory close: sex as a shared experience. Wonderful. And probable the most addictive experience he had ever enjoyed.

He awoke to the smell of tomato soup. He sighed against the pillow and opened his eyes.

"Lunch?" Byrne was holding a tray, waiting.

Stirring, pushing himself up to lean back on the headboard, Peter rubbed his eyes. "Is it?"

"Mmm. You looked so peaceful, I thought I'd let you sleep on for a bit."

"I do feel better."

"Still hungry?"

"I hope that was an industrial size tin you opened."

"There's plenty more, here - " Byrne moved, sliding the tray across Duncan's lap. There was a bowl of soup, a plate of buttered bread, a mug of tea and a handful of biscuits. "Take your time."

"This looks wonderful." He sighed happily and picked up a spoon. "What about you?"

"I've eaten." Duncan just looked at him. "Okay, I had breakfast, then it was lunchtime, so I had some soup, too. And maybe the rest of those biscuits with coffee. Hey! I had to do something while waiting for you to wake up!"

190

"Must be how you keep on all that muscle."

"I wish. I'd save a fortune on gym membership if it did." He sat down on the edge of the bed. "Tell me, how do you feel?"

Through a long slurp of soup, Duncan considered. "Better, I think. Still tired though."

"You were exhausted. When did you last sleep properly, eh?"

The bread was amazing. All the food was. It tasted like nothing he'd ever experienced; perhaps semi-starvation gave you sharper taste-buds.

"No idea."

"At a guess, about the same time you last enjoyed a meal."

"Thank you, mother."

Byrne laughed softly, and settled himself back, leaning on one elbow. "Okay, I'll try and not be too hen-like."

Duncan paused, a piece of bread half-way to his mouth. Then he shook his head. "No. I can't see it. You don't cluck for a start."

"And thank you!"

A smile, and Duncan went back to eating.

"There's enough hot water if you want a bath or a shower."

"Is that a hint?"

"No. But I could go and get the water running."

Duncan sighed. "Now hot water really will be a luxury. I can't remember the last time I soaked in a bath."

"None on that boat?"

"A shower, which just about managed to dribble cold water that looked like it had come straight from the estuary. I strip-washed in the kitchen; it was warmer."

"What about Dyes' flat?"

"Oh, that had hot water." He'd rarely used it though, the meter eating coins once the immersion heater was on. "How long have you lived here?"

Not even aware that the subject had been changed, Byrne did a quick calculation. "Two years, just about."

"Nice."

"Yeah." Byrne looked around and nodded. "It's comfortable."

Duncan scrapped the bowl clean, licked the spoon and put it down with a contented sigh. "That was good."

"Enough?"

"Plenty." He reached for the mug and took a sip.

"I'll take the tray then." Byrne was on his feet. "And then get your bath going."

A smile in answer. Unshadowed.

"Bubble bath?"

"You don't have any!"

"I might." Byrne tried to look unabashed. "Someone must have left it behind. Yes or no?"

"No."

"Okay. I'll call when it's ready." And he left.

Duncan closed his eyes, amused. Bubble bath. What sort? Did Old Spice do a range for the bath? Not that Byrne usually smelled of anything other than soap and Byrne. Not a bad combination.

Suddenly fed up with lying down, Duncan carefully climbed out of bed. He stood, pleased when the room remained steady. Food really did seem to work. And sleep of course; sleep without nightmares, too. Lovely. He sighed, contented. Barefooted he padded out into the hall, meeting Byrne as he emerged from a rapidly steaming bathroom.

"Hello, I was just coming to get you."

"I wanted to stretch my legs." What with one thing and another he'd been lying down a lot recently.

"We could go for a walk later, just down to the park. It's stopped raining." Byrne offered the suggestion almost hesitantly. "If you're up to it."

"I'll be fine. There'll be benches in the park. I can feed the ducks."

"It's not that sort of park. Though if you really want to annoy the locals you can feed the pigeons. Or the rats."

"Nice neighbourhood!"

"Cheap."

"Ah." Duncan nodded at the succinct explanation. "I wondered how you afforded this place."

192

"South Ken was just a little beyond my reach - "

"Bloody horrible place anyway." Duncan grinned suddenly. "Is my bath overflowing yet."

"Oh!" Turning quickly on his heel, Byrne was leaning over the side of the bath, hurriedly turning off taps. "That was close. I'll just let some out." With a glug he pulled the plug up, waiting while water rushed away and the water level sank enough for Duncan to get in without flooding the entire room.

Duncan simply leaned on the door-frame, and admired curves in an academic way, and wondered at the domesticity of it all.

"There." Plug back in place, Byrne reached for a towel and dried off his hands.

"Thanks."

"I'll let you get on. Unless you want anything else?"

"No, I'll be fine."

"Call if you want your back scrubbed."

"I'll be fine." Firmer.

Byrne gave a quick grin. "I know." And stepping past, left him in peace.

The bath really was wonderful. Peter lay in the warm water and sighed happily as his muscles gradually eased, and even his bruises felt better.

Stripping off and looking at himself in the long bathroom mirror had hardly been cheering. He'd blinked at the stranger, suddenly seeing why Byrne treated him with such care. The marks on his wrists were the worst, angry scabbed weals that circled his flesh like obscene bracelets. He looked at them then turned away, not wanting to see more, stepping quickly into the bath and easing into the water.

Resting his forearms on the sides to keep his wrists from getting too soaked, he just lay still, not really thinking at all. Just being - happy.

So strange. He rubbed the toes of one foot against the other, testing the thought.

Happy.

Certainly as close as he had ever been. And it was worth it, even if the feeling only lasted a day. Or a moment. Or just for the space of time that was now.

He could hear Byrne whistling.

Domesticity. Who would ever have thought it.

He smiled suddenly and reached for the soap.

Duncan walked into the kitchen towelling his hair and dressed in the clean pair of pyjamas.

"You look better."

"Feel it too. What's that?"

"Bolognese sauce." Byrne smiled over his shoulder as Duncan padded across the lino. "Though I doubt if they'd recognise it in Bologna."

"Smells good, but is it dinner time?"

"No. But it tastes better when it's stood for a while. Promise."

"I believe you, though it smells pretty damn good now."

"Are you still hungry?"

"No, not really."

Turning, watching as Duncan yawned widely, hands coming up to cover his mouth, Byrne stilled.

Duncan blinked. "What?"

Byrne put the spoon down and turned off the heat. "I've got a first aid kit, if you want anything on those wrists." A lid covered the pan with a sharp clatter of metal on metal. "Or the burns on your shoulders."

Silence.

Taking a deep breath, Byrne closed his eyes. "Which one of them burned you?"

Silence.

He turned, blinking at the stark lack of emotion on Peter's thin face. "Please, tell me."

"Both of them. Kerrigan first, but towards the end Paget got quite enthusiastic too."

Byrne nodded, breathing deeply. "I had wondered."

"When you undressed me?"

194

"Then, and - You were naked when we found you." He reached out an unsteady hand and touched Duncan's skin, just where his jaw met his neck. He'd shaved, the inch of skin was smooth under Byrne's touch. "I wanted to kill them. Bloodily." He shivered. "I didn't, though. Murphy and Cadell wouldn't let me."

"Good. You couldn't cook me dinner from a prison cell."

A laugh that almost worked. "Suppose not."

"No." Duncan let himself be folded into an encompassing hug, resting his head on Byrne's shoulder while strong hands held him so, so carefully.

"I thought you were dead."

"I thought so, too." Duncan laughed softly. "I'm glad I'm not."

"Me too."

And for a long time they simply stood. Then Duncan went back to bed, and Byrne went too, just to be there, to lie close beside him, to hold him whilst he slept.

Unfortunately, the next day Byrne was up early, summoned to work at some ungodly hour, leaving Duncan asleep in bed. Later the same day Duncan went back to Cadell's office.

He was so much stronger, the long hours of sleep, and the food that Byrne had insisted upon, enough to bolster him for the hours he spent dredging up information. Strengthened, he was able to bear the stress, and even managed a certain lucidity. Every day for a week he went to Cadell, and sat in an office talking to either him or some other officer. Every night he returned to Byrne's flat, only having the energy to eat when Byrne was there to insist.

Except Byrne was hardly there; he was working long hours, often only snatching brief intervals of sleep between various jobs. By the time the last tape had been signed off, the two men had spent only eight hours of the entire week together.

Lying stretched out on the extravagant length of Byrne's dark green sofa, Duncan felt as if molten lead had been poured into his bones.

Tired wasn't the word for it.

He closed his eyes, luxuriating in the fact that it was all over. He'd finally satisfied Cadell that there was nothing else he knew, suspected or even thought. Everything was there on tape, and the recording machine had come to feature more prominently in his dreams than he cared to think about.

His brain felt sucked dry. Every scrap of information in his possession extracted, questioned and dissected, and from where he lay now the idea of any conscious thought was excruciating. Painful. So he lay still and ached, letting his mind drift.

Yet there had been one good part: talking it all out had organised everything in his mind. So much so that his book was already half-written, in thought if not on paper, and even the writing it down part was coming along nicely. All that was needed was to get it all together by the time the case came to trial, then some publisher would jump at it. Bloody hell, they'd be stupid not to, all that scandal. News of the Screws would probably be screaming to serialise it. Though *The Daily Mail* would be a better market; middle England loved its scandal.

He hardly thought about the money, what really obsessed him was showing what the law-enforcing face of the police had concealed. The week with the tape-recorder had brought back every scrap of disgust and revulsion that the cons, scams and crimes had ever engendered in him. As he recalled each titbit for Cadell's eager ears, the depression had flooded back as well. There had been too many hurried, hidden conversations in filthy alleyways with people frightened for more than their lives for Duncan to live easily with either the memories or the guilt caused because he hadn't been able to help.

Eyes closed, body still, he felt raw, almost flayed by the remembered misery. All those people -

But it had been worthwhile. It had to have been.

Would be.

Now, after everything, to be at a loose end was faintly disconcerting. Not a loose end, really, for the book had to be got on with, but tonight he was too tired to think about beginning work.

Sighing, he knew he should get up and do something about food. But he didn't. Instead he lay where he was, listening apathetically to the noise of the distant traffic.

Physically he was almost completely healed, even if the occasional headaches drove him around the bend. The simple fact that the tiredness was from honest exhaustion not from illness made him feel remarkably optimistic. Funny, he wouldn't have recommended time with Cadell for convalescence, but it seemed to have worked.

Apart from the lack of sleep. The erratic sleep pattern he seemed to have fallen into wasn't conducive to being a hundred per cent alert. Dreams, discomfort, memory. They all played with him. Had done for weeks. One day, he hoped to get to the point where he could sleep for more than two hours at a stretch.

Without dreams.

He wondered if that was why Byrne stayed away so often: because he got a better night's sleep with his head down on a bunk at HQ. Duncan sighed and in a desultory way shifted his legs, almost preparing to stand up, then stilling as if thinking better of it.

Even living with Byrne, Duncan felt he hardly knew him any better. Apart from that first day they hadn't even fucked. They'd touched though, held each other. So maybe that was enough. Byrne was good for the nightmares. Comforting.

Not that Duncan wanted to live celibate for ever, especially with Byrne. Okay, so they had both spent the entire ten days in a haze of work and exhaustion, and wryly he supposed he should be thankful that Byrne hadn't just availed himself of the warm body that lay so close by his side, but ... He still wanted more.

Greedy. Of course.

It was Byrne, after all.

Besides, they communicated through sex so much more easily than with speech. With each other, anyway. But what did Byrne want? It always came back to that: what did Byrne want? And would he ever say it?

And he wouldn't be home tonight either.

Damn.

Dragging his leaden limbs upright, Duncan sat and pushed bony fingers into his hair, massaging them into his scalp. Too much tension. Perhaps he should go back to Newhaven. For some reason he didn't even contemplate the safe house.

Maybe it was because the boat had been offered without condition, and increasingly Duncan felt that Cadell was leading up to asking something of him, something other than just straight information. Accepting the safe house would put him at a disadvantage, and the way he felt at the moment he didn't even want to hear what it could be, let alone have to come up with an answer. The last thing he needed was for Cadell to have an upper hand.

Well, more of one than he had already.

Though it had to be admitted that returning to the boat was a bleak prospect. Damp, cold and isolated, it wasn't a cheery place at the best of times and after this much contact with normality it would be positively miserable. Contact with Byrne, he amended truthfully. Even hardly seeing him, just being here was better than isolation. Wasn't it? And sleeping where Byrne should be sleeping was better than being without him.

Certainly.

Romance was clearly not dead.

Or lust.

Or whatever the feeling was that they seemed to share.

He sighed, and told himself that he really should get up. Maybe eat something, do some exercise, anything to try and stir some energy.

Sitting with his head resting on his hands, he wondered about simply going to bed. It was only eight o'clock, but even so, perhaps sleep would be easier than making any decisions. And the debriefing was over, so maybe the dreams would be gone. There was no harm in wishful thinking. None at all. He smiled tiredly at his socks, wiggling his toes into the carpet.

But half an hour later he was still sitting listlessly in the same position, startled when the bell rang. Frowning, he went to the door, peering through the peephole before releasing the bolt and locks.

"Hello, I thought you were working tonight." He tried not to sound anything other than pleased. He had, after all, no control over what Byrne did, but warmth and hope and pain escaped in equal measures.

"So did I."

A kiss, warm and pleasant, and Byrne left him to re-lock the door, wandering though to the main room. He slipped out of his jacket and harness, slinging it across the back of a chair. He stretched, easing his shoulders. "But for once luck was with us; the case got sorted out this afternoon."

"Fantastic." Duncan watched as Byrne kicked off both shoes and picked up the post.

"God, I'm knackered! Three hours of paperwork, my favourite." He tossed unopened envelopes to one side and walked back to Duncan. "Is there anything to eat?"

Duncan blinked, taken unaware.

"You're still not eating, are you?"

"Umm ..."

"Guilt! I knew it. Daft bugger. Come on." And taking Duncan's hand he led him into the kitchen. Still holding tight he opened the fridge door and rummaged inside. "Christ, I'm ravenous."

"Okay, Byrne, out the way. I'll put something together for you."

"Yeah?"

"Yeah." Duncan shrugged apologetically. "I do eat. And I'm happy to cook."

"A surprise?"

"Yes."

Byrne pulled him close, kissed his cheek, then was off, walking backwards for a few paces. "I'll have a bath, okay?"

"There'll be time."

Byrne yawned. "Great."

Duncan smiled. Byrne looked so tired that, for once, preparing something he'd want to eat didn't seem such a chore. And who knew, whatever it was, he might even eat some of it himself.

Emerging from a long hot bath feeling a hundred per cent improved,

Byrne dressed in jeans and a T-shirt and went to find dinner. He got as far as the kitchen door before Duncan's voice stopped him. "No you don't! Go and sit down. I'll bring the food along."

Retracing his steps, Byrne went on into the living room. There was an open bottle of French wine sitting on the dining table, along with two glasses, each two-thirds full. He smiled, picked up a glass and took a long drink. Cold and perfect, tasting clean and rich, heady. He hadn't had time for a social drink in what seemed like weeks. Pulling a chair out he sat down, fingering the place settings, half amused by the elaborate preparations. Once or twice, in the cold, dark hours of early morning stakeout, he'd dreamed of this. Of being at home, with Duncan, sharing food and companionship. He conjured the thoughts so often, that it was hard to believe this was real.

He'd cursed Cadell roundly for taking up so much of his time with work. Why now, when he was needed here? It was so typical. He had almost been able to feel Duncan slipping away from him with each day that passed, and short of packing in the job he wasn't sure how to stop the rot.

Though it had made him think of his priorities.

Carefully.

Frowning into his glass, he looked up as Duncan came in and, with a flourish, placed a plate in front of him.

Closing his eyes, Byrne inhaled deeply. "Curry!"

"I don't suppose they'd recognise it in Calcutta."

They both grinned. Byrne picked up a fork. "Don't suppose I'd fancy a curry in Calcutta. And I bet they wouldn't serve it with chips. Home-made chips at that. Where's the ketchup?"

"In front of you. Eat up before they go soggy."

Byrne rubbed his hands together enthusiastically. "Peter, you really know the way to a man's heart." He was fighting with the ketchup which seemed to prefer its residency in the bottle to being on his plate, so he didn't notice the flicker of pain that crossed Duncan's face.

"Yeah, well hope you like it; I'm not an expert on chips."

Byrne sampled the wares, dipping a fat potato finger into the ketchup, then the curry, before blowing on it and popping it whole into his mouth.

Slightly muffled, he spoke around the heat. "Where's yours?"

"I'll get it." Duncan was gone for a moment, returning with a second plate, less burdened than Byrne's. "Is it okay?"

"Perfect."

He settled and they ate in silence. Almost at ease. Duncan poured wine when their glasses emptied. The food slowly disappeared.

Duncan pushed his plate away first, though Byrne wasn't far behind, his plate left clean and near to shining. "Lovely!" He sighed happily, and took another drink.

"We aim to please."

Byrne looked up and stared intently, suddenly absolutely serious "You do that, Peter. Always." He watched some of the tension in Peter's shoulders ease. "I'm sorry it's been such a bad week." Reaching across, taking hold of a hand, cupping his fingers around it, he held it lightly, stroking with his thumb as if trying to quiet a wary animal.

Ten days of living together and it still had to be like this.

And he had no idea how to put things right.

Duncan must have been feeling the same, for he gave a sigh and looked up. "None of it could be helped, you had to work, I had to see Cadell."

"Doesn't help though, does it?"

"No."

Their eyes met. They smiled. Concord at least.

"D'you want to go to bed? I feel like I could sleep for about a year." Byrne yawned, the food and wine weighing him down. It wasn't that late, but he didn't want to do anything but be wrapped around Duncan.

"Yeah, I'll clear up first."

"No. I'll do it, you go on. Warm up the sheets for me."

Byrne watched as Peter hesitated, then nodded. "Sure." He stood up and walked towards the door. Byrne was already clearing up, yet by the time the washing-up was done and Byrne finished in the kitchen, Peter was in bed, curled up.

Turning off the light, Byrne stripped off and eased under the covers. He hesitated then gathered Duncan into his arms. Still skin and bone, but he fitted into Byrne with perfect ease. Breathing deeply of Duncan's scent, Byrne snuggled down.

For a while there was no sound but their even breathing. Then he slept.

11

Woken by daylight, Peter stirred sleepily.

Surrounded by Byrne's arms, held by his warmth, his life, he still managed to feel uneasy. The trouble was, he had absolutely no idea how Byrne would react when he finally woke up.

Duncan knew he would let Byrne do whatever he wanted, and accordingly despised himself very slightly. He felt so unsure, as if the last few months had left him without any certainty. About anything.

The answer to at least some of his problems lay next to him, and was quietly oblivious.

This bed. Christ he'd been fucked here so often. It had mostly been enjoyable, some of it sublime. The dark cotton sheets that showed off Byrne's strong, tanned body to such advantage could tell a few stories. God, the amount of times he'd lain here trying to find the energy and will to leave in the cold, small hours of night.

He had known who he was then. Now? What was he now? He had been comfortable as Byrne's whore. It had all been so clear, so reassuring. Except that he'd wanted more, of course. Now, he wasn't sure of anything, least of all the thoughts of the man who slept next to him.

He sighed, and felt the change in muscle tension as Byrne stirred out of sleep. Twisting his head, Duncan found himself face to face with a smile that made his heart do a double somersault.

Which was so unfair.

"Morning, how are you feeling?" Duncan spoke first, moving slightly away, hiding uncertainty in words.

"Wonderful." Byrne moved, lifting his arms in a stretch that worked its way down to his toes. "And I've got today off."

Duncan licked dry lips. "Yeah?"

"Mm." Byrne snuggled back into the pillows. "You know, I think this is the first time in weeks that we've actually woken up in bed together."

"Byrne, it's only the second time ever!"

"What?"

"Today is only the second time we've woken up together."

"Are you sure?"

Sighing, Duncan curled onto his side and made a list; a very short list. "There was that time about a week before Dover, and today. Any other night we've managed to snatch some sleep, that bloody RT of yours has sounded and you've had to be away being Batman, or whatever it is you get up to."

"I know this last couple of weeks has been busy, but - " He whistled. "Christ, you're right."

"Yeah."

"I'm sorry."

Duncan shrugged. "Just thought I'd point it out."

"Yeah. I know Cadell's been working my arse off. In fact I can hardly believe he's let me have today. How about if I throw the RT in the bath and we turn off the phone. Sound good?"

"I must be dreaming, I was sure I heard you offer to cut off the umbilical cord. No RT? You'd be twitching in thirty minutes." Duncan teased, but truth underlay the humour.

"Watch me. Move over." Byrne hopped out of bed, walked out of the bedroom. In a moment he returned, holding his RT. With a ceremonial bow he turned the switch to mute and tossed it onto the chair.

"Must be my birthday." Despite his sarcasm, Peter was completely disarmed. He watched as Byrne, all naked skin and a grin, came back to the bed. It took little to acknowledge that Byrne's body was nigh on perfect: saved from stockiness by athleticism, the powerful planes and curves of muscle in movement deliciously appealing. The fact that the smooth lines of his body were interrupted by a semi-erect cock was only a slight additional appeal.

Slight, he laughed to himself. Oh, yeah. The quiver of lust that arrowed straight to his own groin had nothing to do with that, did it? Must've been a change in the wind direction.

Jesus, his hands, his eyes, his mouth; every part of Duncan knew every nuance of skin and vein, every touch-sensitive pore, every pulse that counted on the way to pleasure for that particular shaft of flesh. He knew his own with less skill.

"Hey, wake up."

Duncan breathed out the air he was unconsciously hoarding and shifted back so that Byrne could climb into bed, sliding down until they were level.

"There, no interruptions." Byrne turned to lean his elbow on the pillow, looking almost shy. He hesitated, then let out a sigh. "Peter, do you want to make love?"

Duncan heard the words, yet it took a heartbeat of time before he realised he'd been offered a choice.

"Is that an invitation?"

Dark-eyed, solemn, Byrne nodded. "Yes. Whatever you want."

Quite suddenly, Duncan realised that he'd meant it; the choice really was there. Absolutely there. He felt Byrne shiver, and understood the doubts that made the other man so wound-up with tension. They were both so bad at communicating. Two grown men who managed to understand each other so imperfectly. He reached up, and touched a finger to Byrne's lips. "I want you. And yes, I want you to make love to me."

They stared at each other and a long sigh escaped Byrne. "Sure?"

Duncan nodded and closed his eyes as a hand smoothed its way down his cheek, Byrne's skin rasping softly across his beard-roughened jaw. He wanted to purr as a thumb rubbed against the grain, caressing, moving down to touch more skin, neck, chest, nipple. He gasped, a short breathy sound, as the fingers dipped further to pull teasingly at the fine arrow of hair leading to his cock.

Then the hand was back, cupping his face. Byrne's voice was warm, soft. "I don't think I've ever wanted anyone in quite the way that I want you. You're beautiful."

"Byrne - "

"Shush." Byrne rested his lips on Peter's, skin against skin, warm breath against warm breath. "What d'you want me to do?"

Duncan shivered, arching into him like a cat, one leg curving around him, pulling him close. He smiled, voice thickened with desire. "I want you to fuck me."

"But, don't you want - " Byrne paused, and sort of wriggled.

"Have you ever?"

A quick nod.

Duncan could hardly believe what he was being offered. Couldn't believe. It was too much, too complicated when all he wanted now - this minute - was Byrne fucking him and obliterating the need that was so close to pain that it made no difference. "Yes, of course. But please, now I want you inside me."

Byrne moaned aloud, as if desperate just from the words. "Yes."

And they kissed, tongue against tongue. Delicious taste, delicious sensation. Breathing erratically, Duncan pulled back, then dipped his head to savour Byrne's neck, tasting the salt hollow that dipped between the solidity of collar-bones, nibbling up to bite gently at an ear, hearing the gasp as the strong body bucked in his arms. Back to soft skin over bone, then further, to tongue one dark nipple until Byrne was clutching his shoulders, moaning in hunger. Then the other; the same effect, the arousal dizzying, the heat and weight of his own cock pressing against a heavy thigh, slicking the dark hairs with his own need.

He backed off, letting Byrne slide his body partially on top, thigh heavy across his legs. A hand closed around his sex, gentle and firm, sliding down to gently massage the tight-drawn sac, squeezing rhythmically until Duncan was so close he was gasping, lost.

"Byrne, please!" Duncan pulled him up; kissed him, mouth open and wet and needing. His hand was flailing about on the bedside cabinet, seeking and finding the blue and white tube of lubricant, holding it above Byrne's head so that he could see to undo it, squeezing it, twisting madly to shift Byrne's weight so he could anoint himself. Shifting again, wrapping his legs high around the strong waist, finding Byrne by touch, drawing the heat and hardness home in a choreography that was without conscious thought other than the need to be one.

"Peter ..." As the tip of his cock slid past the tight barrier, Byrne gasped his lover's name, bound, enslaved, and quite beyond sanity.

"Kiss me." And Byrne did, the kiss clumsy, more open mouth against open mouth as their bodies were joined by breath and by flesh as Byrne slid home in one glorious movement, filling him, stretching him beyond pain and straight into the wildest pleasure. With his legs, he pulled Byrne closer, pulling him down until they were so close that only sweat separated them. Then he arched back, shifting, loving the sound of Byrne's helpless voice as muscles closed tight. Loving even more the abandonment of caution, of restraint, as Byrne pulled out until his cock was almost free, then let his weight take him back, so deep that Duncan groaned, the hard press of ball-sac against skin utterly intoxicating.

Needing to touch, to feel, Duncan held on tight to heated skin, his hands holding, kneading, reaching. Curled almost double he found Byrne's arse, held the luscious flesh in his hands. He shifted again and found the cleft, and his finger brushed against puckered skin making Byrne shudder and hunch over Duncan's body.

Duncan clawed at Byrne, and raised his legs up over strong shoulders, making himself utterly open, ready, loving the reality, the submission. He knew he was making sounds, but nothing like language escaped his mouth, merely the simplest identification of need as Byrne's muscles gathered and then suddenly the waiting was gone and he was being fucked extravagantly. Long drawn out strokes that shook the bed again and again until gasping, with an echoing sob, the tension snapped and in a rush they both spilled into orgasm.

Later, beyond thought, Duncan wetted dry lips and groaned. Byrne shifted and with a shudder slid from his body and lifted his weight away.

Being flat was delicious.

"Peter?" Byrne had slumped to one side.

"Mm?"

"You okay?"

"Lovely."

"Good." Duncan found himself pulled close, kissed, slow and easy; friendship without need.

They parted mouths, and Duncan rested his head on a sweat-damp shoulder, murmuring softly as a hand rubbed gently though his hair. "Thank you."

"What on earth for, Peter?"

"Granting my wish."

"Your wish? Oh, it was a real trial."

"I noticed." They grinned, and were suddenly giggling like boys.

"Idiot."

"Daft."

Duncan touched a finger to Byrne's lips and traced their contour like a blind man reading braille. "It was good."

"Oh, yes." A nod of absolute agreement.

Duncan looked up speculatively. "And I will get around to you one day." He would, if Byrne really meant it. Not every man liked to be fucked after all. "If you really want it, that is."

"Yeah, I do. You've just never asked, and I've, well, let's put it this way, I've enjoyed you quite a few times."

"Enjoyed? How sweet." Duncan grinned at Byrne's sudden coyness, then just as suddenly frowned. "Hey, I hope you're not offering out of some misguided sense of balancing the books?" Duncan glared at the abashed look that fleetingly touched Byrne's features. "You stupid bastard, if I'm going to fuck you it'll be because you want to be fucked, not because you're offering yourself up as sacrifice to my pride."

"Peter, Peter ..."

Duncan ignored him, and Byrne found himself pressed to the sheets and kissed. Which did shut him up, rather successfully.

"Now listen, hasn't it occurred to you that I might like being buggered?"

"You?" Duncan blinked, his mind quite unable to cope with the idea. "Have you been?"

"Well, not recently. But once or twice, yes."

"Well, I never."

"Not yet anyway." And they were both giggling again, sobering slowly. "I mean it."

"But you never asked before."

Byrne seemed mildly exasperated. "No, because every time I saw you I wanted to fuck you through the floor! Later, by the time I'd finished fighting with myself about being in love with you, that bastard had kidnapped you. So next time, just do it. Okay?"

Duncan nodded, content. "Okay."

"Right, that's settled. How about a shower?"

"Of what?" All wide-eyed disingenuity, Duncan looked edible.

"Minced Duncan if you're not careful."

"But sweetie, I can mince ever so well already." The Stevie lisp was perfect, and he yelped as Byrne's palm connected accurately with his bottom. "Ouch, careful, mate, you might need that later."

"Yeah, you might just be right."

Turning to walk away, Duncan grinned. "Sunshine, I know I'm right." And he exited to the bathroom, sashaying as he went.

Byrne was humming to himself as he went to work; life being remarkably good. He smiled broadly at two secretaries, wanting to share his enthusiasm with everyone, unwittingly causing the women to spend the rest of the day arguing over which of them the smile, and its promise, had been aimed at.

Completely absorbed in his own thoughts, Byrne didn't notice, and couldn't have cared less. He went to his desk and began some routine paperwork, his thoughts utterly involved in the convoluted problem of Peter Duncan.

And who got to be on top in bed.

It was all very well for Peter to be wary, but the idea of being taken by him gave Byrne goosebumps. And he had spoken the truth, the one time he'd been the so-called passive partner in bed it had been good. Hardly earth-shattering, but not such an appalling experience that it put him off wanting to try it now, close to ten years later. Peter was, after all, a good advert for the experience, so much so that Byrne had to curb his enthusiasm and not push his lover too hard down a road he seemed reluctant to take. Lover. His lover.

Who happened to be about the most skilled person in bed that Byrne had ever known. And it couldn't just be practice and experience, though that was a very pleasant bonus. It had to be more. A depth of commitment maybe, of giving. Physical grace and strength too. And passion -

Byrne sighed softly.

Still, when Duncan eventually got around to it, Byrne would be ready and waiting. There was no one else in the world that he could imagine trusting enough to do it. Trust, and lust after. And love.

Byrne grinned to himself, and gave up on trying to quantify the experience, though there was no doubting its effect.

A knock on the door made him jump, and colour slightly as one of the secretaries brought in an armful of files.

Sighing in relief as she left, Byrne gave himself a shake and concentrated on work.

An hour later the door opened again. "Hello, Aidan."

"Byrne. How's things?"

Murphy came and sat on the edge of his desk, clearly in no hurry to be anywhere.

"Including or apart from the paperwork?"

Murphy made a revolted face. "I've been up to my ears in it. No, I meant with Peter Duncan."

"He's fine." Byrne nodded, very cautious. "Why?"

"Because I've seen him flat out twice, I don't know!"

"Oh, sorry." Byrne waved an apologetic hand. "He's fine, physically much better."

"Great. The poor sod was in a right state."

"I know." He laid down his biro. "Have you heard any more about Paget and the others?"

"Not a peep. You know how it is: rush, rush, panic, then nothing until the trial."

"Yeah."

"Still, thanks to your friend we're got the scum stitched up nice and tight. I hope Cadell remembered to say thank you."

They looked at each other and grinned. It wasn't a likely thought.

"I did some of the interviews with your man. Very interesting he is, too." Murphy straightened a pile of papers. "Is he still living with you?"

"Yes." Very wary.

"Good." And with a blinding smile Murphy stood up, stretched and wandered back to the door. "Look after him, all right?"

"Sure."

And Byrne was left looking at a closing door. Utterly confused.

Though however curious Aidan Murphy was, he'd never gossip. And he had liked Duncan. Was interested enough to be looking out for him. Which was nice.

It made him surprisingly jealous.

It was good to have someone to go home to.

They'd settled into a comfortable routine; pleasant company, good food, and even better sex. They talked about nothing of importance. Laughed quite a lot. Duncan clearly spent his days writing; the papers strewing the flat were mute testimony to that. Byrne almost ignored the whole thing, finding to his own dismay that he was faintly contemptuous of the entire undertaking. Writers wrote books. Peter wasn't a writer, not that Byrne had read any of the carefully hand-written pages.

Still, it was something that Duncan needed to do, even if only as a form of catharsis, and Byrne respected that; at times in his own past he'd used far more arcane forms of the same indulgence.

But writing all that by hand …

The idea had truly been like a light-bulb switching on in his head.

After a morning of no-hope interviews he took an early lunch, nipping out to the shops and taking far too long. The afternoon was spent working conscientiously under Cadell's eagle eye, and it was close to seven o'clock by the time he was knocking their prearranged code on his flat door.

Inside, glumly preparing another meal that he was sure Byrne would gulp down in five minutes flat, Duncan pottered around the kitchen, half-listening to the radio, half-waiting for the doorbell to ring.

At least the book was progressing in leaps and bounds.

And he hated being broke. He even spent part of the morning nosing around some old haunts, trying to get some work, anything would be better than scrounging off Byrne. Not that it had quite got to that, Byrne's flat was kept well-stocked with food, and mostly there was nothing to spend any money on, even if he'd had any. But with only one pound and a bit between himself and penury Duncan knew something would have to be done soon.

It had never occurred to him before, but Byrne must be either well-paid or well-heeled. Okay, so the flat wasn't huge, but the furnishings and personal effects that defined Byrne were all expensive and in surprisingly good taste. He wondered who had chosen the colours, the fabrics.

Stirring the cheese sauce, he frowned at himself, knowing jealousy for what it was, and being equally sure that with his own past he could hardly comment.

But none of his indiscretions were flaunted under Byrne's nose. And this flat was full of Byrne's past: books with inscriptions from old lovers, even clothes that could never have belonged to Byrne but must have been left behind after a night or week or whatever of passion in that huge bed.

Every day he told himself it was time to move on. There had been no invitation for permanence. Nothing to make this anything but a short-lived, pleasant interlude.

Not that Byrne seemed to object. He didn't say anything about it at all. He was considerate, amusing, sexy and aggravating as hell. The fact that Duncan felt like he was a cook-housekeeper, and that Byrne treated him like a housekeeper-cum-bed warmer managed to irritate Duncan daily. Until, of course, Byrne came home and then it just didn't seem to matter.

Not that he was at all sure about what he did want, anyway.

More. Certainly.

But what else?

Pouring the sauce over the prepared vegetables and pasta, he sprinkled grated cheese over the top and shoved it under the low grill. Opening a bottle of wine from Byrne's store he placed it in the middle of the table and then went about setting places for them both.

He'd just finished when he heard Byrne's knock on the door.

Opening it he could hardly see the wickedly grinning face for a very large parcel done up in Mr Men wrapping paper.

Standing back while Byrne manoeuvred the box in, Duncan asked, "Wow, who's the lucky kid? I didn't know that you had any."

"Don't be daft. It's for you."

"With Mr Men paper?"

"I liked it. And Mr Messy looks just like you first thing in the morning."

"Oh, cheers." Duncan was smiling as he followed into the living room, watching as the parcel was carefully put down on the coffee table. Then he caught up with the first part of the statement. "Did you say it's for me? It's not my birthday."

"Really?" Not fazed by this news, Byrne grinned, his white teeth showing the extent of his amusement. "Come on, it won't bite, open it."

The parcel looked huge, bright and ribbon-wrapped. Duncan sat down and, with a quick glare at Byrne, tugged at a loose ribbon end, watching it fall away in a tangle. There was sticky tape too. He picked at it, pulling it off carefully.

"Bloody hell, what are you trying to do? Re-use the paper?"

"Anticipation, Byrne, some of us find it exciting."

Byrne watched the intense concentration, and felt his stomach tighten with recognition as he saw the boy Peter might have been, wide-eyed with excitement on Christmas morning. He remembered the feeling well himself and was glad that he'd bothered to have the damn thing wrapped up.

The last piece of tape conceded to Peter's fingers and the paper fell away.

"Byrne!"

Worried by the blank pallor that had swept all emotion from the thin face, Byrne sat next to him, reaching out to touch a scarred wrist. "Don't you want one?"

"Yeah, but it must've cost a bloody fortune."

Byrne shook his head. "I didn't have to hock the family silver, if that's what you're worried about. You do like it, don't you?"

Duncan sighed loudly and bit his lower lip. "I'd be lying if I said anything else, but ..." He tried to frame words to tell Byrne that he felt as if he were taking advantage, that accepting expensive gifts made the imbalance between their lives even more acute, but they wouldn't come and suddenly he saw that his silence was hurting his lover.

He looked up, true thanks in the smile that warmed his eyes. "Byrne, it's the best thing anyone's ever given me." The large lump in his throat made denying the pleasure very difficult. "And it'll make life so much easier."

Lifting the electric typewriter out of the box, he put it down on the table, touching its cream plastic, brushing the tips of his fingers over the keys. He was quite still, then suddenly, in an easy flex of muscle was straddling Byrne's lap. Leaning his hands on the sofa on either side of Byrne's head he bent forwards. "Thank you very much." That his smile was tinged by melancholy Byrne didn't see, as it was masked by the sweetness of the kiss.

They had progressed no farther than a deepening of the same kiss when Peter sat bolt upright, causing Byrne to wince and move to protect his more tender sensibilities. "Ouch."

"Fuck! The dinner!" Pushing himself off he did further damage as he leapt toward the door.

Soothing his wounded flesh, Byrne followed as the smell of burnt cheese finally reached him. With contentment he watched the economic grace of Duncan's movements, propping himself against the kitchen door with his arms folded as the remains of dinner were removed from under the grill.

"Take-away?" He offered the easiest solution.

"This'll be all right," Duncan was poking at the dish, removing the blackened crust, "it's only the cheese on top, the rest's fine."

Moving to stand close behind him, Byrne rubbed his face on the warm skin between T-shirt and hair. Suddenly food could wait. "Peter ..." He whispered the name and his breath caught as sexual fire licked at his groin and his balls moved and tightened.

"Watch it, Byrne." Hands in oven gloves, Peter manoeuvred the dish over to the table while Byrne ground his teeth in exasperation. When Duncan turned back, he was hijacked into waiting arms.

Wide, surprised eyes that glinted more amber than hazel greeted Byrne's stare and in a second had summed up the situation. "Oh, no. We eat first." Duncan waggled his forefinger at Byrne. "Or the pasta will get cold."

"Put it in the oven."

"Then it really will be inedible!" He tried to take a step backwards but Byrne only tightened his grip and, leaning forward licked at his ear.

"Byrne ..." The name was spoken on a sigh that broke in the middle. "Oh, hell!"

Half-clothed, too impatient for total nudity, hands fumbling with zips, buttons, skin, they made love standing up. A kitchen unit supported their weight as bared flesh met the same, cock burning against cock, soft skin and hard need, Byrne's hand pushing Duncan's shirt high, touching him, pulling him close, groin tight to groin. They rocked together. Kissed. Gasping around the deep tangle of tongues as it all was there so fast, and Byrne came first, head thrown back in simple ecstasy that sharpened as strong teeth bit his neck, and Duncan shuddered in his arms, heat spilling against his belly.

Breathing hard, they held each other up.

Duncan lifted his head, his eyes still dreamy. "Nice."

"Yeah."

Too content to part, they held still.

"What about dinner?"

Duncan sighed and straightened. A brief kiss on smiling lips and he let Byrne step away. He looked utterly disreputable; cock bare, lips bruised. Delicious. Even now he was aware of the possibility of arousal. As if he were sixteen again.

He was hungry though. "Go and wash."

"Come with me?"

"And eat at midnight?"

"Ah, you have a point." Byrne came back to him, rubbing a thumb over his cheek. "Though sometimes I think I don't need anything but you."

"Idiot."

"Maybe."

"Go and wash."

A last touch and Byrne went to the door, watching as Duncan sighed, pulled up his jeans, not bothering with the fly, and went to inspect the dinner.

Duncan served the pasta into bowls and they carried their plates into the living room, settling at the dining table.

Lifting his glass, Duncan held it to the light, watching the lustrous liquid turn to ruby fire in the lamp-light. A silent toast and he took a long swallow, letting the wine blend with the taste of Byrne in his mouth.

"Go on, eat!"

He smiled, and obeyed. The pasta was fine after all.

Later that night, coffee made, settled on the sofa next to Byrne, he made himself ask about Paget. "Any more news on the trial?"

"No, not yet. Cadell's pushing hard but it'll still be weeks, if not months. At least they've got the bastard tucked safely away in Brixton."

"That's one good thing, at least."

Byrne sighed into his coffee, making the dark liquid scud into eddies. "He won't be going anywhere for a long time, the drugs alone would see to that. Then there's you. Cadell's been like a terrier with the information you gave him, and even if he didn't say anything to you, he was really pleased. And Kerrigan's been talking as if his life depended on it; we've nabbed five others just from his evidence alone." He leant forward and put his mug down before easing back.

"Miserable creep, he'd say anything to save his own skin." Duncan remembered Kerrigan's pale eyes devouring the agony he'd caused. Remembered more than was comfortable.

There was always more than he wanted to remember. Always. Blindly, he stared down at where his hand held the edge of a cushion, amazed that the grip was so tight bones showed stark under skin. He jumped when Byrne covered the hand with his own, and blinked up, shivering as he came back from the darkness of memory.

"Whatever he did to you, it's done, gone."

A nod.

Byrne squeezed gently, reassurance in his touch. "Did he rape you?"

The question was so sudden that Duncan almost gasped, his gaze flicking to Byrne's face then darting away. "No."

"But?"

"How do you know there's a but?"

"Because I know you. And I know how they would have hurt you."

Duncan shivered, his breathing so shallow it hurt. "No. He didn't rape me." He swallowed hard, almost whispering. "Neither did Paget." He paused, so tense, so hating this, that there was almost nothing but pain in his voice. "But they came close. And there were other things. Kerrigan was a sadist, Paget just wanted me to crawl."

Byrne growled, the sound involuntary.

"I don't think I did."

"Peter!"

"But I can't remember some of it. Does it count if I can't remember?"

"No. Nothing matters anyway. There's no shame."

"No?"

Meeting the stark dilation of fear in Duncan's eyes, Byrne showed only certainty. "None."

After a moment the tension eased. He lifted Duncan's hand and kissed it, letting his lips move to trace across the livid scars.

"Byrne - "

"I could kill them."

"No." Duncan took hold of Byrne's hand, let his fingers rub over the callused ridges that told of skills he really knew nothing about. The threat could so easily be reality. "It isn't worth it."

"Promise?"

"Promise." Duncan shrugged slightly. "I'll get over it. Besides, I like you here, and I'd be lousy at prison visiting."

"I doubt if Cadell would let it get that far. He's far too much money invested in me."

Duncan raised his brows. "Has he covered up for you before?"

"No." Byrne was almost laughing, then he just shook his head. "No, I'm a good boy. Besides, the boss likes you; I think he was almost as angry when they snatched you as I was."

"Yeah, all that evidence disappearing into the wide blue yonder."

"More than likely. Not fond of waste, our Mr Cadell."

"Surprise me again."

Duncan pulled his legs up, curling them under him. "You know, I never really wanted to believe that you were one of them. I ... I just couldn't see it any other way. Thinking you'd tricked me almost made me more miserable than Paget did."

"Do you remember talking to me in the car, when we were taking you to hospital?"

Narrowing his eyes, Duncan thought back. "No. All I really remember is warmth all around me. I was so bloody cold and then you were there." He looked down, more than mildly embarrassed. "I felt safe."

"I thought you were dying." Byrne's hands tightened around Duncan's fingers, as if willing him to understand. "I really thought we were too late. Then you came to. Told me you loved me."

"I what?"

"You were out of it. But you did say that."

"I did." There were so many memories, many so hazy he couldn't be certain which were true and which were lies. But this, this he was sure of. "You were holding me."

Byrne nodded. "Then I bloody well cried all over you. Didn't even care that Cadell and Murphy and half of Kent could see me."

"Daft." He smiled as he said it.

"No. Finally in my right mind about you."

They sat in silence for a while, then Duncan spoke. "I'm sorry about what I said at the hospital."

He remembered all too clearly the words he'd thrown at Byrne, each of them having returned to eat like acid at his gut. His need for forgiveness outweighed anything else, even pride.

"Stop it. You weren't exactly feeling your best, and it must have looked pretty incriminating. Besides, I'm not very proud of some things that I've said to you." He leant sideways and planted a chaste kiss on Duncan's unsmiling lips. "Call it quits?"

"Yeah." Duncan grinned suddenly. "And Paget can rot forever."

"Absolutely." Byrne nodded. "And *Match Of The Day* starts in a minute." He winced as he was thumped. "Spurs are playing."

"Why didn't you say so! Let's watch them get a pasting."

They smiled, in accord. The shadows lifting, the past close to being cured.

Another cup of coffee made, they settled down to the match, joking their way through a mediocre performance, dissecting every player's style, agreeing that none of them deserved to play anything more important than ping-pong.

Afterwards, Byrne clicked off the television, and they prepared for bed. There was a new ease between them. A certain depth of friendship that had been missing before. Sleep came easily, and the night was without dreams.

The week slipped by.

And despite the ease of it all, Duncan came closer and closer to the certainty that they needed to live apart. Not because anything was wrong, but because he was afraid it was all going too right.

One night he even went so far as to speak his thoughts out loud. "Byrne, don't misunderstand, but do you think Cadell will still let me have that flat he offered?"

"Why?" Byrne was totally taken aback. "Aren't you happy here? I thought we were doing okay."

"We are." Duncan gave up on chopping carrots and went to sit next to Byrne at the kitchen table. "It's almost too good. I want it all to last, and I don't want this to become boring."

"Is it? For you?"

"No." Duncan shook his head. "But I need to work."

"Is that all?" Byrne looked relieved. "I don't want you to go. God, we'd have to date like a couple of teenagers. I want you here, with me. Don't ..." He shook his head, grasping for words. "You don't really want to go, do you?"

"I just thought it might be good for us."

"Are you unhappy?"

"No."

Byrne stood up, pulling Duncan with him, taking hold of his hand, walking over to the window. It was dark outside, rain hazing the street-light. For a moment he frowned, as if searching for the right words. Then he sighed. "Look, out there. Millions of people. Yet I've never met anyone like you." He turned Duncan around, held him lightly. "Is there something I'm doing wrong?"

Being too proprietorial, maybe. But Duncan didn't voice the words, and was suddenly unsure if that was a fault at all. He shook his head, in a way that was somehow neither yes nor no.

Drawing Duncan very close, Byrne sighed deeply. "You know, I come home every day wondering if you'll be here."

"Why?"

"Deep insecurity."

"Oh, yeah!"

A smile tugged at Byrne's lips. "Maybe." He gave Duncan a gentle shake. "I want you here as part of my life."

A smile answered him, as Duncan lightly touched the centre of Byrne's chest with the tips of his fingers. "No I don't want to leave you. And if you can put up with me ..." He stopped because Byrne was shaking him again - none too gently.

"Jesus, Peter! I think I can cope! For chrissake, why do you think I've done all this, for the good of Cadell?"

"Well, your boss can be very persuasive."

"Oh yeah, and I'm a martyr to the cause. Peter, as far as I know Cadell is still plotting something dire for me because I never got around to telling him that I was seeing you. I really don't think he'd be encouraging us this much."

"But he knows that we're living together at the moment?"

"Yes. I doubt if he'll have forgotten, I don't think he ever forgets anything. Though he probably thinks that making us live together will prove how incompatible we are. No, I'm maligning him, he's more likely saving on heating bills. Look, please stay, just relax, it'll be all right."

Duncan sighed and stared into the earnest depths of Byrne's eyes and still wasn't quite convinced. "I didn't think that I was here on sufferance, you're big enough and ugly enough to throw me out if you wanted to. But I don't want to ..." He stopped, for he was being shaken again, and he had to laugh. "You learn these persuasive techniques from Cadell?"

"Nah, he believes firmly in bamboo under the fingernails."

"I thought that was next."

"God, and you say I'm kinky. Come on, Peter. Stay. I'll have no one to keep my feet warm if you go."

Duncan fell for the offhand humour far more easily than he had to seductive blandishments, especially as he caught a glimpse of the very real doubt hidden behind Byrne's easy facade. "All right, but don't blame me when you don't like my cooking."

"I love it."

"The chips anyway, you heathen!"

Soulful eyes stared back at him. "It's the only thing my auntie could cook; brings back memories."

"And you're shameless. Wipe that fatuous smile off your gob, you win; I'll cook you the occasional plate of chips. Occasional, mind! We wouldn't want that smooth skin getting all spotty."

"Don't worry, I never had spots even as a kid."

"You wouldn't. Just out of curiosity, do you admit to any failings?"

"Only one. That I didn't realise how much you meant to me before all this began."

Sobered, they stared at each other then gently kissed, feeding on each other's presence. Breaking away to nibble at an earlobe, Byrne whispered, "Do you think we can make it to bed this time?"

"Dunno." Duncan was already losing his grip on reality.

"You're a lot of help!"

"Mmm ..."

"Bed."

They did make it, though neither of them was exactly sure how.

12

It was eleven in the morning. Alone in Byrne's flat, Peter Duncan heard the announcer's modulated voice and stood quite still. He shivered once, then dropping the sheaf of papers he had been reading through, went over to the radio. Abruptly very cold, he listened. It wasn't a very long report: a prisoner on transfer from Brixton to Pentonville had escaped.

The prisoner was Paget.

His legs were suddenly shaky, and he sat down in an arm-chair. Blank-faced.

Horrified.

No one rang, nothing happened all day, except that the news ran though slight hourly variations as more about the escape became clear.

Lost in thought, Duncan was only aware of anything at all when the news was on. He sat very still, his body stiff in the wide, soft chair, his mind wound as tight as it could be.

After everything, for Paget to be free.

Like gall the knowledge ate into him, and he cursed the world thoroughly, the police particularly, and Paget above all else.

And wondered where he was.

Paget.

Free.

Sometime in the afternoon, he stood up and used the bathroom, wandered from room to room, drank a glass of water. Then went back to the deep chair, staring at cream walls, furniture, pictures, but seeing none of it at all.

All that wasted effort.

All that misery.

For nothing.

Shadows gathered early, the night closing in fast on a cold, cloudy day. It didn't matter. Duncan wouldn't have bothered to turn the lights on even if he had noticed the darkness. There was enough light from the street for him to see shapes. And there was really no need for him to see even those.

He sat. And wondered if there was any point at all.

Byrne came home late. And he was very drunk.

Key just making it into the lock, he pushed the door open and peered into grey darkness. "Peter?"

He could hear a tinny voice, radio or TV he wasn't sure. That was all.

Byrne frowned, closing the door behind him and clicking on a light. Slipping keys into a pocket he tugged his jacket off and dropped it onto the floor.

"Peter?" He called out again, walking a slightly unsteady path into the living room. The light snapped on, very bright.

"Hello."

Duncan blinked, and turned his head. "Have you caught him?"

"Oh, you've heard."

"The radio." He pointed vaguely.

"Oh." Byrne made it to the sofa and sat down, hard. "Oops. That was further down than I thought - " He licked his lips, and peered at Duncan. "You okay?"

"What do you think?"

"I think you're pissed off." Byrne squeezed his eyes shut then opened them wide. "And I went round the pubs, trying to get some information."

"Did you succeed?"

"Only in getting plastered." He giggled, then hurriedly sobered. "Sorry."

Duncan shrugged. " I wish I was drunk, too. Do you know where he is?"

"No. There's not a trace. Bastard might be anywhere. France, Spain, bloody South America for all we know." He was slurring, the words falling ungainly from his mouth. "I was going to ring."

"Why didn't you?"

"I - " Byrne stopped. Then closed his eyes. "I was too bloody afraid to tell you. Too bloody afraid. And I thought, every minute, that we'd get him back."

"Really?"

"Had to think it. Had to - " He pushed himself up, righted, then walked to Duncan, kneeling by him. "Had to."

He stank of beer, of cigarette smoke, of pubs. Duncan shook his head. "I wondered where you were."

"Being a coward." He had two stabs at the words, then swallowed hard.

"Just like me."

"Why?" Bleary eyes widened.

Duncan just sighed, slowly shaking his head. "I should have been out there, talking to people. Someone might know something."

"Don't!"

"What?"

"Think about putting yourself at risk!" Byrne was kneeling up, hands reaching for Duncan's shoulders. "He might be after you."

"And risk his chance of getting away? I don't think so."

"He might." Byrne licked his lips. "Don't risk anything until we know where he is."

"What if you don't ever know?"

"Then I'll keep you safe."

"Oh, that'll help."

"It will!"

"For God's sake! What are you going to be, my keeper?"

Byrne nodded solemnly, then fell backward as Duncan stood,

pushing him out of the way. "Hey!"

"Good night, Byrne."

The room spinning unhealthily, Byrne pulled himself up to lean on the sofa just in time to watch Duncan leave the room. "What?"

"Don't forget to turn the lights out." The disembodied voice spoke from the hallway and there was the sound of a door firmly closing.

"What the fuck!" Byrne blinked, then scratched his head. Leaning back he tried to think it through, but his thoughts were ducking and diving just beyond reach. And the tilt of the room was getting worse. He closed heavy eyes.

Just for a moment.

And fell fast asleep.

The next morning his hangover was priceless.

Falling into a hot bath he soaked some of it away. Fried egg on toast helped, as did the coffee and the aspirin. Just about ready to face work, he crept into the bedroom, found some clean clothes, every movement very quiet in case he woke the still figure curled on one edge of the bed.

For a moment he considered saying something, but in the end just tip-toed out, dressing in the bathroom. He closed up carefully, and went off to work, feeling more than slightly ashamed.

The pub was so unchanged that Duncan might not have been away at all. The same customers sat in the same places, the barman wore the same grey shirt, even the jukebox was still playing *Layla*.

As a reassurance that, come what may, life went on regardless, The Black Lion was a pearl beyond price.

Nodding in greeting to a few faces he knew, Duncan walked over to the bar. "Morning, Pat, how's things?"

"Peter, it's good to see you! Are you after a drink? Come on, the first's on the house." The ruddy-faced Irishman made no comment on Duncan's long absence; he was quite used to his customers making unexplained trips away.

"Cheers, a pint of best then."

The beer was taken expertly from one of the old, china-handled pumps. "There you go and the best of luck to you." Pat leant his elbow on the counter. "I read in the paper about Paget doing a runner. Nice to have friends like that who'll leave your cell door open."

Duncan sipped his beer and made a face at Pat's words. "Yeah, makes you sick. All that effort and then he just saunters out as if he owns the place."

"Well, he did have the front door keys."

"Yeah."

Still sour about the whole thing, Duncan blamed Cadell for not foreseeing that putting Paget in the charge of the police was like politely shaking his hand and waving goodbye. It was unlikely he would ever have escaped Cadell - and if he had then the culprit would have been flayed alive.

And Byrne hadn't helped.

"They won't catch him, he'll be off abroad. Bloody cops, too sure of themselves by far." The landlord sniffed. "Don't know why you ever joined up, Peter."

"Looking back on it, neither do I," Duncan agreed whole-heartedly.

"You're better off out of it, that's for sure."

Duncan smiled, then sipped his pint, content to feel at home, not to be judged in any way. It was always a relief to come back here and find himself still accepted. Ex-copper or not. Mind you, they'd all seen for themselves the shit he'd taken from the police. A discredited copper was one thing, but a discredited copper who couldn't even walk down the street without getting harassed was another. Harassment they all understood.

And bruises.

He had a lot to thank these people for, not least their friendship.

"Listen, Pat, I was wondering if there are any jobs going?"

"Here you mean?"

"Yes."

"Have you done any bar-work before?" A nod that was almost the truth. "Then there's a job if you want it. Lunchtimes only, mind. Will that do you?"

"Brilliant!" Duncan was surprised, overwhelmed with thanks. "When do you want me to start?"

"Tomorrow." Pat grinned at him. "And you get to keep any tips." He was laughing as he went off to serve a fresh group of customers.

"Okay." Duncan was speaking to himself.

He had a job.

He sipped his beer and felt quietly stunned. He'd have some cash again. And something to do other than fret about Paget and finish the book - which was nearly done. Written anyway. There was still the problem of getting it published. Still, between that and working a few hours a day here, he'd be occupied while Byrne was off chasing information about Paget.

Bloody hell. Serving behind a bar. Still, it was better than nothing. Better than sitting in Byrne's flat like a drooping flower waiting for a few moment's attention. He ordered a refill and went to sit at his old table.

And it would be a good place to pick up information.

He sat for a long time, just idling, not thinking. It even worked for a while. He watched, listened, talked football with a pensioner he'd never met before.

Then he was alone again, and there was no more ignoring his thoughts. Fully aware that most of his mind was working hard at ignoring the implications of Paget's escape, the rest of it wanted to pick incessantly at the details, the knowing itching him like a scabbed-over wound. It was unlikely they'd catch the bastard a second time. With his contacts, he'd be off and gone already, probably sunning himself on the Costa already.

Paget on the loose ...

No, it didn't bear thinking about.

Suddenly too edgy to enjoy his second pint, Duncan left most of it and, with a nod and a see-you-tomorrow decided to walk back to Byrne's. The long way around. The exercise would do him good, he'd spent far too long recently sitting down. He felt sluggish, stiff.

Pulling up his collar he stepped out onto the street.

The freezing weather had eased up, and the mildness of the afternoon air tasted more of spring than winter. It was pleasant, walking with purpose through the back-streets, gradually working his way up until he stood above the city. Skirting around Whitestone pond, he decided against going across the Heath, the pavement was a far more direct route and he was getting hungry enough to forego the delights of nature for the more immediate pleasure of dinner. It was getting dark as well, close to the shortest day.

The windows of Byrne's flat faced the back of the mansion block where he lived, so it wasn't until Duncan reached the front door that he realised that Byrne was home. Mildly irritated by the surge of pleasure this realisation produced, he rapped sharply on the door, not even bothering to try his key.

"Where the fuck have you been?"

As the door opened, Duncan's mild greeting died on his tongue in the face of Byrne's grim-faced fury.

"Out, where d'you think." He bit the words off tersely, and pushed past Byrne, not trusting his own temper with a longer explanation.

He heard the door slam, and Byrne was at his shoulder. "I've been back for hours. You didn't leave a message."

"A message?" Astounded by the words, Duncan felt the tension in his gut twist one notch tighter. "No, I didn't. Though if I'd known you wanted an hourly itinerary I'd have been sure to make one out for you. What did you want? Duplicate or triplicate?"

"Well I bloody well need something. I can't worry about where you are all the time."

"Worry! Why should you worry?" Duncan turned to face the irate glare. "I'm not a dog off its lead, you know. I can remember where I live."

"You stupid idiot, Paget is out there on the loose, probably gunning for your head and you're off swanning about London without a care in the world. What are you, thick?"

"Yeah, I reckon I must be - to put up with you!"

"I reckon I'm the one doing the putting, mate!"

"God, you arrogant ..." Pale-faced, with two high spots of colour on his cheekbones, Duncan choked on his words, turning on his heel before the fist that had been his hand let fly at Byrne's face.

"What are you doing?"

"If it's any of your business, I'm looking for something."

"I can see that, but what?"

"Nothing that has anything to do with you."

"Fuck it, Peter, everything about you has something to do with me."

Duncan turned, rage and emotion wiped clean from his face by icy calm. "Really? How did you work that out?"

"Because I love you!"

Not even considering a reply, Duncan scarcely paused before continuing his way through the flat. What he wanted wasn't in the living-room so he headed for the bedroom.

He'd started going through drawers when Byrne's hand fastened on his wrist. For a brief second Duncan looked at it, then slowly transferred his flat stare to Byrne's face. After a moment while time stood still, the hand was removed.

"Don't you ever touch me like that again." Duncan was breathing hard, his glance focused on the marks around his wrist, the new as well as the old. "I'm not your property, Byrne. You can't force me into anything." But he kept his voice even and rational, trying to keep the situation under what slight control was left, battening down the pain that was welling up inside him.

At that moment he found the object of his search: a bunch of keys with an address tab linked to them. Holding them clutched like a talisman, he turned and began to throw his few belongings together. The neat movements were therapeutic and he managed to ignore Byrne.

"Peter, stop it. I didn't mean it, I was worried, that's all."

At the words Duncan paused and turned to look at Byrne, almost flinching in the face of fear so real that it took the last of his anger and shredded it into utter misery. "No, it isn't."

"But - "

"What you really want is to own me, Byrne, and despite evidence to the contrary, I'm not for sale." He picked up his bag and walked back into the main room to jam his notebooks and manuscript away, ignoring the shadow that dogged him.

"Peter, that's not true, I don't think I own you. I don't even think I've bought you!"

"Think harder, Byrne."

"I've thought. You're overreacting, I was worried about you, that's all!"

Duncan took two steps forward and silenced him by brushing cold fingers against his lips, turning away before the bigger man could try and turn goodbye into something else. "This is for the best. Believe me."

He smiled fleetingly, then picked up the bag and headed for the door. Byrne got to it before him.

"No. You can't go."

"Why?" Mild curiosity was all that tinted the word.

"Because you belong here, especially while Paget is out there."

"Very persuasive!"

"I love you!"

"That's not a reason, Byrne. I love you too, but if I stay here," he shrugged, "I could end up hating you."

"Why didn't you say something before?"

Duncan sighed, dragging his free hand through his hair. "I thought you'd get over it, over needing me to be what you want, over treating me as if I was either helpless or here to bend to your every whim. But it's not happening. I don't want us to split up, but we need some space. That's all."

"Space?"

"All I'm doing is moving to the flat that Cadell lent me. I've got a lunchtime job at The Black Lion in Kilburn." His face softened. "Look, this has got to be for the better."

They stared at each other, and Duncan bled with regret that it was so impossible for Byrne to understand. It wasn't as if he were asking for the moon, was he?

231

"I love you, Byrne, more than I've ever loved anyone. But I want to be your equal. Think about what you want from me, and when you want more than a whore, when, and if, you decide you want me as I am, I'll be waiting."

There, he'd said it. Enunciated the word that lay in the shadows of his mind, though bringing it out into the cold light of day hurt just as badly in reality as it always had in his imagination. Guarding his face against any reflection of pain Duncan put his head up. Byrne was reaching out a hesitant hand. "Just let me go."

Slowly, Byrne lowered his hand. "Peter, please - "

"You know where I'll be." He couldn't look at Byrne in case what he saw destroyed his meagre resolution.

He watched as Byrne gave a jerky nod. "Yeah, see you."

"Yeah."

Duncan pulled open the door and stepped outside. The door closed almost at once, and he listened as the locks were turned and the bolt put across. There was no other sound.

Blinking to clear his eyes, Duncan turned and walked slowly away.

The first lunch-time shift in the pub had been a doddle. Numerate, and conversant with most of the drinks that the pub served - it hardly went in for cocktails - Peter sailed through.

He hadn't lied when he told Pat that he had worked in a pub before, just hadn't explained that it was ten years ago and that he'd lasted exactly a week. Luckily he had his temper under better control these days so there was little likelihood of him going for any of the customers, whatever the provocation. It was only Byrne who seemed able to strip all him of all his hard-earned composure. And Paget, but he didn't count.

The fact that it was busy enough to keep his mind off his depression was a bonus, above and beyond the tenner that Pat slipped into his hand after closing time.

One of his customers had been Rosie, still frowned on by Pat but blithely unaware of his disapproval. She was overjoyed to see

Duncan, his obvious health and humour cheering her, especially when he told her that the job was semi-permanent. He'd passed the word through her that he was still Paget-hunting, though it was hardly necessary as, thanks to the blanket newspaper coverage, Paget was, after the football, everyone's favourite topic of conversation. Tabloid headlines had screamed loudly about Law and Order, and after the escape *The Sun* had mounted an anti-corruption campaign that had led to questions being asked about police accountability in Parliament.

Though Duncan knew that meant nothing. What was needed was for the police self-regulating system to be overhauled, and that was extremely unlikely.

Perhaps Paget's escape would, in the long run, be a good thing. His trial alone would have been enough to cause controversy, the escape was well-nigh explosive.

Having money in his pocket, Duncan treated himself to a bus-ride home, and after stopping off at the corner shop, went to Cadell's idea of a place to live. At least the heating had finally kicked into life. Unseasonably mild as it might be, Duncan still felt the cold to a ridiculous degree, and had spent his first solitary night muffled under clothes and duvet, miserably regretting his decision to leave Byrne, if for nothing else than his exceptional proficiency as a hot-water bottle.

Leaving him had been the right thing to do.

It had.

Byrne needed to understand about equality. Even if such egocentricity as Byrne possessed had its own appeal, it wasn't ideal in someone you quite fancied spending your life with. Or hoped to.

Hope. Now that was an interesting concept, perhaps one that he should give up trying to encourage.

After heating some soup, he curled up in the moth-eaten armchair to eat, idly scanning the room. Whoever had done the interior design wouldn't be winning any awards. The north-facing room should have been painted in light, bright colours, not in heavy dark browns.

He wondered about Cadell's other safe-houses. Were they all the same colour? Maybe Cadell had bought a job lot of brown paint, the thought made him smile.

It was all very different from Byrne's.

He sighed so heavily that he almost spilled soup on his jeans. No, Byrne's flat was light and airy. Comfortable. Softly cursing he put the empty bowl down wondering, just out of curiosity, what he'd do if Byrne decided he wasn't worth the effort.

He was chewing on that when the doorbell sounded.

Yes!

A day, not bad.

But the distorted figure glimpsed through the spyhole wasn't who he wanted it to be. It was Graham Cadell.

Probably come around to find out why he'd upset one of his agents. He bit down on a smile at the preposterous thought and opened the door.

"Good evening, Mr Duncan."

"Evening." Peter was curious and defensive all at the same time. "Don't you ever go home? Oh, I am presuming that this is a business and not a social call. Anyway, I only have open house on the first Thursday of the month."

As an attempt to put someone off-balance, it failed. Cadell simply continued as if Duncan hadn't spoken. "I've been meaning to visit, may I come in?"

Duncan nodded, he had no real reason to deny the other man entry. Especially as it was his flat. "Make yourself at home." He closed the door and gestured to a chair. "There's a loose spring but as long as you don't wriggle you'll be fine."

"Thanks for the tip." Coat tails settled around him, Cadell was inspecting the younger man. "You're looking better, work must agree with you."

"How ...? No, don't tell me, I don't think I want to know." Duncan sat on the sofa and tutted disgustedly. "Yeah, the work's okay even though, as you obviously know, I've only been there for two days. Feels better than sitting around waiting for Paget to appear."

"I'm sure. How is the book coming along?"

234

"I'm publisher hunting. Why, do you need someone to ghost your memoirs?"

"I doubt if they'd survive the libel laws." Cadell's voice was dryly laconic.

"I suppose the Official Secrets Act might pose a few problems too."

Cadell let his amusement show, and not for the first time Duncan found, despite the fact that he blamed this man indirectly for Paget's escape, he couldn't help but like him.

"So what do you want?"

"Do I have to want anything in particular?"

"I think so. Besides, I'm not the type you'd normally socialise with, and I'm all out of malt."

"I just wanted to see how you were getting on."

"Really."

"You have a suspicious mind, young man!"

"And I suspect you have a devious one."

Cadell smiled. "That might have been commented on before. How's Byrne?"

Duncan unconsciously averted his eyes, staring at the wildly patterned carpet. "I haven't seen him."

"Really?" Cadell looked around, then focused on Duncan. "I've been thinking a lot about you. And I was also wondering if you wanted a job. We're not police exactly and I think we might suit you."

"What? You're joking!"

"No. Didn't Byrne say anything?"

"Not a word." Duncan shook his head in utter bemusement.

"I am serious. You could be useful to us, you have a network of good contacts and you're tenacious, to say the least."

"Oh, hell."

Duncan stood up and paced across the floor, jamming his hands in his pockets before turning back and glaring at the seated man. "I thought you were going to try and make me stop seeing Byrne." He raked one hand through his hair and fumed. "Not try and get me to join your lot." He frowned suddenly. "What is it, do you need a queer on your payroll so that none of your nice upright young men will have to give it up for Queen and country when you need pillow talk from a faggot?"

"No, that's not a reason." Cadell was apparently unmoved by theatricals.

"Oh." The heat was gone from Duncan's tone. Staring at the calm, lined face he asked more reasonably, "Then why? You know all about my past, it hardly makes me ideal, and you already know I don't want to go back to the police."

"That was what decided me. As for the rest, we're not the Guards, your past is less important than your present: you have intelligence, courage, obstinacy and above all, a sincere regard for justice. I think you should seriously consider my proposal."

"I can't say I'm not flattered, because I am, but the answer is no." He frowned. "Thank you, anyway."

"Just 'no'? Don't you want time to think about it? You don't have to make up your mind now."

"But I have."

Cadell nodded. "Ah, well, I tried."

"And you don't sound surprised."

"I'm not."

"Then why did you ask!"

"Because there was an outside chance, and I don't mind taking the odd risk."

"Sorry." Duncan wasn't sure why he was apologising.

"What will you do? I'm sure you won't want to remain a barman for ever."

"No. It depends on the book, really. I might try journalism, if I can ever learn how to spell."

"I wouldn't bother, most journalists can't; that's why they have editors." Cadell tucked the ends of his scarf inside his coat. "Are you and Byrne still lovers?"

The question was asked in the same tones that Cadell probably used to ask the vicar if he wanted tea, and even as he resented its

236

intrusion Duncan could appreciate the stratagem. Now if Cadell had asked that question a week ago, he might have got more than he bargained for. Duncan was almost smiling as he answered, "I don't know, you'll have to ask Byrne that one."

And when he gives you an answer, let me know.

Slipping a pair of trainers on his feet, Duncan walked with Cadell back to his car, standing in the street as the Jaguar drove smoothly away. He still wasn't certain he knew why Cadell had visited and it worried him: devious wasn't a strong enough word for Byrne's boss.

Slowly he went back inside, locking up, settling back onto the sofa. He still wanted the phone to ring.

For the next week Duncan spent his time hawking his manuscript around various publishers and conscientiously doing his shifts at the pub. In his current mood of remote expectancy it suited him fine, and Pat congratulated himself on helping out a friend and doing himself a favour at the same time - not only had he employed a good barman but he'd acquired the most effective bouncer that he'd ever had.

Duncan didn't see Byrne at all, and by the Friday was convinced that Byrne wouldn't come looking for what he obviously considered should be his by right.

Even the editor who was so enthusiastic about his book at the left-wing publishing house couldn't dent his depression; getting rid of the whole thing was now closer to being a relief than a joy. That, plus the fact that it was now doubtful if Paget would ever answer for the crimes catalogued on the A4 pages, made the whole issue rather academic.

Returning home from the second meeting he decided that he felt rather sorry for the editor, she'd been so enthusiastic that it had been a shame not to be able to reciprocate. But even though he'd tried, it was a level of involvement that was beyond his grasp.

Slinging his jacket onto the sofa, he turned on the radio before making himself a basic supper of fish fingers and tea. Sitting at the cramped kitchen table he slowly ate whilst listening to *The Archers*, something he hadn't done since he was a child, but there was no TV in the flat and tuning to a different station would have involved making a decision.

And he couldn't. About anything.

He could go back to Byrne. Or he could wait.

But -

If only Byrne could understand!

Of course, there was always the heartbreaking idea that what Byrne wanted out of their relationship was exactly what he'd had: a compliant, complaisant companion, who acted as wife and sex-toy all in one.

But maybe being just those things would be worth it, to be with him.

Though surely if that was all Byrne wanted from a partner, then he'd have found himself a nice little piece of domestic bliss years ago.

And there was always the possibility that Byrne had just misread what Duncan wanted. Though if that was so, where was he to set it all to rights?

The problem just wound itself tighter and tighter the more he thought about it.

Disgusted with himself he squirted Fairy Liquid into the washing-up bowl with unwarranted enthusiasm, and ended up elbow deep in a froth of bubbles.

It was undeniably one of those days. He sighed deeply.

Washing up and rinsing done, he'd just about finished getting the last of the bubbles to go down the sink when the doorbell rang. His stomach did an Olympic standard double somersault and landed somewhere under his throat.

Byrne. It had to be -

Unless Cadell had decided to have another go.

Mentally crossing every finger and toe in his body, girding his loins and blithely invoking the help of St Jude, whom he hadn't even thought of since he was ten years old and Jayne Mitchell turned him down, Duncan went to the door.

13

Darkly saturnine, closed-faced, dressed in unrelieved black that enforced the physical power of his body, Byrne leant on the wall opposite Duncan's flat. His arms were crossed and if body language spoke louder than words, Duncan knew he should be intimidated.

Damn it, he very nearly was.

Scarcely trusting his voice, Peter cleared his throat. "Hello, Byrne."

"Peter." Byrne spoke Duncan's name as a greeting and as an observation.

"D'you want a cup of tea? There's a pot on the table." Always there with the right words, Peter. But he couldn't think of anything else to say.

"Ta."

Byrne levered himself off the wall and walked through the open door, his demeanour so closed-off, so remote, that Duncan had to remind himself forcibly that this was Byrne. His Byrne. Not some maniac.

His lips quirking at the fantastic thought, Duncan shut the door and turned back into the room and inadvertently into Byrne's arms.

Even if his life had depended on his ability to resist, Duncan could not have done so. He returned the exploratory kiss with a sigh of confusion. After a moment Byrne stepped back and some of the tension escaped from his face.

"Well, at least that settles that."

"What?"

"That you weren't lying about still loving me."

"I don't lie. Not often anyway."

Byrne nodded, his gaze still utterly intent.

"And I don't tell just anyone I love them," Duncan added.

"No." Byrne smoothed his palms over Duncan's shoulders as if cataloguing the bones. When he continued, it was quietly. "Have you ever said it before?"

"Only to my mum."

"Oh."

Byrne blinked, his hands stilling, then pulling the other man close. They leant into one another and might have kissed, but Duncan shook his head.

"I've been waiting for you. This week's been bloody miserable."

"I wasn't sure what you wanted."

Byrne insecure? Duncan blinked as the knowledge sank in. "Just you."

"I'll stop being such a pig."

"You weren't a pig!"

"No, I just took you for granted. You'd think the last few months would have taught me better." Byrne kissed Duncan's mouth, softly. "The night when I was drunk ... I was clumsy. And when you left, I really believed I'd gone past the point where I could make it all right."

"It takes both of us to do that."

"I worked that out." He smiled, the fine lines around his eyes crinkling. "You know, I had a long speech worked out where I was going to say everything up to, and maybe including, going down on my knees, but ..." He looked for a moment very lost, the strain of the last few days suddenly visible. "But now I can hardly talk."

"You're doing fine."

Byrne took a deep breath, as if inhaling Duncan's presence. "I missed you."

"Yeah, me too."

They stood in the hall, in silence, just touching.

Duncan sighed, a weight lifted from his world. "You're such a mystery, Byrne."

"You can talk."

"All on the surface, me." He suddenly poked Byrne's arm. "Come on, let's pour the tea before it stews."

They moved to the kitchen, still slightly awkward. Duncan poured thick tea into mugs, then sat to watch as Byrne stirred sugar into his. There were still questions. Even though he was happy. Happier.

"Byrne?"

"Yeah?"

"Tell me really, why did it take you so long?"

Byrne's jaw tightened and Duncan watched a pulse beat suddenly at his throat. "Truth?"

"Yes."

"I did think it was over. But, deep down, I also thought you'd come back to me."

"Ah."

"You wouldn't have. I knew that after a day or so. Then it was hard to know what to do, how to be here."

"It took all my self-control, staying away."

"It made me realise something; I fell in love with you as you are, self-sufficient, independent, strong. I was trying to deny all that. I'm surprised you stayed as long as you did."

"It wasn't that bad," Duncan protested. "Besides, I thought that you would ease up after a while."

He reached across the table and stroked a white-knuckled hand where it gripped the mug. "If we are going to live together then let's do just that, together. Talk to me, love me, but don't pretend that I'm either half-witted or don't matter. I want more out of living with you than just sharing your bed."

"Yeah." Byrne's voice was gruff as he slipped his fingers out of the handle to entwine them with Duncan's.

"We're both beginners at this game, give it time."

They met each other's eyes. Duncan smiled. "You know, if a

gypsy had told my fortune the day that I met you and predicted that I'd feel this way, I'd have laughed in her face."

"Me too." Byrne squeezed a thin-boned hand, his grip met strength for strength.

"And I was supposed to be sleeping with you for money." Duncan grinned. "Love? No way."

Byrne nodded in agreement. "You were a whore, I was a punter. And we were both fools. Peter, let's start again. Come back. Nothing matters except you."

"What about my past?"

"It's part of you. And whatever you are, that's what I want."

"Byrne. I've a slight confession."

"Yes?" Byrne sounded relaxed, but his shoulders tensed and the pulse was back at his throat.

"I gave up being a whore a long time ago, hardly was one in the real sense. But since I met you, well, you're the only person I've been with." Why this should seem an almost shameful revelation he wasn't certain. "There's no way I'm anything approaching snow-like purity, but," his lips twisted mockingly, "I'm not that much of a bad bargain."

"Do you think I'd care if you were?"

"Maybe. You're a traditionalist about the strangest things."

"Yeah, well, I don't care about your past." He smiled, a rueful look in his eyes. "Though I can't say I wasn't jealous, before."

"Good. I like that."

"And every cloud has a silver lining. Come here …"

They kissed, long and leisurely. Then parted with a breath, a sigh, warmth.

Watching the square thumb that traced and retraced over his knuckles, Duncan was content. Still curious though. "You ever lived with anyone before?"

"No. Never had the time. Or found the right person. I've paid for sex from time to time, worked my way through the typing pool, dated a few girls who meant a bit more."

"What about men?"

"No one in years. I thought I'd struck gold when I found you, even though you cost me a bloody fortune." Byrne shrugged and squeezed an apology.

"Yeah, well, I was broke, and informers don't come cheap."

"Well, I needed something to spend my salary on anyway. Though come to think of it, if that money was spent on information, perhaps I can get reimbursed by Cadell. Ouch!"

Duncan thumped him. Quite gently, really.

Money. Duncan considered the concept wistfully. "He might give me some cash, I'm still broke."

"Don't take this the wrong way, and I do want you to stand on your own feet, but in the meantime, how about a loan? I ..."

"Byrne, Byrne, stop it! I appreciate the thought, but I don't need it. I wouldn't be kept by you if you were richer than Croesus. I told you, I don't want to be bought. I can only give myself away."

"And will you?" Byrne almost stopped breathing.

Duncan looked up, mischievous. "Yeah. Of course. Now drink your tea."

"Yes, mum." But Byrne was grinning as he drank, finishing it down to the dregs. He carefully placed the mug down. "Will you come back with me tonight?"

"Yes." No hesitation.

And in the end it was as simple as that.

All that Duncan needed now was a real job, an income, the book published, Paget caught and a nuclear arms freeze. Not much to ask, was it?

Roused from his amusement by Byrne's questioning squeeze of his hand, Peter shook his head. "Just an idle thought; you know me, never happy."

"What's wrong?"

"Nothing a decent job and unilateral nuclear disarmament wouldn't settle." He laughed at Byrne's face. "Told you, my brain runs on an erratic course sometimes."

"Erratic? Bloody hell! Never mind, you can explain it later when we're in bed, it'll give us something to do."

"Oh yeah, as if we've ever needed any assistance."

"Well, we're a couple now. They say it's never the same."

"Are you taking bets?"

"You wouldn't get any odds." Byrne smiled. "I bet we last longer than my parents did."

"How long was that?"

"Six months."

"Oh cheers, what a target." He picked up the mugs and stood up to take them over to the sink. "Which one of them brought you up?"

"Neither, an aunt did. Bloody good job too, my mum's a born-again Christian and my dad was a sailor. I'd have gone round the bend with either of them; come to think of it, I still do. More than half an hour of family life and I'm climbing the walls."

"Oh, so they're all still alive?"

"Yeah, I've even been known to go back for Christmas. What about yours?"

"Dead."

Waiting, Byrne was offered only the stiff set of Duncan's shoulders as he washed up. Mugs set to drain, finally Peter turned, leaning back against the sink. "Okay. My mum was a prostitute, she never knew which of her punters got her pregnant. She died when I was thirteen." He smiled, softly, sadly and offered a truth he had rarely shared. "I loved her a lot. I miss her."

"She must have been something."

"Yeah. I tried never to be ashamed of what she did. Succeeded mostly." He was frowning when Byrne's hand cupped his face, not even having seen him move.

"I'm glad there was someone for you." He stroked his thumb over the pale scar by solemn eyes.

"Yeah, she was always that."

"And after?"

"Homes. Fostering." He shrugged it all away.

"And this?"

Duncan blinked, then realised what Byrne was touching. He licked his lips and shrugged. "A fight, sort of. It was what made me think, realise I was doing something wrong with my life." He trapped Byrne's hand in his own and pulled him close. "So I came to London and became a good boy, and then I joined the police. Now you know everything."

"Everything?"

"Mostly. No more really dark secrets."

Not really. But there was dark and darker. Duncan pushed away the thought that Byrne still really didn't understand. Though maybe he didn't need to.

Besides, Byrne was suddenly managing to look very sneaky. "What?"

As he watched, Byrne reached into an inner pocket, drew out a gift-wrapped package. "I forgot, I bought you a present."

"Byrne!"

"Yeah, okay, I shouldn't have, but I saw it and ..."

"All right, all right!" Peter looked at the package, then took it. He waited until Byrne gave him some room and sat back at the table.

"I was walking past this jeweller's and there it was. If you don't like it you can always give it to Oxfam." He was watching Duncan's fingers explore the square packet, then begin to unwrap it.

"Byrne - "

Inside was a twisting circle of gold; heavy, unadorned. Holding it for a moment poised between his fingers, Peter absorbed its simplicity, feeling its cold perfection and absolute craftsmanship. After a moment's hesitation he slipped it over knuckles and hand, onto his arm, where its patina glowed against the pallor of his skin, its clean lines somehow defining the thin strength of his wrist. It was beautiful.

"I'm not trying to buy you. I just couldn't leave it in the shop."

"What a feeble excuse!" But there was no way Duncan was going to throw this back into Byrne's face. "Hey, gifts are allowed, sometimes! It's perfect. Thank you." For a fleeting moment he knew himself to be almost on the verge of tears. Then Byrne touched him.

"I thought it would look good."

"Good job you're always right, isn't it?" A smile took any bite out of the words and suddenly what he wanted to do had nothing to do with crying. He wanted to be home.

Byrne took hold of his hand, a finger running across the gold. "I could have waited, maybe should have done. Sorry."

"Idiot." Duncan sniffed, and took a deep breath. "I'll go and pack." He was already standing.

"Peter?"

"Yes?"

"I love you."

"I know. I love you too." He gave a sound that was close to laughter. "Sentimental, daft pair that we are."

"No roses though."

"That's true. Does that make us safe?"

"Without roses we can still officially be macho."

"Good." A grin, a shake of his head and Duncan turned on his heel.

Half an hour later the safe house was locked up, and together they went home.

Unfortunately home was a mess. Peter unpacked while Byrne read the paper. He looked up as Duncan walked into the living room and had a proper look around.

"Hey, what happened here? You sack Mrs. Mopp?"

"No, she's on holiday."

"Holiday?"

"It is almost Christmas."

"Oh. Yes."

"Not a high point of your year?"

"No, never even thought much of it when I was a kid. My mum always had to work twice as hard and I hardly ever saw her. Then later on ..." He shrugged it away. "What about you?"

"I like Christmas."

"You would. Don't tell me, you like the tree, the turkey, and all the trimmings on both."

"Yeah, not that I normally bother as I'm on call most of the time;

the blokes with families get the time off. And there never seems much point in decorating a tree just for the mice to enjoy."

"Just out of curiosity, how old are you?"

"Twenty-seven, why?"

"Well, leave out the twenty and you might hit your real age." Peter ducked as Byrne was on his feet and a cuff flew past his ear. He was laughing as he backed away.

"Peter!"

Byrne moved but, eel-fast, Duncan dodged behind the sofa, then with an inch to spare made it to the door. He was almost hiccuping with laughter as he ducked into the bedroom where Byrne's flying tackle knocked what little air was left out of his lungs.

Both men were laughing, wrestling on the floor. Byrne knew exactly where to tickle to make Duncan squirm, and he did, until the man underneath him was gasping, red-faced. "Stop! Stop! Oh God ... I'll get a stitch ..."

"Come on then!" Byrne too was breathless, though as much from lust as laughter. "Give in."

"All right! Anything ..."

"Anything?"

"Yes ... yes!"

The hands stopped.

"Okay, then fuck me."

All hilarity gone, Byrne straddled the suddenly still man and waited with breath bated, watching the hazel eyes darken as realisation swept away everything but desire.

"Yes. But don't you mean make love to you?"

Byrne shook his head. "Whatever we do, it'll always be that. But I've got a feeling that if I dress this up in any other way it just won't happen."

He watched Duncan's face, seeing emotions flickering across it. After a moment, Duncan gave a short laugh. "Sussed, eh?"

"Yeah. Now come on, let's get into bed, get out about a quart of KY and get on with it."

"Smooth-tongued bastard, you." He grinned.

247

"Yeah, that's me." And with a flare of need, Byrne lowered his mouth to Duncan's, kissing him, taking it wet and deep and fast. After a minute he eased away, blinking.

Duncan just shivered. "Keep that up and I'll be doing anything you want." And a smile tugged at his glistening mouth.

Byrne just growled and stood up, pulling Duncan after him.

"Byrne. Just one thing."

"Yes?"

"If you don't like it, tell me."

"You think I'd suffer in silence?"

"Possibly, Mr Macho." Duncan nodded.

"I'm not a virgin." He ignored the splutter of Duncan's laughter. "But, yes, okay, it's been a long time."

"Seriously, you might not like it. And I might not be very good at it."

Suspicion made Byrne stop still. "Are you saying what I think you're saying?"

"Maybe."

"Peter - "

"Yeah, well." He looked mildly embarrassed. "At least one of us is virgin at something."

Byrne was more than a little shocked. "You mean all those men and not one of them - "

"No."

"Why?"

"I never wanted to. The guys I fancied were always happy on top, or even just doing other things. The punters? I certainly never found one who wanted to let me have a go; not that I'd want to have touched most of them with a barge-pole. I guess I must see the active part of sex as being something different; more like love. Stupid really."

"No, not at all." Oddly enough it all made a skewed sort of sense. "Though for me it's the other way around. "

They held each other's eyes and smiled in a moment of perfect understanding that needed no more explanation.

Then Duncan sighed forward, brushing Byrne's lips in an almost kiss. "Well, that's all right then."

"Quite." And with that Byrne drew close, pushing the door shut on the world. A soft kiss and he backed away.

Duncan looked serene, happy. He wrinkled his eyes and laughed softly. "Well, I think the first step might be to take our clothes off."

Byrne was about to agree, then paused, watching as Duncan's fingers curved around the hem of his T-shirt and, in one movement, pulled it off, the soft cotton falling to the floor.

The day was getting late, the bedside light the only illumination in the room. Gold tinted, it painted pale skin, touched the flex and glide of fine muscle under thin flesh. Duncan was so desirable. So beautiful. Utterly so. All grace and balance, pale skin, red hair touched into fire by the light. His jeans rode low on his hips, and as Byrne watched they were unfastened, stripped off along with shoes and socks and underwear, all of it kicked aside leaving nothing but Peter Duncan, naked.

A knot deep in his belly, Byrne watched as Duncan ran his hands over his own skin, palming from chest to shoulders then to belly, slowly to groin. Eyes fixed on Byrne, he held himself, cupping the weight of his sex in one hand, pulling on his cock with the other.

Byrne watched and was hard, aching just from the sight of him. "Peter - "

"Clothes, Byrne."

"Oh." Byrne blinked and reached for the small buttons on his shirt, fingers thick and ungainly, fumbling as he watched the slow pull of Duncan's hand over the length of his cock. Trousers were next, pushed down, shoes unlaced and tugged off, all of his clothes abandoned.

And they were both naked.

Erect.

"Come here." Duncan jerked his head. He smiled as Byrne stepped closer. "See this?" He glanced down at his cock, and Byrne followed his gaze, seeing the solidity of it as if for the first time, the darkness of stretched, over-heated skin, the size and weight and strength of it where it jutted so imperiously from Duncan's body. "It will be inside you; fucking you until you come."

Byrne just moaned softly.

"Still want it?"

"Jesus, yes - "

"Touch me then." And he released his own hold, letting the spear of muscle push arrogantly into the air.

But Byrne didn't reach out. Instead he fell to his knees, mouth open, devouring. Hands around Duncan's body, feeling it arch as if electrified.

The carpet rough against his skin, Byrne tasted his lover, swallowed him deep and whole and without restraint. He tasted of salt and desire, of sweet musk. Sliding the cock from his mouth he licked it, lapping like a cat, tonguing the fat vein that snaked down, following it, sucking just where the skin changed to a rougher texture. He heard a moan, and fingers were tugging at his hair.

"Don't, please, I'll come!"

Byrne closed his mouth, and then pressed his face to the red hair at Duncan's groin, breathing deep, pressing his lips to the soft crease where torso met thigh. A kiss pressed to skin and he was on his feet, held close, kissed quickly, grinned at wickedly.

"Bastard! I thought you wanted me to last!"

Byrne grinned lopsidedly. "I just wanted a taste."

"Yeah."

Another kiss. This one was longer, deeper, altogether different, with Duncan's hands defining the shape of Byrne's skull as he explored his open mouth, sucking lips and tongue, biting, grinding their mouths together until Byrne's knees were shaking. Only then did Duncan graciously relent.

Byrne blinked, then took a deep breath. "Let's do it."

He watched as Duncan reached down, curling his fingers around the heat of Byrne's shaft, watching the foreskin slid back by expert fingers, watching the weight of his cock pulse, lengthen greedily.

"Yeah." Duncan nodded, and Byrne found himself pushed down onto the bed, followed, arranged until he was lying in the middle of the cover, just where Duncan wanted him. "Don't move."

Byrne didn't. He just lay still and watched as Duncan found towels, lubricant, tissues, then was back.

"Turn over."

Byrne blinked, and obediently rolled onto his belly, finding his hips bolstered by towel-covered pillows that raised his arse into the air.

"Lovely ..."

He felt Duncan run the flat of his hand down the length of his spine to cup the muscled buttocks. He followed the path of his fingers with his tongue, skilful, arousing with the lightest, surest of touches, licking long and slow at the dip where the spine ended, then down, into the cleft. Byrne felt himself parted by a gentle hand on each cheek. He jumped when Duncan licked him, shuddered when the tongue probed deeper, tantalising, tasting. Slow licks, over and over, until Byrne thought he might not survive to be fucked at all. Then, just when he thought it was all too much, a hand circled his balls and pulled back, just as the tongue pushed into him.

Byrne cried out. He wasn't going to come, but the sensation!

He tilted his hips back greedily, wanting Duncan to have more, hardly feeling as a finger was pushed inside. The second he knew about, but it only made him more hungry. He knew he was writhing, but there was so little thought in him, so much sensation. A third finger, fucking him slowly, the pain not there, not really. Until it truly was gone, and the hand slid from his arse and he could have wept at the emptiness.

Distantly he felt Duncan plant a final kiss before moving. Hands came to rub over his back, long strokes that ended at the curve of his arse, and made his muscles tremble each time.

KY, cold on his skin, warmed by heated flesh, pressed into tightness, pushed deep, one finger again, eased in to the knuckle. Eased out. Again. Again, this time two fingers, sure and certain and curving down, stroking the soft insides, finding such pleasure that Byrne called out in supplication.

A third finger and Byrne had to fight to breathe and finally Duncan took pity, easing his fingers away.

Cool air, then the bed shifted and Duncan was between his thighs. Another shift and something large nudged against sphincter and pushed in against the resistance. Byrne hunched his shoulders and tilted his hips back. He opened himself with every ounce of will-power in his possession and then, with a jolt that made him gasp, he was stretched wide, taken.

"Byrne - " Duncan's voice was a thread of tension. "Is this all right?"

Byrne growled, the sound beyond eloquence. There were no more words, nor need for them. He pulled back, knelt, pushed his face into the rough cotton sheet and opened himself. He groaned as Duncan pushed deep, and they were joined as close as it was possible to be.

A flex of muscle, and Duncan was pulling almost free, then was back, deep, the stroke harder, more angled. Again. And again.

Taken, opened, filled, Byrne felt something change inside him, felt himself open, flower. And somehow, what had been simply pleasure was suddenly beyond anything he had ever known.

He shouted out loud, spine arching as Duncan found a rhythm, used it, fucked with it, lost him in the primal need of it all, until nothing in the world existed but the moment, nothing but the slap of skin on skin, nothing but the need.

Taking and giving. Oblivious to everything else.

Breath sounds, the suck and slap of skin and flesh, sweat, murmurs of need and want and love.

Blind, lost, found, Byrne came first, gasping, shuddering, his body nothing but wanton sensation as the world whited behind his eyes, and the pleasure hit like a knife in his balls, wiping everything away. He came, screaming out loud, just aware of Duncan pumping deep, deeper, crying out, planting his seed and claiming the world.

Byrne awoke to a chilly trickle down his thigh, he shifted slightly and smiled as his body nudged him into remembrance.

"Sore?" Duncan was peering at him warily.

"Yeah." The huge smile gave no doubt that Byrne was blissfully happy.

Duncan smiled too and together they settled back, easily wrapped around each other, the damp discomfort ignored.

"You were very tight." It was more an enquiry than an observation.

"Mmm ..."

"Are you sure I ...?"

"Peter ..."

"Okay, okay!" He grinned smugly. "It's good, isn't it?"

"Yeah." Byrne sighed the word with pleasure.

"Think you'll be up to doing me later?"

"Hah bloody hah." Byrne yawned. "Maybe for our tenth anniversary."

"The ten minute one's been and gone. How about ten hour?"

"Okay."

There was silence for a while.

Then Byrne shifted as if uncomfortable.

"You okay?"

"Yeah."

"Then what?"

"Peter?"

"Yes - "

"The first time we met, did I hurt you very much?"

"What on earth are you talking about?"

Byrne wiped a hand over his face. "The first time we had sex, I wasn't exactly careful."

"No, you weren't at your gentlest, but I really wasn't complaining. I would have said something, you know. And I did come back ..."

"So it was all right?"

"Are you fishing for compliments?" He gently pinched a fold of skin and laughed softly as Byrne wriggled. "It was very good. I won't break, you know. And if you ever did hurt me, I would tell you."

"I know, but, well, I'm sorry about that time."

"Idiot. I don't think you have it in you to really hurt me."

"I should hope not." Byrne sounded slightly shocked at the

thought. Then he paused, some of the ease gone from his muscles. "Enough people have had a go at you."

"What d'you mean?"

"Paget. This." Byrne rubbed his thumb over the scar by Duncan's eye.

"Ah, that."

"Tell me ..." Byrne twisted so that he could look into the other man's eyes.

"God, you're tenacious."

"You said it was a fight."

"Sort of."

"How sort of?"

Duncan sighed. "I was a cocky kid, thought I knew everything, could handle everyone. Then I met these guys, loaded with money, who really worked to impress me. They did. I went to their house for the night."

"And - "

"And found they got their jollies from the rough stuff as much as the sex. I fought them, lost, but lived to tell the tale."

"The bastards."

"I was off sex entirely for a while, and I got out of Manchester and the whole group I was running with. Cleaned up my act in all sorts of ways." He shrugged, dismissing it all. "The scar's a reminder, that's all. And it was a very long time ago."

"I could find them, kill them."

Duncan sighed as Byrne's hand lightly feathered over his cheek-bone. He lifted his head and met Byrne's intent eyes with a serene smile. "You would, too. But don't. I'm over it, and I wouldn't have told you if I thought I could have got away with a fib."

"I'm glad you told me."

"Promise me, Byrne, no vendettas. Don't even think about settling things with those men, they were just scum."

Byrne squirmed then nodded. "All right, I promise."

Duncan yawned, contented. "Good. And can we save the rest of our life histories for another time, I'm bloody knackered."

"God, what stamina ..."

"Stamina yourself." He patted Byrne's limp and sticky cock. "Let's get some shut-eye and see who's got the stamina later ..."

Growling under his breath, Byrne closed his eyes, and with little effort they were asleep.

14

Christmas Eve had decided with typical perversity to be mild and sunny, and the crowds in Oxford Street sweated their way around over-heated shops wearing their best winter coats.

Parked in a backstreet, Byrne ventured into the heaving masses of people, feeling overdressed in cords, polo-neck and dark-brown leather jacket, and feeling very sorry for everyone else who seemed wrapped up in layers enough to cope with Alaska.

Bombing around Selfridges in record time, he made two other visits before battling back to his car, making it there just before the meter nudged over into 'penalty'.

Remembering Duncan's disinterest in the seasonal festivities he'd decided against a tree, but at the last minute couldn't resist crackers, mistletoe and a Christmas fairy that he was going to put in pride of place on top of the Yucca plant. A fairy for two fairies. Very droll. But he thought it might make Duncan laugh.

Not that Peter Duncan wasn't happy. To Byrne he seemed more relaxed and content than at any other time since he'd known him, but Duncan laughing as if he meant it was something to hear, and finding ways to provoke him was fast becoming a hobby.

Packed into the boot along with the other presents were six bottles of Moet; for even if Peter didn't want to celebrate the combination of Christmas and the arrival of a cheque that covered the advance on his book, Byrne did. In fact when Peter had finally got around to

257

showing it to him he'd done a war dance through the flat in celebration.

The fact that the author was left cold by the whole thing was a puzzle, but then Byrne was more or less resigned to the depths to which Duncan could take him in confusion. Just when he thought, yes, this is it, Peter will see it this way, the cussed sod would declare that black was white and that this week he was going to see it as blue anyway.

Never one to let a conundrum beat him, Byrne was content to persevere, however long it took.

Even the rest of their lives.

Bloody hell.

Smiling widely at a thwarted traffic warden, he drove off towards home. Who would have thought it? Even after weeks of reassurance he was still almost awed.

Convinced that by now Paget was sunning himself in warmer climes, Byrne had decided that life was good, talk was cheap and that they were going to have a good holiday despite the worst that the weather, the TV and Cadell could throw at them. With any luck they'd see none of the weather or the TV, and with even more luck neither hide nor hair of Cadell.

Driving up the Edgware Road, Byrne decided to pop in and see Duncan before going home. A quick hello and a pint of Christmas cheer to keep him going until the end of Duncan's shift.

Locking the car and setting its alarm Byrne risked life and limb running across the High Road and dived through the swing doors of the pub.

Glaringly bright with Christmas decorations, The Black Lion still managed to be just about the seediest place that Byrne had ever voluntarily stepped into. Crammed with people all shouting above the blare of Irish music, it was overpoweringly alive, reverberating with a peculiar North London ambience that indulged a party spirit with jubilant abandon. Even the labourers, still in their work clothes, were part of the festivities; as if it wouldn't be long before one of them got up on a table to dance a jig in his steel-toe-capped boots.

Fighting his way through the crowd, most of whom to his knowledge he'd never seen before in his life, he found himself returning a multitude of Christmas greetings as he made his way to the bar. Finally reaching his destination his heart lurched and he knew that the grin plastered all over his face must be inane. But Byrne didn't give a damn. The sight of Duncan made him want to give a whoop of elation, let alone smile.

Dressed in faded jeans that looked as if one more turn around a washing-machine would be their last, and a tatty old green T-shirt, Duncan looked so different from the elegant hustler he'd first met. Not that it mattered. Old, soft denim enhanced the sweet curve of arse and swell of sex, and the T-shirt was tight across a flat belly and straight back.

Bending and straightening to fill the orders that were flung at him, Duncan's easy grace was delightful. It was only when an old biddy tutted over her Guinness that Byrne realised that he was being blatant.

Half-shocked at himself, he began to turn away but then Peter saw him and the blazing flash of smile riveted him to the spot, weak-kneed, and beyond such mundane things as embarrassment.

"Byrne, didn't expect to see you here today." There was more than pleasure in the warmth of Duncan's smile. Nobody would think that they'd only been apart for about five hours.

"I was passing by, thought I'd nip in for a pint." He lowered his voice and leant forward. "And to leer at you, gorgeous."

"Idiot." Duncan brushed his hand over Byrne's, the touch seemingly accidental. "Pint of best, or are you after havin' a Guinness, sor?"

"You know, I never knew this was a Scottish pub! No, I think I'll have a light ale, in a straight glass, please."

Duncan sniffed. "You'll be ordering a pink gin next. And talking of ..." His eyes searched around the room. "Come over to the other side, there's someone I want you to meet."

He disappeared, leaving Byrne to battle through the throng to the far side of the bar. His drink was on the polished oak counter when he arrived, standing next to a wineglass full of creamy, frothy liquid. Duncan was talking to a bleached blonde in a skirt too tight and far too short for her thighs.

"Byrne, I want you to meet Rosie. Rosie ... Byrne." Duncan grinned at both of them.

Gallant to the end, Byrne summoned his most James Bond-like smile. "Rosie, pleased to meet you." He shook her hand lightly. "Any friend of Peter's."

She giggled, clearly liking what she saw. "Yeah, likewise, I'm sure."

Peter was shaking his head in tolerant amusement. "Rosie's got to be off in a minute," he explained to Byrne. "Shame you've got to work today." She nodded and Byrne just controlled his wicked impulse to ask her what she did when he caught Duncan's eye on him and shut his mouth, suitably abashed.

She continued, "My bloke, he'll be in looking for me if I'm not careful. Still, it's been a great lunchtime, ta ever so much, Peter."

"'s okay, any time. But before you go I've got something for you, hang on."

She hesitated and Byrne watched, seeing her affection and concern for Peter written clearly on her over-painted face. Anybody who felt like that about Duncan couldn't be all bad, he admitted. Maybe she could have been quite pretty, but the make-up and the street clothes took away any of the charm that her seeming naivety should have given. Though that was certainly the idea. Shame though, in another world she could have been happy and married and not on as many drugs as she clearly was.

With a flash of pain, Byrne realised what Peter had escaped. Finally saw what strength it had taken. Strength and courage.

Duncan emerged from the back room with a ribbon-festooned parcel in his hand. Finding a dry patch of bar he placed it down in front of her. "Happy Christmas, Rosie." He touched her hand, and blew a kiss across the bar, hoping she'd understand that it was for far more that he was thanking her.

"You shouldn't have, Peter, really it's lovely ..."

She was overwhelmed, and through the smoky air Byrne thought that her eyes were over-bright. Not understanding what his lover was up to, Byrne waited in amused affection. Whatever she'd done for Peter he obviously felt very warmly towards her, he was tense with anticipation, but happy.

"Well, go on, open it. It isn't a joke, you know." Duncan gave the curling ribbons a tweak.

She touched the bright package hesitantly and then grinning to show lipstick-smudged teeth, began to rip the paper off.

It was a bottle of perfume.

Her mouth fixed in an 'O' of childlike delight. She glanced at Duncan for reassurance and when he nodded, tore open the cellophane and opened the box. Taking the top off the bottle she sprayed herself luxuriantly. "Chanel! Peter, it's lovely!" She giggled into her wrist, sniffing the heady scent with abandon. "Wait till the girls get a whiff of this." And kneeling up on the bar-stool, all white thighs and glimpsed knickers, she reached over to give him a huge hug.

Emerging tousled and with a big pink lipstick kiss on his cheek Duncan was laughing. "You like it then!"

"Love it!" Taking one last sniff from the bottle she replaced its cap, putting it, its box and all the wrappings carefully into her bag. Looking up, she smiled brightly at the two men. "Happy Christmas, Peter, and you, Byrne. Mmmm, I feel all posh now, and dead sexy." She tried to vamp at him but spoiled the effect by giggling.

"Happy Christmas, and you don't need perfume to be sexy, Rosie, go on with you. Try and have a good time, won't you."

"Yeah, and you." She sniffed her wrist again in delight.

"Go on, off with you or you'll be here till closing time." Peter waved her away, smiling as he said it.

"I know. Still," she brightened, "they won't be able to say no with me smelling like this, will they? I'll make a fortune an' we can all retire to the seaside. See you after the holiday. Bye." And finishing her drink in one gulp she gave her skirt a cursory tug, and disappeared into the crowd.

When she had gone Byrne turned and sipped his beer, wrinkling his nose before putting it down. "Peter, unless they've started brewing this with a dash of Paris's best, your Rosie was a bit enthusiastic with her spraying."

Wafting his hand in front of his face and coughing Duncan agreed. "Sorry, Byrne, but I had to give it to her before she left; I won't see her again until after Christmas."

"Who is she?"

Duncan considered what she was against what she'd actually done for him and found that he couldn't really put it into words. Eventually he'd sort it out and tell Byrne. All of it. "Somebody I've known for a long time. When we've got a couple of hours to spare I'll tell you all about her."

Byrne nodded, and forgetting what he'd already discovered took a gulp of his beer. "God, that's disgusting." He made a pained face and wiped his mouth.

"Want another, is it too weak?" Duncan's laughter was scarcely hidden below the surface. "I could put a double shot of perfume in it next time, or would sir prefer Yves Saint Laurent?"

"Comedian."

"No, seriously, do you want another drink, because I'd better be getting back." Pat was already making pointed gestures at his watch. "Or I'll be out on my ear."

"No, it's all right, I'll go home and clean my teeth." Byrne smacked his lips, tasting the inside of his mouth.

"See you later, then." Duncan made a flapping movement at the landlord. "I'll try not to be late."

"Yeah, I've got a couple of surprises for you."

"Idiot, love you." The last words were mouthed so quickly that Byrne almost missed them and then Duncan was gone, fending off a barrage of orders as he went back to his job.

Driving home, Byrne felt blissfully happy. When Duncan got back from his shift they would have four whole days off together. In amazement Byrne realised that it was probably longer than they'd managed to spend with each other since, well, ever.

Four days, with any luck they'd only have to get out of bed in order to stock up on food and alcohol. Maybe a walk in the park. Or maybe not.

Considering some of his purchases, and contemplating the uses to which the odds and ends he'd bought in Soho would be put to, the distance back to his flat telescoped, and he was parked outside before he got to the end of their possible variations. Byrne gathered his belongings, locked up the car and headed for the stairs.

At his door, juggling packages, he got as far as inserting the key into the deadbolt when the touch of cold metal against his neck stilled every muscle in his body and the faint hairs on his neck lifted in absolute fear.

"That's it, Byrne me old chum, take it really easy, but hurry up with opening that door."

Dry-mouthed as adrenaline poured through his system, Byrne obeyed.

Paget.

You bastard, he thought. But he was really cursing himself and the pathetic laxness that had let Paget take him.

"Get inside."

Byrne obeyed, listening, aware, waiting for a chance. He heard the door close. "Paget …" He started to speak, but the words ended in a gasp as something hit him hard, and pain burst like a firework behind his eyes, taking all consciousness away.

"Cheers, Pat, and all the best to you as well."

"Peter, have a glorious time, you hear. 'Tis the season to be jolly …" He was singing as he locked the pub door. Walking away, Duncan shook his head. It wasn't often that Pat had a drink at work but when he did, well, he obviously liked to make it worthwhile. Not exactly sober himself, Duncan decided he wasn't too far gone to drive, and by half-four he was home.

Patting his top pocket to reassure himself that Byrne's present was still there, he was walking up the corridor to Byrne's flat reaching for his keys when, at the door, he stopped and glanced down.

Outside, next to the mat, were three carrier bags.

He stilled, instantly.

Maybe Byrne was inside and had forgotten them.

Maybe he couldn't carry them all at once.

Or maybe -

He crouched down, carefully peering into the bags.

Six bottles of champagne, various parcels, some already gift-wrapped.

Damn.

Byrne would never have left this outside for passers-by to pick up. He liked his champagne and it was far more likely that the bottles would be chilling comfortably in the fridge.

Unless he was just coming back, maybe he'd had too much to carry.

Hardly breathing, Duncan waited, listening.

Nothing.

So.

Paget. It had to be.

But where? What if he was still here, in the flat with Byrne -

Tension shivering along his nerves, Duncan stood up. Should he go and call Cadell? Or just knock?

He breathed out slowly through his nose, and wished earnestly for a gun, some sort of weapon. Sweat prickled under his T-shirt, and with a decisive movement he took out his keys. As silently as possible he inserted the key into the lock. It turned with a sharp click of metal moving metal.

And the door was open.

Standing to one side of the frame, his heart beating fast and loud, he narrowed his eyes, peering into the slice of darkness that widened as it swung open. Weighing his chances, half-convinced that gunfire would greet him, he stepped through the door.

And switched the lights on.

Empty.

He swallowed, scanning around, and his eye was caught by something shining on the floor. Crouching, he touched cold fingers to the mark, lifted them, and could have wept when he saw they were red, covered in the darkness of drying blood.

He swallowed nausea, and forced himself to stand, to check every room. Only then did he reach for the telephone. It took six rings before a voice answered, yet his breathing still wasn't back to normal.

"This is Peter Duncan, I need to speak to Cadell."

"I'll put you through to his secretary, one moment please."

Another voice. "Graham Cadell's office."

His patience was wearing thin and the hand grasping the telephone was slippery with sweat. "This is Peter Duncan, I need to speak to Cadell urgently."

"I'm afraid that he's in conference at the moment, would you like to ring back later or ..."

"For fuck's sake, can't you understand, this is urgent! Let me talk to him now. I'm not messing about, this concerns Byrne."

"I'm sorry ..."

"No. Are you listening to what I'm saying, woman? I need to talk to him now. Look," he took a deep breath and tried hard to sound sane. "Please, you must!"

She relented. "I'll see. Please hold the line."

Thirty seconds later, a sharp voice filled his ear. "Mr Duncan..."

"Cadell, I'm at Byrne's, I think that Paget's taken him."

He wasn't sure what reaction he expected but it wasn't the measured, "Why?"

"Because there's blood staining the carpet and half of Selfridges' Christmas department out in the hallway! For Christ's sake, just believe me and get over here." And he crashed the receiver down before he said anything he would really regret.

Wiping his mouth on the back of a shaky hand he went to crouch by the bloodstain. There wasn't much, but it was fresh; even in the centrally-heated flat it was scarcely drying at the edges.

Standing up he slowly walked from room to room; the only thing he could find out of place were the bags out in the hall. He brought them inside, but couldn't bring himself to open any of it.

265

Slowly the blind, thoughtless desperation left his mind, leaving him implausibly calm. He wanted Byrne very much; to touch him, feel him, cry on his shoulder, even look a fool for panicking about his absence, anything rather than cope with the thought of no Byrne at all.

Ever.

Because of Paget. Which meant because of himself.

Sick with guilt, with grief, with fear, he sank into an armchair and closed his eyes. Bent forward, elbows propped on his knees, he stared into nothing.

There was only one tiny sliver of hope; Byrne wasn't dead. There would have been more than blood to come home to. Sickened, he closed his eyes.

Why hadn't Paget waited? He could have had Duncan as well, here, now, no waiting.

Unless this was all just to make him sweat, suffer.

If so, Paget was succeeding very well.

The bastard had to be round the bend though, to give up on escape just for revenge.

Unconsciously, he reached up and rubbed gently at one series of small round scars just under the neck of his shirt. They were raised, the skin still red when he looked in the mirror. He could remember the pain. Remember Paget's face, and the smell of his own burning skin.

Now Paget had Byrne.

Rather than face that, he stood and began blindly to pace the room. Three turns later the doorbell rang.

"Duncan." Cadell pushed into the room, Murphy right behind him. "What's this all about?"

"Paget must have taken Byrne, I'm sure of it." He couldn't find the right words and settled for plain desperation. "Do something."

"Sit down and tell me about it." Cadell was assessing the man in front of him. After a moment he tutted softly under his breath. "Aidan, make a cup of tea, will you, and get the technicians up here for a phone tap."

Duncan watched as Cadell sat down, easing the knees of his trousers as he lowered himself into the chair. His explanation was short, and was listened to intently.

It didn't take long. Cadell had his mouth open to reply just as the phone rang.

They both stared at it, then Cadell gestured for Duncan to pick it up.

"Peter Duncan speaking." Better to be clear, just in case.

"Hello, Peter." His skin crawling, Duncan could hear the gloating smile spread on Paget's face. "Is Cadell there yet? I expect a fast worker like you would've managed that."

"Paget."

"I want you, faggot. Byrne here's no fun, but he's still alive and if you want him to keep on living you'd better do exactly what I want, when I want. Instant obedience, and your playmate survives. I might even let him go. Once I've got you. I'll ring back in two minutes with instructions, be prepared."

And the line went dead.

Cadell was standing over him. "What did he say?"

Duncan mutely looked up, then carefully replaced the receiver, mildly interested to see that his hand was quite steady.

"Come on, man, spit it out."

Seeing Cadell's impatience only deepened Duncan's calm. He carefully wiped his palms down the pale denim of his jeans before replying.

"He wants me." Duncan looked up. "He's going to ring back in a minute with instructions for what I've got to do." There, it was easy to be calm and collected. With any luck Byrne would behave in the same way when, and if, Paget released him.

Cadell turned on his heel. "Damn it, where's the equipment?"

"They're caught in a jam about a mile away, sir."

"Jesus."

The telephone rang, making all three of them start and Duncan lunged for the receiver.

Paget, of course.

"Still no little clicks, Peter, not been able to get a monitor in yet? Not that it would matter if you did. Not while I've got what you want, right?"

"Paget, tell me ..."

"Tell you what? Where Byrne is, maybe? Or how he is? Oh, I'll do that. Maybe. When I feel like it."

Paget sounded as if he were enjoying every minute, his voice edged with cruel triumph.

Bleakly, Duncan knew suddenly that Paget was really quite mad. What else but insanity could mean that revenge came before freedom.

Paget stopped chuckling. "Is Cadell there?"

Duncan hesitated, but decided on the truth. "Yes."

"Well, tell him to go fuck himself." Paget laughed uproariously, then suddenly his voice was hard and cold, breathy as he forced his lips against the mouthpiece. "Now listen, be at Charing Cross, by the monument, in an hour. Someone will meet you there. Oh, and don't bring anyone along, we don't need any company. Don't be late."

"Paget ..."

But he was talking to an empty line.

Duncan carefully replaced the receiver, avoiding meeting Cadell's intent gaze. He had the glimmer of a plan, but how much rope would Cadell allow him? Enough to hang himself, without a doubt; but Paget as well? A shame English law was so picky about such things.

He tried to keep all speculation off his face as he stood up. "I've got to get to Charing Cross. I'll be met there, I don't know who by."

At that moment two men were let into the flat by Murphy. The three of them started talking in low voices as Murphy filled them in on what was happening.

Cadell interrupted. "It's too late to do anything with the phone. Just get Duncan here wired."

"No. Paget's too wised up, I'll be body-searched."

"Not outside Charing Cross station. Listen, Duncan, we need to know where he's taking you."

"No. I don't want anything. Any hint of surveillance and Byrne will be dead." They both would be, but that wasn't an issue.

"At least wear a tracer."

Duncan was unconvinced, but in the end gave in with the thought that what could be fitted could be un-fitted. He let them attach the tiny transmitter to the collar of his old leather jacket, standing silently while the technician did his job, concentrating on the dark speckling of beard on brown skin, on the slight smell of sweat that wafted up when the man moved. Anything other than think beyond the now. If he just dealt with it second by second, then maybe he could cope.

"There."

Duncan smoothed his collar back, and turned as Cadell spoke. "We'll follow you, discreetly."

"All right."

"We'll get him."

"And Byrne?"

"Of course."

Duncan merely nodded, and wondered silently exactly how much Cadell was prepared to sacrifice in order to get Paget.

Excusing himself he walked along the hall and into the bedroom, closing the door quietly, moving to sit on the bed.

In a moment of silence he sat still, one hand resting on the bed-cover, the other relaxed on his knee. He wished he could be sure of Cadell, at least sure enough to share his plan. But the letter of the law wasn't, in Cadell's eyes, something to be played with. And Duncan was going to do that, and more. He wanted both himself and Byrne out of this alive. Simple. He also wanted Paget dead.

If he got the chance.

So, no Cadell, no back-up. Paget the policeman would be expecting that, and it was always best to do the unexpected. Or whatever it took to keep Byrne alive. Alive and well and out of Paget's sadistic reach.

Duncan shivered convulsively.

Setting his jaw he stirred, rolling his shoulders in an effort to unlock their tension. Sliding back one of the wardrobe's glass doors, he crouched down to rummage. With a grunt of satisfaction he pulled out his canvas hold-all, unzipping it to pull out various bits and pieces. On his feet, he pulled the bedroom door open a crack, listened, then walked steadily across to the bathroom, shutting himself in and locking the door.

Let Cadell think he'd got a bad case of nerves; it was better than him knowing the truth.

He stripped off his jacket, letting it fall to the floor. His T-shirt followed. Naked to the waist he sat on the edge of the bath. The objects he had retrieved from the bedroom were on the side, and he picked up an oilskin wrapped package and, very carefully, unfolded the layers of cloth, revealing the stark shape of a knife; a hunting knife with a wicked, edged blade.

He stared unemotionally at it, resigned.

A long time ago, in a different life, he'd taken the first money a man had ever given him for the use of his body and exchanged it for this. Protection. Safety. It had even worked, most of the time.

Solemnly, tender as a lover, he pressed a finger to the glinting edge. Then raised his hand and smiled emptily as a thin beading of blood welled where the steel touched his flesh.

He sucked the blood away.

Cadell wouldn't be happy. Not that it really mattered.

He'd brought along tape and scissors too. Concentrating, frowning, he cut off a series of strips, and then strapped the knife to his forearm. The metal was cold against his skin, though it warmed quickly. Enough tape to keep it in place, not too much so it would pull free when it was needed. He hoped he'd gauged it right.

He flexed his arm, nodded. The knife was small enough to fit easily between his elbow and wrist, flat enough not to show once he was dressed. Unless Paget wanted to waltz with him it would be hidden, safe.

He stared at the blade, touched it. Such a slim hope. Though better than none.

Better than none.

He dressed again, pulling on his T-shirt, tucking it in, easing into his jacket. The tape he hid in a cupboard, and went out to face Cadell with all the acting ability that he possessed.

He walked into the living room, straightening as everyone turned towards him. He shrugged. "I'll be off, then. I wouldn't want to be late."

Cadell nodded. "We'll never be far behind you. As soon as we know where Byrne is we'll get you both out. Just keep Paget occupied until we're ready. Good luck."

Duncan stared at the hand that was extended towards him and cautiously reached to clasp it in return. "Thank you." He released Cadell's hand and backed away, unnerved by an intent stare that seemed to follow him through the walls, all the way out of the flat, down the stairs and into the street.

Duncan parked in Villiers Street. Locking up, he paused. From somewhere he could hear carols being sung, though the raucous laughter coming from a pub almost drowned them out. It was dark, late enough.

Avoiding groups of merry-makers, he walked up to the brightly-lit station, edgily wondering what would happen; who would meet him; if they would take him to Paget or just hand over an address. A bubble of fear kept rising in his gut, but he held it back, swallowing it ruthlessly.

Turning left, he was there, in the wide space in front of the station and instead of pavement under his feet there were cobblestones. Expectation made him sweat and, as he walked across to the monument, he looked into the face of every person who passed him by. No one reacted; except for a suited man who clearly thought he was being picked up. Though he wasn't mistaken for long.

Duncan ignored the curses and went back to waiting.

It was surprisingly quiet. In the distance he could hear shouting, more laughter, the rumble of trains going in or out of the station. All the shop-workers would have been let off early, and anyone who wasn't already at home would be snug in pubs and restaurants, holding out until the last minute.

He leant against the elaborate stonework and wiped his hand across his mouth. He was on time. Unless the contact had been early.

Though there was always the possibility that Paget was cruel enough to make him wait all night and then arrange something else tomorrow.

Christ knew what he'd be doing to Byrne in the meantime. Sweat trickled down his back despite the evening chill. He was at the right station. On time. He only had to wait.

Moving slightly so that he placed himself in a pool of light cast by a street lamp, he tried to concentrate on not thinking at all and had succeeded so well that he jumped when a voice spoke his name.

"Peter Duncan?"

What looked like an unmarked police Rover had drawn up in front of him, and the driver, still inside, was holding out a piece of paper. The man shook it impatiently and Duncan walked forward to take it, just as the car drove off.

"Hey!" He shouted in frustration, smelt the acrid stink of burning rubber, and cursed thoroughly. He'd wanted someone to take him to Paget; another body to use as bargaining power. Well, that was that. He took a deep breath and unfolded the paper. All that was written on it was an address, one he didn't recognise at all.

Jogging back down Villiers Street, he unlocked the car and got in. A rummage in the glove compartment unearthed a battered A-Z for London and he clicked on the overhead light to peer at it. Cursing his lack of speed he finally found the map reference and the right page, following his finger down the curling path of the river to a maze of streets he knew to be half-derelict.

Byrne was being held in one of the old warehouses. Not a bad choice: miles of abandoned buildings flanked on one side by the Thames and the other by slums. You could stay lost there for days, maybe longer; even kids wanted more interesting places to vandalise.

Tossing the A-Z onto the passenger seat, he tapped his fingers on the steering-wheel and came to a quick decision. Deftly he unpinned

Cadell's tracer, holding it for a moment, turning it in his long fingers. Then, window wound down, he dropped the tiny silver disc into the gutter.

From now on there was going to be no law: only justice.

Calm, ice-cold, he turned the key, starting the engine. Putting the car into gear, he drove away, cutting back to the Embankment and following the river east.

15

Waterloo, Blackfriars, Tower; he passed bridge after bridge, sometimes driving along the very line of the river, sometimes taken on detours inland by the no-entry signs and one-way streets. Always he came back to the water, the darkly moving mass of it following as he drove.

Away from the prosperous centre the city became darker, grimier. A few high-rise estates, garish with tinsel and artificial snow caught his eye, then he was past them, into streets untouched by the developers, where terraced houses edged together and the few shops were mostly boarded up, empty. Further on and there were lights; sweat-shops still working, even tonight.

The streets were quiet, hardly anyone around. He drove past Wapping and turned south, into the Isle of Dogs and past the old West India Docks.

Here the street names changed, became evocative of another time; a time when the river had been worked, when a thousand ships had sailed from the now- abandoned quays and the spoils of an empire were sold from her wharves. Jamaica Street, Havannah, Masthouse, Cuba, Spindrift, Empire, down to where the river folded back on herself and there was nothing at all but abandoned, broken warehouses.

There he slowed and turned into a tight maze of streets, parking by a corner, shutting the engine off to sit back, eyes closed as if in thought or prayer.

After a minute, he climbed out of the car and, caught by superstition or foreboding, quickly crossed himself, forehead to belly, shoulder to shoulder.

Swallowing hard, he wiped his palms on his jeans and locked up the car. Someone might come back for it. If he was lucky.

Byrne, maybe.

Byrne.

They hadn't had enough time. Not nearly enough.

His chest ached at the thought; of never holding that strength again, of never being held by it. Touching the alien comfort of the knife taped to his skin, he knew what he had to do.

Somehow.

Faced with the darkest of possibilities, he found that, perhaps for the first time in his life, he really wanted to live. Wanted to so badly that it hurt, the need a physical pain in his body, in his bones. But he needed Byrne's life even more. Wanted that with absolute conviction.

His mind was quite serene as he moved away from the car.

There were a couple of street-lamps illuminating the narrow street, and he walked along peering at the tall buildings with their huge doors, until he came to one displaying a faded legend on its split and peeling green paint: Dawson & Son. Tea Importers.

Dry-mouthed, he stood and stared. Listened. Then, before his courage could give way he walked up to the small door set within the larger one. Reaching out he put his hand against it and pushed. With a loud creak of ancient hinges it swung open and he stepped inside into utter darkness.

Still, nerves prickling under his skin, breath tight and shallow in his ears, he waited for his eyes to adjust. Listening hard he could hear nothing but a silence so absolute that the air itself seemed muffled, dead, stinking of rot and disuse.

The floor creaked as he shifted his weight. Nothing else stirred.

Slowly his vision returned, and enough light spilled in through the open door for him to see around. He was standing in a large room;

floor, walls and ceiling all made from rough wooden boards. The floor was filthy with dust and worse. Piled in one corner were rags and old papers, the remains of some tramp's bed. Bottles, all empty, mostly broken, lay along one wall. There was nothing at all of any worth, no furniture, no Paget, and no Byrne. Just dust and decay. No windows, no doors other than the one he had walked in through. And, on the far wall, a single flight of shallow stairs that led up into shadows.

Blood drumming in his ears, he stepped forward, the old floorboards groaning softly as he walked. If Paget were here, then he'd know he had a visitor. If he were here. If Byrne were here.

Fifteen paces to cross the room. There were more shadows here, less light. The stairs looked rotten, but he set foot on them anyway, weight set down cautiously with each upward step. He was so on edge that he was scarcely breathing, adrenaline pulsing through his veins, every primal urge telling him to run away, to be safe. Instead he went on.

The stairs led to a short corridor. And another door.

It seemed far more difficult to open than the last. Wiping sweat from his eyes, hesitating only slightly, he turned the handle and pushed the door open.

Onto darkness.

"Paget?"

Duncan winced as his voice cracked. But there was no answer. He stepped though, finding floor where he had half expected emptiness, and closed the door behind him.

Just as the overhead light suddenly clicked on.

Heart trying to beat its way out from his ribs, half-blinded, Duncan backed into the wall.

"Hello, Peter."

Paget. At last.

Duncan took a steadying breath and, blinking past the brightness, looked across a dingy, bare room that might once have been an office, past the walls with their rotten plaster, into Derek Paget's mocking face. The big man was leaning casually against the far wall, one hand by the light-switch, the other holding a gun that pointed unwaveringly at a bound man lying by his feet.

Duncan took a step forward, then stopped as the gun muzzle lifted. Tied with rope, ankles hitched to wrists pulled tight behind his back, Byrne was very still, limp, a gag wrapped tight around his mouth. Duncan couldn't tell if he was conscious. Or even alive.

"Nice of you to call, faggot."

Duncan ignored him. "Is he all right?"

"He's still alive, yeah."

Duncan clenched his hands into fists, and held still by will alone. In the stark light cast by a naked bulb he was white-faced, grim. He dragged his gaze from the bruised and bloodied form of his lover up to Paget's relaxed and grinning face.

"Then let him go." He held both hands away from his body in surrender. "Come on, I'm here now, you don't need Byrne any more."

"How sweet! But do you really think that I'd let flash Harry here run off to get reinforcements? Oh no, I'm hanging on to him until the last minute. And even then - " He shrugged.

"But you promised!" And as soon as the words were out of his mouth, Duncan regretted them, knew he sounded like a child.

Paget laughed. "Ooh, are you going to have a tantrum?" His voice changed, and he was suddenly angry. "I said that if you did what I want, then he might survive. And he might. Besides, he's quite happy, aren't you?" He stepped forward and kicked Byrne, hard enough to force a grunt of pain past the gag.

So Byrne really was alive. Even if only partly conscious.

"Byrne?" No answer. Duncan looked back at Paget. "Let me check he's all right."

"Ah, such sweet concern. Been missing him, have you?" He crouched down and ran the gun barrel across Byrne's cheek. "I don't think I'll kill him. At least he had the excuse of only following orders. Unlike you!" Paget glared, then just smilcd. "Well, you enjoyed watching me squirm, now I'm going to enjoy you."

"I didn't enjoy it, Paget."

278

"No?" Paget stood up. "You know, I sat in that fucking cell and dreamed about killing you. In my fantasies I've topped you every way that's ever been thought of and, because I'm an inventive bastard, a few that haven't. I'm glad you came. Though you might regret it, might even regret that the dope didn't finish you off. It would've been a lot less painful than how you're really going to die." He looked squarely at Duncan and smiled, the blond stubble on his chin glinting brightly.

Duncan looked at him, noting the greasy, overlong hair, the unkempt and unwashed clothes. Paget must have been sleeping rough. Maybe even here. Maybe that bed was his. And the bottles.

He didn't look reasonable. Certainly not sane.

Duncan swallowed on the lump in his throat. "Paget, you've just admitted that you only want me, so let him go. Please." He forced the plea out of his dry mouth.

"So you can beg for him, can you? You know, in all the time that Kerry and I had you, we couldn't get you to beg for yourself once. Not once! Little cunt like you, should have been easy. Now, a couple of minutes up here and you're begging already. Begging me. So do you really think I'd let Byrne go, when I can make you do anything I want just by hurting him?"

Feeling quite sick, Duncan closed his eyes.

"Anything I want. And I can prove it. Come over here."

Duncan went. Feeling as if every muscle in his body had turned to stone, he went across the room, past a boarded up window, walking under the light; the creak of boards under his feet the only sound as he obeyed Paget's order.

"Very nice."

Duncan stopped a few feet away, Byrne's body between him and Paget.

"Now face the wall, you know the routine."

He did.

A foot or so away from the wall he stopped and reached forward, pressing his palms to the plaster, leaning his weight onto outstretched arms. Waiting.

279

Paget's footsteps sounded loud as he approached. Duncan tried not to think, but Paget was touching him, and the sour, whisky-reek of Paget's breath was cloying in his nostrils, and the stink of his body was far too strong.

The skin on the back of his neck crawled as, very gently, Paget brought the gun to rest against his neck. "You can do better than that."

Duncan widened the spread of his legs.

"Better."

The gun cold at his neck, Duncan held still as Paget searched him. Splayed against the wall he could only wait as fingers insinuated intimately, making him squirm.

"Don't you like being touched? I bet you like it when lover-boy does it. Though I still think you should try it with a real man."

Duncan gasped as a big hand gripped his genitals and squeezed.

Paget was laughing, and his hand tightened until Duncan was shuddering, hissing with the pain that stabbed up from his groin. Pressed into the cold wall Duncan held quite still, sweat dripping down his face, knowing that Paget was watching, wanting, loving his reaction, but quite unable not to show how much it hurt.

Paget suddenly let go. Duncan gasped in relief, then held still as the gun barrel ground hard into his side. "How does he treat you? Like a girl, I bet."

"None of your business."

"No? I think it is. Does he fuck you, get you to lie there like a woman while he gets off on using you?"

"We're lovers, Paget. Ever been to bed with someone who cared for you, or do you only ever pay for it?"

"Lovers." Paget spat out the word. "He fucks you because you're there, that's all."

"No." Duncan forced his head round, met the insane, pale eyes. "We love each other, we make love to each other."

"Pussy faggot, you're nothing but a whore!"

Duncan smiled, his eyes still locked with Paget's. "I'm *Byrne's* whore."

"And mine." Paget was suddenly laughing, no humour in the sound at all. "Mine. Get undressed."

Making no move, Duncan twisted his face away, but the gun cracked across the back of his head, scraping skin from his cheek as it hit the wall.

Paget was hissing in his ear, body close, but not close enough. "Come on, Duncan, or I'll shoot bits off your sweetheart for you, starting guess where."

"Back off then, I can't move."

Paget shifted a fraction. Though still Duncan remained pressed close to the wall, breath tight in his lungs, apprehension like a hand squeezing his heart.

"Two seconds, whore."

Duncan shuddered. Then cried out loud as Paget turned suddenly and fired, the sound shockingly loud.

"Byrne!" He tried to turn, but Paget's heavy weight held him tight against the wall, the metal grinding into his ribs, the hardness of arousal pressing against his arse.

"There, like I said, I keep all my promises."

"Byrne!"

"Shut up. This time I just fired at the wall. Next time - "

The gun was digging hard into his ribs as Paget's left hand wound tightly into his hair. Clenching his teeth as Paget gave him an inch of space, Duncan brought his hands down to his waist and slowly unfastened his jeans.

"Come on, get a move on, you've done it before."

Yes, he'd done it before, even in similar circumstances, but none of that made it any easier. He prayed that Byrne was unconscious, that he would know nothing of this. If he survived to remember anything.

Awkward, Duncan pushed his jeans and underpants down past his knees, straightening to let his unsteady hands rest on the wall, his forearms flat to crumbling plaster.

"That's better. And when I'm finished you can tell me how good I was."

Gun to Duncan's neck, Paget was breathing fast as, with his free hand, he unzipped his own trousers.

Taller, heavier than Duncan, he had to spread his own legs wide to find a usable angle, pushing and fumbling between cold arse cheeks, cursing, using muscle and cruelty, until finally he forced his cock-head inside.

Slammed against the wall, Duncan strangled a scream, hating himself, knowing he was mewling from the pain, knowing the sound excited Paget but unable to stop it escaping. Sickened, he bit his lip, tried for silence, but had to whimper as the dry cock was shoved deeper into his body.

And his fingers crept closer to the knife.

When Paget finally began to fuck in earnest, the driving hurt of the gun in Duncan's side eased. Almost beyond recalling what he had to do, Duncan swallowed dryly, tasting blood from his lips. Beyond the pain there was something he needed to do.

The knife. He brought his arms down, slid ungainly fingers up his sleeve. Prayed.

And, with a twist of his body that nearly ripped him in two, he pulled the blade free, and rammed it with all his strength back between Paget's ribs.

Too fast for Duncan to follow, the gun fired, exploding plaster from the wall. Someone cried out and Paget choked obscenely, gave a racking shudder and slumped forward, boneless, his weight dragging both men away from the wall to fall to the floor in a heavy tangle of limbs.

Tears hazing his sight Duncan moaned and, revolted by the touch and cling of Paget's body, scrambled clumsily away. He made it to his knees and forced himself to look back.

And stared into Paget's sightless eyes.

In the sudden quiet Duncan remembered how to breathe.

Then he cursed as pain flared from the line of fire that arced along his ribs. His back and side were warm, soaked in blood, most of it Paget's, some of it his own.

Clammy with reaction he found he was shaking.

But he was still alive. Blinking away sweat, he knew it was real; he was alive.

A miracle.

Which left only Byrne.

Biting down on the pain, he crawled across the rough floor-boards, hardly daring to look. At the bound man's side he lifted his head, and met Byrne's anxious eyes.

Duncan smiled. Tried to smile. A few more feet and he was at his lover's side, touching him, feeling the warmth of his skin. Hastily he tried the ropes that bound Byrne, but his fingers only slipped off, useless. He sniffed and levered himself upright, pulling up his jeans, half fastening them.

Sore beyond belief, he made it back to Paget's side and carefully crouched down. He didn't look at the blood that soaked Paget's shirt and jacket, or at the darkness of his own blood smearing Paget's cock. Instead he just took hold of the knife and, after a moment of resistance, pulled it free.

Duncan nodded, and unsteadily straightened.

Back at Byrne's side, he more or less fell to his knees again. But the knife cut through the ropes at wrist and ankle, and Byrne groaned as he moved. The gag took a moment longer, then he was free. He turned over, rubbing his arms, and looked up.

Duncan forestalled any tirade by simply leaning forward and kissing Byrne's bruised mouth.

After a moment he sat back on his heels.

"Peter."

A hand touched his skin, and Duncan closed his eyes, sighing.

"Hello," Byrne said.

"Hello yourself."

"Hey!"

Duncan blinked, and found he was crying. With the back of one hand he wiped his face and sniffed. "Sorry."

Byrne shook his head, his fingers stroking damp skin.

A deep breath, and Duncan met his eyes. And saw how terrible it had been, to watch impotently. "I'm so sorry - "

Byrne just shook his head, his hand warm against Duncan's face. "I love you, Peter."

Byrne's words were so far removed from what he had expected that Duncan laughed, though the sound was close to tears. "I love you, too. But I'd love you even more if you refrained from getting kidnapped by maniacs."

"You can talk."

"I know." Duncan smoothed the short, ruffled hair back into a semblance of its usual sleekness. "Are you really okay?"

"Yeah, I'm absolutely fantastic. Same as you by the looks of it."

"Fantastic."

They grinned weakly.

Duncan sobered first. "Can you stand up?"

"In a minute. Peter?"

"Mm?"

"How much of that blood is yours."

He blinked. Then shrugged. "I don't know." Sighing he took the hem of his shirt and peeled it upwards, watching as Byrne winced.

"You'll need stitches."

Giving in to curiosity he peered down; the bullet had cut a curving path across his side. It looked as painful as it felt. "Oh." Duncan nodded, and looked away. There were other hurts too, nothing he wouldn't get over.

Byrne reached out and with a single finger moved his head back. "How long before you got here had you got all that worked out?"

"Got what worked out?"

"You planned everything, goaded him into it. Yes?"

Duncan sighed and gave up on lies. "Yes. It seemed the only way." He blinked and looked at his hands. They were filthy. "I wish I could have thought of another, so you didn't have to watch."

"Idiot. You just saved my life, and your own. I can cope with the rest. As long as you can."

Duncan just looked at him and nodded.

And Byrne was on his knees, easing him up into a careful embrace, his face in the chilly curve of Duncan's neck. "Okay?"

"Yeah." Duncan sighed, and the breathy sound was of ease, not despair. "Thank you." He felt the shudder ripple into his bones.

"I'm glad you killed the bastard."

Duncan nodded.

"And it was absolutely self-defence."

"Absolutely," Duncan agreed solemnly. Then shivered again, leaning his weight into the warmth of his lover. "Byrne. Please, can we go home?" It was a whisper.

"Come on." Byrne levered them both to their feet. Duncan straightened painfully, his eyes drawn back to the ungainly jumble of limbs that was Paget. Byrne just shrugged. "I'll call Cadell, he can deal with this."

"Cadell won't be talking to me."

"Why?"

Duncan let himself be turned away, guided towards the door. "I threw one of those expensive bug things away."

"Don't worry, he'll probably take it out of my salary."

"And this was meant to be his show."

Byrne smiled. "Don't tell me Cadell thought you'd follow his orders?"

"I think so."

"What an idiot."

Duncan just concentrated on getting down the stairs.

"Anyway, Cadell will get over it. You did the right thing, Peter."

"I know. Cadell would never have let me kill Paget."

"No. It might have been seen as unwise."

"But necessary." It wasn't quite a question.

"Yes. If it had been you he had taken, I would have wanted him dead. No question."

Simple. Byrne understood. Nothing else mattered. Duncan nodded, and went back to the task of walking.

They left the warehouse without a backward glance.

Strangely, Duncan found the street wavering under his steps. There wasn't much pain any more. Not too much. He wanted a hot bath and tea and Byrne under warm blankets and to sleep forever.

Until they woke and made love.

Gently.

"What are you smiling at?"

"I was thinking about what I want, about you making love to me, and how you'll have to be gentle for a while."

In the middle of the street, Byrne stopped him, took his hand, and brought him close. "As long as it takes." Almost of a height, they leant into each other. "After you get checked out in hospital."

The jerk of alarm almost pulled Duncan away. "No!"

"Yes." Byrne pulled him back. "Just to be sure you're okay. The bullet wound, too."

"If I go then you do too." He peered at the bruises on Byrne's face. "I suppose the rest of you looks the same."

"Guess so." Byrne almost shrugged, then stopped himself. "But I'll be good if you are."

"Okay."

"Now. I'll drive straight to the nearest casualty."

A deep sigh. "Fine. Though you'd better ring Cadell first."

"Oh, yes."

"Had you forgotten?"

"No. But there are more important things than him."

"Gosh."

Byrne laughed softly. "I'll drive."

"Don't think I could." His perception was slowly narrowing, the world cutting down to Byrne and the strip of road that led to the car. "Not unless we want to end up in the river."

Byrne watched as Duncan turned very pale. "Keys?"

"Pocket."

They were. He opened the car, eased Duncan in. The road to the hospital had better be clear.

Duncan settled gingerly into the seat and sat back with a sigh. "God, I'll be glad to get home."

"Me too."

Byrne got in behind the wheel.

Alive! If he'd had the strength Duncan would have shouted the thought out loud. He smiled anyway.

Byrne turned the ignition and the engine caught. The heater started to work immediately.

Duncan wrapped his arms around his body, and heard a soft crinkle. He reached into his pocket.

"Byrne, don't go anywhere; sit still a minute." He waited until Byrne took his hands off the wheel. The heater was making the car nice and warm. "Guess what day it is."

A frown of concentration, then enlightenment. "Christmas?"

"Bingo. Here - " He held out a very slim parcel. "Happy Christmas."

"That was in your pocket the whole time?"

"Just forgot to take it out." A half-shrug.

"Idiot." Byrne was smiling almost shyly, as he took the present.

"Yeah."

Duncan watched as Byrne stripped off bright red and green paper to reveal an envelope. Frowning he glanced up, then opened the flap to pull out a sheet of paper. He scanned it, then his eyes were bright.

"Is this for your book?"

"They said I could have a dedication page. Well, there it is."

"It's for me." He blinked as Duncan recited the words printed on the single sheet of paper: "To Byrne, in lieu of roses."

They held eye contact then simply came together, the hug gentle and utterly beyond meaning.

After a while, Byrne sat back. He wiped his face. "Right, better get you to hospital."

Duncan groaned. "I thought you might have forgotten."

"Wishful thinking!"

Duncan settled back.

"You're smiling again."

"Can't stop."

"Well, I expect I'll cope." Byrne found first gear. He was smiling too.

END

Watch out for -

Perfect Trust

S.Hardy Brondos

When Jason Swedborg and Daniel Reilly agree to work as top-secret agents for the US government, they expect to encounter danger and death. What they don't expect is to face a twisted web of conspiracy which includes shadows from Daniel's past and the ominous beat of voodoo drums.

Nor do they expect to fall in love with each other. Life is full of surprises.

The first Swedborg and Reilly mystery

This novel will be published on the 1st February 2001.

Available from our website:
Waywardbooks.com

Watch out for -

Kind Hearts

Evelyn Martin

Peter Ryan's life is an open book for anyone to read; on the other hand Edward Ashton, his partner in the successful Burford's Detective Agency, is more of an enigma.

Together they get results, but then a new case threatens to drag Ashton's past into the limelight.

This novel will be published on the 1st May 2001.

Available from our website:
Waywardbooks.com